I0708850

Seers of Light

A Novel by
Jennifer DeLucy

OMNIFIC PUBLISHING
DALLAS

Omnific Publishing
P.O. Box 793871, Dallas, TX 75379
www.omnificpublishing.com

First Omnific ebook edition, February 2010
First Omnific trade paperback edition, February 2010

Library of Congress Cataloguing-in-Publication Data

DeLucy, Jennifer.
    Seers of Light / Jennifer DeLucy – 2nd ed.
    ISBN 978-1-936305-03-2
    1. Supernatural—Fiction. 2. Vampires—Fiction.
    3. Spirituality—Fiction. I. Title

10 9 8 7 6 5 4 3 2 1

Book Design by Barbara Hallworth

Printed in the United States of America

This book is dedicated to my brother, John — sweetest and handsomest of men — and my sister, Katie, who insisted that I mention how lost I'd be without the wellspring of her perfection.

*"No one saves us but ourselves. No one can and no one may.
We ourselves must walk the path."*
-Buddha

Prologue

Michael,

There is no question now that I am a danger to you both. Leaving is the hardest thing I'll ever do, but if anything ever happened to either of you, I would die. Go ahead and hate me. It's better that way.

And please do not look for me at Abram's, I won't be there. Take care of our little one, and find love again.

Yours forever,
Elizabeth

One

Frank poked his head into the storage room.

"Hey, kiddo, toss me a roll of paper towels, would you? Goddamn cola exploded all over the floor out here."

"Sure, Grandpa."

The back room of Connie and Frank's corner store had taken on a multitude of purposes over the years. There was the expected, of course. This week's inventory was Coke, pretzels, Slim Jims, energy drinks, lottery tickets, breakfast bars, and (between Frank and me) *Playboy* magazines. By next week we'd probably need to restock the Budweiser and cigarette lighters, too.

This past evening, the room had played host to the most exciting game of poker Scranton, Pennsylvania, had ever known. With everything on the table, I'd bluffed my way to victory once again, taking Frank's old buddies Leo and Oscar down once and for all. In fact, the table remained assembled still, legs crooked and cards in disarray.

I grabbed two rolls of paper towels—these messes always required more supplies than anticipated. Frank wasn't up front, so I opened a roll and started cleaning the spill myself. The door ringer sounded, and I looked up to see a young man leaning against the frame. He reminded me of James Dean, his hair combed perfectly into an oily wave and both hands in his pockets, watching me.

"You didn't call last night, Maggie," he said in a voice so low it was almost a whisper.

I looked around, but the store was empty. "I … I'm sorry?"

"You said you'd call. We were supposed to go to O'Malley's. Why didn't you answer the phone?"

What the hell was he talking about? He was looking *right* at me.

I stood up, sopped paper towels in both hands. "Look, I think you've confused me for someone else," I said.

"Don't screw with me!" he snapped, stepping forward. "I know what you've been doing, Maggie Ann. I've seen you with him."

Instinct told me to take a few steps back. "I'm going to get someone who can help you, okay?"

"Baby." He smiled, his expression suddenly calm. "You're not leaving."

"No, I'm not, I promise." I continued to back away.

"Don't bother, Maggie," he said, all the emotion gone from his voice. "We don't need them. I know how to help us …."

He reached into his pocket and pulled out a pistol, and the wet balls of paper towel fell from my hands with a thwopping sound.

"*Please*," I whimpered, begged. "*Please*, I'm not her. My name is Lily Hunt. Do you understand me? I'm not who you think I am."

"No more lies."

I was frantic, crying, but terrified to move. "Somebody *please* help me …."

"Lily?"

I shot my head around to see Frank holding spray cleaner in one hand and a mop in the other. "Kiddo, what's wrong?"

"Grandpa, he's got a …" I turned to face the door. "…gun," my voice trailed off.

"*Who* does, honey?" Frank glanced around, alarmed.

The door ringer hadn't announced his leaving, but the stranger was gone.

☙

My life, all twenty-eight years of it, had been a quiet event until tonight. I'd gone to college, then worked in my grandparents' store, eventually managing it. Everyone I'd ever known was satisfied with the ordinary, mindlessly at ease with their own little things in their own little houses. The *un*usual was shunned, and I had long since given up on the idea of escaping the same fate. Now I was the talk of the community, and I would be for months.

"So we don't know who he is or where he went," said the officer, reviewing my statement. "But at least we have a description, and we'll put it out around town. Plus the security video." He held up the tape. "I'll have a look at this once I get back to the station."

"And what if he comes back?" I asked.

"I'll have Michael man patrol the neighborhood for a few days, make sure he doesn't," he claimed. But it occurred to me that he was full of it. I just knew he couldn't care less. Whether it was the look on his scruffy, pasty face or the tone of his voice, his nonchalance didn't escape my notice. He was itching to close the conversation and get somewhere else. God, people were so transparent.

After the officer had gone, Connie stood, attempting to appraise my state of mind. "Why don't you go home and get a decent night's sleep. There's no point in staying here," she suggested.

"I'll go home…but *sleep*?" I scoffed. "Not likely, Grandma."

"Another reason why you need a good man in your life, Lillian. It's high time you—"

"Connie, for Christ's sake," Frank cut her off. "She doesn't need that right now."

"I'll be fine," I assured them again, and kissed Frank's forehead before grabbing my purse from behind the register. "Night," I added, heading out of the store.

"Lily, lock your doors!" Connie shouted after me.

"Always!" I called back.

Settling into the driver's seat of my car, I examined my reflection in the fold down mirror. My mascara was smudged. Why did I even *try* to wear makeup? It didn't look right on me anyway. Connie had always said so. Mature looking women wore makeup, whereas I was a perpetual baby face, Cupid's bow lips and all. My only saving grace was my dark blue eyes. They were almost feline, with curly lashes.

Pulling my mess of black, wavy hair up into a bun, I flipped the mirror back up and looked at the clock: 10:00 p.m. "Free Bird" blasted its way out of my purse and I jumped, hitting my forehead on the mirror. Wincing, I rummaged through my wreck of a purse in vain; the cell phone had already gone to voicemail. There was always too much crammed in there for me to find anything quickly.

"Damn it."

I checked caller ID and chose number three on speed dial.

"Lily?" A hyper voice greeted me.

"Yup, Kate, it's me."

"Fantastic! A bunch of us are meeting up at Heil's in about fifteen minutes. You wanna join?"

"Ehn. Not tonight, my friend. I've had all the excitement I can handle for one evening."

"Why's that? Worn out playing Go Fish with the old man's club?" she laughed.

"It's poker, and don't diss my homies. Besides, no games tonight. I was a little distracted, what with being held at gun-point and all."

"Homies? Woman, what did I say about trying to talk street? You sound like an idio—wait—I'm sorry, *what*!?"

"A gun. Pointed at me."

"What the hell, Lily?! Are you kidding me?"

"I wish."

"Oh my God. Wow, *I'm* the idiot."

"Yes, you are. And it was really weird, because he thought I was someone else, some girl named Maggie."

"God, a mental case. Did he take much?"

"No, he didn't take anything. He just wanted to confront her. He was dressed like someone from a fifties movie, Katie. It was bizarre."

"And where is he now? You called the cops, obviously?"

"Well, yeah, obviously. But he'd already run off."

"And you're *sure* you don't want to come out tonight? Sounds like you could use it."

"I'm positive. You know me. I'm not as big of a lush as you are."

"*Oh*! I'm deeply offended," she joked. "You know I abhor the devil's drink."

"Mhm. Just call me if you need a ride home."

"Will do. Hey, you feel like going walking with me tomorrow?"

"You mean…at the lake?"

"Yes. At the lake. Where else? It's been months. I'm getting a double chin, Lily."

"Not tomorrow, Kate, okay? I'm a little messed up right now. Or we could just go to the gym."

"Woman, what's the difference?! Trail, gym, fresh air versus recycled air. Lily, at least the trail is free!"

"Kate, give me a break, all right? I just don't like those woods. They're … claustrophobic."

She sighed loudly into the phone. "Jesus. We'll go to the gym."

"Thank you."

The doorbell rang and my black tabby skittered from my lap, digging his claws into my thighs.

"*Arrgh*, Rufus, you *spaz*!" I called after him.

Frank was the only one who played a doorbell to the rhythm of shave and a hair-cut.

"Mornin', kiddo," he said.

"Hey, Grandpa." I smiled at him, but his typically happy greeting was strained at best. He looked exhausted and anxious. "What's wrong?" I asked.

"Lily … the … " he began, then paused, frowning.

"What?" I asked again, and he sighed, his face settling into something uncharacteristically serious. My mind raced through worst case scenarios. "Is Grandma okay?"

"Grandma? Sure, honey. Sure, she's fine."

"Well, you're scaring me. What is it, then?"

"Let's just go in the house, all right?"

"All right … yeah," I agreed, letting him pass.

Frank had always been fast on his feet, even in his old age, and so my heart broke as I watched him shuffle heavily toward the couch. I took my favorite position, curled tightly into a ball in the corner of the sofa, and said nothing, waiting for him to speak.

"The police reviewed the tape," he said finally.

"And?"

"And … honey, how have you been lately? I mean, have you been feeling okay?"

"Fine. But quit beating around the bush. What's the story?"

He sighed. "Lillian, there was nothing on that tape."

I stared at him. "You mean it was blank?"

"No. It recorded just fine. But the man with the gun? He wasn't there."

"You've lost me. It skipped that part?"

"Lily." He put his hand over mine. "Honey, it recorded you, reacting, talking, crying, but … there was no man, no gun. There was no one but you."

I shook my head. "That can't be possible," I said, chuckling, but his face remained sober, his eyes glued to mine, straining in search of something he'd never noticed before. It scared the shit out of me.

"That's not *possible*," I repeated more forcefully. "He was *there*, for God's sake. I'm not losing my mind!" Oh, God. I was *so* losing my mind.

"I know, I know," he insisted. "I know you're not, Lily. You had to have seen something. But, well, what do you expect us to make of all this? Your grandmother is convinced you're on some kind of drugs. She's afraid you've been sniffing the crack like those hooligans on COPS."

"This is absolutely insane!" I laughed. "Grandpa, I am *not* on drugs. I've never even been drunk!"

His expression lightened with relief. "Of course not, kiddo. I told her she was two drops short of a bucketful, but …." He dropped his gaze.

I put my hand on his shoulder. "Listen, I don't know what happened last night, but, whatever it was, it was real. You have to believe me."

He lifted his gaze. "I believe you," he said.

My shoulders slumped and I relaxed. "You do?"

"Yes, Lily. I know you. If you said he was there, he was there."

"Thank you, but I still have no idea why no one else saw him."

"Beats the hell out of me, but … I wonder," he began.

"Hmm? What?"

"Lily, do you remember Mrs. Cartwright?"

"Erm, refresh my memory."

"Your imaginary friend, kiddo, from, oh hell, you had to be three or four years old. I never mentioned her?"

"No. But go on."

"Well, you and Mrs. Cartwright were inseparable for a year. You had tea parties, watched movies together, collected rocks, all kinds of things."

I nodded. "Rocks, huh? Exciting stuff, my childhood." I smiled patiently.

"Well, I remember one night I asked you if you wanted me to read the *Curious Little Kitten*. You loved that damn book. Drove me crazy with it."

"I remember that!" I grinned. "Aaah, crazy kitten. Whatever happened to that book?"

"I threw it out," he said seriously.

I laughed. "*What?*"

"That's right, and that old rocking chair of yours, too," he said.

"Grandpa! Why?"

He sighed again. "I can't believe I'm actually telling you this." He chuckled self-consciously.

"What?"

"Well, that night, like every night, I asked if you wanted me to read to you, and to my surprise, and I have to admit, relief, you refused. You said Mrs. Cartwright would do it. You told me to lay the book on the rocking chair for her. So I did. I left the lamp on, and closed the door."

I watched as the color in his face seemed to wash away. He went on.

"Later, when Connie and I were getting ready to go to bed, I remembered your light was on."

"Okay," I said.

"And, well, I heard this noise, this rhythmic squeaking on the way down the hall to your room. I figured you were awake, playing."

"Was I?" I asked.

"No, Lily. You weren't. I opened the door, and … oh hell, this is going to sound ridiculous." He stopped.

"And after last night, who am I to judge?" I peered at him.

He smiled, sheepishly. "Well, you were sound asleep, but that damned rocker was going, and the book, it was opened, opened in mid air. Then it dropped on the chair and the rocker stopped."

Every hair on my body stood at attention.

"Hell, I took that chair and smashed it to bits, threw it in the garbage," he said.

"Shit. That's creepy as hell," I said, astonished. "Thanks, Grandpa."

"Anytime," he offered. "And I never told you, or your grandmother, or anyone else for that matter until now. There have been little things over the years, Lily. I always wondered."

"Like what?"

"Oh, smaller stuff that I could just explain away when I needed to. Like how you managed to move an entire buffet table across the room when you were knee high to a grasshopper. Or how you always knew the exact moment when your dad would round the corner from work."

"Bizarre. And you're telling me that Grandma never noticed *any* of this?"

"No. It hardly ever happened around her. Besides, she lived in a haze for a while ... after we lost your dad."

I frowned. "You know, my memories of him are fading."

He shook his head. "I'm sorry, honey. But I'll tell you, your father loved you so much, Lily. When your mom left ... well, you were just about all that kept that man together. You, you were all he had to remember ... " He stopped, turning from me to wipe away a tear I wasn't meant to see. "They were too damn young when they got married, you ask me."

"Do you think she's still alive, my mom?" I wondered out loud, my mind drifting to a distant memory. Throughout the years there had been repeated dreams. The most cherished and vivid of these was of my mother, smiling eyes, shining waves of black hair, rosy cheeks.

"I have no idea," Frank responded. "When she left, Michael wouldn't talk about it. He never would say a mean word about her, though, not a one, and Jesus help anyone else who did!"

My father had died when I was seven years old, and thank God for Frank and Connie, they were the best sort of people. But there was a lost history to my life, a giant gray void, and it left me feeling empty. The urge to know myself through my parents remained a painful ache.

"So let me get this straight," I said, staring at him through narrowed eyes. "You think ... you think that the man in the store was ... *what*, exactly?"

"Well ... ."

I waited for his answer, but his face changed.

"I tell you what," he said. "Let's just chalk all this up to a bad tuna sandwich and I'll handle your Grandma, okay?"

Handle Connie. Only Frank could pull off such a feat. I wrapped my arms around him, laying my head on his shoulder. "We *will* talk about this again," I said. "But I suppose I can let you off the hook for tonight, seeing how you've agreed to tackle the old woman."

"Appreciate that, honey."

"I love you, my Grandpa."

"Love you more."

I woke to a fiercely howling wind, the kind that makes you shiver, even buried snugly under a blanket. You could hardly call me a deep sleeper. In fact, most nights it didn't take much more than a thump of Rufus's tail, or a muted roll of thunder to rouse me from slumber. But this wind, this was no breeze.

Pulling my covers more tightly around me, I closed my eyes in hopes that pretending not to notice would quiet the noise. No luck. Now the waves of air were whooshing against the side of the house.

I grabbed the remote from next to my bed and clicked on the television. I would just have to drown it out. On went the Home Shopping Network. *This'll put anyone to sleep*, I thought. The prim-looking woman on screen held up a bright gold chain-link necklace polished to an unnatural sheen. Crooning over its quality she declared that no one would be able to tell that it wasn't real gold.

"*Trust* me ladies," she began, "you wear this gorgeous piece to your next dinner party and I guarantee you'll be the talk of the evening."

Soon the jewelry designer was chirping in with some babble about "lifetime guarantees" and I sighed into my pillow.

"It's probably made of aluminum," I said. "You open it up, try it on, your neck turns to dust, and your head falls off."

About ten minutes of this did the trick. I didn't even notice the wind anymore. Dozing off to the tinny tune of a "masterful" music box that had to be seen to be believed, the television abruptly turned to snow.

"Ugh" I moaned, thickly.

Groping around my crumpled bed spread for the remote I turned the station. *Mama's Family*. All right then.

Two seconds in and the screen cut to snow.

"What the hell?"

I switched to the weather channel. Windy, but cloudless, and then snowy as the screen went out again. I squinted at the bright white static, then flipped channels.

The Andy Griffith Show. Andy was looking awfully distorted. What was with his face?

Two pictures seemed to be layered over one another. In the background, Andy lectured Aunt Bee on the dangers of driving, while a nearer, subtler, more shadowy figure seemed to squat with arms outstretched as if holding either side of the screen apart. And was it watching me? I could almost detect elevated cheekbones, a smile. A sneer?

Two stations overlapping?

Snow again. I got up from the bed, my feet etching their clammy way into the soft carpet, and approached the television. Crouching down, I examined it, hit it on the side. I scratched my forehead, blinked, and turned around.

The figure that had just plagued the screen was now on my bed. It was only a shadow of something human, crawling on all fours to the foot of the bed, closer to me. Its head tilted to one side, and every few seconds I could swear it was smiling. It remained quiet, but stalked around like a caged animal.

I stood completely immobile. The man-creature approached the foot of my bed again, dropping its head down over the edge, and then cocked it up at an unnatural angle, looking at me. Its eyes were red embers. This had to be a nightmare.

It let its arm fall to the floor, never breaking its gaze from mine, and my body seemed to have lost all motor function. I tried lifting my foot. Nothing would move.

Dropping the other arm, it pulled itself from the bed, its legs falling behind it soundlessly. Then it stood. If the thing was taller than me I couldn't tell, as its stature remained hunched and distorted.

A saving burst of anger at this intrusion upon my sanity woke me from my haze. I knew I wasn't asleep.

"What do you want with me?" I found my voice.

It stopped its sickly slow progression and straightened its head, twisting it to the other side, still looking at me.

"Why are you here?"

It shifted toward me again and feeling returned to my body. I took a few quick steps toward the door. The creature tilted its head, reflexively, adjusting its gaze. A sound almost like sifting sand grew in strength and emitted from its chest. Was it breathing? My heart beat out of control. The sound died away only to begin again seconds later.

Reaching behind me, I groped for a door knob but found only air. I grasped further and my hand greeted cool hard wood. I dared not look away from the thing, but rather slid my fingers over to the knob and gripped it. By now, the creature stood less than two feet from me, transfixed, breathing his gritty breaths and grinning senselessly. The air was frigid.

I jumped to the side and pulled open the door, and a burst of warmth swept through the room. My visitor began to dissipate like frost, first at the edges, then its arms and legs, its center, and finally its face, still grinning.

☙

I camped out in the living room for the rest of the night, the television off, and the lights on. Who could I call that would possibly know how to help me? Grandpa had enough on his mind, Grandma already thought I was hitting the crack pipe, and Kate… Kate would assume her poor best friend had finally lost it.

Then it dawned on me. Maybe I *had* lost it. Thank you, God, that had to be the answer! I grabbed the phone book, flipping through the P's for local psychiatric clinics. "Private Investigators, Pruning Services, Psychiatry …."

I glanced up at the clock. Quarter till eight. They wouldn't be open this early. Settling into the carpet with the phone in my lap, I waited, my head on the wall behind me. My eyes drooped, the sleepless night catching up with me.

Fighting the urge to nod off, I popped my head up and looked at the clock. Ten minutes to go. I closed my eyes again, and suddenly I was on a lake trail. Veering off the path into the trees, further and deeper, I finally broke through. Out in the distance, in the center of the lake, stood an old man, and he walked across the water toward me, stopping at its edge.

"Well, hello, Lily," he said, his voice kind. The space around him was a globe of golden light that engulfed me in an instant. I felt supremely happy.

"You again?" I asked, dumbfounded.

He laughed out loud. "You remember me."

"Yes."

"Good. Some people forget their dreams the second they wake. I must have made an impression."

"You keep coming back here," I said.

"No, Lillian, *you* do," he corrected.

"Oh. Why do I?"

"Don't you know?" He smiled.

"You're protecting me?"

"No. I'm preparing you."

"Am I going to die?" I said, totally at ease.

"Not at all. But do keep a keen eye, child." He motioned behind me, and something moved in the woods. A pale, sinewy form broke through the tree line and stopped suddenly, shielding his face against the light around us. At first glance, the creature appeared to be human, but the ivory color of its hair and skin blended too perfectly. It wore a translucent cloak, and the flesh beneath revealed bright blue veins that webbed along its legs and torso.

It hissed at the old man and I flinched.

"Not to worry, Lillian. He cannot harm you here," the man assured me.

The creature shrank away from the sound of his voice, whimpering like a child, and then took off running into the woods.

"Lily," said the old man. "Wake up."

My eyes snapped open and the cat was padding at my chest, flopping his tail in my lap. The clock read 8:13.

"Off, Rufus," I said, plopping him aside, and picked up the phone, my hands shaking.

"Northeast Counseling Center, Kimmy speaking," answered the chipper voice on the other end of the phone.

"Hi, Kimmy. I need to schedule an appointment with one of your doctors."

"Sure, what's your name?"

I paused. "Lillian."

"Okay, Lillian, your last name?"

"Hunt."

"And your date of birth?"

I gulped. Did they really need to know that? "November seventeenth, 1979."

"Mhm. And what do you need to be seen for?"

"Uhm, I, I think I might be hallucinating."

"Okay. Are you hearing voices?"

"Sort of... but not really ...."

"Are they telling you to hurt yourself or anyone else?"

"No. No, it's not like that. I mean, I'm seeing things, very realistic things that I can't seem to tell apart from real things, you know? And my vision is strange, there's... blurry light ...."

"Sure," said the patronizing voice. "Do you have a history of mental illness in your family?"

"I … I don't know." *Maybe*, I thought. "I don't think so," I said.

"Okay, have you ever suffered from depression, addiction, or anxiety disorders?"

"No."

"So you're not on any kind of psychotropic drugs?"

"No." I laughed. This was ridiculous.

"All right, Lillian. Our first opening is with Dr. Labbabadahan."

"Dr. Labba … I'm sorry?"

"Labbabadahan," she repeated effortlessly.

"Right, can you spell that?"

"Sure, it's L-a-b-b-a-b …."

"Wait! I need to get a pen," I interjected, fumbling around the phone stand for something to write with. All I could find was a Sharpie.

"Go ahead," I said, poised to write on my hand.

"From the beginning?" she asked with a huff.

"Yes, please."

She sighed, spelling the name again.

"And when can I see him?" I asked.

"His first opening is the sixth of September, at nine a.m."

"Sixth of September? But that's five *months* from now," I said, appalled.

"Yes. He's a very good doctor."

"And that's great, but what do you do in the meantime? What about people who have fallen off the deep end? Do you suggest they tell the voices to shut the hell up?"

"I thought you said you weren't hearing any voices?"

"I'm not!"

"Well, then, if you're in immediate crisis you might consider admitting yourself to the Community Medical Center for acute care, or you can call our hotline and speak with—"

"No. You know what? That's okay. I think maybe this was a mistake. I'm sorry." I hung up the phone. Sliding down the wall to the floor again, I lay my head in my hands and began to cry. "Oh, *fuck*!" I yanked my hand from my eyes, realizing too late what I'd done. It would take days to scrub the ink from my face.

Two

How silly I'd been, avoiding the trail. I had loved to come here. Tall birch and maple trees lined the path on both sides, moist brown earth overflowed onto the pavement, and to the right, through the trees, you could see the lake. Four miles of blissful walking trail circled it.

Oh, it was always beautiful, but the feel of it had changed for me. The weight of the air made it hard to breathe sometimes. It felt claustrophobic, crowded even when I was all alone. If only I could put my finger on it, the inexplicable disorientation that seemed to find me in places like this…an alien awareness, like the trees and grass and wind knew I was there. If I listened hard enough, I could nearly hear them buzzing.

Frank was glad when I finally took him up on his many offers to come in late. I was cloistered, a recluse, that was my problem. I needed to get out more, absorb some fresh air. There was no need to panic, really. Kate had told me once that I had to learn to exist in this world, out of my head. Maybe she was right.

The trail was misty today, and the sun glowed through the trees in soft white light. Weekday mornings were not the most popular time for walking, and I was alone. It all smelled so good, like moss and wet leaves. If I was supposed to think logically, why did everything have to feel so surreal? I would just have to think boring thoughts—like metric system conversion—or military time. Ooh, geometry!

I was about to graph a line in my head when something rustled in the trees beside me.

I halted, listening closely, but the trail remained a peaceful mix of breeze and birdsong.

With some effort, I sought to clear my mind. Concentrating on breathing, I inhaled and exhaled with great deliberation. My head was swimming pleasantly, and my body seemed weightless. I closed my eyes. Then, the sound of someone else's breath, vast, echoing, and dark, swirled around me. I gasped and my eyes shot open.

The thoughtless peace was failing as a tide of beautiful and troublesome images crowded my consciousness—thoughts of strangers with guns, menacing shadows, a dark haired woman with smiling eyes, an old man with worn, ebony skin. And thoughts of my father, memories that I had never been able to conjure before.

Everything pulsed electric and my body tingled uncomfortably. It was as if my blood was slowing, my muscles failing. I couldn't move another inch, and the rustling stopped. The air again turned to static, and I knew I wasn't alone.

It's behind me.

Whipping my head around, I met my pursuer. We gazed, eye to eye, yet there was no real sight to his vacant, black stare. His hair fell in straight sheets down his shoulders, and blue veins crossed the near transparent skin of his neck and face. I understood then that he was ancient, though how I knew this I couldn't say. No normal signs of time sullied his skin.

He spoke to me, but only in my head, whispering that it wouldn't hurt, it would be over before I knew what was happening, quick, painless. What did he mean? And why was I so happy with it all? Shouldn't I be afraid? He smiled, and my knees trembled. Half of my brain demanded I scream, but the other half was a gelatinous wasteland, incapable of feeling anything short of total contentment. Quick and painless, he'd said. What a nice way to go. I tried to speak, but my tongue was an immovable leaden prop. He leaned in, and the voice in my head said not to struggle.

Of course. Why would I? Everything was wonderful.

But still something vague and distant pricked at me, growing in strength and clarity. An alarm sounded and for an instant, I knew something was terribly, terribly wrong. I blinked, my hand poised with an inexplicable urge to move the collar of my jacket aside, when a perplexing noise erupted around me. If everything was so terribly pleasant, what *was* this unsettling sound? It was nothing like the soothing voice I'd heard in my head. It was high pitched, frenzied.

I was screaming.

He seemed surprised with this turn of events, and he narrowed his eyes in concentration. My limbs felt heavy again. Nothing more than his two hands held me to the ground, but my feet were as good as planted in concrete. There was no escaping this, and whatever kind of nightmare I was having. I braced for the incomprehensible, managed to close my eyes, and prayed to God that it would be quick.

There was sudden movement in the green beside the path, something like twigs being broken, and my captor's attention was again interrupted. He lifted his head and seemed to sniff at the air.

Call for help, I told myself.

"Don't waste your breath, dear," said the sweet voice in my head.

"Please… help me!" I pleaded hoarsely, to anyone at all. It was all I could manage, though the sound was strangled and forced.

A few seconds passed and, satisfied that nothing was there, he tilted my head sideways, and lowered his lips to my throat, intent on finishing what he'd started. I knew what he was, though everything in me said it was impossible.

It all happened in an instant. There came a sudden burst of wind, then a whopping force sent my captor soaring off into the woods to my right. I caught a glimpse of blue in the brush before everything went still. The lake wind lapped at my face and, as if I'd risen from deep waters, I gulped for air and began to scream in earnest. My legs gave out and I collapsed to the earth below in a heap, weeping. I knew I needed to move, to escape, but I was paralyzed with fear. What was the point of running? He would just catch me again. I would die here.

There was new movement in the path ahead and my sobs caught in my throat.

"Leave me alone!" I shouted. The effort seemed futile, but at least I would die with some pride intact.

"It's… it's okay," someone responded. The rustling increased as the man behind the voice made his way free of the brush. He stood some twenty feet ahead of where I lay on the ground, his hands held up in surrender. He had a youthful face and wide blue eyes. His hair was the color of sand, his build trim but muscular in the arms. Something about his shirt, smudged with mud and ripped down the side, struck a chord of recognition.

"I'm not going to hurt you," he spoke with a British accent. As he continued up the path toward me, I felt the static building again, but it was milder, more controlled.

"Stay away from me. Don't you *dare* come near me," I ordered, my words losing their volume, breaking, falling apart.

The man stopped. "I promise I'm not dangerous. I swear it," he said, and he continued his approach, stopping to bend down on one knee in front of me, examining me carefully. His tactics were different from the other man's, and his face was natural, human. I explored his gaze and could see no signs of ill will. He didn't *look* evil.

"Can you walk?" he asked

"I … I don't know."

"You shouldn't have come here alone. It's not safe."

"No kidding."

The blue of his shirt caught my eye again. "Are you the one that stopped him?"

"Yes. I took care of it. He should never have known you were here, though. This should never have happened," he said apologetically and smiled. "Well, there'll be no hiking these paths anymore; I hope you understand. Do you need me to carry you?" he suggested.

"*Carry* me? Are you serious? No, I'm fine."

I placed my hands on my knees, pushing myself up, only to feel my legs buckle again. In an instant he was there, my frame a rag doll in two very strong arms. I suddenly felt safe, and the path was much brighter than before, the area all around me emitting a warm, golden heat that penetrated through every surface.

"Walking seems like a bad idea to me." He frowned, still holding me up.

"No. I can walk now. I won't fall again," I assured him. Only then did I notice how tall he was. He must have stood a good ten inches above me.

"Can we go then? I'll escort you out, if you don't mind."

We began down the path. I knew I shouldn't have felt so secure, considering the nightmare that had only moments before come to life at my expense, but I could not bring myself to panic, engulfed in this strange calm. Once or twice

I'd slow the pace, enjoying the beauty of the woods, until he took my hand, urging me along.

After a little while, the lights engulfing us began to fade and certain very unsettling thoughts crept their way back into my head. I felt like I was waking up.

"Why aren't they?" I asked him, stopping abruptly, my hand slipping from his gentle grip.

"Pardon me?" He turned only his head to face me.

"The woods. The trails." I motioned around us. "Why aren't they safe anymore? What's out here? And who was that man? Who are *you*?" The fear was returning.

"Later." He grabbed my hand again and pulled me forward.

"No! Come *on*! What is this all about?" I was getting frustrated.

"Not now."

"Why not? Tell me!"

He winced, stopping in front of me with an exasperated look on his face, and leaned in close to my ear, speaking in a low voice, almost a whisper. "Too many questions to safely answer here, Lily. I don't know how many of them followed him. They'll be angry now I've done away with their friend. If you don't mind, I'd like to wait until we're in the clear before doling out any explanations."

"You know my name."

"Yes, I do." He dragged us onward.

"How? Are you a stalker or something? Let *go* of me, dammit!" I yanked my hand from his again and crossed my arms, glaring at him defiantly.

"Ugh," he moaned, deftly lifting me from the ground and cradling me in his arms like a child.

"Are you crazy!?" I struggled to free myself, but only half-heartedly. The strange calm was returning, despite his behavior being highly unorthodox.

"Look, Lily." He sighed. "The more you fight, the longer it will take us to get out of here, and consequently, prolonging the time it takes me to get to your explanations."

The light around us grew stronger, and so did my level of calm, but at this point, I knew better than to trust that. I let a few moments pass, but then it was time for another vie for freedom.

"If you let me walk, I promise, I'll come along without a fuss. Just answer one question for me, just one. And it's harmless, I swear!"

He looked down, examining me for all traces of deception, and seemed convinced of my sincerity.

"All right then." He gave in, letting me down. "What is it?"

"What's your name?"

His mouth was shut tightly, poised to evade, when he realized the benignity of my request.

"I suppose I could manage that one."

"Mmhm. Your name?"

"Christian Wright."

"Christian. I guess I don't need to introduce myself, now do I? How *do* you know who I am?"

"That's more than one question," he chided, taking a step down the path, pausing only to turn his head back and hold out his hand. "You promised. You have to keep your half of the bargain."

I hesitated, but kept my mouth shut, allowing him to lead me the rest of the way in silence until we'd reached the clearing at the start of the trail. The trees spreading apart at either end allowed the morning sunlight in. Christian stopped walking once we reached the parking lot. He turned to me.

"I can't let you go home, Lily."

My pulse quickened. He was a serial killer, I knew it. A psychopath. I recoiled, balled up my fists and took a deep breath, ready to scream and fight.

"Lily, it's okay." His voice was steady as more of that inexplicable light circled around us. He looked into my eyes with an expression of sympathy, and I could tell he was working not to frighten me. "I know who you are because Abram saw it all happening. He saw you, in these woods, being attacked by a vampire. It was *never* supposed to get that far, but somehow he found you. Your energy must be off the charts."

"Is this some kind of joke? A vampire?" I scowled.

"The dreams you've had—you've seen Abram in your dreams, remember?"

My mind reeled. I *had* been dreaming a lot lately. And the old man ... .

"How could you possibly know that?" I took a step back, prepared to flee.

"*Please* don't run. Surely you were more prepared than this? I know it's all a bit much, but—"

"A *bit*?" I interrupted.

"It's not safe for you to stay here! Just let me take you back to Abram and I'll explain it all to you when we get there."

"*Take* me?" I shouted. "If you think that I'm going even *one* step further with you without my promised explanation, you're insane! And don't even *think* about picking me up again!" I said, as he made a move toward me.

"I won't! I'm not, Lily. *Look* at me," he pleaded, speaking very deliberately, his eyes locked with mine. "I am *not* a psychopath. I am not a killer, a stalker, or any other form of assailant or abductor. I am strictly here to get you away from what was out there." He flung his arm toward the trees. "There are things you don't know yet, but they *will* be explained to you. Now, however, is not the time, or the place."

I stared back at him, stunned, as the dreams played over in my head. Either I was crazy or this man was telling me the truth. Which option did I prefer?

"Then … then I'm not losing my mind? I'm *not* schizophrenic or any-thing?"

Again his eyes softened with understanding. "No, you're not." He laughed. "I know it's a lot to ask of you, to trust a stranger and follow him on blind faith. But you know you need to come, Lily."

This last line was delivered as a statement of finality, of something mutually implicit.

I released my long held breath and nodded, while a current of euphoria bowled me over. I knew I should follow him, wherever he was leading me. I knew because from the moment I'd stepped foot on that lake path, the empty nothing in my gut had left me. Something extraordinary was going to happen. Maybe something, *anything*, would finally make sense.

"My car is just there." Christian pulled me to a nearby aisle.

We stopped at the rear of a black vehicle far too nice for me to ride in.

"A Maserati?" I said, intimidated.

"It was my father's," he explained, then jetted to the passenger door and opened it for me.

"Well, wait a minute. What about my car? How long will I be gone?" I said, a sudden rush of logic swaying my resolve.

"We've got it covered, and your things are already in my trunk, see?" He pushed a button on his key remote and the trunk opened soundlessly. My purse lay there along with a suitcase and duffel bag.

"Are you kidding me?" I laughed in amazement. "Are you James fucking Bond or something?" The revelation of my things in his trunk didn't faze me as much as it should have.

"Later," he pressed, closing the trunk and redirecting us to the passenger door. I got in.

The car started and purred contentedly. We pulled smoothly out of the parking space. I wondered if it was his driving or the vehicle that was so impressive.

"So how far is it, Abram's?" I asked. "Or am I not supposed to ask questions in the car?" I peered at him, ready for an argument.

"No, it's fine. Actually, it *is* sort of a drive," he admitted.

"How much of a drive, exactly. Are we talking Pittsburgh or the Philippines?"

"Er, for now? Atlanta," he muttered

"Wait, *what*?" My heart thudded erratically against my chest. "I can't go to Atlanta!"

"Wow, you *do* panic." He sighed.

"Well, of course I do! What did you expect? Why Atlanta?" I demanded.

"Honestly, I thought you'd have known *some*thing," he said, clearly frustrated.

"Right." I scowled. "But as you won't *tell* me anything …. If you'd just tell me *why*—"

"Because, Lily," he cut in, sighing heavily. "It's time for you to learn what you are."

Three

So, Abram. Who is he?" I asked.

"He's an ancient soul," Christian said. "A Seer."

"A Seer? Like, a psychic?"

An amused smile played at his lips. "Hardly. Psychics, as you know them anyway, are a fraction of Abram in about every aspect imaginable. They're the beginnings of a spark of him."

"So, what does he want with *me*? Surely I haven't done anything to upset the course of the universe," I joked apprehensively.

"That I can't say, exactly."

"Well, great then. So, I just got into a car with a strange man, who is taking me to see a psych … er *Seer* and doesn't know why. And I should simply, go with the flow then?"

"A strange man who saved your life," he reminded me politely. "And I didn't say I didn't know why. I said I couldn't say. Hasn't it occurred to you that if I meant you any harm, you'd be dead by now?"

I considered for a moment.

"Fine," I said. "But I can't believe I'm going along with this. And do you always drive this slowly? You're five miles an hour below the speed limit, Christian."

"You know, you're going to feel terribly foolish for being so contrary."

"And this saving and kidnapping business, do you do it often?"

"No. You're the first I've ever retrieved, actually."

"Retrieved?"

"Yes. There aren't many like us in any given region. And, at times, it's inevitable that one of us is born outside of the circle. When you're ready, the Seers send for your retrieval."

"God, it's like *X-Men*. So what am I?"

"It's not my place to say beyond that you're one of us." He grinned. "And if it makes you feel any better, I believe I gave my retriever a black eye when he came back for me."

"This happened to you?"

"In a way."

"What do you mean *back* for you?"

"Never mind that."

"Well, can you at least tell me what I'm being 'retrieved' for then?"

"Not specifically. As I said before, I'm afraid I don't know the details. We don't all carry the same abilities. Only Abram knows what your endowment is."

"My endowment. Wow. Really, Christian, could this be any more *Lord of the Rings*? Do you always talk like this?"

"Are we *The Lord of the Rings* or *X-Men*, Lily? Make up your mind. And it is what it is. Only Abram really knows how—"

"Yeah, I've got it. Abram knows all. Abram is good, Abram is wise," I mumbled. "You know, this better not be some kind of a cult, because I warn you, I am no sheep."

"It's not anything like that!" Christian screwed up his face in displeasure. "Do you know how many of those things we've fought to wipe out? Don't be offensive, Lily."

"Whoa, sorry." I exhaled quickly through pursed lips. "Touchy subject?"

"Sort of. What I mean to say is that most cults are not as they seem to the casual observer."

"We have a while. Explain," I prodded.

"Are you sure you really want to hear this? It may be a bit hard to swallow."

"Look, I just got attacked by a fucking vampire, Christian. I suppose I'm up for bending my old perceptions. Besides, I'll take any information you're actually willing to give me."

"All right. Most cults are begun by dark spirits."

"Dark spirits? You mean evil ghosty types?"

"No, not necessarily a ghost. It doesn't usually involve a human spirit. Usually, it's a leech, an energy drainer."

"Oh. Where does this kind of spirit originate, if not a human?"

"There's more than one place, but I've seen a lot of parasites that were man-made."

"Man-made?"

"Yes. The energy of the masses is a force to be reckoned with. Any prolonged negative human event experienced by many can cast off a dark energy. Hell, it doesn't even need to be experienced by many. One mind with an emotional force strong enough can create a new outside energy. It has to go somewhere, after all. And once it's free, it needs to replenish itself through sheep-herding, as you would put it."

"How do you know all this?" I asked. "Abram, right?"

"A lot of it." He smiled.

"How long have you known this man?"

He hesitated. "All my life."

"Are you saying that literally or are you being philosophical?"

"I have known him since I was very young, quite literally."

"Then you wouldn't have dreamed about him?"

"Actually, I did for a while. He was very persistent. I knew what he wanted. But I was hardly as inclined as you to come along for the ride." He laughed. "Like I said, my retriever winced every time he saw me for quite a few months."

This was an amusing thought. At first glance, Christian hardly came off as the knock-your-lights-out type. He was far too proper looking, and the accent gave him an air of constant formality.

"I have another question," I said, "but I don't know if it's too personal."

"I suppose if I said it *was,* you'd just find a way to get it out of me anyway."

"Maybe, but that's beside the point. May I?"

"What is it, Lily?"

"Okay. Well, the light that surrounded us in the woods—where did it come from? It seemed like…were you kind of…glowing?" I cringed, not knowing how a guy would feel about such a thing.

To my surprise, he smiled happily. "Is that all? It's protective energy. You can see that?"

"Yes. Of course. It was … nice," I said, blushing.

"Releasing it helps to calm people. I'm surprised you can detect it already," he said.

Well, protective energy. I could get behind that.

The rest of the trip was sprinkled with answers to only the most impersonal questions, vague descriptions of people I would meet. Any time I asked anything remotely related to myself, however, such as why I was going there, what about me Abram knew, Christian would decline to answer. It was something Abram had to explain, he'd tell me.

Mercifully for Christian, we reached the Atlanta area with a bit of daylight to spare.

"So you live here?" I asked, curious to know the extent of Abram's little commune.

"Not permanently. There was an uprising of vampires that caused a riot under the city and threatened to infest the residents. It's taken a while to get things under control, but eventually we'll move on."

"Oh. Then, do you all stay together?"

"Mostly. But it's not the way it sounds," he pressed.

"And you travel around, looking for trouble, then?"

"We don't usually have to look very hard."

He took an exit marked "Landsfield" and we drove for a while through a winding country lane, tall grass on either side. "We're nearly there," Christian said.

I watched as houses became sparse, turning to trees, and the trees to fields. "What's with the wide-open spaces?" I asked. "This isn't Atlanta. Where's the smog?"

"This is Landsfield, a speck on the map about forty minutes outside the city. The country is best. Some discretion is well advised in this line of work, Lily."

"You all remain to yourselves a lot, then?"

"Mmhm. It can be very lonely, really. We only see other Sentients a few times a year, and the circumstances are often unpleasant. But there is real danger in exposing ourselves, Lily. It's happened before, and we've been kidnapped, tested, interrogated, even tortured. The powers that be and the populace as a whole have no true concept of reality and are nowhere near ready to work alongside us. So we keep our lives to ourselves."

"But what about religions? I mean, you'd think they'd be all over this, proof of the supernatural."

"Quite the contrary," he said. "It's most frightening to them, I think. They'd have to change their entire belief set, uproot a complete ideology, and first and foremost acknowledge that they'd been wrong all along. Not likely in many lifetimes."

We veered to the right and turned a corner, passing rows of massive and wild growing cottonwood trees. Then a lovely white farmhouse came into view. It was only one story, but it sprawled across an impressive width of land. Hanging ferns decorated a porch that wrapped entirely around the building.

"We're here. This is it." He turned to face me. Whatever my expression read, he sensed it. "It's all right," he assured me.

I laughed breathily. "Whose *house* is this?" I asked.

"It belongs to one of Abram's friends. He only comes here on holiday."

"He's got some impressive friends, huh?"

"You could say that," he said smiling. "He tends to create a few wherever he goes."

Christian got out and waited for me to do the same. "You won't need carrying, then?" he teased over the top of the car.

"I will not, thank you very much."

"Good. Let's get your things out of the back."

He headed for the trunk and offered me a duffel bag, taking my suitcase. "That's that, then." His voice was light and casual. "Let's go." He closed the trunk, glanced up toward the house, and froze in a look of amused irritation.

"What is it?" I asked, examining his expression.

He rolled his eyes toward the massive porch. "It appears we have an entourage."

I followed his gaze to the porch to see a crowd of about ten faces gathered there. The one striking point about each of them was that same golden light, swelling out in rays from their collective outline. They wore friendly, but cautious, expressions. If they were trying not to overwhelm me, it was too late.

A few stood out more than the others. In front there was a young girl, mid-twenties at most, with an enviable mane of strawberry blond hair and a peaches-and-cream complexion. She wore a fearlessly happy smile. Next to her was an older woman, about the same height, who looked very much like the younger but for few gray hairs.

I turned to Christian, anxiety twisting at my gut.

He smiled at me and sighed quickly. "Come on. They're harmless, really. It'll be fine!"

Reaching over, he placed his hand on my back, walking me toward the porch. The faces grew more expectant and more encouraging the closer we came, until finally we stopped in front of them.

"Lily," Christian began. "This is my mother, Clara." The older of the two strawberry blondes smiled, and I immediately liked her for no more reason than the light around her. It was brighter than the rest.

"Welcome, Lily. We're all so very happy to have you here," she said, reaching out and wrapping me in a strangely familiar embrace.

"And this," she went on, directing my attention to the young woman at her side, "is my daughter, Annalise."

"Please, call me Anna!" She grabbed me up for an enthusiastic hug. "Thank *God* you're here. I have been going mad with only the testosterone and these old biddies around all the time!"

"Anna!" Christian chastised her. "Don't scare her off before she's stepped foot over the threshold!"

"That's right, you minx, watch yourself," Clara chimed in.

"You must forgive my sister, Lily. She is exceptionally lacking in tact," Christian cautioned as he smiled nervously.

"Nonsense," said Anna, messing the back of his hair. "I am simply exceptionally bad at bullshit."

Clara put her arm around Anna. "Yes, well, same thing, I'm afraid, dear," she said.

"It's all right, Anna. I'm a lot like that myself," I spoke, and the group went silent. They were hanging on my every word. This was going to be interesting.

"Can she come inside or will we be setting up camp out here this evening?" Christian asked, shaking his head at the eager faces edging ever closer.

A very tall, very muscular older man ducked quickly through the crowd toward the door, clearing a path on his way. "Okay, folks, show's over, let them through. We can all make our introductions inside," he said, holding the door open. His voice was booming and jolly.

Clara took my arm and led me into the house with Christian and Anna in tow. It took my eyes a moment to adjust to the deeper, wooden interior of the round reception hall. Bouquets of wild flowers were placed at each side of the door, and a well-worn, circular Asian rug was spread out across the floor. The ceiling was higher than I'd imagined from the outside, with painted white beams running the length of either side. A long hallway veered off to the left, while a large kitchen opened to the right. Straight ahead was the living room. Two windows stood floor to ceiling. Through them, I glimpsed the grounds in back. If anything, I would enjoy exploring them.

The group filtered in behind me, forming a haphazard line against the wall. First to step forward was the large man who had cleared the way for me. He had a graying beard and stood a solid foot above the men around him. He reminded me of an old lumberjack.

"I'm Demetre Phelps," he said, taking my hand and shaking it vigorously, a wide smile on his face. Up close I could see that he was older than I'd thought. His face was leathery and deeply wrinkled.

"I'm Ginny," said a very small brown-haired girl, offering her hand.

"I'm Lily," I said as I smiled back.

"I know. Are you really a path crosser?" she asked, her eyes wide.

"Am I … a what?" I found myself looking at Christian for an answer.

Demetre sighed. "Now, Virginia, you were not supposed to say anything like that." His accent was clearly American, with a slow twang.

"I'm sorry, I couldn't help it! It just came out," she lamented.

"It's okay," I said quickly. "I just don't know the answer to your question, Ginny. I'm sorry."

"Oh. That's okay. Abram will know. He always says he isn't that smart, but he knows lots more stuff than me, and maybe even Grandpa!"

Demetre cleared his throat, and the room burst into laughter.

"Uh … I have a memory endowment, Lily," Demetre explained. "I remember everything I see and hear. I can relay it back perfectly like a map or a recording. So, my little monkey here thinks her old Grandpa knows everything!"

"Which is plainly not the case, I promise you," said a plump- faced woman at his side. She wore her silver hair tucked primly into a bun behind her head. "I'm Ophelia, Demetre's wife. And Ginny is our granddaughter," she explained. "It's not clear if she has a gift yet, but Demetre does, so we hope that she will too, someday."

I desperately wanted to ask what she meant by a gift, but I was distracted by a dark-haired man, around my age. He was tall, and a bit on the gangly side, with some of the palest skin I'd ever seen. While the calming light of the others had faded minutes before, a blue glow remained with him, and he stood at the room's perimeter, out of the limelight.

"Who's that?" I asked Christian.

He glanced at the man with little interest. "Maddox," he said.

"Oh. And, shouldn't I meet him?"

He shrugged. "If you want to."

I waited good-naturedly for Christian to heed my request, but more time passed and he continued speaking with Demetre as if I'd never asked. I looked away from the main group again, toward the stranger, and we locked eyes. His smile was warm and guarded, with a hint of amusement. Without even thinking, I ducked through the bodies toward him.

"Hello," I began. "Christian is lost in conversation so I thought I'd make my own introductions. I'm Lily."

"I know," he chuckled, taking my hand. "I'm William Maddox." He gazed at me thoughtfully through moss-colored eyes. "Abram saw you well, Lillian."

"Did he? This guy must have some fantastic eyesight. And call me Lily. I'm not a fan of Lillian."

"I'll keep that in mind," he said, half-smiling. "So, is it true that you can see lightlines?"

"Lightlines? You mean the glowing?"

"Not necessarily. You're probably confusing an aura with a lightline."

"Well, whatever they are, I...I actually went to an optician." I cringed, covering my face with my hand. "That's when I started getting worried."

"Ah, yes. Thought the lunacy had set in?" he said with a laugh.

"Absolutely."

"Well, things will be clearer from now on. Vision develops as it's needed, Lily. Your experiences draw it out."

"Good to hear." Mother of God was this an actual answer? I decided to press my luck. "So, these lights appear when people are trying to calm me down, right?"

"Yes. But Abram thinks they'll be more prominent, more detailed, for you at other times as well. I suppose we won't know until after you've...well, later," he said.

"After I've what?" I was evidently and hopelessly in the dark.

"Eh … I assumed you'd know more by now."

"That seems to be the consensus." I frowned.

"I guess I'm not *too* surprised," he continued. "I realize you had no guide. That makes for some uncertainty. But your endowments should be more pronounced by now. Haven't things been happening to you?"

"Oh, definitely. But I just assumed I was imagining them and blocked them out."

"Some things are difficult to dismiss when you're a path crosser. How did you explain away being visited?"

I blinked. "Visited?"

He blinked back. "Have you really never been visited?" he asked, flabbergasted.

"Well, maybe, but, what do you mean by that?"

"Didn't Christian explain *anything* to you? What did you two talk about for eight hours?"

"Abram wanted me to tell her only what was necessary." Christian was at my side, an instant tension building in the air around us. "We don't need to overwhelm her. She doesn't know this life, Maddox."

"And obviously you haven't done much to remedy that fact," William contested. "What *have* you told her?"

"She knew the dreams."

"You of all people should have an appreciation for a decision made with full consent. Let me guess, Lily, did he pull any strong-arm tactics? Threaten to tow you to Georgia if you didn't agree to come?"

I stammered. He *had* carried me. Oh boy, this was awkward.

"No, it was fine," I said. "I'm sure Christian was simply doing what he thought was best."

"That's right," Christian said. "After all, someone had to keep her safe," he said in a tone too polite to be sincere, and William's face fell.

"If you'll excuse us," Christian went on, "Lily has a few more introductions to make before dinner."

William nodded slowly. "Of course. And Lily … ." He turned to face me, forcing a smile. "It was nice to meet you," he said.

"Nice to meet you, too" was all I had time for as Christian took my arm and all but dragged me away toward an older man standing next to Clara.

"Thomas has been friends with Abram for years," Christian said quietly as we walked. "He's an old Sentient."

"Aaah, Christian, you have brought the lady of the hour to us at last." He grabbed my hand with both of his. "A pleasure to meet you, my dear. I am Thomas Ward."

Thomas was a small, white-haired gentleman wearing thin, wire-rimmed spectacles. Like Christian and his family, he spoke with a British accent, and his presence was uniquely warm, just as Clara's had been.

"How was your trip? Was it terribly awkward for you, dear?" Thomas asked, patting my hand.

I laughed out loud. "Awkward?" I passed Christian a kind glance. "Not more than I could handle," I finished.

"Abram knew she was coming?" he asked Christian.

"Yes. We ran into some complications and had to retrieve her earlier than planned."

"Were you prepared, Lily?" Thomas asked.

"Prepared for what, specifically?" I asked.

"Mmm. That answers my question. But we're more than happy to show you the ropes when you need it."

"Thanks," I said with a smile. If only I knew what "the ropes" were.

"Hey, Golden Boy! Abram's back." I turned toward the source of the heavy New York accent to see an olive-skinned young man in a muscle hugging shirt with short brown hair crossing the room. He, like Christian, seemed to be in exceptional physical condition. His muscles were a tad too much for my taste, though, like he spent an exorbitant amount of time kissing his triceps in front of a mirror.

"Hey, the newbie!" He strutted up to us, a Cheshire grin showcasing bleached white teeth.

"Yes." Christian took a step closer to me. "Lily, this is Paul DePrimo. Paul, this is Lillian Hunt."

"Lillian, nice." He looked me up and down, nodding in approval.

"Just Lily, please," I said uncomfortably.

"My pleasure, Lily." He reached for my hand and kissed it. "Perhaps, if you'd allow me to be so kind, I could show you around town one of these evenings."

"That would be ... nice," I said weakly.

"She'll be busy," Christian interrupted. "With Abram, I mean."

"Aaah, I get it. Don't worry, bro." He nudged Christian's shoulder.

Thomas cleared his throat. "Well, I think Abram will want to meet her. Christian, why don't you take her to the study."

"Sure. Lily, shall we?"

"Yes!" I said a bit too eagerly.

He took my arm and we ducked through the crowd toward a nearby hallway, slowing the pace once we were out of Paul's sight.

"Was that guy for real?" I giggled.

"As real as they come." He grinned. "He's got a good heart; he's just a bit of a Casanova. Abram had him retrieved from a foster home in Queens ten years ago. Right here." He nodded toward a worn wooden door on the left, lifting his fist to knock. I grabbed his arm.

"Wait!" I whispered.

"What is it?"

"I'm … I'm nervous," I muttered.

"About Abram?" he asked with a laugh.

"Yes."

"Lily, believe me, Abram is the last person in this world you should be anxious about. The moment you meet him you'll understand why. Now, I'm knocking," he said in a warning voice.

I frowned, but I didn't attempt to stop him again.

"Come in!"

Christian opened the door and stood against it, waiting for me to pass. I glanced at him anxiously and stepped inside. The room was exactly as you'd picture a study. It smelled like cedar and pine cleaner, and bookshelves lined nearly every wall, their contents stacked sideways, upwards, and at a leaning angle. These books were obviously not for show.

"They haven't frightened you off yet?" asked a gentle voice from the right. An elderly black man stood two rungs up a librarian's ladder, a book in each hand.

"They're doing their best." Christian closed the door behind me. "Lily, this is Abram Saru."

"Welcome, Lillian." The old man smiled. He stepped down and placed the books on a cluttered desk, then turned to me and placed both hands on my shoulders, examining me with the warmest of expressions. Anyone watching would have thought he'd known me all my life.

"Good to see you again. You look even more like your mother in the flesh," he said.

"You're him," I whispered, dumbfounded. The face before me was utterly recognizable: the gray eyes, snow white hair, even the softness of his smile.

He pinched my cheek. "You came with Christian. Fearless girl!" he said, pleased.

"He didn't exactly give me much choice in the matter," I said laughing.

Abram patted Christian's shoulder. "Yes, he's a man of action, this one."

"Definitely." I smirked.

"But she's here, all in one piece, right?" Christian added.

"Yes, but you look a little worse for the wear, son." Abram nodded at Christian's torn clothes.

"See, now that was the only trip-up. It seems a blood-sucking vermin got wind of her. *Someone* wasn't keeping their post," Christian grumbled.

"Now, now, I'm sure any of us could have missed it," Abram said. "The vampire acted abruptly."

"Who wasn't keeping their post?" I asked.

"Abram," Christian went on, dismissing my question, "he had one purpose there, and it was to watch over her, and he couldn't even get that right. Why do you trust him?"

"Because I choose to, Christian." Abram's words were perfectly civil, but final.

Christian opened his mouth to argue, deliberated, then changed his mind. Whoever they were talking about was a sore subject, but, even after just meeting Abram, it was clear to me that he commanded respect without even trying. His unfailingly patient countenance was, ironically enough, quite intimidating.

"Lily, would you mind terribly keeping me company for a short while?" Abram asked.

"No, of course not," I said.

"Good. Christian, see you at dinner, then?"

Christian nodded at Abram and headed for the door, but turned to smile in my direction.

"Bye," I mouthed. He waved in response and left the room.

Abram sighed. "It's been a long day for you, Lillian."

"I've had longer, believe me," I said.

"Yes, you have. I *am* sorry I couldn't be of more comfort to you in recent days. I realize you must have been in great distress."

"So you know what's been happening?"

"I do. And I know it has been escalating. I did *not*, however, anticipate any imminent danger for you, Lily. I apologize for this oversight and for the need to bring you here so abruptly. In fact, I had hoped you could remain with your loved ones for a longer time, but, obviously, this is impossible."

"Yeah. I understand … okay, no, I don't, but I believe you."

"Thank you for that."

"You're welcome. Though, if Christian wasn't supposed to be my retriever, who was?"

"Ah, pardon my withholding that detail at the moment. It is better revealed, I think, when you are more acclimated to this life and less vulnerable to the ideas of those around you. Now, Lily, have a seat, won't you?" He motioned toward a large leather chair next to the desk. I did as he asked and watched as he turned an identical chair so that it faced me. He sat down and leaned in, his forearms resting on his lap.

"You must have many questions," he said, and I listened intently, trying to determine the origin of his accent.

"Yes. More than I can think of," I said.

"Naturally. And you mustn't try to think of them all tonight!" He laughed. "I have no intention of overwhelming you. In fact, I'll answer only a few questions this evening, so choose carefully. No doubt your housemates will be filling your head with all sorts of things in my absence."

"A few? How many is that? Three?" I complained.

"Three sounds sufficient."

I scrunched up my face, thinking hard. What could I ask that would seem like one question, but in fact, result in several answers?

"Okay. I've got one, and I'll start small," I said.

"A clever decision. Do go on," he urged.

"What am I?"

"Ah, and here you said it would be simple!" he said, beaming. "But you've begun with the most difficult. Still, I'll answer it according to your needs. You are, first and foremost, a human being. This is, always remember, the most important thing. Shall I go a step further?"

"Yes, please."

"I thought as much," he chuckled. "You are also a human Sentient, as Seers have named you. Your soul has carried with it the perceptions of many lives."

"So, what does that mean?"

"This is your next question, then?"

"Oh no." I pouted. "I s'pose it is."

"It simply means that the vision of your mind is multi-dimensional. You can sense many veils of reality."

"Doesn't sound so simple to me," I said.

"This is one time when the practice is easier than the theory," he agreed.

"I'll just have to trust you on that one, Abram. I'm not feeling too able at present."

He nodded. "And you're utterly confused as well."

"Completely."

"Fantastic! You're beginning with a clean slate. You see, Lily, you have a unique advantage over the rest of the Sentients here. You have yet to be jaded, yet to be molded by the minds of others like you! Your point of view will interest me greatly, I'm certain."

"That's very flattering," I said.

"But sincere. I mean every word of it," he insisted. "Now, do you have your last question ready?"

"Yes, I do, actually."

"Let's have it."

"Why am I here?"

"Hmm. I could tell you, but… forgive me, child, that deserves more than a verbal explanation. Would you mind if I deferred it until tomorrow? I'm afraid I have a dreadful weakness for surprises, and I'd like to deliver a practical demonstration."

"All right. Then I have a back up question."

"As would I." He grinned.

"What are these things coming after me? The other night, this black… thing… shadow, whatever it was decided to hang out with me. *I* had to leave my own bedroom!" My admission made the experience real, and I shuddered.

Abram gazed at me with understanding, and warm light gathered around us. It wasn't as bright as Christian's had been, but it felt better. I suspected Abram didn't have to try as hard.

"Yes. I dare say you would be more prone to these sorts of visitations while away from other Sentients," he said. "A shadow you say?"

I nodded.

"How did it behave?"

"It was sort of just staring at me. It didn't seem like it was in any kind of hurry to get *too* close, but it was testing the waters, that much I could tell."

"Hm. Would you say it was observing you?"

"Yeah. I guess it was."

"Did it say anything?"

"No. The most noise it made was this awful rasping sound. I couldn't tell if it was breathing or trying to talk to me."

He shook his head. "I should have suspected as much. Your dark visitor was, I'm fairly confident, a Scout. That would explain how the vampire found you so quickly."

"A scout?"

"Yes. Vampires can create them to lock down a Sentient's location. And perhaps more than that, these energies get to know you most intimately. They study your thoughts, your reactions. They gage your strength."

"So, it was spying on me?"

"Indeed. And once it established a mental connection, you were as good as wearing a tracking device."

"Nice."

"Most disturbing. But you should know that the cumulative energy that surrounds us here is a great deal more difficult for dark spirits to penetrate, so rest at ease."

I sighed, relieved.

He continued. "I would, however, take care when on the grounds or away from the house. You are the most attractive sort of Sentient, Lily, and you have few defenses built up at this stage."

"How should I take care? What do I do?"

"Shall we make an accord? If you'll be so tolerant as to allow someone to accompany you for a while, I'll see to it that you learn to protect yourself in the meantime. Is this acceptable?"

"You mean a babysitter?" I raised an eyebrow.

"Think of it as your own personal security guard," he countered.

I sighed. "Christian?"

"If you'd prefer," he said.

"I don't have a preference." I fumbled uncomfortably. "It's just that he seems to have taken over the role. It's natural that he'd be resuming his position."

"Indeed. I shall foist him upon you, then." He nodded, standing.

I laughed. "Thanks."

"Dinner? Clara is making one of her delightful chicken pot pies, and I cannot resist."

"Sure." I knew I liked Clara. Aside from a root beer and bag of pretzels on the car ride here, I hadn't eaten since breakfast.

☙

With the exception of Abram, who was helping Clara carry food to the table, nearly everyone was seated and chattering loudly. One voice, in particular, was instantly recognizable. Paul regaled Anna with a story of how he repelled three vampires at once in Vancouver.

"They were huge!" He spread his arms out and elbowed Demetre in the shoulder.

"Uh-huh, and were you blindfolded with your hands tied behind your back?" Demetre grunted.

"Yes … wait," Paul stopped, confused. "No, but I *was* suffering from a bout of heartburn, having just partaken of some potent marinara," he rambled, trying to sound eloquent. "Nevertheless, rest assured, despite this setback," he continued, "with right on my side, I was victorious in the end."

"Yes, yes, rest assured," Thomas said, clearly amused.

"What? You don't believe me?" Paul pointed at himself with a forkful of salad. "You have my word, as a gentleman and a Sentient."

"You hear that, Thomas? He's a gentleman," Anna said. "Just keep that in mind, Romeo, the next time you decide to harass a sorority house."

"I am insulted!" Paul put his hand over his heart. "I was merely doing my job. There were evil spirits present. I felt them!"

I took a sip of iced tea as Christian leaned into my ear. "He's confusing ghosts with breasts again."

The tea rushed out my nose back into my glass, and I gasped for air, coughing.

"Whoa, you okay there?" Demetre raised his voice over my choking.

I nodded feverishly, trying to compose myself. Christian smirked and patted my back.

"She's good. Just a little bit down the wrong pipe is all," he said as Anna eyed us suspiciously.

Abram stood up and cleared his throat; the table went silent.

"Evening, my friends," he said, happily. "Now, I know it's not customary to make speeches at the dinner table, but I thought, in this particular instance, it would be fitting. As you all are quite aware, Christian was kind enough to retrieve a new Sentient, Lillian Hunt." He nodded to me and everyone smiled. Anna put her hand on my shoulder.

"Most of you have had the benefit of a guided life, knowing all of your years what you are and why, and have been supported by others like yourself. But Miss Hunt cannot claim such luck, and so, bearing this in mind, I am certain you will all do your best to make her feel welcome and safe. I know she will be a refreshing addition to the Society."

"Here, here! To Lily." Thomas raised his glass and the rest of the table followed suit.

Christian glanced at me, smiling subtly until his eyes reached the door. Following his gaze I saw that William had joined us. He looked utterly handsome, pressed against the wood frame, his arms crossed. I wondered how long he had been standing there.

"William," Abram waved him forward in greeting. "Have a seat."

Christian's face hardened and he looked away, picking up his glass of water and taking a mechanical sip. William sat back in his chair, observing the scene.

"So, William, m'boy, how goes the surge in Philadelphia?" asked Thomas. This caught my attention. Philadelphia was in Pennsylvania. And that reminded me of … shit … my grandparents!

"They're stronger than I thought," William said gravely. "And their numbers are greater."

Thomas nodded. "It's the remnants of Vancouver, isn't it?"

"Yes. It is," Abram said. "They're licking their wounds and rebuilding."

"Wait, Abram," I cut in. "Are you talking about vampires?" I'd been so wrapped up in the events of the day that I'd barely considered Frank and Connie. Until now. The idea that there were monsters out there, anywhere close to them, froze my blood. What the hell was I thinking, sitting here eating fucking *pot pie* (though, *God*, it was really good) hundreds of miles away when there were *vampires* in Philadelphia?!

"I'm afraid so, Lily." Abram turned to me, biding his words. "But we need not discuss these matters over such a delightful meal," he said.

"But, I have family there," I said.

William opened his mouth to say something but Christian spoke over him.

"Don't worry, Lily. We'll wipe them out, just as we always do. I promise." He squeezed my hand under the table and threw an angry look at William. "No help from him," he added.

"Christian, do be reasonable," Clara began.

"What?" He bristled. "Would it really surprise any of us if he were helping them?"

"That's enough," Abram said calmly, and Christian fell silent, but the seed of distrust had been planted. I would view William with more suspicion now.

I ate dinner as quickly as I could without looking impolite, and waited anxiously for someone else to finish. I didn't want to be the first one to leave the table. Paul got up, and I grabbed my plate and all but ran into the kitchen, turning on the sink and scrubbing maniacally.

"Hey, what's the emergency?" Paul approached the sink.

"I have to call home And Rufus!" Sudden realization hit me. What about my life at home? What about the store, my grandparents, my obligations? What was I going to tell everyone?

"Rufus? Is that your boyfriend?" His face fell.

"No," Christian corrected, walking up behind us. "Her cat."

"You have to call your cat?" Paul asked.

"No, no, I just, I need to call home. Dammit, I don't have the charger for my cell phone! And how do you know about Rufus?" I asked Christian, again amazed at how knowledgeable he was of the details of my life.

"We pay attention." He shrugged. "There's a phone in your room, Lil. You can use that one." My lifelong nickname slid off his tongue so naturally you'd think we were old friends.

"All right," I said, turning on my heals immediately, then stopping. "Eh, I have a room?"

"Come with me." He chuckled.

I followed Christian out of the dining room and across the main reception hall, now dimly lit. He led me down the same corridor where Abram's study was. We passed it and several more rooms until we'd nearly reached the end.

"Here it is," he offered. I turned the crystal knob and entered the room. A lovely fragrance filled the air.

"Apples?" I said, noticing the glowing jar candle on the nightstand.

"Anna knew you liked them," Christian answered. "So she went out and bought one. Oh, and here … ."

He took a few quick strides toward what looked like a closet door and pulled it open.

"Here's your bathroom, and … ." Just then a black tabby bounded out of the tub and into my arms.

"Rufus!" I squealed, nuzzling him close. "When and *how* did you guys do this? Did you break into my apartment?" I paused, turning my attention back to Christian.

"Well … ." He lowered his eyes, shuffling his foot against the floor. "Perhaps a bit. But we had no choice!" he added, immediately. "You were in danger."

"Uh-huh," I said sternly, but I decided he had a point. "And how did you pull it off?"

"It was all Anna. She drove your car ahead of us to Atlanta, brought the cat with her. I'll just bet she's gotten attached to him already," he said, reaching out to pet Rufus's back. I opened my mouth to warn him, but it was too late. Rufus snapped his head around and sunk his teeth into Christian's hand.

"Shit," he cursed, grimacing.

"Christian, I am *so* sorry! He doesn't like people," I apologized, plopping a disgruntled Rufus on my bed and grabbing Christian's injured hand.

"It's all right. It's okay, Lily." He laughed warmly. "A small scratch, practically healed over already, see?" He rested his hand in mine, allowing me to examine the damage more closely.

"It looks okay," I said.

"It feels fine," he said smiling. Warmth emanated from him as it had before and the moment was pure tranquility.

"Lily?" he whispered.

"Yes?"

"You can let go of my hand now," he said, the corner of his mouth upturned.

"Oh, right," I said, my face flushing as I freed his hand. "You need to stop messing with me that way, I mean, the calming thing. It's very disorienting!"

"Yes, horribly disorienting being so very ... peaceful." He grinned. "Do you feel more at home in a panicked state?"

"Ugh. It's more familiar to me than anything else anymore." I sat on the edge of the bed and sighed.

"You know," Christian began, taking a seat next to me. "Everything that's been happening to you is perfectly normal ... for people like us," he said.

I laughed. "And I'm sure that would be very reassuring if it didn't scare the shit out of me," I said.

"Ah, should I whip out the calm, then?"

"No, no," I said. "You'd better watch yourself, Christian. When I start getting all skilled with the glowing lights of bliss, you're going to be a serene mess. Payback's a bitch."

"Then I'll remember to keep my distance whenever I prefer a really foul mood." He laughed softly.

"Wise," I said.

"Well, then. You'll be wanting to call your grandparents." He stood up.

"Ehn. Dreading it, actually. I have no idea what to tell them!"

"Hmm. I wish I could help you with that one, Lily. But I'm afraid Abram was right. It's unique for a Sentient to be raised outside of the inner circle." He shook his head. "I can't begin to know how you'd explain this."

I nodded solemnly.

"Demetre and I will be going downtown in a bit," he began. "We probably won't be back until late, but if you need to talk, knock on my door. It's the second one down on the left."

"Thanks," I smiled. "But I think you've had about enough of me for one day."

"No, Lily, really," he insisted.

"Don't be such a gentleman. It'll make it harder for me to kick you out." I jumped up, crossed the room to the door and opened it for him. He went along cheerfully, but stopped in the doorway.

"No use putting off the inevitable," he said. "You should get that call over with."

I moaned, my nerves finally catching up to me. "I guess."

"Night, then. Good luck," he offered.

"Thanks. Goodnight, Christian," I said. He started down the hall. "Thanks for the rescuing, by the way," I called after him.

"My pleasure," he called back. "Oh! And if I had to pick, I'd say we're more like *X-Men*."

"Is that right?"

"Yes. Those hobbits are absolutely unnatural … with the hairy feet," he muttered before he rounded the corner and was gone.

A swarm of butterflies pounded their wings in my stomach as I glowered at the phone. Exhaling sharply, I closed the door behind me and sat on the bed next to the nightstand. *Should I think this over or just dive in?*

"Ridiculous!" I jumped up and paced the floor. "They just don't do this. Normal people *just* don't do this!" I scolded myself. "Why am I even here? I mean, they all seem harmless enough, but fuck! I'm going to end up on my back covered in a sheet with my Nikes sticking out!"

But no. I knew I was mistaken, and I felt immense guilt. These people weren't mindless followers. They were real. And I was one of them, more and more one of them every day. There was no functioning in my old world as I was now. I could claim a fractional understanding of what was out there, and even less of an idea how to deal with it. I needed them, and the thought frustrated and encouraged me at the same time. From this phone call on, nothing would be the same, no matter what I told my grandparents.

I picked up the phone and dialed. Frank answered.

"Hello?" His voice brought my new and old realities crashing together. I jumped off the cliff.

"Grandpa. It's me."

"Oh, hey, kiddo! Thank God! I told your grandmother that you'd decided to take the whole day off, but in the meantime, I've been worried sick! Where've you been?"

"Grandpa, I'm so sorry. I didn't even think about…God, I just wasn't thinking," I sighed.

"You all right, Lily? And where are you calling from? The number looks long distance," he said.

"*Shit,*" I mouthed. Caller ID. "Well, Grandpa, I decided to take a vacation," I cringed.

There was silence on the other end. "A vacation? To … where, exactly?" he asked, pronouncing the words carefully.

"To Georgia." I shut my eyes, scrunching my shoulders together. Of course Georgia. Why the hell not? That was just like me.

I could nearly see his expression on the other end of the phone. The mouth wide, the brows narrowed.

"Lillian, what in the hell are you doing in Georgia?" he said, finally.

"I just…" *Think quickly, think quickly!* "I wanted to see the beach." I'm sure my face was a comedy of expressions now.

"Well …." He was laughing. "Of all the…Lily, there are closer beaches than that! That must have been, what, six, seven hours on the road? And with gas the price it is …."

"Yeah, but, you know, the beaches closer to home aren't the same. I wanted to see a Southern beach. I decided to be spontaneous!" I lied.

"So you drove to Georgia? Alone?"

"Yes," I lied again. "But I brought mace and a first aid kit," I joked feebly.

"Lily, honey, when are you coming back?"

"I don't know. Grandpa, I'm so sorry. I know I'm complicating things for you guys, with the store. I know it seems selfish."

"No. Lily, baby, don't worry about that. Look, if you need a vacation, and Christ knows you do, then by all means take it. But, just, be careful. I hate the idea of you being all alone out there."

"Well, if it makes you feel any better, I met some really nice folks familiar with the area and they've been very hospitable."

"Good. Well, you just don't trust anybody too soon, though, okay?"

"No problem. You know me."

"Yep. Well, any idea how long you might be gone? No pressure or anything, just curious what to tell your grandmother."

"Uhm, it might be a while," I said, forcing the words out.

Another moment of silence. "Like, a week, a few weeks? What?"

I sighed. "I don't know yet, Grandpa. I've got some things to figure out." It was all I could say, but it was honest.

He sighed as well. "Okay, kiddo. And I know the answer to this already, but you're not in any kind of trouble, right?"

"No! No, of course not," I said, unsure if this was wholly accurate.

"Yeah, I'm sorry to ask. Just an old man worrying. I'll miss you around here."

"You too. Every day." A lump formed in my throat. "I'll call you all the time."

"You'd better, or I'll send a search party."

"I know, I know." I laughed lightly. "Thanks for trusting me."

"Well, your choices have always been a little *too* safe in my opinion. If this is what you need, it's what you need. I want you to be happy, Lil." His voice broke. "You've never really seemed happy with life, just tolerant of it."

The truth of what he said ripped open a carefully sealed package and warm tears slipped down my face. "I love you. I'll make you proud, I promise."

"Already have." Damn me. More tears.

"All right. I'm going to go. I'll call you tomorrow!" I said, willing myself to sound casual.

"All righty. Night, kiddo."

"Night, Grandpa."

I doubted that my first night in my new room would be restful, though someone had gone to great lengths—I suspected Anna—to try and make it so. Sheer pale blue curtains hung from two floor-to-ceiling windows, and a snow white comforter, with matching blue pillows, decorated the bed. The floor was solid wood and cold on my bare feet, but the weather here was unbearably muggy, so I was sure I wouldn't mind it.

Turning off the lamp, I pulled up the blinds. To my delight, a huge portion of the floor, as well as my bed, was immediately bathed in moonlight. The surge of euphoria returned, and I laughed softly. Taking a step forward, I stood in the light, tilted my head back, and closed my eyes. It held my face and wrapped its arms around my shoulders, and for the very first time, I let hope in.

Four

*I*t was still early when I woke. I stared out the window of my new room, the sun just beginning to show over the trees, the clouds a luminous, rose-hued spread. Opening my suitcase, I found that Anna had done an exquisite packing job. She'd managed to fit the bulk of my wardrobe into the main compartment, along with toiletries in various pouches, and stuffed a duffel bag with shoes—brilliant girl. She'd even remembered to put my cell phone charger into a side pocket. Admirable as it all was, my amusement was somewhat tainted. How on earth had she managed to get into my apartment so easily? And how did they know where I lived? In fact, it seemed they knew more about me than I did. Even more, Abram had acknowledged my mother. My list of questions was mounting extensively.

After a long shower, I put on my favorite sundress, smiling as it fell gracefully to my knees. Kate had always teased me, saying that my clothes were too girly, but I lacked the boyish lines and sharp edges that ruled the fashion world, so I had a particular hatred for anything terribly modern, preferring timeless and feminine to cutting edge and risqué.

In keeping with my trend toward rebellion, any attempts to really straighten my hair were futile. The stubborn waves re-emerged in minutes, only half-tamed. I assumed my mother had struggled with the same hair, the same dilemma. Sometimes, I'd catch a glimpse of myself in the mirror and I'd swear it was her face looking back, the same face I'd dreamed about years before. It made no sense that I should feel this way, since I'd never seen a single photograph of her anywhere; Frank figured that Dad couldn't bear to look at them. But nonetheless, the woman in my dreams had seemed so recognizable.

I slipped into some ballet flats and sat at the foot of my bed, wondering if anyone else would be awake this early. Already my nerves were getting the better of me. I'd been shut up all night in my own fantastic trance to contemplate everything that had happened the day before, and now it all felt unreal. Naturally, denial was ludicrous—after all, here I sat, the evidence at hand. But my new world, with its colorful inhabitants, was still asleep, and some part of me feared that I was as well. If I got up the nerve to open that door, would it all blow away? I put off the action as long as possible, but there were only so many ways to refold your clothes before risking a diagnosis of obsessive compulsive disorder.

"Voicemail," I remembered, grateful for the distraction.

1:37 p.m.: *"Lily, it's Grandpa. I tried your place but you didn't answer. Where are you? Did you decide to take the whole day off after all? Let me know."*

4:21 p.m.: *"Lily, it's Grandpa again. I'm getting worried now, kiddo. Give me a call."*

6:02 p.m.: *"Hey, Lil, it's Kate. Where the hell are you? Frank called me and said he hasn't seen or heard from you all day. Call somebody, woman!"*

9:11 p.m.: *"Lillian Elizabeth Hunt! I just got off the phone with Frank, who informed me that you are in Georgia! What the hell are you doing in Georgia?! Love you! Call me back!"*

I winced, shutting the lid on my phone. Talking to anyone back home about what had happened—especially Kate—was completely out of the question. Strange, how unwaveringly I'd embraced the sudden proposition of a new life, and how easily I had given up the old one. Maybe it was a sign of weakness or boredom. But no. No, I couldn't swallow that. There was something more to the restlessness I'd concealed so carefully. It's not that life hadn't been good as it was—it's just that it wasn't *right*. Everything was out of place and, as a result, I'd felt lost. Now, it was as if all the mislaid parts of me were coming together, and though I hardly understood any of it, I suspected I had everything I needed.

Lost in my thoughts, I barely registered a quiet knocking. The door! Hallelujah, I was saved from an awkward solo emergence, and by a little girl, at that.

"Good morning, Ginny." I smiled down at her.

"Hi, Lily!" she sang. "You look pretty. I brought you a present!" She held out her tiny hand with a proud grin of anticipation.

"You did? For *me*?" I chuckled.

"Mm-hm."

I took the object from her and examined it. It was a smooth, speckled blue stone.

"Oh, Ginny. How beautiful," I said. "But, why are you giving it to me?"

"My grandma said I could," she smiled. "It was my mom's. She said it was a worry stone. But I don't worry much, and Grandpa says you look nervous, so I asked if I could give it to you. Look ...." She took the stone and held it between her delicate fingers. "See where it sinks in? That's from my mom. You keep it in your pocket, and when you get scared or worried, you can take it out and rub it between your fingers. It helps!"

"Wow. That's so nice of you! I don't have one of these, you know."

"I didn't think so," she said confidently.

"Thank you, Ginny."

"Welcome!" She grinned. "Did you eat breakfast?"

"No, not yet. I was going to wait for someone else to wake up first."

"I'm awake! And so is William and Clara. Want some Froot Loops? We have Cheerios and Shredded Wheat too, but, bleh." She made a face.

I stifled a laugh. "Well, I certainly don't want any of *that* awful stuff. Froot Loops it is."

We tiptoed past the bedrooms, Ginny pulling me by the hand. When we got to the kitchen, Clara was standing over a sizzling frying pan, and William sat at the table, frowning over a crossword puzzle. He looked up for a moment and smiled in greeting. The smell of bacon permeated the room.

"Good morning, love!" Clara greeted me. "Care for some breakfast? An omelet?"

"Actually, Ginny has won me over on the idea of sugar for breakfast this morning," I said.

"Oh dear. I see," she laughed then sighed. "Well, top shelf then, just above the dishwasher."

"I can get it!" Ginny exclaimed, grabbing a chair and pulling it over. I watched nervously as she slid it into place and climbed up, deftly retrieving the cereal and hopping back down. The bowls she could reach without the chair, but only barely. I got the milk and spoons, and we took a seat. I reached for the milk carton.

"I can do it!" Ginny pleaded.

"Uhm …." I laughed. "All right, then." I slid my bowl over to her. Surprisingly, very little milk and Froot Loops were sacrificed to the table top, but I was too late to stop her heading for the sugar bowl with my spoon. I gawked as she sprinkled a hefty amount on top of my cereal and pushed it back toward me, smiling. William raised an eyebrow and smirked behind his puzzle.

"Thanks, Ginny," I said, hiding my dismay.

"Welcome!" she said. Then she took a huge spoonful of her own cereal and attempted to fit it all into her mouth. Half of the contents fell back into the bowl.

I laughed to myself and took a bite. *Mother of Jesus!* Fighting the urge to gag, I swallowed as quickly as possible. Ginny looked at me.

"Yummy, huh?" she asked.

"Delicious," I said, choking on a particularly large lump of sugar. William got up from the table and a moment later returned with a glass of water. He sat down to his puzzle again and cleared his throat. I looked up to see him sliding the glass over next to my bowl. I smiled into my Froot Loops. After a moment, William was again scowling over his puzzle, tapping his pen impatiently.

"A nine letter word for 'a book of rules,'" he said to anyone. I thought for a moment.

Oh, that was an easy one. "Catechism," I offered, and then took another bite of Diabetes.

He examined his paper quizzically. "Hmm." His face relaxed as he nodded and wrote the word in.

"Look, Lily!" Ginny had her spoon hanging off her nose.

"Amazing!" I gasped.

"You do it!" she insisted.

"Oh …. Uh, I don't think I can." I squirmed.

"Sure you can! Come on, try it! It's easy."

I sighed, ready to give in.

"Eleven letter word for 'seedy fruit,'" William said suddenly.

"Seedy fruit?" This one required a bit more contemplation. I twirled a section of hair around my fingers, sure to display deep concentration as Ginny watched my face. Watermelon wouldn't do it. Neither would cantaloupe.

"Oooh, pomegranate?" I said.

"Are you asking me or telling me?" William said, pen still hovering over the paper.

"Telling you?"

He smirked and shook his head, but filled in the blanks with my answer, nonetheless. I worried that I should have stretched out the answer, bought more time, but Ginny seemed to have moved past the spoon trick.

"Done!" she squealed, tipping her empty bowl toward us.

I gawked. "Holy …."

"Impressive," William nodded, the corner of his mouth upturned.

"Wow, kiddo." I laughed. "I feel sorry for your grandparents later."

"How come?" she asked.

"Just …." I stumbled. "You're going to be tough to keep up with."

"Oh. You mean hyper? Grandpa always lets me go outside and run around in circles! You wanna come with me?"

William snickered.

"Gosh, Ginny, that sounds like fun, but I don't think I'll be able to today. Abram wanted to show me something," I answered.

"Oh. Well, maybe tomorrow, then!" she said.

I laughed feebly. "Maybe."

"Okay. I'm gonna go watch cartoons now. See you later, Lily! Don't forget to rub your stone!" Ginny grabbed her bowl and spoon, dashed to the sink, and dropped them in unceremoniously before skidding out of the kitchen.

It took me a second to realize William was staring at me, an amused expression on his face. "I'm sorry? What did she just remind you to do?"

"What? Oh!" I said, giggling. "She gave me a worry stone. See?" I held it out and William looked it over.

"Ah-ha," he said.

Clara sat down next to me. "I've made plenty of eggs and bacon if you'd like some, dear," she suggested, ruefully eyeing my sugary, sopping pile of cereal. The food on her plate was considerably more appealing, but I'd given up on breakfast for the day.

"No, thank you, Clara. I'm not that hungry," I said.

"Suit yourself," said a voice from behind me. "But my mum's cooking is exceptional in every way." Christian bent down and kissed Clara's cheek.

"Morning." Clara smiled.

"Morning, Mum, Lily." He left William out, but at this point I wasn't surprised.

Christian sat down at the end of the table and grabbed a loose section of newspaper, sorting through as he chewed on a piece of toast.

"Has anyone seen the crosswords?" he asked.

I eyed William nervously as he flipped the nearly finished puzzle over to face Christian. "You should start waking up earlier," he said.

Christian's face went sour. "You should start sleeping in."

William looked at his watch. "Or you could buy an alarm clock."

I concentrated ardently on my glass of water.

"Piss off, Maddox," Christian said.

"Gentlemen," Clara broke in.

The two men shot each other a final look before William pushed away from the table and stood up. "Lily, thanks for your help," he said.

"Sure … thanks for the beverage."

William nodded and walked out of the kitchen as Christian stared after him, then turned his attention to me. "Help with what?" he asked.

"Eh, nothing," I muttered, still ardently sipping from my glass.

Clara spoke up. "By the way, Lily, Abram is in his study this morning when you're ready."

"But, it's still so early. Maybe I should give him some time?"

Clara chuckled. "Oh, I doubt that's necessary. Abram has been quite eager to have you here. The sooner the better, I think."

"Why *is* that, exactly?" I laughed. "I mean, how do any of you know anything about me?"

"Well, your mother, of course," said Clara. She eyed me oddly. "Lily, did your grandparents tell you *anything* about your mother?"

"It's just that they didn't know anything. My dad never talked about her."

Clara nodded in understanding. "Yes, I *am* sorry, Lillian. I don't suppose any of us were fully aware of your history. Abram, of course, would be the exception to that, but he's hardly one to expound upon the details of other people's lives."

"It's all right. Though my hope is that he'll be willing to expound upon the details of my life with *me*," I said.

"I trust that will be the case," she assured me.

"Well, then. What am I waiting for?"

"If you're waiting for my good looks to fade," Christian began, waving his toast in the air, "it's a futile waste of time. Give up at once."

I snorted. "All right, then, that's my cue." I smiled.

"See you later!" Christian said after me.

"And looking just as striking as you are now, I'm sure!" I shouted behind me.

The sound of Clara's happy laughter faded as I crossed the reception hall and headed toward Abram's study. The door was open. I peeked around the corner.

"Hello?" I said, quietly.

"Lillian! Come in, come in!" Abram sat holding a book in one of his large wing chairs, his glasses low on his nose.

"Is this a good time?" I asked.

"Oh, most definitely! It is always a good time. Let there never be a question of that."

I stood in front of him awkwardly. He chuckled and shook his head. "Lily, we are not strangers, you and I," he insisted. "Sit with me. There's so much to talk about."

I did as he said. "Good book?" I asked, peering through his fingers at the cover.

"Quite good." He removed his hand so I could see. "*Jane Eyre* ... have you read it?"

"Aah. Yes. It's kind of depressing, actually."

"Ha! Well, I suppose it may be. Though, I do adore a good love story."

I laughed softly. "Same here."

"Very good," he said with a smile. "Now, then. Literature aside, shall we begin with questions? Have you been compiling a list?" he asked.

"Are you kidding?"

"Ah, but of course you have. And no need to hold back today. Ask away."

"All right. I want to know about my mother."

"I'm surprised you didn't ask that one last night!"

"You know, so am I. I guess I wasn't thinking very clearly. But I am now."

"Indeed. No one can fully understand their present, if they know nothing of their past. And this story has several beginnings, you know." He looked eager now, leaning forward as he had the night before.

"Your mother, Elizabeth Vivian Norris, was born in Newport, Connecticut, in 1956. Her parents, your grandparents, James and Vivian Norris, were Sentients. Elizabeth was immensely evolved, like you. Her endowments were similar to yours, though no two are exactly alike. She was raised to know herself and others of a like nature, and was encouraged to marry a Sentient or remain single, as this life is demanding even for the strongest sort of person. You see, we travel to where we are needed. This very house, accommodating as it is, is not our own. And there are unfailing dangers in our line of work. But, I am straying a bit. Where was I? Ah yes, that was one beginning. The next is as follows.

"As fate would have it, she met your father, a non-Sentient, they fell deeply in love, and were married in the late seventies. Elizabeth decided it was not safe to raise a family in our Society, and she and Michael moved to Scranton, his home town. A few years later, they had a child, and she was charming little thing, if I do say so myself. If I recall correctly, the very first time you smiled, it was at me!" He beamed proudly. "At least, that's what your parents *told* me, anyway," he chuckled.

"Well, they were exceptionally happy in Scranton, Lily. Your father built houses, and your mother stayed at home with you, and for a while everything was as it should be. But Elizabeth knew the risk of raising you away from us. She knew that certain protections could not extend beyond our group. And she became increasingly nervous as more and more entities were drawn to her, alone in that house with her baby. As we discussed last night, when we're together, the protective strength of our energy is nearly impenetrable. Safety in numbers, you see. But when we're separated, there are anomalies that are a great deal more threatening, and moreover, creatures such as vampires that cannot be reasoned with—only battled."

Abram paused, then sighed, as the mood in the room changed. The nature of his story was taking a sinister turn, and I knew there would be no happy ending.

"Your mother's energy was an unmistakable beacon in the darkness to them, and when you were barely ten months old, a vampire smashed out the back door of your parents' home and made to attack Michael in his bed, with Elizabeth laying right beside him. She was able to repel the creature, and he fled, leaving the three of you unharmed. But your mother could no longer deny the gravity of the situation, and soon after, Elizabeth left you both and flew to London to live with some Sentient friends."

I let his words sink in briefly before speaking. "Why couldn't we just have moved in with her parents? With other Sentients?"

"That was Michael's argument, as well," Abram explained. "But Elizabeth wouldn't hear of it. Your father had no way of defending himself against those types of threats, and until you were grown, there was no telling if you did either. To her, leaving was the only realistic option."

"Then what happened? Where is she? Is she still in London? Is she still alive?"

Abram's eyes dropped from mine. "She was attacked by a coven of vampires less than a year after she left Pennsylvania."

What thread of hope I'd babied since childhood snapped painfully, and I began to cry. Abram sat up straight, and amber warmth encircled me. It was more powerful than the strongest embrace.

"Your mother was an honorable Sentient, Lily. She loved your father, though he was beyond what she knew, what was familiar. And she continued to cherish you both to the end, even across the globe."

"But she left us," I said. "And what good did it do? She ended up dying anyway!"

He put his hand over mine. "Lillian, I cannot say that I would have chosen the same course, but there are innumerable paths one may choose in this life— some that, at first, appear flawed. Yet, if lived with love and honesty, they will always render the greatest fruit. They will serve as a lesson to us all."

I shook my head, wiping tears from my face. "I lost my mother, my father. My grandparents lost their son long before the cancer took him. What kind of lesson is that?"

"Oh, but child, if only you could see!" he said, his eyes boring into mine as he bent in closer. "If only you could see."

"See what?" I sniffled.

"How your life will mend our wounds."

I stared at him. "What are you talking about?"

"No matter the deviation, all things come full circle. You begin and end your journey in the same place, but with a different set of eyes. Both your mother *and* your father fulfilled their purpose here according to their very own choosing. And because of that, here you are, alive and well … and unspeakably important to us. Do you not feel the pull of your own destiny?"

To deny this would have been a lie, and so I said nothing.

"Lily, think, for instance, of all the times when your spirit was drawn to the woods, when, with no sound, no indication of danger, you were overcome with fear, or happiness—compelled to follow an unknown force. Any other person wouldn't have returned. Any other person wouldn't have known there was something to return to."

I released the breath I'd been holding for far too long. "I felt so stupid thinking that one day it would just … reveal itself to me. I told myself to snap out of it."

A smile spread across Abram's face, knowing and warm. "I tried to reach you many times before, but you were quite resistant."

"Yes," I agreed. "Because I couldn't have handled the prospect of being wrong. It scared me to hope too much, to carry around this wish that what I saw wasn't the end of all there is. I figured I'd either go crazy or devolve into a mindless, numb half-human who didn't care anymore."

"And you are not the only one, child," Abram added. "To a certain degree, most people feel this way, but do not know why. If you had insisted upon mimicking the world around you, searching outside of your own heart for meaning, you'd not have found it. It is good that you recognized this."

"Abram, don't give me too much credit. When Christian came for me, I was *not* very cooperative."

At this he laughed. "Well, this *is* fitting, as he was quite the thorny retrieval himself."

"Yes, Christian had mentioned," I said, but didn't press the issue.

Abram went on. "You must know that the knowledge you craved has always been at your disposal."

"Has it?" I frowned.

"It has. Let me give you an example. Do you recall, as a child, there were certain pieces of music you could not bear to listen to alone?"

"Yes."

"The notes were too unsettling because you were feeling the sensation behind them, the impression of the author. Where other observers merely listened, you relived the actual emotion.

"And further, you were impatient with the emotional limitations of your peers…an adult trapped in a child's body. You are still overwhelmed with the feelings of the many, aren't you, Lily? You believe you cry too much? People have accused you of being too sensitive? Over-sentimental? In fact, wouldn't you say that, in spite of your best efforts to quell that empathetic little girl, these qualities only grow stronger with age?"

He wanted an answer, but I was too stunned by this intimate awareness of my life, my weaknesses, to say anything in response. He didn't push me, which I appreciated; he simply laid his hands in his lap, smiling contentedly. One got the impression that he had all the time in the world. There was no impatience in his demeanor.

"And do not believe," he continued, "that you are alone in your dissatisfaction."

"I hope not. But call me a skeptic. People can be so closed off."

"Indeed … at ease in a dreamlike state of indifference, and so do not know to value anything beyond their material lives, their flesh and bone, human needs. Have you wearied of others' inability to grasp what you suffered to ignore … the anguish, pain, bliss, joy, euphoria, feelings that were more than one soul could shoulder without a like mind to share them with?"

"Then, why? Why is it like this?"

He sat back again. "Lily, it will not be easy for you. You'll have to trust me."

I furrowed my brows. This was becoming a frequent request. "Okay," I whispered.

"Let me ask you," he went on. "Have you ever experienced a feeling of disembodiment washing over you? And you could only wait for the feeling to pass? While at rest, perhaps? Half-asleep?"

I gasped. "Yes! And I've tried to describe it in words, but it never sounds right. What is it?"

"Most likely a trapped spirit was passing too near you, and you sensed its consciousness. It is nothing too pleasant to be lagging here after death, Lily. The earth plane is no place for a disembodied soul. You'd have felt its detachment from the source. Of course, that is only one of many energies you're capable of sensing. No small surprise that your attempts to express this were futile. If you didn't know what was happening to you, those around you stood little chance."

I grimaced, thinking of the times when I'd tried sharing these feelings with others, searching for an explanation. "Everyone was so patronizing," I said. "I just learned to keep this stuff to myself. It wasn't worth the ridicule," I finished, hardly shielding the bitterness in my voice.

"And for that you mustn't judge too harshly, Lily," he interjected. "People are, after all, as they are content to be. It is not an easy path, walking around as a Sentient being. Few are prepared for this."

"What makes *me* prepared for this?" I laughed in frustration. "Hell, I don't even know what it is I'm preparing *for*. A few dreams? Knowing when to run? Does that sound like the makings of a … whatever I am … to you?"

"Most certainly. You saw me where others could not. That was all the convincing I needed of your preparedness. And Lily," he continued as his hand rose to silence my next objection, "there is something you should see. It will help you, I think."

He stood up, his withered hands pressing into the chair's arms for support. Fragile as he seemed, Abram moved with grace. I could see that in his youth he must have been an imposing figure.

He turned to me. "Will you join me, then?"

I hesitated. To the core I understood that following this man was nothing trivial. I would not return as I was before. Still, my curiosity outranked my fears. "Well, as long as I've come this far," I said, standing.

Abram's expression remained the same. "Yes. I agree," he said.

We left the room's amber glow and entered the hallway, rounding a corner to the back of the house. My eyes struggled to adjust. On either side of the new passage were tall open windows with gauzy white curtains billowing to the floor in a feathery pile. At the end of the hall were simple French doors. The sunlight shone through them, and the whole scene reminded me of a story I'd read once about a near death experience.

Abram approached the doors and opened them both at once with a single sweeping gesture. It was a vision to see the man nearly one with the light as he lowered his arms and stepped to the side. A new breeze poured down the hall toward me, fresh and clean. Everything surrounding Abram seemed to come to life.

He smiled expectantly in the doorway. "To the grounds?" he asked.

I nodded, following. The man knew how to set a scene.

We stepped out onto a path with tiny crystals embedded in the pavement. Whoever tended these grounds did so with great care, as the grass was lush and deeply green without being overgrown. The lawn spread in either direction until it met the edge of the grounds which were surrounded by trees. Maple and birch, my favorites.

Our path split around a stone fountain, an angel at its center, and trailed off into the distance. We walked along in silence for a while, though I couldn't say how long. Time seemed relative with Abram. From the moment we'd met till the present, I couldn't say if it had been minutes or hours.

Finally, he wandered to the right of the path toward a gray stone bench placed at the mouth of a shallow, graduating pond. He took a seat before the water, leaving enough room for me to join him.

I took my place noiselessly on the bench, feeling more than a little unworthy. The very air around him seemed a loftier space than my frame deserved to occupy. For a moment more he sat serenely staring over the surface of the water.

"You know," he spoke at last, "intriguing thing, water. It is the stuff of myths and legends. Have you heard of Narcissus?"

"I think so. It's Greek, right?"

"Mmm." He nodded. "They had it all wrong, you know… he was not smitten with his own face, but rather, what he saw reflected in the water."

I found myself examining the same stretch of pond as Abram, hoping to realize even a whisper of what he saw. "But, the story goes that he saw his face in the water, right? I'm … I'm honestly not sure what you mean," I admitted.

"Oh, but surely you know," he urged.

"I do?" I fumbled. Oh, how small was my mind.

"Surely."

"Eh …." I chuckled. "Huh. So he wasn't just … oh so very vain?" I suggested.

"So they say. But do keep trying; there is a better answer," he said.

"Uuuhm." I hedged. Good grief. I had no idea. "He had a tadpole fetish?" I laughed.

He shook his head, grinning. "Not at all, though tadpoles tell their own story," he said.

"I'll bet they do." I smiled back. He probably had a story for everything.

"All the same," he continued, "we must not lose sight of the question, as the answer is most clear to you." He spoke with complete assurance in his voice, not a speck of doubt.

"Right."

He said nothing, only contemplated peacefully the water's surface once again, waiting.

I thought harder. If I were Narcissus, what would glue my face to that water, what would keep me coming back for more, hours on end, days and nights wasted by the water's edge? What's the drive behind any such obsession? Then, in an instant of realization, it occurred to me.

"Maybe … maybe he saw another life, another reality, where he was someone else, someone better."

"Indeed! Please, go on," he insisted.

"He could have been obsessed with an alternative to his life." I stared at my hands. Suddenly Narcissus seemed like every one of us. "Maybe it wasn't a reflection he was staring at, as much as a window … to a world he pined for," I suggested.

"That's right. Perhaps it was," he said. "Until now, you've only ever sensed the depth of Narcissus's fixation. I have brought you here that you might glimpse it with your own eyes. Glimpse it without, of course, losing yourself in it. Live along side it with wisdom, lest it absorb you.

"We've spoken of spirits who, in their attachment to a reality which is not their own, refuse to leave here. They are obsessed with another kind of life, unaware of their own intended course."

He reached out and grasped my hand. Perfect calm claimed me.

"I will show you what you have already known was there. I will show you why you are here, and whom you must help. As long as you are grounded, a sacred flesh-bound being on this earth, it is your endowment to help these spirits see the path to their own reality, and dispense of those which would do us harm." He nodded toward the water again, still holding my hand.

"Lily, look and see Narcissus's true reflection."

As my eyes followed Abram's back to the water, I felt a familiar charge rising up from the earth below my feet. It spread through me, and every hair on my body stood on end. The water's clear reflection of sky and green turned to gray, while forms—human in shape but not substance—seemed to press their hands from beneath the surface and gaze upward as through a pane of glass. Their features grew more distinct, and I stared, mesmerized and terrified, into eyes wide and pleading.

"Are they trapped down there?" I asked, frightened of and for them in the same moment.

"You needn't fear," he said. His light grew in strength, and my trembling ceased. "They are not beneath the water. They are everywhere at every moment."

"How? How does this happen?"

"We are, all of us, born of light, Lily. It is our natural state. But these souls are lost, and so they suffer in shadow. They peer into our lives, some out of mere curiosity, and others oblivious in their longing to return to what they knew. You are a path crosser and an empath. Not only astral, but living energies of every kind will be drawn to you for comfort, sanctuary. They will seek to halve their pain, and express their joy, through you. What's more, you possess the unique ability to progress a spirit forward using your own guiding light. Of all the endowments you could have carried with you into this life, these are the most troubling and rewarding."

My world, till now, had been a small one, a lonely one. Feeling ever out of place, the days had flown by like wasted moments. And now, even knowing that the bided time would finally mean something, fear and purpose battled for an answer.

"I'm scared," I said.

"Yes."

All or nothing, Frank had always said. "But I can't go back to a false life."

❧

Abram and I spent a good part of the day talking about what my new life would entail. He endured the myriad of questions that followed my first vision, but he often left some aspect of the answer for me to discover on my own.

"It's quite vital that you learn defense," he said, the sun high in the sky above us.

"Defense? Like, fighting?"

"Well, in a manner of speaking," he said. "You won't be learning to throw a punch or paralyze your opponent with one finger, but your defenses will be lethal nonetheless."

"What *will* I be learning?"

"You will learn how to detect your enemy before he is aware of you."

"Sounds hard."

"Not terribly. And it is essential that, before you've ever learned to guide a spirit, you know how to contend with it. And, moreover, how to tell if it is, in fact, human or otherwise. That shall make all the difference."

"Difference between what?"

"Between preparing for action or preparing for conflict." These last words were spoken with no more intonation than any others, but they rang alarmingly in my head. What exactly was I signing up for?

"How will I know one from the other?" I asked.

"You must be taught, and taught well. I shall have you begin lessons in a few days, here, on the grounds."

"With you?"

"No, I dare say not. I have someone in mind, though."

"Who?"

"Forgive me, but I would rather not say at the moment. I must ask that person first, you see."

I nodded.

"There is an area of the woods where the trees are not so densely grown together, at the very end of the grounds, you see?" he said, stretching out his arm and pointing down the long path. "Perhaps that should do in the beginning."

In the trees? I'd become leery of trees. Wouldn't a theory book, desk, and chair be just as effective? As if reading my mind, Abram nodded.

"Yes, it does seem a rather odd set up, does it not? But I am confident it will serve you well." And as he grinned, I'd have sworn there was something of mischief in his eyes.

Five

I sat at the dinner table and crushed chick peas with my fork. The evening had passed with the same happy chatter that greeted me on my first night in the house, but I was hardly aware of any of it. My mind was in a hundred places at once—with my grandparents, fending off the various surges of complicated sensation coming from the people around me, and relentlessly replaying the images of all those lost souls. Luckily, if anyone had noticed the serious drop in my sociability, they didn't let on.

After a while, Christian got up from the table and grabbed his plate. Tapping my arm to get my attention, he paused in the kitchen doorway and waited. I picked up my plate and followed behind him, and we took turns rinsing them in the sink.

"Want to go for a drive?" he asked.

"Sure." This would be my first time out of the house in two days, and I was starting to feel a bit detached from the world. A drive was exactly what I needed.

The night was warm and breezy as we stepped outside, the air thick with jasmine and wet earth, and the fragrances sent me into a whirl of emotion. Though a mystery every time it occurred, I was used to this particular phenomenon. Scents had often done this to me, evoked a gut reaction … as if I were reliving a powerful moment. No doubt there could be some physiological explanation for it, but not always … and not this time.

"I figured you'd like to escape for a while," Christian interrupted my bliss as we walked toward the car.

"Sounds about right. So where are we going?"

He shrugged.

The cool of the leather seats was soothing, and I relished the silence as we drove. We hadn't traveled very far before Christian turned off the road and up a wooded hill. At the top was a paved lot that overlooked a river at the bottom of a ravine. The view was amazing, but the drop was unsettling.

"So." He exhaled. "Are you all right?"

"I don't know. Am I? You're better qualified to answer that than I am. How am I supposed to be right now?"

"Right. You're grossly overwhelmed then."

I considered his response. "Well said."

"I'm sorry I didn't tell you more the first day. I just, to be perfectly honest, I wasn't terribly happy to be retrieving you."

"I'm touched, thank you."

"No, no." He laughed. "I don't mean it personally. It's just that this is not an easy life, Lily. There are so many risks, and I feel responsible for you now. I mean, I brought you here, after all."

"Well, no obligations, Christian. I'm not completely powerless."

"No, you won't be for long, anyway," he said. "But that doesn't change how I feel. You'll have to put up with me, Lily. I'm insufferably stubborn, you know."

I sighed. "Just avoid the caveman crap."

"Yes. I'm sorry. I'll watch that bit."

"Thank you," I said, and then I paused. "Christian?"

"Hm?"

"Where's Abram from?"

"Well, let me think. I know he was born in South Africa—the Eastern Cape, though it wasn't called that back then. Why do you ask?"

"His accent, I couldn't place it."

"Ah." He nodded. "Yes. From what my mum has said, his childhood was extremely difficult. I'd imagine he must have seen the worst that apartheid had to offer. I don't know much about his history, but mum says that at some point he left to attend University in England, and it was there that another Seer recognized what he was."

"Does he have any family?"

"I don't think so, no. Just us. I really don't know many details. Abram doesn't speak much about his past. He believes that the present is the only real thing and everything else is an illusion … a distraction."

"I see. Do you agree with him?"

He shifted in his seat. "Sometimes … but other times …" He stopped mid-thought and went quiet, staring intently out the windshield.

"Other times?"

"I don't know." He shook his head. "Lost my train of thought. By the way, Lil, I do have one sort of slightly ever-so-caveman-ish request to make."

"What?" I asked, eyebrow raised.

He turned to face me again. "Stay away from William. He's not to be trusted."

"Oh?"

"That's right."

"Why? He's a little snarky, yes, but what's wrong with him?"

He laughed, but there was no humor in his voice. "He's not one of us. Just stay away from him, okay?"

I looked at him, astonished. "Then why is he here? I mean, Abram wouldn't allow someone around who wasn't trustworthy."

"Wouldn't he? Abram is forgiving to a fault, Lily."

I considered this. Christian knew the intricacies of this strange life, and the histories of the people in it. I, on the other hand, was completely green. What justification could I have for doubting his word?

"Please," he insisted again.

"Well … . All right."

The relief on his face was instantaneous. "Good, then. Let's get back. They'll have noticed we're gone by now, and we wouldn't want to start any vicious rumors." He smiled.

❧

Lounging on the edge of what was now my bed, I stared out the window at the garden. My head reeled with the events of the last few days and the images Abram had made known to me. My heart ached for these lost souls, but I feared them nonetheless. Abram promised this would pass, that this life would fit me perfectly, just as it did every Sentient. But I felt weak, small, stupid. What right had I to direct a spirit when my very own felt superbly lost?

There was a knock on the door. "Uh … come in?"

Anna opened the door and peered around it. "You're back!" She bounced into the room and plopped herself on the bed next to me.

"I am."

"I was afraid you'd decided to go home."

"Nope. Still here."

"So, how badly wigged are you?" she asked, smiling cautiously.

"Pretty badly," I admitted.

"Has Abram discussed lessons yet? He said something about lessons."

"Unfortunately."

"Ha! That eager, are we?"

I shook my head slowly. "I always thought I was brave, Anna, but I was fooling myself."

"Oh, now, don't say that!" she scolded. "Besides, did Abram tell you about my mother?" she asked.

"He said she'd be a helpful guide. That she's a path crosser, too."

"Yes."

"Are you? A path crosser?" I asked.

"Not quite. My endowment is more suited to emotional management than anything else. You really should have a talk with my mum, Lily. She can ease anyone's mind."

I believed her. Clara's force was stronger than the others, and powerfully good. I'd have to shove my preemptive fears in the closet until I could speak with her, gain just a sliver of her perspective.

"This business aside," I continued, "can I never walk a trail again without a monster harassing me?"

Anna let out an appreciative groan. "William could tell you best how to arm yourself against attacks. He knows how their minds work. Of course, Christian would have to let you near enough to actually *talk* to him for that to happen."

I was starting to get that. "But I suppose I can see where Christian is coming from," I said. "There's just something different about William that I can't put my finger on."

To my surprise Anna laughed. "Yes, it's a pretty normal response for a Sentient to feel that way around a vampire."

My heart leaped into my throat as the connections were made.

"He's one of them? Living *here*?"

"Yes. But before you have an aneurysm, there's something about him that you don't know. William is unique among other vampires. In fact, I don't know that one could fairly call him a full-fledged vampire, anyway. He has a soul, Lily. He has a conscience."

"And vampires don't normally have souls?"

"No! That's the whole point. They're the remaining flesh of what once housed a soul, an incredibly intelligent, warped animal, but nothing human."

"So, William is human now?"

"Erm, not precisely," she said, evoking a frown from me. "But sort of!" she corrected. "I mean, that is … I think."

I shook my head, unconvinced.

"But let me say this," she continued. "When William's soul was restored, the memories of what his vessel had done were such that he came to my father, begging to die. Dad refused to kill him." Anna looked down at her hands. "My brother has never given William a chance."

"If your father trusted him, and Abram trusts him, then why doesn't Christian? There *must* be a reason."

Anna paused for a moment, and a shadow seemed to dull her features. She was no longer with me, her mind had traveled elsewhere.

"Why didn't he just tell me what William is?" I asked

She stared at her lap. "He was trying to protect you. He'd rather William not be here. My father didn't survive to see us vote on William's staying. I think if he had been, Christian's feelings would be different."

"How did your father die, Anna?" I asked, dreading the answer.

She hesitated. "Christian … he was there. We all were." She examined her fingers even more closely now. "It's been harder for him, though."

"Harder?"

"Yes. There was a time when my brother wanted nothing to do with a Sentient's life. When we agreed to let William stay, Christian left. He hated Abram for allowing it. He saw it as an act of betrayal, after what happened to Dad."

"That's why he needed retrieving?"

"That's right. But Mum wouldn't let up, though Abram asked her to. He said he would still visit Christian's dreams, but maintained that it was my brother's choice to return. Mum wasn't so accepting of the situation, though, as you could well imagine. You've met the woman."

"Yes," I said, grinning. I could imagine.

A new question, a difficult one, remained to be answered. If I was ever going to understand these people, turn them from alien to kin in my mind, I would have to know what they had known, see what they had seen. I was, after all, making up for lost time.

"Anna," I began. "Tell me what happened to your father."

She sighed, a weak smile on her face. "It's so much easier not to think about it."

"But how long can you keep up the Pollyanna act?"

"As long as they need me to."

"Well, here's the rub." I closed in the space between us, placed my hand on her face, and smiled. "*I* don't need you to. So don't be brave."

"I can't talk about it," she said, the strength gone from her voice. "But ... there's something ...." She stopped, shaking her head. "God, never mind."

"What? What is it? Please, Anna."

"Lily. Hell, I know how selfish this is," she began, tears filling her blue eyes and spilling down her cheeks. "But my experiences are communal when I share a vision. I can't lie to you. It's a terrible thing to ask of someone, and I'd love you still the same if you refused, but ...." She was sobbing quietly now. "I could tell you what happened," she said, suddenly lifting her head, "or I could show you." Her eyes burned into mine, questioning my courage. I knew what she wanted. She wanted me to see what she had seen. She wanted me to share the burden.

"Show me," I said.

Her sobbing intensified for a brief moment, a look of astonished gratitude washed over her, and she took my hand. "I'll repay you for this someday, Lillian Hunt. I swear on my life," she said.

She was holding both my hands now, her eyes and mine locked together, and the room began to spin fiercely. It felt like I'd lifted off the bed, was flying through the air, and everything around us was a brilliant white glare, everything but Anna's eyes. Abruptly I was being pulled forward into them at light speed, my hair whipping behind me, my arms flying backward. I shut my eyes instinctively and landed. When I opened them, I was in a dark, graffiti littered tunnel, and the stench was unbearable.

"Anna?" I whispered, my voice trembling.

No one answered, but I could hear voices in the distance behind me, and as I turned, I saw Anna standing with her face in her mother's shoulder, crying. Clara held her daughter close and stared ahead at something, her face stiff with horror.

I let my gaze follow Clara's. In Christian's arms, there was a writhing, twisting, shuddering form. I willed my legs to carry me there, though I don't remember walking at all, just thinking. In a second, I was next to Christian.

"Christian, please. *Please*," the man cried.

"No, Dad." Christian shook his head, his eyes full of fear.

"You *must*," the man begged. "Please, son, you *must*."

"*No*." Christian's voice was a drawn out, agonizing plea, his face twisted up, tears streaming freely. "I can't, Dad. I can't, I can't." He rocked on his knees, his fists balled up tightly.

"Son …." The voice was a rasping moan, rife with pain. "Do this for me … please. Don't let this … happen. Just spill the blood. Don't … don't be afraid … let me go." His head fell back, a strangled scream ripped through him, and his body convulsed and curled up.

Christian grabbed his father around the shoulders. "Dad, it's okay. I'll do it. I'll do it."

"Your gun, son. *Now*, Chr … Christian," he sputtered.

Christian sobbed, reaching to his side and pulling a gun from the ground, his hand shaking violently. His father's breaths were harsh, his neck arched backward in his son's arms.

Christian took the gun in both hands and pressed it to his father's chest, weeping.

"I love you, son," his father wheezed.

"I love you." Christian lifted his gaze and his eyes went blank.

I looked away, crying. Seconds later a muted shot sounded, and a moment of agonizing silence followed. Then, the air was cut through with Christian's screaming. I dared myself to look back as he wept, rocking the lifeless body of his father on his knees.

In the foreground, Anna and her mother stood, Anna's head still in her mother's chest, Clara's face buried in her daughter's hair.

I was overwhelmed, blinded by stinging tears. Everything began to spin again and I was thrown backward with great force. When I landed, Anna and

I were sitting on the bed, clinging to each other. I held her this way for a long time, just as her mother had.

"Oh, Anna," I whispered at last.

"He had to do it," she whimpered. "Dad had been attacked; his body was changing."

"What do you mean?"

"Into a vampire," she said, a shudder coursing through her and into me. "And Dad wouldn't allow another of them to populate the earth while we had the power to stop it, even if it meant leaving this world, leaving us."

"When did this happen?"

"In Vancouver. They'd been holding him in the sewers. By the time we found him, it was too late."

Powerful revulsion swept over me. Not only had one of these creatures tried to take my life, but they had stolen my mother, destroyed my parents' lives, and devastated an essential part of what was now to be my family. To add insult to injury, one of them was dwelling right within these walls.

℘

Thursday came quickly, since time tends to fly when you're terrified and awe-struck. I'd done my best to stick by Christian or Anna at all times, avoiding even the suggestion of William's company. But today I would have to brave it on my own, at least for a little while.

As Abram had requested, I followed the path to its end and entered the wooded patch. It all felt terribly silly to me, this mysterious business. Why Abram couldn't simply tell me who he had in mind for training seemed pointless, unless .... .

"Hello, Lily." I knew that voice, and it wasn't Christian's. I stiffened, turning around to face him.

"William," I said, with little effort to sound friendly.

"From the look on your face I'd say you're disappointed. Abram didn't mention you'd be working with me?"

"No. He didn't specify."

"Well, he does tend to keep things to himself, remember. Of course, most people like Abram's way of doing things."

"I don't know *what* I like. In fact, why the hell am I here right now?"

"Sensory training, self protection," he answered.

"No, I mean right *here*," I spoke of the place where we stood.

"You're following a directive? Look, am I missing something, Lillian?"

"Do *not* call me Lillian," I seethed.

He sighed, crossing his arms. "You know … *Lily*," he stressed, "this isn't going to work so well if you're non-compliant. Do you not trust me?"

"I don't trust monsters," I said emphatically.

He winced at the last word, and his expression hardened. "Christian's been setting the scene, then," he said.

"No. But that doesn't matter. I'm just glad someone did."

His voice went icy cold. "Wonderful. Perhaps this was a mistake."

"Damn right." I glared. "Tell Abram to send a human next time."

He scoffed. "Any particular human?"

"What's that supposed to mean?"

"Don't be so naive," he said, his tone biting. "Saint Christian just might disappoint you."

"Go to hell."

"Been there, didn't care for the company." He smiled, more pleasantly this time.

We stood in silence for a moment, William grinning defiantly, his arms still crossed, waiting for my next move, and me refusing to budge.

"Ugh!" I groaned. "God *damn* it, Abram!"

William raised his eyebrows. "Uncle?" he said, a pleased look on his face.

I opened my mouth to protest and my breath caught in my throat. He had no right to be so good looking. What self-respecting male, vampire or otherwise, had eyes that pretty? Like grass … or, maybe more like a forest canopy … wait, *why* the *fuck* was I analyzing the possible color variations of his eyes? Jesus. I scrunched up my face in disgust. "Yeah, whatever. Who better to teach me the inner-workings of evil, right? And I'll never trust you," I assured him.

"I think you will," he responded, beaming at me.

I rolled my eyes. "I'm here to learn. Stop wasting my time."

He had the audacity to whistle … as if *I* was the one being unreasonable.

"All right. Down to business, then," he said, circling me a few times.

I stood rigid as a stone. "Is this really necessary?" I complained.

"Shh!" he scolded.

I scowled. "What are you doing, exactly?"

"Lily … ," he warned.

"Fine!" I crossed my arms.

"Please don't do that," he complained.

"What?"

"Cross your arms like that. I can't read you as well."

"Well, good!"

"No, not good! The better I can read you, the better you learn. So, free your energy, please. Open your arms."

I sighed and let my arms fall to my sides.

"Hm. Nice. I can tell why the vampire found you so easily. That aura of yours … it's intensely attractive. No surprise, though, considering what you are."

"This is what's attracting things to me? What exactly is an aura, anyway?"

"It's the extension of your soul's energy beyond what's flesh, the physical manifestation of wisdom gathered from former lives."

I looked at him incredulously. "Like rollover minutes?"

"I suppose so," he answered with a chuckle. "It's the universe's process of sifting out unnecessary elements."

"How does anyone know this?"

"There have been innumerable generations of Seers, Lily. They've learned a few things."

"So what is a Sentient, really?" I asked. He may have been the adversary, but my curiosity was insatiable.

"Anyone whose energy is advanced beyond the norm," William began, "and is capable of using that energy in an atypical way is considered a Sentient."

"So, magnified senses?"

"Exactly. The closer you get to the true state of the soul, the more you're capable of seeing. A Seer has achieved levels of sentience beyond what you or I are capable of in this life."

"Like Abram?"

"Precisely. Eventually his path will be complete and he won't have to return to the human form."

"Can you see things?" I said, hardly imagining that he could be advanced in any way.

"Yes."

"Can you see lightlines?"

"No. But I can see auras."

"What's the difference?" I asked.

"Lightlines are emotionally driven. Only an empath can decipher their intricacies. An aura, however, all Sentients can see. We can even produce light when necessary."

"So, you can see my aura?"

"I can. But it's easier to feel."

"Can you feel mine? Right now?"

"Very well." He smiled warmly, and for a moment, he seemed like he could possibly be a little less horrible than I thought.

"So, what's it like?" I asked.

"You want me to be honest?"

"Yes," I said, crossly. "Why wouldn't I? Is there something wrong with it?"

"No. It feels like … well …." He seemed to struggle to find the words.

"Like?"

"Almost like … like being held," he said finally, then

looked away, clearly embarrassed.

I fought back an awkward smile, barely concealing the upturn in the corner of my mouth. "Oh," I said, quietly. "Well, why would anything evil be attracted to that?"

"For a very different reason than human souls, you can be certain," he said, darkly. "Your enemy seeks to absorb that kind of force and use it to manipulate the world around it. In succeeding, he would render one of three scenarios. The first two, I might add, are considerably more pleasant than the last."

"What are they?" I said, stricken with morbid curiosity.

"Possession is the mildest," he answered.

"Wonderful," I said, my heart pounding.

"Death is a possibility as well, though when you're well prepared, it's also a rarity."

"And that isn't numero uno on the bad scale?"

"No. Death is nothing; it's simply waking up."

"Well, then, what's worse?"

"Turning," he said.

"Turning?" I shook my head, not comprehending.

"The result of a vampire attack, Lily."

"You mean …." The word sounded so small next to its insinuation, as if the Seers had purposely chosen it to sound less hideous. It would have seemed more natural for me to react, but only a distant acknowledgment of the truth had sunk in. The rest had yet to break the surface.

"Do you understand what I'm saying?" he asked.

A thought occurred to me. William had been turned. He had been human once. He was probably well trained when it happened, too. I could be him, any of us could. Then the fear set in, a rush of hysteria.

"This is insane! All of it!" I paced in front of him. "What if I can't do this? I'm not brave enough, William. I'm not ready for this." My strength again deserted me and my eyes welled with tears.

"Lily." William's voice was calm.

"Shit," I cursed, shaking. He took a step forward and put his hand on my arm. I winced but remained still.

"I'm sorry to upset you," he started, "but once you've learned to detect them, once you've learned to defeat that kind of threat, you'll lose most of the fear, you'll feel empowered. And you *are* brave, Lily! You're here with me, aren't you?"

There was no Christian here to manipulate my sense of well being, and fear could easily have seized my will. But wasn't now the best time to be courageous, knowing there was so very much in this world to be courageous about?

"I overreacted," I said. "I freaked out. I'm okay now."

William thought for a moment. "I want to show you something. Stay where you are, keep facing forward," he said, walking behind me.

Instantly his footfalls went silent. *He's stopped*, I thought. I stood still, listening intently. What was he doing? Impatience gnawed at me, and I gave in to temptation, turning my head back quickly. He was gone.

Disregarding his orders, I turned full circle, peering into the trees, down the path. Had he just left me there? Was he screwing with me, laughing while I waited like a sheep for however long I was fool enough to do so?

"And the lesson for today is how *intolerably obnoxious vampires are!*" I shouted to the trees.

"That wasn't very nice," he whispered, inches from my ear. And to think I'd always considered screaming a juvenile response to things.

"Not good!" I said, my hand on my heart.

"What?" he smiled.

"How the hell did you do that?"

"You really ought to mind that potty mouth of yours, Lily," he teased. "It is uncharacteristic of a Sentient."

"Yeah, well, I'm a beginner."

"Excuses, excuses."

"Can we get to the point, please?"

"No problem. The point is you weren't paying attention."

"I was, too! I looked for you! I mean, you didn't even make a sound!"

"And what did you expect?" He laughed. "You know, looking and listening are great tactics for human detection, but they won't help you here. Your adversary isn't going to wave and call your name before an ambush. Use your senses, Lily."

Oh! He was just *infuriating*! "And do you care to explain how the hell this is done?"

"Just trust yourself. It's in you to know this stuff."

"Ugh, please, Mr. Miyagi, spare me the wax on, wax off."

"Must you *always* be so unpleasant?"

"No. Not always," I clarified. "Just with you."

"Clearly," he said.

Was it my imagination or had I actually hurt his feelings? A pang of guilt tugged at my conscience, but I pushed it away.

"Let's just get on with this," I said. "How did you disappear and appear like that?"

"I walked."

"So you're invisible now?"

"Hardly. As I said, you're just not paying attention."

"Well, as you obviously have all the answers, how do I pay attention?"

"Let's try this again, shall we?" He grabbed me by the shoulders, spinning me around to face the path. "Now, this time, don't peek, don't move, don't say anything. Just wait until you *feel* me coming before you react."

"*Feel* you coming. Fine." I rolled my eyes.

Again I heard a few footfalls and then silence. A moment went by without a sound. What was the protocol for "feeling" vampires, anyway? I sighed, closing my eyes. An image, the memory of a trail, the woods, a dark-eyed killer came into view. I was on that Pennsylvania path again, running. I could feel something then, couldn't I? I had to make myself feel it again.

I kept my eyes shut, lifted my head, and spread my hands, palms out. Giving every inch of my flesh full attention, I waited.

My fingertips began to tingle, only slightly at first; then it spread into my hands, up my shoulders, my neck, my face. The sensation of someone watching me progressed until it was fully physical, an energy focused on, zeroing in on mine … straight ahead. I gasped, my eyes shot open. William was about ten feet in front of me.

He smiled. "Well done."

My body still reeled with the sensation of his approach. Why had I never felt that around him before?

"I knew you were coming," I said in wonder. "For a while, before I even opened my eyes."

"Yes." He nodded. "I know. You were putting out a tremendous amount of energy."

"More holding?" I cocked an eyebrow.

"More like a warning beacon that you weren't a force to be trifled with."

"You're serious?"

"Absolutely, Lily." He examined me, shaking his head. "Impressive."

There was an awkward silence.

"Again, then?" he asked.

We went on like this for close to an hour, him coming at me from every angle, every distance, until I was exhausted. Despite the definite lack of physical exertion on my part, I couldn't remember the last time I'd felt so fatigued.

"I think you've had it for today," William said, chuckling as I swayed questionably in place.

"I think so."

"Abram wanted you to go on a cleansing with Anna and Clara tomorrow. Are you up for it?"

"I don't know. What's a cleansing?"

"One of many things we're called out to handle. But this one in particular is suited to your endowment."

"Still not telling me much," I complained.

"It's a house clearing, Lily. There's a local family suffering from a haunting, and Clara has been working with them for weeks now."

"She's going to kick a ghost out?"

"Yes. It's a fascinating case."

The idea *was* exhilarating. "Yeah, I'll be good for it."

He laughed again. "You're not scared of ghosts, then?"

I shrugged.

"All right," he said. "I'll see you the same time tomorrow."

I hesitated before confirming, wrestling with a perplexing concept. I didn't *want* to be civil, but he was almost likable … when he wasn't being an ass. Still, I trusted Christian, and I'd made a promise.

"How much longer do we have to do this?" I asked, inserting as much annoyance into the words as possible.

William frowned. "Still think I'm the enemy, I take it?"

Thoughts of my mother and the pain of Anna's vision still burned like a salted wound.

"If Abram thinks we should, I will, but … ." I clenched my fists.

"What, Lily? Speak your mind."

"But I've seen what your kind can do."

"My kind … ."

"That's right. This innocent bullshit, well, for all I know that's all it is … bullshit. I haven't forgotten what you are."

It would have been so much easier to hate him if he'd said something rude in response. Instead, he stood motionless, examining my face. "I'm sorry you feel that way."

There was no trying to conceal my astonishment.

"Are you serious?" I laughed at him. "How did you expect me to feel? Am I supposed to believe that you're trustworthy? Why? Because you said so? You know, Christian didn't want me around you at all, so there *has* to be a reason for that. For all I know, you aren't any better than that thing that tried to kill me!"

"I wouldn't—"

"Save it." *I can't hurt him.* I repeated the words like a prayer. I had a vendetta to uphold, damn it!

"Lily, I know you have little faith in me as a person of character … as a *person*, really," he said. "But put that aside for now, do what you must to learn, and then you'll never have to look at me again."

Why was he being so diplomatic? He was a creature, after all. He wasn't a *real* human. Who knew if there was really any good to be found in him? I would not, could not, allow myself to be duped. Still, he had a point. I could choose to shut him out completely once these lessons were over, and I needed to know how to protect myself.

"Tomorrow," I said.

He nodded, relieved.

"I have to go," I said.

"All right."

When I got back to the house, Christian was waiting on the back deck, reading a newspaper. He sat up when he saw me coming.

"Did it go well?" he asked.

"Went fine."

"What did he show you?"

"How to sense him coming."

"Hm. Can you do it?"

"Yes."

"Good," he said.

"I think I'm going to tag along with your mom and Anna tomorrow."

"Eh, are you sure that's such a good idea?"

"Why wouldn't it be?"

"Well, you look a bit worn out, Lily."

"Nah. I don't feel that bad. My energy is coming back. By tomorrow I'll be fine."

"But being in a place like that can really sap you dry," he argued. "Maybe you should wait for the next one."

"Not necessary." I shook my head. "Really, I'm feeling pretty good right now." And I meant it.

"All right, but maybe I ought to come along."

"Suit yourself." I smiled.

William walked up the porch steps toward the back door and gave us a quick glance.

"I don't think you should work her so hard," Christian called after him. Then he stood up, tossing the paper onto the swing. "She looks exhausted."

"Christian, I'm all right." I tried quelling him, but it was too late.

William turned slowly. "Lily, would you like me to take it easier on you next time?" he asked, looking only at me.

"No. I said I was fine."

He smiled and shot a look at Christian. "She seems to have made up her mind. I won't force her beyond what she's comfortable with."

"No, you won't," Christian answered ominously. The two stood staring each other down, waiting for the other to crack.

"I'm going inside," I said, glaring at them.

I pushed past William. His whole demeanor had changed. His speech was more calculated around Christian, his words cautious and generic. Christian's hatred for vampires aside, these exchanges seemed especially volatile with me in the mix. I would have to try very hard to ease Christian's concerns. After all, he felt obligated to me now. And I, in turn, would do everything in my power not to make his life any more complicated than it already was.

℮

I knew what needed to be said, but saying it would break my heart. Frank had been so good, so understanding of my traverse into the unknown. Could I really expect him to accept any more? The space between what *was* and what *would* be had been a nice sort of cushion, a safe limbo for everyone involved. But there was no dragging this out forever. The time had come for me to break the news to my grandparents.

The conversation started out much the same as it had for weeks. Frank tossed around the usual questions about the southern heat, my friends, my health. But he always seemed to sense where to stop, where my limits were.

"So they want me to stay, Grandpa. They want me to work with them."

"I thought as much," he said, quietly. "I would if I were them.

You'll be making a good living?"

"Yes. We'd have to travel a lot, though, go where the need arises."

"It sounds like a hell of an opportunity," he said. "It's about damn time those student loans started paying off."

"Right." I snorted. If only he knew what a waste they'd been. "By the way, I'll have to hire some movers to get everything out of my apartment and into a storage unit. Would you mind making sure they don't destroy anything?"

"I'll be on them like a bitch in heat, kiddo."

I giggled.

"You know," he began, "life has a funny way of working itself out. Your Uncle Jack is happy enough managing the store. Aunt Vicky always wanted him to work closer to home, anyway. I'll retire in a few years, and if he wants the place he can have it. I'm getting tired, kiddo."

"I know, Grandpa. I'm sorry I had to muddle things for you. Everyone must think I've lost my marbles."

"Never mind what they think," he retorted. "You've always had it in you to be more, Lily. That's all we've ever wanted for you. You've given up too much for too long, and I'll throttle anyone who tries to hold you back."

How could you describe a man like Frank? He was just as good as any Sentient, that much was certain.

"I still haven't told Kate. I'm afraid of her reaction. When I first talked to her about this she freaked out."

"Yep, I can see it now," he said. "She's been by the store several times trying to convince us we need to conduct, what the hell did she call it, an intervention?"

I laughed. "Oh, Lord. Thanks for the heads up."

Six

*P*reparing for a cleansing was, evidently, no simpler a task than healing it. Anna and Clara buzzed around the house, gathering things, checking off a list of equipment, then checking it off again.

"Do you really use all this stuff?" I asked. "I thought only amateurs used dowsing rods and EMF meters."

"It's for effect," said Anna, deciding between a Bible and a tube of water.

"For effect?" I giggled.

"Yes. Don't laugh, Lil! People can deal with the invisible. They can cope with what they can't really see, can't fully prove … like ghosts. But they can't handle us. There's no way for them to safely fathom a human who can throw an object across the room with their mind, or stop one for that matter. Most people aren't meant to see the complete picture at once. It has to look more like the equipments' doing than ours. So we bring these," she held up a crucifix, "to detract from ourselves."

It made perfect sense once she explained it. What would I have done if, just weeks earlier, someone had tried to convince me of what I knew now? I'd have had them committed.

"All right then, girls, shall we be off?" Clara entered the room carrying five bags at once.

"If you'll let me carry some of those, absolutely," I said.

"Well mannered *and* beautiful." She smiled, reneging control of her handfuls.

"I know." Anna sighed. "Isn't it sickening? She'll positively ruin it for the rest of us."

"Are you referring to the swarms of men out there petitioning to be with a lost cause?" I retorted, trudging out to the front porch.

"And humble!" Anna threw her hands in the air. "Beautiful, well-mannered, and humble!"

"Now I *know* you weren't referring to yourself," said Christian, jogging up the porch steps to lighten our load.

"Absolutely not," said Anna. "We were listing Lily's virtues."

"Ah." He nodded. "Why don't you ever list *my* virtues?"

"Because you're already a cheeky-arsed bastard," Anna answered, hopping down the stairs.

I snorted and slung my duffel bag over my shoulder.

Christian cleared his throat. "No comments, please."

"What? You're marvelous! You're a god and a king," I said.

"And *you* are the epitome of grace and agreeableness."

"Why do I get the feeling you didn't really mean that?" I frowned.

"Oh, come on, then." He chuckled, shutting the door behind us and heading down the stairs. He paused for a moment, looking back. "You really are quite beautiful, though, Lily."

I waited for the redness in my cheeks to subside before following him into the car.

Spring in Atlanta can be every bit as sweltering as the summer, and this day was no exception. By now the rains had passed and the sun burned away the last of the clouds, beating down and drying out the earth. Despite the steady breezes, my skirt stuck to my thighs on the super-heated car seat. I felt lethargic in the sun's glare, and laid my head against the window.

Clara sat in the passenger seat and Anna next to me in the back.

"Are you sure you're up for this?" Christian had been monitoring me from the rear view mirror.

"Christian, I swear I'm fine. It's just the heat of the car," I insisted.

"Okay."

"It's not too far, Lily," Anna said. "And here, I brought us water bottles."

"Great, thanks." I smiled, taking the sweating bottle from her and laying it against my neck. Looking up, I caught Christian peeking at me in the mirror again before glancing away.

"These people we're going to see, I should warn you, are kind of official," he said.

"Official? Who are they?"

"The governor," Clara answered for him.

"Get out! Why?"

"His wife, really," Clara corrected. "Morgan Montgomery would never let us step foot in his home, but his wife is quite another story. She contacted a local parapsychologist's group who went in on the sly but couldn't budge the spirit. Word spread to a friend of Abram's and voilà. We're on our way to round number two of Project Evacuate The Pig-Headed Specter."

"Is that how it typically happens?"

"Mainly," she continued. "Sometimes, though, Abram will see a local news article about something and send us out to survey its validity. Of course, Abram has so many sources of information at his disposal. He's a tremendously well-connected man."

"A little too well-connected," Christian muttered.

"Yes, well. Someone has to keep tabs on AWOL Sentients, dear."

"Believe me, Mum, you're enough to get the job done."

"Let's not get into all that," Anna whined. "Look, we're nearly there anyway." A sign directing tourists to the governor's mansion zipped past my window.

"Have you guys scoped it out, then? Do you know what you're dealing with?" I asked, redirecting the conversation.

"I should say we do," Clara said. "And what a treat for your first time out. Not something you see every day," she said, prolonging the anticipation.

"What is it?" I sat forward in my seat, placing my hand on the back of her headrest.

"A full bodied apparition."

"Uh … I see." My pulse raced.

"Have you experienced any yet, Lily?" Clara asked

"I think so," I said tensely.

"What was it like, then?"

"Well, he pulled a gun on me."

"*What?*" Christian gasped.

"Yeah. Just whipped a gun out. Thought I was his cheating girlfriend, I think, and … ." I shivered.

"When did this happen?" he asked.

"A few weeks ago."

"Well, good timing on our part, then," Clara added. "It's usually after the twenty-fifth birthday that these things really start escalating, so I'm not surprised."

"And this apparition at the governor's mansion, is he … unpleasant?" I asked, trying to swallow.

"It's a she, and at the very least she's quite bold about the whole thing," Clara went on. "She feels she has the right to call whenever she pleases. I've tried reasoning with her, explaining that she wouldn't have liked this happening in her lifetime. But she ignores me, just looks away. Anna's the only one who's been able to get anything out of her. She's not a residual haunting either. We're not dealing with some imprint of her life replaying itself. She's there, in real time."

"Who is she?"

"Miss Price, she calls herself. She was the niece of Governor Chandler in the late 1800s. It's puzzling, because she shouldn't be attached to the place. The mansion that stands now is not the same one she knew. It survived a fire and a tornado before it was rebuilt from the ground up in the sixties."

"And they see her?" I asked.

"Yes, but only the women. The governor has never seen her, or I doubt he would take the stubborn stance he has on the matter."

"Has she caused trouble for them?"

"The fact that she hasn't fully made a transition after all this time is the trouble. If she were even remotely reasonable, she'd feel no need to appear to others. As long as she's so hell-bent on remaining in that state, she could simply walk the halls undetected any time she pleased."

"So what reason does she give for appearing, then?"

"That is what I've yet to determine. Just here, Christian," she said, reminding him of a turn, and then she continued. "So often full bodied apparitions are the result of a spirit wanting help, but she shows no signs of that."

"Do you think we'll see her?"

"Oh, I *know* we will," Anna chimed in. "So far she hasn't been able to resist our energy. With you in the mix now, she'll be popping up all over the place."

I breathed out nervously. "This was more appealing in theory."

"Don't worry, Lily. We won't let anything bad happen. Besides, she seems harmless enough, just obstinate," said Anna. "I can only imagine what she was like when she was alive."

"Probably a lot like you, dear." Clara smiled.

Anna laughed. "Well, do me a favor, will you? If I ever start haunting things, give me a good swift kick in the phantom arse, will you?"

"Can I do it?" Christian asked.

"Oh, piss off, you," said Anna, flicking the back of his head.

"Not while he's driving!" Clara scolded. "You may be haunting things a lot sooner than you think if you keep that up, Annelise."

"Oh, fie." Anna sat back and pouted. "No matter how old we get, Lily, she'll always be mum."

I smiled, thinking how lucky they were.

Clara grabbed her cell phone out of the pocket of her jeans and dialed.

"We're here," she said to whoever answered. After receiving clearance onto the grounds, we pulled up in front of a Grecian looking building with a rust colored brick exterior and tall white columns that ran around the entirety of the building. If I could have imagined an ideal southern mansion, this would be it, right down to the wide circular fountain in front.

"It's big" was all I could think to say as I craned my neck to take it all in.

"Yes, it is. But don't be too intimidated, dear. At this point, Mrs. Montgomery is all too happy to have us."

I nodded, unconvinced. I felt like an intruder and I hadn't even stepped foot on the grounds yet.

Christian pulled up to a suit-clad man standing out in front of the building and rolled his window down.

"Evenin' folks," the man said.

"Hello, Tim." Clara smiled at him.

"Terry asks that you pull the car along the left side of the building, just in case …." the man said with a thick southern accent. Christian nodded and drove on.

"In case what?" I asked.

"In case her husband gets home early." Anna smirked. "He really doesn't approve of 'our type.'"

"Ah-ha. What exactly is 'our type'?" I asked in earnest as we pulled to a stop alongside the building.

"Same as his type," Christian started, grinning as he got out of the car. "Only smarter and much more attractive."

The four of us walked around the front of the building. By then Mrs. Montgomery was waiting on the porch. She was the perfect image of a politician's wife in a powder blue cardigan set and shoulder length red hair that flipped out at the ends. She was younger than I'd expected, but her face was creased with worry as she walked along the elegant front porch toward us.

"I'm so, so very glad you came back," she said, her accent enchanting. "She's been behaving differently ever since you left. I don't know what you said to her, Anna, but she's been visiting my bedroom instead of Carley's the last few nights. It's like she knows I'm alone!" She shivered and went on. "I just wish Morgan was home to see it himself."

Anna turned to me. "Carley is Mrs. Montgomery's daughter," she explained.

"Oh, please, please call me Terry," Mrs. Montgomery said eagerly, taking my hand.

"I'm Lily." I smiled.

"Where *is* Carley?" Anna asked.

"I sent her to a friend's, like you suggested," Terry said.

"Good, we can go at it full force, then," Christian said.

"Do you expect your husband home anytime soon?" Clara asked.

"I don't think so. He's been gone away for about a week, and he's got a meeting with our financial planner in Savannah this afternoon. I don't expect him home until late, but, I apologize, I can never be certain," she said.

"No need to worry, dear," Clara said as a suspect wave of calm passed through me. She was working her magic on the poor woman, no doubt.

Terry smiled. "My, you are all just so wonderful," she said. "Let's go inside. It's hot enough to fry an egg out here."

Through the main door we entered a huge front hall. To the right was a library, and to the left another room with its door shut.

"Upstairs," Terry said, leading the way.

We followed her further back to a smaller, circular hall with a large grand staircase at its center. There was a dining room off to the right and a living room to the left. Terry started up the stairs and we followed. Christian, Clara, and Anna seemed to know exactly where she was going and kept pace with her. She stopped a few rooms down the main corridor and opened the door.

The room didn't seem like the site of a haunting. It was bright and modern enough, with white carpet, a white bedspread, and white paint on the walls.

"Here. Right here," she said, pointing to the foot of her bed. "This is where she's been standing every night now for days."

"Hm." Christian's forehead wrinkled in thought. "Last time we were here, you said she'd never been in your room."

"No. Only Carley's."

"Almost protective," Clara murmured.

Christian nodded in agreement. "How long does she stay?" he asked.

"It's the same damn thing, same damn time every night … pardon my French. Three o'clock on the dot she comes in, stares out the door for a few minutes, then disappears."

"Strange," Anna mused.

"If only I could sleep through the ordeal! But I can't. I hear the door open, I see her waltz past, everything goes ice cold, and I know she's here. The first night I was so scared I cried the whole time. The second night I didn't dare look up. And last night I just lost my temper! I told her I was going to stop sleeping in here and she'd have to haunt herself!"

Christian burst out laughing. "And how did that work out?"

"Well, it was simply infuriating. She just kept looking out the fucking door, completely ignored me … do pardon my language." She had slung the last few lines together in one breath.

"Quite all right," Clara assured her. "Has she been around during the day anymore?"

"Yes, in the bathroom a few times, and Carley saw her in the family room the other afternoon while Morgan and I were out."

"And neither of you have seen her together yet, have you?"

"No. It's still only been one or the other of us."

"Well, then, we split up again. How about if I give the bathroom a visit," Anna suggested. Till now she had said very little, just observed the conversation, occasionally glancing around the room.

"And I'll go to the family room," Christian said.

"Good enough. Lily, you stay here with me, then," Clara said.

I nodded readily.

"I'll just let you all do your thing," Terry said. "There's a stack of thank you notes downstairs waiting for my signature. Call me if you need me," she said.

Clara and I sat on the bed. "I certainly hope she pops around for a bit. Would be terribly disappointing for you if she didn't," Clara said.

"Uh, not *that* disappointing, trust me," I laughed.

"Oh, come on, now." She patted my leg. "You'll do very well."

"Will I?"

"Certainly. I can see that."

"You can?" I was utterly disbelieving.

"Let me tell you something," she said. "You've got more courage in that button nose of yours than I had in my whole body the first time I came along on one of these. You know how I know?"

"How?"

"Well, I'd been preparing for this sort of thing all my life, you see. I knew what to expect, but I was still quite the stick up the arse. Fragile, my mother called me, God rest her soul." She snickered. "Despite the knowledge base, I begged my way out of these things the first few times. I was simply terrified! But after so long, my father had had enough, and simply *would* not let me stay behind! The first time I saw an astral, I fainted."

I giggled. "Seems like a reasonable reaction to me."

"Yes, well, the point is that you've had little formal preparation, but here you sit. William said you seemed excited at the idea of coming!"

"Ha, well, maybe not excited, but eager, yes. Of course, it isn't real to me yet. I haven't seen her. I'll probably scream like a banshee if that happens," I admitted.

"But you didn't scream when you saw your gentleman caller," she reminded me.

"Yes, well, that was before I knew what he was."

"True," she said.

"And you should have seen me after the vampire incident," I said.

"Oh, but in all fairness though, love, that was quite the proper reaction for one of those. Nasty little bastards they are. You don't want to take them lightly."

"No. It was horrible. I don't know how you can get used to fighting them. I couldn't even move!"

"That will get better, with William's help, of course."

"Hmph. Ironic." The words came out more angrily than I'd intended.

She raised an eyebrow. "Been talking to Christian, have we?"

"I know what William is, if that's what you mean. But Christian wasn't the one to tell me," I said. "I do wonder something about William, though."

"Yes?"

"Well, the vampire I saw back home, he was different; he looked hideous, inhuman. What's with William? He looks normal enough."

"The boy is a handsome little devil, isn't he?" She nudged, fidgeting with a temperature gauge.

"No! I didn't mean *that*," I said, appalled. "I meant he looks like a human; no veiny growth, no ugly eyes."

"Oh, that!" she said. "Well, exactly how much do you know about William?"

"I know he has a soul."

"Yes. And that soul allows him a certain level of humanity. Had he remained on his original path, he'd have been just as bloody ugly as your friend in the woods someday."

I nodded.

"Christian doesn't realize you're aware of William's history?" she asked.

"No. Christian has no idea how much I know," I said sadly.

"How much *do* you know, dear?"

The conversation was cut short as Anna dashed around the corner and halted in the middle of the room, looking around.

"Where is she?" she said excitedly. "She came in here!"

"We haven't seen anything," Clara answered. "She's not made an appearance yet, but I suspected as much. The temperature's dropped nearly ten degrees."

Now that I thought about it, it had gotten awfully cold in here. I balled myself up on the bed, looking around quickly.

"What happened? Were you in the bathroom?" I asked, enthralled.

"Yes! Well, the bathroom turned frigid, and I knew something was happening. Then she walked through the door, looked at me, and darted out again. I followed her in here, but where the blazes did she go?"

Clara smiled. "Right there, dear."

I whipped my head around to where Clara's eyes were resting. A lovely young woman stood in the far corner of the room, dressed in a green and white gown. Her blond hair poured down in ringlets along her shoulders, and the look on her flawless features was no less than irate. My spine tingled as I gripped the comforter to steady the shaking. It was all I could do not to hide behind Clara.

She glared at Anna, her fists clenched tightly. "Why do you insist on following me? Won't you all please let me do as I must?" Her words sounded far away at first, then grew in clarity as I focused harder.

"It's not that we're following you," Anna began. "We're just trying to get a handle on why you're here."

The apparition turned her head toward the bedroom door. "You're making it worse," she said.

"Making what worse? You mean we're angering you?" Clara asked, frustrated.

The girl stood perfectly still, unresponsive.

"Please," Clara begged. "Why are you visiting these people?"

The girl whipped her head back toward Anna. "It's better if she's not here!"

"Who?" Anna asked.

"The older one. He's angry when she's here. It makes it worse."

"When *who* is here?" Anna fumed. "*Who* is angry? What are you talking about?"

"You!" She pointed a finger at Clara, and cold air immediately shot across my face.

"Who do I make angry?" Clara asked.

"Shhh," the girl whispered, facing the door again. We stood in silence, following her eyes to the exit and waited. Nothing. She turned her head slowly back to us. This time, her gaze fell on me. I froze.

"He's watching you," she said, her eyes worried. "He knows you're weaker than the others."

"Who?" I said, transfixed. Hold the phone. Had I spoken to her?

"A monster," she answered, shaking her head.

"Who do you mean? Who's a monster? Who else is here?" Anna asked.

Again we waited in silence.

"You needn't be afraid, dear," Clara said at last, standing up. Warmth emitted in a ray from her chest. The light coursed across the room and filled the girl's form, transforming her appearance immediately. The pale, smoky skin glowed more naturally and she smiled.

"I'm not afraid," she said. "He can't harm me. I fear for the women."

"Why? Who is he? What attachments does he have here?"

"I fear for the women," she repeated, her words echoing strangely.

Then, in the blink of an eye, she was inches from Clara's face. "Fear for the women," she whispered pleadingly, and again it echoed off the walls.

"What is he?" Clara asked, concern finally registering in her eyes.

"Not human. He lusts for their flesh," she said with a sob. An instant later she was gone, and the air around us warmed almost immediately.

Clara's face went dark. "Incubus," she said, backing up and sitting down on the bedside.

"No, Mum, not possible." Anna shook her head.

"Yes, Anna. She only appears to the women. She watches their beds at night, guards the bathrooms. She protects them when they're most vulnerable."

I thought for a moment. Incubus. I'd heard the word before.

"Anna, get your brother," Clara demanded. But Anna stood in place, her eyes wide with fear.

"*Now*, Anna!"

Clara's tone shook her, and Anna took off without a word.

"What's going on?" I asked.

Clara scooted over close to me and took my hands in hers. She spoke in a hushed voice. "Something I've seen only once in my life ... and hoped I'd never see again."

"What is it, Clara? Tell me!" I whispered back.

"It's the vilest kind of energy. Most dark spirits crave power, drain humans for the sake of sustaining their own existence," she said. "But an Incubus is the manifestation of something much lower than that. I wish there was an easier way to say this, Lily. But ... ," she hesitated. "An Incubus is the astral world's version of a sexual predator."

Her words floated on the rim of absorption. I struggled to push them away as long as I could, but they found an opening, and the sick revelation settled in.

This was straight out of the worst sort of nightmare. Surely nothing so despicable existed. I knew I should say something, anything to indicate that I understood, but bile rose in my throat and I clenched my jaw.

Christian and Anna entered the room. "Are you sure?" he asked his mother.

"Not positive, but I'd put a wager on it."

"Well, that settles it. Next time, we're bringing Paul."

"Nonsense, dear. I think between the four of us we can handle it."

"Lily? No way." Christian objected. "She shouldn't come here anymore."

"Don't underestimate her, Christian." Clara rubbed my back as she spoke. "She's stronger than you think!"

"I don't doubt her abilities, Mum, but she's nowhere near prepared. You should have seen her after training yesterday."

"Eh-hem, in the room," I grumbled.

"Oh, Christian, don't be such a horse's arse," Anna scolded.

"Do you think you could handle it, Lillian?" Clara asked

It was strange, really. Though I was disgusted by the idea of this spirit, I was not afraid of it. Rather, a surge of vengeful hatred sent me reeling. I wanted it dead—I wanted it to suffer.

"Where do things like this come from?" I asked.

Christian sat next to me. "Lil, you remember the conversation we had on the way to Atlanta? About the way mass energy creates … offspring, so to speak? The human race would be overrun with negativity if that didn't happen."

I nodded, understanding. So this is where humanity's toxic runoff went once it reached maximum capacity.

"What do we do?" I sighed.

"First thing to know is that these creatures hate a male presence. They feel threatened by it," Clara said.

"That would explain why Miss Price never felt the need to visit Terry or Carley while the governor was around," I said. "This Incubus," I shuddered, "must not have the guts to come too close when he's here."

"Exactly! Now you're thinking like a pathcrosser," Clara smiled.

"So, it's more inclined to cooperate when faced with a male Sentient," Christian remarked. "Which is why I say we bring Paul into the mix, and nix the whole thing for you this time around, Lily. No offense intended."

"I don't know. I feel safe with you guys. At least let me stay for some of it." I frowned.

"She'll be completely fine!" Anna argued.

"And if you're going to insist on *two* men accompanying us, then there's certainly no need for alarm on that account," said Clara.

Christian seemed perturbed for a moment, but then his expression relaxed in defeat. "Impossible women," he grumbled. "But you're staying in the same room with me, Lily. No arguments."

"Fine, fine," I said to patronize him.

"In the meantime," Clara began, "we can't do a thing while the family is around. Let's go have a talk with Terry."

Mrs. Montgomery was downstairs, seated at her writing desk, just as she said she'd be.

"Terry? I'll need a word, if you'll be so kind," Clara said.

"Why certainly." Terry looked up from her invitations.

"Shall we take this to a more comfortable area?"

"Of course. Come with me."

We left the study and followed her to a formal living room. A graceful oval rug was spread across the center, and the couch and loveseat were upholstered in wine-colored velvet—refurbished antiques, no doubt. I sat between Christian and Anna on the larger sofa, while Clara and Terry faced each other on the loveseat.

"Terry." Clara sighed. "I wish I could say I had good news."

Terry shook her head. "Oh, Clara, please don't tell me that. Does she still refuse to cooperate?"

"I'm sorry, dear. But I'm afraid we're dealing with more than a mere haunting."

"What in hell is she?"

"That's just it. It's not her, you see. She's actually quite desirable in this situation. But something else is here. And Miss Price has been protecting you and Carley from it."

Not surprisingly, Clara's light broke its boundary and ebbed toward Terry. I knew she was preparing her for the news.

"I need to ask something of you. It's no small favor, Terry, and I'm sorry, but I must insist that we have access to the house when no one else is here. There's too much risk involved as it is."

"Whatever you need," Terry responded. "But why? What's so risky? You still haven't said what we're dealing with here."

Clara's light grew in strength, and Terry smiled serenely. She had no idea what was happening to her, and despite the gravity of the situation, I sniggered to myself.

"I suppose I can't, in good conscience, keep it from you, but damned if I know how to say this," Clara said.

"Oh, I'm sure it will be all right." Terry grinned contentedly. "You're all so very good at this."

Clara sighed again. "Putting it in layman's terms, there's a creature living in your home, and he wants to harm you and Carley. I would insist that you not leave her alone in the house until we've cleansed it. In fact, both of you should avoid this place whenever you can until we come back."

For a fleeting moment Terry's brow furrowed in concern, but Clara was too well-practiced with her energy. Where she should have panicked, Terry simply nodded her head. I knew that even after we left, she would continue to feel the inexplicable calm, the confidence that I had felt with Christian and Abram. It was a wonderful thing, until you learned that it was only an illusion. There was very real danger here.

"When will you be back?" Terry asked.

"Tomorrow, if possible."

"No, tomorrow won't work." Terry sighed. "We have dinner with former Governor Boyd and his wife. They've sort of taken us under their wing." She rolled her eyes. "I'd *love* to get out of it, but Morgan would be livid. He idolizes the man."

"Okay, well, as long as Morgan is home, you should be all right," Clara said. "But when *can* we come back?"

"How much time will you need?" Terry asked.

"It could be very difficult," Clara admitted. "Ideally an entire day."

"Well, we leave for vacation next Saturday."

Christian nodded. "Perfect. We'll have the whole house to ourselves."

"And no doubt we'll need it," Clara said. "In the meantime, I would look differently upon your female house guest. Miss Price has been an angel in disguise."

"How about that. So, precisely what kind of creature are we talking about? A ghost? A demon? Please say no to that last suggestion."

"It's an entity that defies the norm," said Clara. "It's not human, and demons don't exist. Not in the way that we've been taught to believe, anyway. You may or may not know it as an Incubus, and it's particularly ... fond ... of lone females."

Terry's eyes narrowed. "Jesus Christ. Why in the hell would it be here? Excuse my language."

"Most likely it attached itself to you somehow. Have you been anyplace particularly unpleasant lately? A hospital, an asylum?"

"No. Nothing like that."

"And it was roughly three months ago when all this started?"

"Yes, that's right."

"Can you think back further? To just before then?"

"Hm. Let's see, just before the ghost started showing up, Morgan had taken office. There were so many places, so many things we had to do. I don't know that I can recall them all but ...." She blinked and took a gasping breath. "Oh, Jesus. I wonder ...."

"Yes? Out with it!"

"The men's prison. Morgan and I visited the Metro State Prison right after he was elected."

"Shit," Christian said. "Appropriate place for something like that to spawn off."

"Isn't it, though?" Anna added. "It must have been attracted to you. Attached itself to you and followed you home."

"Now that I think about it ... ," Terry offered, "this puts a whole new light on my first encounter with Miss Price. I had just gotten off my elliptical—those things work miracles on your thigh muscles, I am *not* ashamed to say that mine are like stones! But, anyway, afterwards I was a real mess, so I jumped in the shower and half way through, God damned if something didn't have me by the shoulders. And that's when our ghost girl first appeared. I just connected it with her."

"Has anything touched you since then?" asked Clara.

Terry reflected for a moment. "No, nothing concrete. Though a few times I'd have sworn someone was following me. Silly, I know, but there's been more than one occasion when I just ran past a dark corridor or a room with the lights off. It was almost like I could see something move out of the corner of my eye. What a silly notion," she pondered, giggling nervously.

"Not so silly," Christian said. "People are too quick to discredit intuition and blame things on an overactive imagination. If you get a strong gut feeling about something, I'd recommend you heed it."

"I will," Terry said.

"Good," Clara said. "And what time shall we get here on Saturday?"

"We leave around noon, so, anytime after that. I'll have Tim let you in," said Terry.

Seven

So, we avoid close proximity to vampires why?" William asked.

I narrowed my eyes at him.

"This is important, Lily. Stop glaring at me," he reprimanded.

"Well, you're quizzing me like a four-year-old!" I looked away, watching a bluebird flit from one tree to the next.

"I am not," William said. "I'm simply trying to drive the point home. If you remember nothing else, remember this. Close proximity is bad why?"

I sighed loudly. "Physical contact allows for enthrallment."

"That's right. In fact, if the vampire is powerful enough, he can gain control without even laying a finger on you."

"Hm," I considered. "So what's *your* defect?"

"I'm sorry?"

"*You're* close in proximity, William. Shouldn't I be all glazed over and catatonic?"

"Only if I wanted you to be."

"So you could ...."

"I could." He nodded, a suggestion of a smile on his face. "If I chose to."

"But you wouldn't dare," I threatened.

"Of course not," he said, and then he smiled in earnest. "Unless you're particularly discourteous, in which case it would probably be the only solid method of shutting you up."

"Fuck … you …." I said.

He raised an eyebrow. "Keep dreaming."

"*Oh,* you *arrogant … stupid* …." I stuttered. Where were the words? Where were the goddamn words?

He crossed his arms and shook his head. "Stupid?" He snorted.

"I'm thinking!" I blurted, and he chuckled at me. "*All right,*" I said. "I'll save that for a later session after I've had time to root through the universe and find a colloquialism vile enough to be applied to you. For now, let's talk shop. If a blood sucking asshole—such as yourself—should come within any kind of close range of me, I'm to do what exactly?"

"Supposing I told you, would you try and use it on me?"

"Absolutely."

"I thought as much. So we'll avoid that discussion for a while."

"Fine. Then we're done here," I snapped.

"If you say so. Though you're only shorting yourself, Lily. There's a lot more you need to know."

"No point in rushing things." Christian broke through the tree line, walking up beside me. "Is everything all right, Lily?" he asked, giving William the evil eye.

"Fine," I said, sneering along with him.

"Fantastic." William grinned.

"Is that right?" Christian took a step closer to my trainer, staring him down.

William shook his head. "Is this supposed to benefit her, Christian? Lesson disruption?"

"It sounded like you were finished to me," Christian said.

"We are. Let's go," I said, giving William one last seething look before turning to leave.

"Colloquialism!" William shouted after us. "Good word."

I fought the urge to laugh, then scolded myself inwardly. It's not like I needed compliments from a fucking vampire anyway. Christian stalked up behind me as I booked it to the house.

"Has he hurt you in any way?" he asked accusingly.

"What? No. Why would you think that?" I halted in my tracks. Was he finally ready to tell me what I already knew? He looked at me appraisingly. Why was he hiding this from me? Did he think I was so fragile, so incompetent, that I couldn't survive the truth? And how long did he expect I could go on living here without finding out?

"Never mind," he said. "But he's obviously done *something* to you."

"He's just … aggravating."

"Not surprising. I *knew* this was a bad idea."

"He just," I began, slowing my pace. "He tries to act … like … like he's not …."

"What?" Christian urged.

"I don't know. You said not to trust him. But he acts like I should!"

Christian laughed bitingly. "To be expected."

"But why, though?" I baited. "I mean, give me one reason in particular why I shouldn't?"

He shifted from one foot to the other, then took a deep breath. "Lily …."

I watched and waited.

He sighed through his nose. "Some things are better left in the shadows."

"Come *on*, Christian," I groaned. "When are you going to stop being so vague with me?"

"Christ! I said just *drop* it for now, okay?!"

I stared at him, shocked by his outburst and uncertain how to respond. The fact remained that it was getting harder for me to view William as a monster, despite my frequent cracks at disdain. Christian needed to give me something concrete to work with, something William-specific to chew on, and he needed to do it quickly, because William's responses were exasperatingly organic—even human. Did I want to believe that his soul made no difference with regard to his nature? Perhaps not. In moments of weakness, when I could feel myself trusting him, even enjoying him, fear took hold of me. And yet, when, in the light of empathy, I snidely cursed him, shame followed. On which end of the scale could a Sentient's heart rightly lie?

"All right," I said. "It's dropped." *But it's your funeral*, I thought.

☙

"Oh, this is splendid," Abram beamed. "So very many syrups to choose from. Is this boysenberry?"

I giggled. "I think it's blackberry."

"Mm. Well, regardless, a plethora of flavors and so little time. What a wonderful place. We must tip the waitress well."

Thomas smiled. "I don't know that she has anything to do with the variety of syrup selections, Abram," he said, pouring creamer into his cup of coffee.

"Well, she is exceedingly good at pointing them out," Abram replied with enthusiasm and cut into a stack of pancakes.

"Has anyone noticed my six-pack?" Paul asked, lifting his white T-shirt over his abdomen. "It's really coming in."

"Keep your shirt on during breakfast!" Anna covered her eyes.

"Well sor-ry," Paul huffed. "I'll just have to show you *after* breakfast then."

"Lucky me," Anna grumbled.

"So did *you* catch it, Lily?" he asked, eagerly.

"Uh, yes, very six-packish. I'm in awe, Paul," I said.

Paul grinned like a kid with a lollipop.

Christian rolled his eyes. "So, did Mum tell you about the governor's mansion, Abram?"

"Yes, indeed she did. Very grave situation," he said, dumping half a container of peach marmalade onto a biscuit.

"Then it probably wouldn't be the best idea for Lily to attend," Christian added, and I gave him a look.

"On the contrary. I believe it will be quite beneficial for her. Perhaps William should attend as well?" He looked at me.

"I …."

"Not necessary," Christian spoke for me.

"Well, we shall discuss it later," Abram said. "By the way, Lily, would you kindly ride home with me? It's a lovely day for a drive, and I have a few questions for you."

"No problem," I said.

After our meal, Abram and I rode in his car—a white four door coupe from the1940s—with the windows rolled down.

"I'm surprised Clara allowed for the breakfast out." Abram chuckled. "She has been so smitten with having a kitchen that she's insisted on cooking at every turn."

"Ah," I said, understanding. "Well, she is a good cook. It's use it or lose it I guess."

"Indeed. And speaking of using it—are you finding the defensive lessons helpful?"

"Uhm, sure. They're great," I said, biting my tongue.

"Splendid. And is William explaining things well?"

"Yes." I had to acknowledge this fact. If nothing else, William did always answer my questions.

"Wonderful, wonderful. Tell me something you've learned," he said.

"Well, he's explained enthrallment, auras, and the path of a soul."

"Ah, yes. Basic but important. Understanding one's soul is essential."

"And that reminds me … ." I'd thought of a perplexing question. "I've been wondering about animals."

"Yes?" Abram responded brightly. "What have you wondered?"

"Are humans the only beings with souls?" I asked.

"Certainly not," Abram answered. "Anything that lives and dies has a soul, Lillian. But some souls are collective. You've witnessed the phenomenon of bird migration many times, I'm sure?"

"Mhm." I nodded.

"And you are aware of how unanimously in sync their movements are? How hundreds, thousands of them can fly together, turn on a dime, reshape their flock in the same instant without a second's hesitation?"

"Yes!" I was excited now. "I have. How is that possible?"

"Because, they share a group soul," he said. "A connected mind. Modern day science—inspired as it is—has yet to explain the issues of instinct and migration because these concepts are beyond what is confined to a lab specimen or wired to a machine."

"So, shared souls … that's amazing. What about other animals? Like dogs or cats?"

"No, their souls are quite uniquely their own," Abram explained.

So, Rufus has a soul, I thought. Considering his surly nature, this was hard to believe.

"Okay. One more," I said.

"Let's have it."

"Well, what about Ginny? I mean, does she go to school with other kids? How do Ophelia and Demetre manage that while we're moving all over the place?"

"Mm." He nodded. "As you probably noted, a good number of Sentients are retrieved … usually in their twenties, when paranormal occurrences become more recognizable. This tends to allow them the opportunity for a normal childhood. Unless, of course, you are Mr. Paul DePrimo, in which case your childhood was rather terrible, regardless of location." He frowned. "But as far as children born in a Sentient household, they are home-schooled ... or more appropriately, road-schooled."

"That's what I guessed."

"A very good question, Lily. I see your list has yet to exhaust itself." He winked.

I laughed. "Nope. Nowhere near exhaustion."

"Marvelous," he sang. "One should show infinite interest in the world around them."

I snorted. "Tell that to Christian. I'm pretty sure if I ask him one more thing, he's going to cover his ears and start singing."

"Oh my, that would be a dreadful consequence indeed, as he cannot hold a note. But don't be discouraged! Be fervent in your questioning, Lillian. It is the natural route to perceiving oneself."

&

Midweek was muggy and overcast, with a strong wind sifting through the trees on my way to training. A slow drizzle of rain started to fall. William was already waiting, lounging against a low hanging branch.

"You're late," he said.

"*Please*. Like you have anything more pressing to do. I haven't seen you leaving with anyone lately. What exactly *is* your job, anyway?"

He spoke slowly, smugly. "*You* are my job, Lily. Or I would be staking out an encampment of vampires right now."

"Figures. Hanging around with murdering bastards in your spare time?"

He stood up quickly and took two long strides in my direction, hovering over me. "You have no idea what you're talking about. Quit while you're ahead, Lily."

Patient William was gone. Just as well; it was easier to fight him this way.

"Or what? You'll bite me? You're no better than the rest of them, are you?"

"Lily ... I'm warning you." A sheet of rain cut through the treetops.

"You move another inch, and I swear to God ...." I threatened.

"You'll what?" He took a step closer, smiling.

I gathered up every ounce of energy in my body and hurled him a vicious look. In an instant, he was thrown backward. He landed with a thud on his back, groaning.

"Oh, *shit*," I said, battling laughter.

He sighed painfully, boosting himself up on his elbows to look at me.

"I hadn't planned on advancing your lessons that quickly yet," he said.

I shrugged, grinning sheepishly. "I had no idea that was going to happen! You should have warned me before you pissed me off like that."

"If I remember correctly, I tried to." He turned to his side, panting, and pushed himself up. "*Now*, maybe we can do what we're both here to do, if you can keep from breaking my back in the process."

"I could if I knew what the hell that was." I giggled. There was no hiding my giddiness.

"You can repel very well, apparently." He limped back to me.

"So, that was repelling, then?"

"It was. Congratulations," he said with avid sarcasm.

"When can we do it again?"

His hand shot up. "*Not* right now, Lily."

"Oh, come *on*. I enjoyed it!"

"Shocking," he said, glaring at me.

I pouted. "Please?"

His eyes softened and he sighed. "Well, I suppose now that I know what you're capable of, we could bypass the kiddie pool."

"I'm ready," I said, poised for combat.

"Naturally, but can we focus on another subject?"

I frowned again. "Fine."

He kicked a stone in the air and caught it. "We'll start smaller this time. Knock it out of my hand."

I blinked, suddenly confused. How did this work again?

"You have to throw your energy into it. It starts at your center … right here," he said, maneuvering around to place his hand on my stomach. "Then work it outward through your chest, arms, until it's concentrated in your hands, in your face."

"Enough with the touching now, William," I warned.

He rolled his eyes. "Just pay attention."

"Center of energy, chest, hands, face. I got it," I insisted.

"All right. Again," he said, holding out the stone.

Envisioning a smoldering coal in my core, I watched it grow into a flame, then spread across my torso. I imagined my hands were balls of fire, my heart a blazing sun. Staring at the stone I willed the thing to move. It quivered a bit and then lay still.

"Not even trying," William goaded.

Clenching my fists I refocused my anger on the object in his hand.

"Move, damn it!" The stone slipped between his fingers and soared off into the woods behind him.

He smiled triumphantly. "During an actual attack, you have the benefit of ripe emotional energy at your disposal. You need to feel something real to pull this off, Lily. Otherwise, we'd be blowing stuff away accidentally night and day around here."

I relaxed my clenched teeth. "Makes sense."

"Yes. Take someone like Christian for instance. With his temperament—"

"Oh, please," I interrupted. "Leave him out of this! I doubt he's done anything to justify that statement, anyway."

"And how would you possibly know this?"

"Because, he's Christian. I can just tell."

"I see. So he's perfect in every way, then. Infallible." He scoffed. "Lily, in this line of work you'll meet time travelers, those who see the future, read your thoughts. And then there's Christian and Paul—soldiers, both of them, and innately hostile. Not that they can't be pleasant enough Sentients, but some handle the aggressive impulses better than others. While Christian has railed against me, he's conveniently neglected to warn you about his temper. It would be a shame to allow his domineering, egotistical tactics to stifle your growth here."

"Oh, hold on!" I raised my hands to stop him. "Isn't it enough that I agreed to train with you? How dare you, even for an instant, pass judgment on anyone? Do you get off on being a hypocrite?" No sooner had the words left my mouth than I regretted them.

"Wow. I can't seem to make any kind of leeway with you, can I?" William's face fell.

"Well, what were you expecting? This ground has been covered. I don't know why you're still so intent on trying to convince me of your merits! What could it possibly matter to you? Shall I trust you so you can use it against me?"

"Do you really believe that?"

"It's a plausible theory! As far as I'm concerned, you need to stick to the basic training out here, William."

"And there's no chance in hell of you and me becoming friends, then?"

I laughed. "Are you serious? Why would either of us want that?"

He narrowed his eyes in frustration. "Why *wouldn't* we?!" He charged forward, then deliberated and turned back a few paces, only to return again, glowering down at me. "When you first got here, you looked at me differently, didn't you? Can't you draw your *own* damned conclusions?"

"Don't yell at me!" I shouted back, tears threatening an emergence.

He relaxed, his shoulders falling. "I realize what you think I am," he said. "But, it's not true anymore. I'm not what I was. All I'm asking for is an inch."

"William. Are you, or are you not, a vampire?" I asked.

"Yes," he said. "But my foundation is human now, and I'd do *anything* to never have been turned. Lily … please." He didn't seem angry anymore, simply defeated.

William was, by any estimation, a proud man, and this kind of disclosure was astonishing. I remembered what Abram had said about empaths. People would naturally reveal their weaknesses, their pain, in my presence. All at once I felt inept to deal with such a prospect. But, ready or not, my well-constructed wall had suffered a crack. How could I not feel for him now?

I took a deep breath, and then exhaled just as slowly, trying to clear my head of all the conflicting thoughts. Perhaps I had been too hard on William. Maybe even vampires had a choice, a chance to be redeemed. Better not to share these thoughts with Christian, though.

"So, I should believe you're not evil, then …." I eyed him cautiously.

He remained silent and perfectly still. Undeniably, his energy radiated a very human sadness. And perhaps a twinge of fear?

"I suppose I know a thing or two about being an outsider," I said.

He watched me expectantly. "So …."

"*So* …." I left it at that.

He narrowed his eyes. "Don't be cruel, Lily."

I moaned. "Ugh, *fine*, William. I'll let up on you. But this won't be easy with Christian in the mix."

He relaxed his form. "We'll be understated with the niceties." He smirked. "So … truce, then?"

I couldn't suppress a smile. "Truce."

❧

"Do these people have a name? Can I look them up online?" Kate asked.

I held the phone between my shoulder and cheek while I tied my hair back.

"Well, not technically. They're more of a privately funded civic organization."

"You're being evasive, Lillian. They have to have a name."

"Just…it's like the Peace Corp, Kate. They travel around where they're needed."

"And your role in this obscurely named Peace Corp-like group?"

"Well, let's just say that my English major is finally being put to good use. I communicate with the clients."

"Communicate?" Her voice was dripping with suspicion. "Oh, *God*, Lil, you're not like a phone sex operator, are you?"

"No!" I laughed loudly. "Shit, Katie. I'm … I'm a conduit between parties."

"Right. What kind of parties are we talking about? What do you do?"

"It's crisis intervention, so to speak. I step in and talk the client into cooperating. But I can't say too much. Privacy issues, you know?"

"How are you qualified for that, Lil? You don't have a degree in psychology."

"Training. They're convinced that I'm the right person for the job, and I'm learning as I go along."

"And why can't you do something like this at home? Why did you have to rush off to Georgia?"

"Because I needed to go away, Kate," I said. "I needed some answers."

"What's so wrong with us?" she snapped. "What's out there that you couldn't find closer to your real life, closer to your grandparents? You deserted them, Lil. You were all they had, and you just took off like some kind of maniac! That's not like you, and I *don't* like this."

I sighed. "Please try to understand. Can't you just trust me? I have no choice but to be here."

"*God*, then they've got some kind of hold on you and I ought to drive out there and drag you back myself! Whatever they've done to screw with—"

"Kate, stop!" I said, and she fell silent. "Everything isn't always so easy to understand. I've never been the person you assumed I was and wanted me to be. Don't tell me you can only fathom what stems from your place in this world, because that's awfully narrow-minded of you."

She laughed. "You're right, Lily! You're not the person I thought you were, and I'm tired of trying to keep up with your fantasies. I'm sorry we aren't enough for you. Call me when you wake up." She hung up the phone.

&

"Straight flush?! Unacceptable. She is heretofore banned from the game," Thomas pronounced with teasing indignation.

The impending Saturday cleansing had created some tension among the housemates, so I'd decided that a good old fashioned poker session was in order. Demetre, Anna, Paul, Thomas, and I sat around an elaborately carved, circular coffee table in the middle of the living room.

"I say she cheats," Paul argued.

"Why? Because she beat you to a bloody pulp? Don't be a shit," Anna said. "Lily, you must teach me to play like that. You've won every hand!"

"No problem," I said. "Step one: Spend countless hours in the company of farty old men."

Thomas cleared his throat.

"What?" I smiled. "I said farty old men, not dashing British gentleman such as yourself."

"Well, then, that's all right." He nodded. "Do I dare deal again?"

Thomas barely had the words out before a loud slam jarred the house and a muffled but angry voice broke through our cozy atmosphere. It came from the direction of the bedroom hallway. While I could make out only bits of the argument, the voice was unmistakable.

"…no *reason* why he should come!" Christian's words were scattered as we all listened intently. "We don't need him. What's wrong with Paul?"

Anna sighed and slapped her cards down on the table and took off toward the source of the commotion.

"Oh dear." Thomas tsked. "Only one subject gets the boy that riled up."

"You ain't shittin', either," Demetre said. "What's he saying?"

I got up and leaned out of the doorway, craning my head into the reception hall in time to hear Anna join the fray.

"…a bloody fool of yourself!" I caught the end of her scolding accusation.

"Let him stick to what he knows; leave the human business to us!" Christian seethed. Then it all fell silent. I assumed that Abram was involved, but I didn't dare investigate myself.

The voices began again and grew clearer, moving to the front of the house. I stepped out of the doorway quickly and back into the living room. Christian stormed into the main hall with Anna and Clara close behind.

"You need to back off!" Anna demanded. "Why shouldn't he accompany us? He's been training her!"

"That argument is asinine considering she shouldn't be going in the first place, so piss off, Anna!" Christian barked, and then he charged out the front door, nearly unhinging it in the process.

"Ugh! He's such a pig-headed bastard!" Anna lamented.

"It's not good," Clara said, quietly. "So out of balance, all of this."

"You know, it might occur to him that we lost Dad as well, and there's no one in this house to blame for it!"

"I fear your brother blames himself more than any other," Clara said, then sighed deeply. "Darling, go back to the game. I'll take care of this."

Anna nodded, glancing into the living room. We sat, pointlessly feigning ignorance, with cards in hand. She headed for the sofa and dropped onto it dramatically.

"He's impenetrably unreasonable." She huffed.

"So we've heard," said Thomas.

"What's he angry with William for now?" I asked, surprised by the touch of annoyance in my voice.

"Oh, it's too ridiculous to address," she said. "But you know I'll tell you anyway."

We were counting on it.

"Basically, Abram wants William to come with us to the mansion. And Christian has blown all to bits over it. But I can see Abram's point. I mean, if you're coming with us, Lily, and William has been training you, it makes sense that he should be there to coach you through your first real exposure."

Paul groaned. "Christian and William together? On the same job? I'm *glad* I'm not going."

"Oh, come on," I said. "How bad could it be? I mean, they're professionals, right? They can keep it together for one night."

Anna snorted, Paul gawked, and Thomas studied his fingernails.

"Er, Lily, they've never been on a job together for a reason," Demetre said. "All the calming energy in the world doesn't seem to make a difference."

"Then *what* is Abram *thinking?*" I complained.

"I know Abram," Thomas said. "If there's a chance for some kind of camaraderie, he'll wheedle it out of them."

"Ah. Well, good for him!" I said. Anna opened her mouth in shock and threw me a questioning look.

"I … don't like conflict." I shrugged.

"Well, it's just that I was certain you'd bought into Christian's anti-William stock," she said.

I glanced around nervously. "This doesn't reach Christian," I warned.

"No problem!" Paul swore.

"Quiet as the grave, dear," Thomas said, and Demetre nodded. I glared at Anna.

"Oh, for heaven's sake, tell me!" She bounced in place.

"There's nothing exceptional to tell," I said. "It's just that I've decided some civility toward William on my part might not be total blasphemy."

Thomas looked pleased. "Good. I'm glad you're remaining neutral," he said. "I know what the boy is. We all do. But he's not without redeeming qualities."

"Besides," Demetre added. "As far as I can see, that could be me or any one of mine. And you better believe I'd have fought to win them back somehow."

"But, on the other hand … as I'm remaining neutral …." I looked at Thomas. "That could be a slippery slope. I mean, every vampire was once someone's child, wife, best friend. But we battle these things and kill them all the time, right? Where's the line drawn? How can we differentiate?"

"A good point," Anna began. "But there is a significant difference between William and most vampires."

"Right. The soul thing."

"Yes," said Anna, gearing up to do the tale justice. "I mean, after a turn, normal vampires are really just animated vessels since the soul has moved on. But in William's case, what with his having a soul and all, he's a person again. And, perhaps more importantly, is *how* he came to get his soul back. You see, before he—"

Paul let out a loud cough. Anna paused and went on.

"Before he was ever—"

Paul interrupted again, gagging elaborately and nudging his head toward the front door. William had walked in.

"Oh," she whispered, covering her mouth.

I realized we were all staring at him about the same time that he did, but it was too late to turn away now.

"Hi, William!" Anna chirped.

"Anna." He smirked, strolling through the doorway. "Am I missing something?"

"Oh, no. Just … playing cards!" She held up her losing hand.

"Hm." He rounded in front of the couch and sat down. "Who's winning?" he asked, leaning forward.

"Lily," groaned everyone.

He smiled at me, an eyebrow raised. "I'm in."

"Is that a challenge? Because I'm not to be trifled with, William," I said.

He just chuckled and accepted the newly dealt hand from Thomas.

"Aces are wild," Demetre called.

William put two cards down. "Two, please," he said.

Demetre winced at his cards. "I'm out." He slapped them down on the table.

"Chicken." Paul shook his head.

Demetre put his hand over his heart. "You know what the great Kenny Rogers said about knowing when to fold 'em."

"I beg you, no singing!" Thomas implored abruptly.

Demetre looked affronted. "I hadn't planned on it!"

"Yes, well, precautionary measures, my friend. I've heard tell of your shower operatics."

"Hmph." Demetre scratched his beard. "Are we gonna play a game here?"

I examined my hand. A two of hearts, a three of hearts, a jack of spades, a six of diamonds, and a seven of spades. Not very promising. I kept the two and three of hearts, but the rest had to go.

"Three for me," I said, straight-faced.

Oh, now I'd done it. A pair of sixes, one a spade and one a diamond, threatened to botch the whole thing. My only hope resided in the ace. Maybe I could pull this off with two pair. I looked around. Paul was frowning at his cards, chewing on the corner of his lip. No threat there.

Thomas dropped four of his reject cards on the pile and drew four more. "Bloody buggering hell," he muttered. I snickered.

Then there was William, his face a composed masterpiece. Dammit. I should have suspected he wouldn't fall so easily. I peered sideways at him, trying to evoke a reaction. He glanced back, unaffected, then returned his gaze to his cards. I blinked, trying to focus on my own. What the blazes? They were a foreign bungle of smudges, colors, and shapes that made no sense at all. With some effort, I cleared my head and the cards were cards again.

"Well, I know a lost cause when I see one," said Anna, and she folded.

"Thomas?" William questioned.

"Ehn. Let me wallow in denial for a bit."

"No problem," William said. He turned to me, eyebrow raised, half-smiling.

Ugh, I should have been used to the handsome thing by now. Why was it so distracting? Was this some kind of creepy vampire game strategy? I sighed. Conniving non-humans.

A silent moment passed, with Paul and Anna looking on, absorbed. Thomas became increasingly edgy, peeking back and forth from me to William.

"Oh, I give up," he finally said.

"Same here." Paul moped.

I allowed myself a subdued snigger before regrouping.

"You're next, William," I smiled sweetly.

"Me? No." He shook his head, grinning broadly. "No, I don't think so."

"Suit yourself," I said.

There was more tense silence, and then William leaned back, lounging on the couch with his cards. I shifted my position. The wood floor grew harder and more uncomfortable as the moments ticked on. I sighed.

"Really, William. You are *completely* bluffing!" I reprimanded.

"Am I?" His eyes widened in surprise. "I could have sworn I was waiting for you to accept the inevitable. I'm a very patient man, Lily."

"And I am a very stubborn woman," I said. "You expect me to cave?"

"No need," he offered. "Let's see your cards." He called my bluff. *Shit*, I thought. *He must actually have a good hand!*

Considering my options, I decided it was better to lay the cards down now, save face. The idea of my losing set, my failing bluff, shamed beside his winning hand was intolerable.

"It is obvious that you are afraid to back down, so I will be the bigger person and withdraw from the game," I declared, setting my cards face down on the table. The room gasped.

William's smile was unreasonably alluring. He leaned in and shook his head slowly. "You really should know better, Lily," he said, spreading his cards in front of me and standing up.

They were a dud, an abysmally losing hand. I gawked.

"No need to doubt yourself. Especially not with me," he said.

I could feel the flush rising in my cheeks. "Good to know." I gulped. *Act casual; no one will notice.*

He laughed. "I think I'd better call it quits before this gets violent. Thanks for the diversion, folks. See you later, Lily."

"Later, son!" Demetre called after him. Anna waved.

"Lily, Jesus, don't pop a blood vessel," Paul said. "Even *you* can't win them all."

To my great relief, I realized that my reaction had been mistaken for anger. Ah, bless my temper.

"Of all the people I had to lose to," I grumbled, sealing the deal.

"No doubt you'll be ready for him next time," Thomas encouraged me.

I shrugged. "I can pay him back in training."

"How's that?" Paul asked.

"Well, I've discovered this magnificent little trick called repelling." I smiled.

Demetre burst into riotous laughter. "You learn quick, don't 'cha?"

"Upon my word," Thomas said, impressed.

"Lily, you can repel?" asked Anna. "You've only been at this a few weeks!"

"Is that not normal?" I asked.

"Nooo," she said. "I mean, I knew what repelling was for years, and I tried doing it countless times, but damned if I could pull it off at first. Piss it, Lily, another month and you could battle that Incubus on your own!"

"Lord, no." I shuddered. "I like this beginner's thing. It's like the first few weeks in a new job. You don't have to do much, just watch everyone else work."

"Yeah, but that gets boring fast," Demetre said. "Especially for a Sentient. You just wait. You'll be raring to go in no time."

"I can see her heading in that direction," Anna said. "She's already spoken with an astral."

"Are you sure you've never done this before?" Paul laughed.

"Yes. But, I don't know. It felt natural. Besides, she talked to me first. What's the big deal?"

"I suppose it's not much for you, Lily," explained Thomas. "You *are* a pathcrosser. But not all of us here can communicate with them, you know."

"*Really?* You can't all talk to them?"

"No. I can't," he said. "I can sense energy from many directions and at further distances than most, but I can't necessarily interact with it."

"That's right," Anna began. "One can see an astral without being able to talk to it. My brother can't speak with the dead. He can battle and destroy an entity, but he can't communicate with it, can't reason with it."

"So, you're saying if he'd been in the room with us, in the mansion, he wouldn't have heard Miss Price?"

"Precisely! It's just that we're required to bring a combatant along in cases where a ghost has ill intent, or worse, … isn't a ghost at all."

"Huh. And is William a combatant?"

"No," Anna shook her head. "No, he isn't, actually. But having him along can be just as useful, believe me. His endowment is nothing short of phenomenal."

"Okay. Spill it then. What can he do?"

"He's a healer." She smiled.

"A … healer?"

"Mhm. You have yet to experience what can happen to a Sentient after an attack. The damage of a few moments may require days of recovery. And that's saying nothing of what results from a really *serious* assault. William is a healer because he has the ability to use his own energy to restore us. In theory, he could be drained quite badly by the process. The more severe the damage, the more energy he has to expend. But I've never been around to see it *truly* put into practice."

Fascinating. So William could heal. What a marvelous gift. I'd been waiting for some deep dark secret to turn up, the key justifier of Christian's loathing. But even knowing how my mother had been killed, the hatred I'd felt for William was ebbing away in the universal wash cycle. Christian would be furious if he knew I'd gone back on my word about trusting William, but I didn't have the heart to use him as a whipping boy anymore.

Eight

So, how have your lessons been going?" Clara handed me a bowl of heavy cream to whip.

"Fine," I muttered, ignoring the flock of birds let loose in my stomach.

"Yes, I knew William would be a good teacher. He's very patient."

"Except with Christian."

"Well, Christian's got his faults too, dear. And his low regard for William is not, in my opinion, entirely fair. Abram knew William when he was human. Did you know that?"

"No, I had no idea." The disclosure made perfect sense once I gave it a chance. Why else would Abram have allowed him to stay? "What happened?"

"Occupational hazard, I'm afraid. Knowledgeable vampires do not kill our kind. They seek us out, in fact, to change us."

My jaw dropped.

"Why not just kill us?" I gasped. "We pose no threat to them dead."

"Oh, but we're so much more valuable to them alive! They possess power enough as vampires, equipped to survive situations that would be fatal to humans. But vampires realize that some gifts carry over, regardless of a soul. Not to mention our knowledge of the inner workings of the Society. Vampires are ruthless in their endeavor to turn us."

"Comforting," I said.

"In fact, the vampire that … ," she began, then hesitated.

"What is it?"

"Well, Christian would be unhappy if he knew I told you this, but you deserve to know."

"Okay. Go on."

"The vampire that attacked you in the woods? He wasn't going to kill you. I'm sure of it."

"Okay. I'm not liking this."

"I'm sorry, dear. Shall I stop there?"

"No. Go ahead"

"All right. No doubt they were seeking you, Lily. They knew what you were, even if you didn't. It was the perfect opportunity."

"You think there were more of them? More than just him?"

"Where there's one there's bound to be many. Thank God for Abram. He knew the day would come when your energy was too strong for them to resist, and he sent someone to keep an eye on things."

"Christian," I said knowingly.

"No, Lily. Christian retrieved you and he killed the vampire. But he couldn't infiltrate their clan. He couldn't know their plans for you. That was left up to someone else, someone who could walk among them and win their trust."

"Who then?"

"Can't you guess?" Clara smiled down at her dough, still kneading with gusto.

"No, there's no way," I said, mortified. The mix of remorse and pleasure was nearly equal.

"Say what you will about William," Clara said, "but he has yet to fail us, regardless of what Christian says."

"Well, why didn't William say anything? I mean, he's all about the abrasive honesty. Why didn't he tell me?"

"I don't know for sure, dear. But one might guess that he didn't want to gain your approval via guilt."

I burst into laughter. "Gain my approval? I find it hard to believe that William wastes any time worrying about what anyone thinks of him."

She stopped kneading and looked me squarely in the eye. "I don't know that I agree with that assessment, Lily. But either way, we're not just talking about *any*one. We're talking about you."

An oddly ecstatic feeling was rising inside of me, a strange but very pleasant suggestion. I wasn't certain what caused it, but my suspicions were enough to send me grasping for a change of subject.

"So, how long did he tag along with the bad guys?" I said.

"Oh, it was four months or so," she said.

I was stunned. William had never let on that he'd played any sort of role in my protection.

"Well, since we're on the topic. There *is* something I've wanted to ask," I said, picking up my bowl and planting myself on a stool in front of Clara.

"I'll do my best." She glanced up quickly, and then returned to the dough, sprinkling it with flour and shaping it between her hands.

"How did he get his soul back? Christian says vampires have no desire to do good. He says the thought actually disgusts them."

"Yes, and he's right. But William's body had housed the mind of a Sentient. And it maintained the memories from his human life. He knew where to come should he ever need saving. As it was, something quite remarkable, quite miraculous, happened that none of us were ready for. It so rarely happens to a vampire that we had never come across it before, only heard tales of it."

I sat, rapt in her words, and my hand had long since ceased to stir a thing.

"Vampires can go several months without feeding, but he hadn't eaten in almost a year. His body was actually dying, Lily." She shook her head as if the idea still stunned her as much today as it must have then. "And for a vampire, there is no afterlife. Their very existence *is* an afterlife of sorts. His soul should feasibly have moved on, so I don't know what compelled him to turn away from that kind of life.

"He was terribly weak when he came to see Abram. Even in his hopeless state, he knew who to turn to for help. Abram took pity on the boy, not the monster. After all, if William had been given the choice, he wouldn't have wanted another vampire to find its way into this world because of him. He fell prey just as any of us could, fighting for our world, our lives. Abram reckoned that the good left in him was so strong that it was fighting back, fighting the nature that had taken it prisoner and would rather be dead than a murderer.

"Our Abram returned William's soul, and is adamant in his refusal to speak of it. He will only say that the spirit which sustains this universe is ever renewing and eternally willing to share itself with one who desires it."

☙

"Do it!" William stood tall, his arms at his sides, fully open.

I swelled the vibrations of my body to the surface, narrowing my eyes in a concentrated stare, willing them out. Nothing happened.

"*Come on*, Lily! Don't flake out on me!"

My whole body tensed and my skull throbbed with the pressure. Still, William remained untouched. If only it didn't feel so contrived. I couldn't muster that kind of emotion out of nowhere. The surroundings were too controlled.

William sighed, relaxing his arms. "Lily, I'm not even trying to block you. You have to do this again. You've done it before. What's the problem?"

"I…I don't know." I shrugged, frowning. "I'm trying, but…I don't feel angry right now."

"Tomorrow night, there's a good chance you're going to encounter an Incubus. Add to that the fact that a vampire tried to *kill* you! Doesn't that stir up the wrath of Lillian?"

"More like the terror. And stop calling me that! You know I hate it."

"Lillian."

"*What?*"

"Lillian." He smiled slyly.

"Oh, mature. The extra long lifetime still hasn't taken the boy out of the vampire."

"Lillian," he repeated, walking up to me. "Stubborn, arrogant, blindly loyal Lillian can't muster the strength to fight a vampire."

"Shut *up*, William."

The edge of his mouth twisted up into a delightfully rebellious smile.

"Make me."

Gritting my teeth together, I stared him down like a mad-woman. My fingernails dug into my palms, my eyes watered, and my whole body trembled…and William didn't budge, not even an inch. Sighing, I sulked and dropped my gaze to the ground.

"It's no use," I said, all the will gone from me. "I'll never survive as a Sentient. They should put me on kitchen detail. I could stock shelves. I'm good at stocking shelves."

"Lily?"

"What?"

"The whole friends thing aside, I still piss you off, right?" he asked.

"Yeah. Sure," I said half-heartedly.

"Good." And then his lips were on mine, his hands on either side of my face, holding it in place. For an inconceivable instant I forgot everything—who I was, where I was—and wrapped my fingers into his hair, deepening the kiss.

Then, my mind exploded. No, no, no, no! Friends we could be, but not this!

I pulled free, breathless, enraged. If there had been words to express the fury, the confusion, and moreover the inexplicable glory of what I felt, I'm certain I would have let him have it. But that wasn't what he was counting on, was it? If real emotion was as powerful and as concrete as a brick wall, and William was looking for some brick throwing, he was going to get it.

There was no need for energy building now, no need for deep concentration. It took the smallest word to do the job.

"Never," I whispered. And he shot up and backwards, slamming against the tree line and falling to the ground, unmoving.

☙

"Hold up, where's the fire!" Paul complained as I crashed into the house, knocking the door into him.

"Sorry," I called back stiffly, my stride unbroken. There was no room for deliberation here. Abram and I needed to talk. I knocked on his door.

"Come in, Lily!" he called. I opened the door and shut it behind me.

"How did you know it was me?"

"Because the ire of an angry female Sentient is impossible to overlook." He chuckled. "I could feel your vibrations all the way down the hall."

"Hm. Well, I need to make a request," I said as civilly as possible.

"Of course. Let's have it."

"I want another trainer."

"Other than William?" he asked. "You've taken issue with him?"

"Yes," I said. I'd have put more effort into sounding hostile if Abram wasn't so very likable. "Completely."

"I see." He studied me carefully. "Do grant me a measure of tolerance, but I must ask what William could have done to warrant such a negative reaction."

"He...he's ...." I fumbled. I was not about to give Abram the gory details. "We just don't get along!"

He frowned. "I must admit I'm surprised. William has always been, in my experience, quite agreeable."

"Yeah, well. I don't care for his training methods."

"You disapprove of them?" Abram's expression changed only fractionally.

"Yes. Can't Christian teach me, or Paul?" I persisted.

"It's questionable that they would be best for you, Lily."

"Why? They certainly have more in common with me than he does."

"Do they?" He smiled, amused by the idea.

"Yes," I defended my statement. "I mean, for God's sake, he's not even human!"

Abram's smile disappeared. "Is there no place in your heart for a more flexible definition of the word?"

"But he's not like us ... he's .... Isn't it wrong?"

"He is more a Sentient than most, I promise you," Abram said. "And moreover, he will push your lines of limitation more effectively than any of the others. This is necessary, Lily. You must grasp so much in so little time, because this life is inevitable. The doors have been opened."

Though not fully understanding them, his words weighed on my heart, and I was ashamed. Damn me to hell the day Abram believed me so petty.

"Abram ...." I shook my head. "I don't claim to be anything better, or even comparatively *close* to any one of you. But, look, I can't tell you why I need to switch trainers. It's complicated. Just please ... please." My reasons for the appeal were unfurling into something more candid, more disconcerting. William had set something in motion and it required distance—total disconnection—to be battled successfully.

And Abram saw it.

He laughed, laying his hand on my shoulder. "Lillian, William will remain your guide, and moreover, you have full permission to not detest him!"

"But, Abram ...."

"I have found that interference is, in fact, a hindrance. Let the chips fall where they may. There will be no judgment from me."

"A hindrance to what? I don't understand!"

"Perhaps not." He patted my back. "But I do," he said, leading me to the door. "Now kindly go and see if William has quite recovered. I dare say you are as powerful a repeller as your mother ever was!"

I gasped, but Abram closed the door behind me, his chuckles still emitting from the other side. How could he know?

Oh, *shit*, I thought, mortified. There was a reason they called Abram a Seer.

I stood, utterly embarrassed, in the dimness of the hallway. If anyone but Abram had asked me to patch things up with William I would have taught them a few choice words. But who could say no to the man? At every turn Abram seemed to know me better than I knew myself. And there it was. Now I understood what William had meant my first day in the house.

"Abram saw you well."

If only I had permitted myself a moment of logic, thought all this through before running to Abram, perhaps I would have come to a sensible conclusion on my own. But my emotions had gotten the better of me. Was it an empath's tendency to overreact—or was that aspect just me? Maybe William's tactic was unconventional, but it had worked, hadn't it?

I headed down the hall and into the foyer. An awful thought crossed my mind. What if he was still out there? Unconscious in the woods? I ran from room to room, hoping to see him there. The living room was empty, and only Anna and Clara were in the kitchen.

"Have you seen William? Has he come back in the house?" I asked, breathless.

"I don't know, dear," Clara answered.

"I thought you two were having a lesson," Anna added.

"We were. Shit … sorry," I muttered.

"Is everything all right, love?" Clara asked, concerned.

"Fine. I'll be back!" I flew out of the kitchen and across the house, down the bedroom hallway and around the corner to the back hall. As soon as I stepped outside I saw him.

He was sitting on the bench in the distance, in the same spot Abram had first shown me my fate. I moved quickly at first. Then the overall humiliation of the circumstances sank in and I slowed down. He didn't seem to hear me coming, and I stopped just a few feet behind him, steadying my breath and gathering my courage. I walked over and stood next to the empty side of the bench, waiting a moment to decipher his reaction. He barely turned his head, but the illusion of a smile was there. I sighed, and sat down next to him, leaving plenty of space between us. A moment passed in silence.

"Did I hurt you badly?" I asked at last.

He chuckled quietly. "Like hell." Grinning, he turned to face me. "You're insanely good at that, Lily! It was remarkable. I ...." The smile faded, and his expression turned uncomfortable. "I'm sorry. I suppose I deserved it."

It was my turn to laugh. "You totally did! What's the matter, William, you couldn't come up with *any* other catalyst?!"

"Well, it seemed like a good idea at the time! I realize I irritate you, so I knew you'd be angry. But my main concern was ... was ...." He stopped.

"Was what?" I smirked.

"Keeping you alive, for God's sake! That vampire was set to destroy you, and where the hell was I?" He stared at his feet. "I've been a miserable failure thus far, and I'm not about to screw up again."

"William, what are you talking about?"

"The vampire," he began, studying a slow moving Koi fish in the pond. "The one that Christian killed the day he brought you here .... It was my job to keep his ass in check."

It was just as Clara had known. "You were supposed to be my Retriever," I said.

William nodded. "Yes."

"What happened?"

"When Abram saw that Lolial was looking for you, he sent me as a mole."

"Lolial?"

"That was his name, the vampire that attacked you."

"He had a name."

"He did. I told him I was a Sentient and that I'd been newly turned. Of course, he was all too enthusiastic about that idea. He actually started looking forward to my visits."

"How long have you been a vampire?"

"It'll be thirty-three years next month."

"And how old were you when you were turned?"

"Twenty-nine."

"So ... you're roughly ...."

"Sixty-two years old, yes." He smirked, glancing at me.

"Wow." I scrambled for a suitable response. "You ... look great."

He laughed loudly. "Thank you. But it's only because I stopped aging once I was turned."

"I gathered that," I teased. William narrowed his eyes at me, but I ignored him. "So you'll always look like this?"

"Actually, I don't think I will. I've been ... aging, I guess."

"You're aging?"

"Yes. Ever since—"

"Your soul," I interrupted him.

"That's right. It was really tricky at first. I'd forgotten how tired humans get."

"Hm." I smiled at my hands, inexplicably pleased. "So, you were a mole."

"I was. And obviously I was lying about the newly-turned thing, but I had no choice. I didn't look much like them. My appearance had normalized with a soul, so I was too human to pass for an older vampire.

I'd visit their camp every few weeks, and each time, they would try to convince me to stay. Obviously that would have blown my cover completely. They'd have expected me to feed ...." He swallowed, looking angry. "It was only inevitable that Lolial should try to recruit my help in pinning you down, so I was forced to pull a Herod."

"A Herod?"

"Mhm. You know. In the Bible? Evil king, kills all the babies?"

"Yeah, I know who Herod is. But I don't understand what you meant by *pulling* one."

"Well, the story goes that King Herod told the wise men to go and find the baby for him, right?"

"Riiight." I lifted an eyebrow.

"Humor me!" He chuckled.

"Okay, go on."

"Well, they know his true intention is to kill it. So when they finally find the baby, instead of sending word back to Herod of his whereabouts, they warn the parents to get him the hell out of town."

I laughed. "I can't believe you're telling me a Bible story."

"*Anyway*, Lolial wanted to find you ... badly. And so I offered to search for you myself. Each time I'd report back that I was sure I was getting closer, but always too obscure with the details to give them anything real to go on. The pretense was only supposed to last a few months, until I came for you and brought you here. But he must have gotten tired of waiting for me to find you. I still don't know how he managed to track you down."

"I think I do."

"You do?"

"Uh-huh. He used a Scout."

"He …. How do you know what a scout is?"

"Abram told me. One visited me the night before the attack. I didn't know what it was then, of course."

"*Fuck*. I'm sorry, Lily. They didn't mention anything about having one. They must not have trusted me as well as I thought."

"I guess not."

"Thank God Abram saw the attack happen beforehand. If he hadn't sent Christian …."

"Well, why didn't he just send you?" I interrupted.

"Because Christian is a combatant, remember? I assume he made easy work of killing Lolial?"

"Well, yeah," I admitted. "It all happened in a matter of seconds, really."

William nodded. "I could probably have fought him, but it would have been harder, and there was no room for error. I don't have Christian's flair for that sort of thing."

"I see."

We fell silent.

"Anyway," I said, "I don't blame you … for the Lolial thing. So don't beat yourself up over it anymore."

He smiled weakly.

"I do have another question for you, though," I said.

"Shoot."

"Why was he looking for me? What did he want with me?"

"He talked about it a lot, actually. He was pretty fanatical. He and his coven had passed through Scranton on their way to Philadelphia, and if he could have stopped to find you the moment he detected you, he would have. But he couldn't. They were still weak."

"You say he was going to kill me. But what you really meant, what Clara thinks anyway, is that he was going to turn me."

"Lily, don't think about things like that." He shook his head.

"I want to know! Just tell me. Am I right?"

"We wouldn't have let it get that far."

"Then, he was."

"Yes. He was."

It was enlightening to learn the truth and the weight of William's role in my life, even before I'd ever known he existed. Christian went to such great lengths to hide this from me, but why bother when knowing the facts made me stronger?

"So, we're still friends?" William checked.

"We are," I said.

Nine

Christian spent most of Saturday trying to convince me not to go back to the mansion. He tried subtle coercion, suggesting perhaps I would rather go with him to the coast and let Paul take his place at the cleansing.

He tried fear mongering, listing the horrors of an Incubus and the reasons why I wasn't prepared to face one.

"You don't realize what they can do to you! How they can ruin you. You don't know how to combat that, Lily!"

"And what are the chances of this thing just making a bold showing with all of us there?" I argued. "I want to see it taken out. Besides, I'm not missing my first crossover."

"That may not even happen if we can't get the damned Incubus out of the house. Miss Price won't budge till we do."

"Good then. I wouldn't want her to. But that's immaterial. I'm going."

And then, he resorted to begging.

"Lily, *please*. Be reasonable! This is too dangerous, too risky."

"Christian will you give it a rest! Everyone else seems convinced that I'll be fine. Why do you have so little faith in me?" I scowled and crossed my arms, my feelings hurt.

He sighed. "Lily." He put his hand on my shoulder. "Lily, it's not that I don't have faith. I have no doubt you'll be as strong as any one of us, but I can't bear the thought of anything happening to you. Before you came here you knew nothing about any of this, nothing. I've never felt so responsible for anyone before."

"Obviously," I grumbled. "And the constant obligation has got to be *horribly* exhausting."

"Oh, Lily, for God's sake. You must know I didn't mean it that way."

"I'm not sure how else you would mean it! The message was pretty clear. Until I'm worth a damn, you don't want me around mucking up the works and slowing you down, right?"

"No," He narrowed his eyes pitifully. "It's nothing like that. I just want you to be safe."

I bit the inside of my cheek, glowering at him, then relaxed. "Christian … I'm coming with you. I promise I'll leave if things get too bad. But at least give me a chance."

He hesitated, staring back just as stubbornly, then sighed in resignation. "I'm sticking to you like glue. I'm going to haunt you worse than any damn ghost, Lily."

"Fine."

"And not just there. Now that I know you're prone to streaks of unreason—"

"I am *not* being unreasonable," I whined. "But again … fine."

He pouted. "Is it that bad, hanging around with me?"

I chuckled. "I s'pose not."

"Thank you. Now, as much as I hate the idea, I think we should get you to Maddox for a crash course in Incubal arse-whooping."

"You mean repelling?"

"Yes, I …. How do you know about repelling?"

"Easy, I've done it!" I smiled.

"You what?" He laughed, astonished.

"Why does everyone react that way? *Geez.* Did I just smack of failure the moment you met me?"

"Certainly not. I just …. When the hell did you repel?"

"Calling to mind one instance, … yesterday."

"*What* did you repel?"

"William." I shrugged a shoulder, smiling delicately.

"Lily!" He laughed again. "That is brilliant! I'd have paid anything to see that!" And he swept me up into a massive hug.

"Mr. Wright, you're being a caveman!" I admonished.

"Ah, my bad." He smiled, but did not let me down. Rather, his wide grin faded into something more gentle, and he stared at me a moment too long before I broke the awkward silence.

"Can I skip the crash course, then?" I mumbled self-consciously.

He smiled again and set me down. "It appears you can."

"Good. I'm feeling a little guilty about the whole repelling incident, really."

"Don't waste your time," he said. "Maddox can't feel pain."

I wanted to say that I wasn't convinced of that anymore. Christian was being a bit short-sighted. But I knew better than to voice such a traitorous view. Having seen the agony of his memory first hand, I couldn't find the will to oppose him.

❧

"Christian… forty-five miles an hour?! Are you barking? We're on the *highway* for Christ's sake!" Anna chided, peering over his shoulder at the speedometer.

"Don't start. I'm buying us time to think," he said.

"Then you're paying for the ticket when we get pulled over. Speed up," she argued.

"Children, children, do try to be civil. No bullshit behavior," Clara warned.

"Does making fun of Christian's shirt count as bullshit behavior?" I asked.

"What?" Christian remarked defensively. "I like this shirt! This is a nice shirt."

"Ugh." Anna wrinkled her nose. "Your attempt at GQ has tragically ended in douche-bag."

"Sod off. There's nothing wrong with keeping up appearances," he defended.

"Well, who in the hell is there for you to impress?" Anna snorted.

An instant of uncertain silence passed. "No one." He shrugged.

"You all are a loathsome lot." Clara chuckled. "And I'm being very serious! Any anger, negativity, hostility," she looked pointedly at Christian, "would only make our job harder."

"So are you saying we can fuel this thing? Our behavior can make it more powerful?" I asked.

"That's right, dear. It's only natural that it should feed off that which made it to begin with. Therefore, Christian, I ask that you kindly try to contain yourself around Mr. Maddox this evening."

"I can promise to try, but I can't promise to succeed," Christian goaded.

"I'm not satisfied with that. He'd be congenial enough if you'd stop instigating things."

"I'll stop when he stops."

"Such an attitude is hardly fetching in a gentleman," she said.

"There's a simple solution to that dilemma," he began. "Being that only one of us counts as a man, roughly *anything* I do in his company would qualify me as one. The gentle part is optional."

"Don't push it, Christian," Clara spoke in a commanding tone. "You know very well my feelings on the subject, and I trust you won't broach the topic again."

"Backing away from the topic slowly," Christian answered.

"Well, I still think it's insane that you made us all ride with you," Anna complained to her brother. "William has a blazing SUV. Why should we squeeze into *this* little dumper when we'd all have fit swimmingly in—"

"Forget it!" Christian cut her off. "He's not driving us anywhere."

"*Stubborn idiot*," Anna growled, sitting back and crossing her arms. "You don't own the world and you can't control everything."

I inched away tightly into my corner of the car. Bristling energy was flying everywhere, and the hairs on my arms prickled uncomfortably.

"I don't claim to own anything," Christian argued. "But since Dad is gone, *someone* has to protect—"

"*Oooh.*" Anna clenched her jaw and her hair feathered outward as brilliant orange light billowed from her tiny form. "You had *ruddy* well better not even *start* with the protecting us business, Christian. You being male does *not* automatically relegate the rest of us to damsel status!"

"Enough!" Clara snapped. "We all protect each other. That's how it's always been, and that's the end of it. Do you hear me? The *end* of it."

No one dared say a thing more until we had reached the secluded grounds of the mansion. Clara dialed a number on her cell phone and handed it to Christian.

"Tell Tim we're nearly here, will you, dear?" She pulled out her wallet and tucked it under her chin, routing through her purse intently.

"Glove compartment," said Christian, putting the phone to his ear.

"Sorry?" She glanced over at him and her wallet slipped to the floor.

"Your glasses."

"Oh. Fantastic!" she said gratefully, opening the compartment to find them there.

"Tim? It's Christian Wright. We're here," he said.

Clara put her glasses on and clambered for her wallet as Christian pulled to a stop and offered her the phone.

"Oops," she said, knocking it out of his hands.

"Mum, what on earth? Are you *actually* nervous?" Christian smiled.

"I suppose I must be." She laughed at herself, flustered.

"My poor mother," he crooned. "I'll really try this evening, I promise." Soft golden light floated from his outline as he bent and kissed her on the forehead.

It was easier for me to understand Christian in moments like these. Wouldn't the safety of my own family usurp any other consideration? I thought of my grandparents. I had left them behind to fend for themselves. The pain of separation was constant, but how could I possibly reconcile our lives without exposing them to the hazards of this world? And how could I make them accept, without hurting them, that I wasn't the person they'd thought I was? That I'd never been that person?

Tim was already in the driveway waiting for us, keys in hand.

"Evenin' folks," he said, opening the door for Clara.

"Hello, Tim." She smiled. "Is everyone gone, then?"

"They are," he said. "I don't know if I can be of any help, but I'd be happy to offer my services."

"That is positively lovely of you, but I'm afraid it wouldn't be for the best." Clara sighed.

"Hm. Well, now I *am* worried." He frowned, escorting us onto the porch. "I figured it was serious when I got the request from Bird's Eye to call Abram …." He stopped to unlock the massive front door and pushed it open. The lights in the great hall were still on, but the rest of the house was in darkness. I felt short of breath.

"Who's Bird's Eye?" I asked Tim.

"An old Sentient friend of Abram's," he explained.

"So, are you a Sentient?" I should have known.

"Me? Hell no." He laughed, roughly. "No, my sister is the Sentient. Bird's Eye's her nickname. I, on the other hand, don't have a gifted bone in my body." He laughed again.

"Are you any good with that?" Clara noted the hand gun holstered away in Tim's belt.

"Why, yes, I'd say I am."

"Then you're already leaps and bounds above me in one arena," she offered.

"Hmph," Christian sniggered. "She couldn't shoot a wall."

"Well, I'd be happy to teach you how one of these days, if you had the inclination," Tim suggested with an eager smile.

"She'd love to!" Anna responded for her mother, grinning wildly.

"I …." Clara flustered. "Well, I don't suppose there'd be any reason why I couldn't," she said, throwing a reproachful glance at Anna.

"It's settled then," Tim said, standing up straighter.

You couldn't miss the energy Christian was giving off. His shoulders had stiffened and his usual warm glow receded, giving way to a new kind of light, something more similar to Anna's fiery bursts. His eyes darted gloomily between Clara and Tim.

Someone say something funny, I thought desperately. But there was no need. William took a few quick strides up the porch stairs and neared the door. Okay, so we'd exchanged one kind of awkward for another. At least this one I was used to.

"Hi." William nodded at Tim.

"Evening. I'm Tim Slater." Tim offered his hand.

"William Maddox." William took his hand, still poised in the doorway. He had a penchant for doorways, that man, always lingering first to feel out the welcome mat. I thought in that moment that it must suck to be a sort-of-vampire.

"Good to meet you," Tim said. "And on that note, there seems to be more than enough backup here. You have my number if you need me," he said to Clara. She nodded and thanked him.

"All right," Christian said. "Maddox can go with you, Mum, and Lily and Anna, come with me."

"Now, wait a moment dear." Clara held a hand up. "That wasn't the plan."

"We had a plan?" he asked, impatiently.

"Yes. You know very well what Abram and I discussed. The plan is that William remains with Lily."

Christian sighed heavily. "He's here, isn't he? Isn't that enough? What assistance can he offer that we can't?"

"She's been working with him," Clara said. "I'd venture to say he knows her strengths and weaknesses."

"That's what I'm afraid of," Christian muttered.

William's lightline became visible, changing from cool blue to blinding white, then faded away again.

"She's got nothing to fear from me, Christian," he said.

"I'll refrain from comment. I have promises to keep." Christian threw William a look, then turned to me. "Like flies to sugar, remember?"

"Yes." I sighed.

Anna tapped her foot impatiently. "Right, then, shall we get on with it, please?"

"Let's go," Christian said, leading the way toward the stairs.

"Leave the lights off, dear," Clara directed as Christian went to flip a switch.

"Do you think that's completely wise?" He sounded worried. "I mean, this thing can come at us from any angle at that rate."

"Yes. And we must draw him out. It won't exactly be easy, Christian. It doesn't like males, remember?"

He sighed, but took his fingers off the light switch.

"Upstairs, then," said Clara.

Christian led the way, with his mother behind him. Anna, William, and I followed. The house was absolutely silent with the exception of our footfalls on the wooden stairs. Moonlight arched through the huge window as we reached the landing, casting a watery glow down the hall. The house was exceptionally cold up here. Didn't cool air usually sink to the lower floors? Nevertheless, the temperature downstairs was definitely warmer.

"Do you think we should separate?" Anna asked her mother. "If we want this to work, shouldn't the girls go off on their own for a bit?" she suggested quietly.

"No," Christian said.

"Now hold on, she has a point, Christian," Clara said. "It does seem the only practical way of starting things out."

"Are you crazy?" he argued, straining to keep his voice low. "If this thing is half what you say it is, I'd be out of my wits to let you alone with it."

"I don't think there's much choice," Clara insisted. "You needn't stay away for long. We'll call you at once if he makes a showing."

Christian stood his ground, glancing from Anna to me to Clara again. "I don't like this," he said finally.

"Neither do we." She laughed. "Now let's all pick a room."

"Lily can't be alone," he reiterated in a raised voice.

"No, no, of course not. She'll go with William and wai—"

"I promised Abram I'd keep her safe," Christian spoke over her.

"Christian, for God's sake!" I scowled. "How bad can things possibly get with you right down the hall?"

"She's right. You're overreacting," William said, crossing his arms and standing beside me.

Christian ignored William's comment and looked at me. "I don't care if you think you possibly imagined even the smallest idea of a hint of something. Call me immediately." Then he glared at William and sulked off to the nearest room, leaving the door open wide.

"All right, Anna, do you want to come with me or are you feeling brave this evening?" Clara asked.

"I suppose I could fly solo for a bit," she said, anxiety evident in her typically fearless bearing.

Our three groups parted ways, Clara taking the main bedroom, Anna one of the guest rooms, and William and I the farthest down the hall.

"This must be Carley's room." I noted the canopied bed and poster of a pubescent boy hanging above the vanity. Even in the darkness, there was no mistaking a teenager's bedroom.

"Nice." William smirked, flicking the draping lace of the canopy top and sitting down.

I sat down next to him. "So," I said, rapping my fingers on the bedspread. "This is boring."

William laughed. "Yes, most of them are. Although … ."

"Hmm?"

"Although there has definitely been something here," he said, eyeing the corner of the room near the closet.

"Now?" I whispered, unconsciously shifting closer to him.

"I don't think so, but there *has* been. Its residual energy is concentrated in that area," he said, nodding again toward the corner of the room. "It must watch from there."

"Great." Though I didn't want them to, my eyes stubbornly returned to the spot William had indicated, and my mind conjured all sorts of menacing images before I could force my attention elsewhere.

"It's freezing in here." I shivered. "I thought it was cold out there, but this room is insane."

"Yes," he agreed.

"Is that a bad sign?"

"Yes," he said again.

"You're big on the one word answers this evening, William." I chuckled.

He shrugged. "I'm being observant, Lily."

"Ah. So, I should shut my trap, then?"

"No." His smile broadened, the expression appealing even in the dark. "You should ask questions."

"Oh. Okay," I whispered. "But now I'm all self-conscious."

Now it was his turn to laugh. "I know full well that you have to ask questions to learn the answers," he said. "Don't be self-conscious. Ask me whatever."

"You don't feel like I'm a liability?"

"A what? No!" he whispered, firmly. "Of course not. Why?"

I shrugged, sighing thoughtfully. "I don't know."

"Lily," he said, sounding injured. "Have *I* ever made you feel like that?"

"No. Not you," I said.

"Hm," he murmured and relaxed.

We sat quietly for a while, and as my ears adjusted, I became more sensitive to other sounds. The alarm clock by the bed, for instance, made a rhythmic ticking that I hadn't noticed before. It was almost comforting. Absolute silence always made me nervous. It lent itself to hearing things I'd rather not. Reasonably, it would have made more sense for me to be nervous, considering the situation, but nothing seemed to be happening and I wasn't alone. I leaned against the bedpost and let my mind drift.

"You know, you're just as good as the rest of them." William broke my train of thought. "In fact, I'd say you could give most of them a run for their money. Just give it a year, Lily. They'll be struggling to keep up with you."

I balked. "I appreciate the sentiment. But for now, I'm a wounded race horse. Sort of worthless."

"Don't say that." His tone was still hushed, but insistent. "There's a lot you're capable of right now, just as you are."

"Like what?"

"Well, for one thing, you've got a hell of a repelling ability," he said dryly.

"Yeah, yeah. Not like I can whip that out on demand."

"No, not yet, but very soon. And your empathic abilities are unquestionably in place."

"You think?"

He laughed to himself. "Yeah, I do."

"You say that like you mean it."

"I *do* mean it, Lily. I have to watch myself around you. Too much time spent with an empath makes you forget yourself."

I frowned. "What do you mean by that?"

"Nothing personal," he went on. "It's just certain things, certain vulnerabilities that you would, as a rule, keep to yourself come to light too easily. Look at Christian. He's even more open with his hostility when you're around."

My initial inclination was to be offended, but I fought the urge to argue and considered his point. This made sense. It had to be disconcerting being so exposed simply because of the pull of someone else's energy. At first, the idea of William as vulnerable had seemed impossible. If there was anything a vampire should *not* be it was vulnerable. But William had a human soul. And human souls were susceptible in every way. That he had proclaimed himself needful of something as basic as friendship only served to prove the strength—and accountability—of an empathic endowment. How much was my presence affecting those around me in a harmful way?

"So, really, Christian might not be such a bitch to you if I wasn't around," I said.

William seemed amused by this idea. "Oh, I wouldn't go that far."

"Well, nonetheless, I *am* sorry. If it means anything, I'd rather that he wasn't."

"Would you?"

"Yes. I ... what was that?" I said, reacting to someone's shouting.

William was already standing. "It was Clara," he answered. "Come on."

We sped out to the hall to see Christian and Anna running into the master bedroom. Clara stood in the middle of the room, her arms at her sides and her hands spread open.

"He's here. Close the door, Christian," she ordered.

"No, first get Lily out of here," Christian said. "Take her downstairs, Maddox."

William nodded quickly and pulled me by the arm out of the room, shutting the door.

"William, what are you *doing*?" I said. "You just finished saying I wasn't totally helpless."

"I know. But there *is* a certain level of danger here that even *we* don't face every day. I don't blame him for wanting you to sit this part out," he said, dragging me down the stairs.

"Why even bring me along, then?" I fumed. "Ugh, God damned Incubus! Miss Price had *better* be crossing over tonight or I'm going to be livid!"

"Yes, of course, Lily." William smiled as we reached the bottom of the stairs. "I'm sure the monster *and* the ghost will play perfectly into your timeline."

"Shut up, William." I pouted.

"I will if you'll come with me," he said.

"Where are we going?"

"This way." He turned to walk toward the front of the house while I stood still, eyeing the stairs furtively. I didn't want to leave them all alone. I may have been an amateur, but I couldn't shake the feeling of guilt. What was happening? Would they be all right? What if there *was* something I could do to help?

"Lily, there's no use tearing yourself up about this," William said, somehow knowing my thoughts. "Take this life one step at a time, okay?" He held out his hand. I sighed, dejected, and let him lead me to the sitting room. William turned on a lamp and we sat down on the same sofa Clara and the governor's wife had shared days earlier.

"I wonder where Miss Price is," I said.

"I don't know. Maybe she's gone to Vegas for the weekend."

I giggled. "Miss Price—a compulsive gambler."

"You just never know with these spirits, Lily. They come and go as they please."

"Sounds nice."

"Ehn. The nomadic lifestyle is overrated," he said in a knowing tone.

"Is it something you get used to? Moving around all the time?"

"Yes. I mean, if it's all you've ever known," he said.

"And you can really learn to feel at home no matter where they are?"

"I guess. I think it's probably easier when you have family around."

"Hm. I don't have that particular security blanket," I said, suddenly depressed.

"Same here."

I turned my head slowly to meet his gaze. "It's odd. We're kind of in a similar boat, you and me."

He nodded. "In a way … minus the vampire thing, of course," he said.

"Yep. Minus that." I smirked.

William reached over to the side-table to pick up a porcelain elephant, and I lay my head back, watching him turn it over in his hands, examining it in the dim light. The moment was almost peaceful, until a muffled crash came from upstairs. Then the yelling began. I was pretty sure it was Clara, but Anna's voice was intermittent as well. William tensed up, ready to act, but everything went quiet again.

"False alarm!" Anna shouted down the stairs. I exhaled, relieved.

William set the little elephant down between us, and I picked it up, just to busy my hands while he peered out into the hall. This was aggravating. Maybe it would have been better if I hadn't come along. At least then I wouldn't have to deal with the worry so closely. I was about to complain when a piercing scream, unmistakably Anna's, broke through the silence.

"Let's go," William commanded, already to the door. I jumped up to follow but dropped the blasted figurine in the process. It smashed into a few pieces at my feet.

"I'm right behind you. *Just go*," I insisted, bending to pick them up.

Tossing the bits on the table as quickly as possible, I left the sitting room and headed for the stairs to see William rounding the corner at the top landing, out of my sight.

I made it to the bottom step when the lights above me flickered. I stopped, jerking my head around anxiously, and that was all the time it took for the air to turn intensely cold, even more so than it had been in Carley's room. As I shivered, my teeth chattering, the lights flickered twice more and then went off. Everything was black for a second as I strained to see, waiting for my eyes to adjust. What was rapidly becoming a familiar static sensation raised the hairs on my body until they could have lifted out of their pores.

"Shit," I squeaked, hyperventilating. "Okay." I breathed out. "Okay. Just keep walking."

"Why did you come back?" a voice whispered angrily from behind me. It wasn't human, the way it sounded. It was like wind. I turned to face it.

Miss Price was glaring at me reproachfully, her misty blue form billowing in the windless room.

"Why?" She asked again, her eyes brimming with anger.

"Why?" I repeated her question. Had I just uttered a word?

"Stupid girl! I *told* you he was watching you. You're a *fool* to come back here! I don't have the power to keep him away from you." Her eyes changed into something more fearful, more hopeless. Then, her gaze fell behind me. "It's too late." She looked at me again. "He was made in darkness. He will take you in darkness," she whimpered. "You must scream."

I tore my eyes away from her, intent on taking to the stairs again, but I couldn't move. Something was holding me around the waist, and it wasn't Miss Price. She was gone.

I tried to scream, but as I opened my mouth, a thick, frozen stench filled my throat and nostrils and choked me into silence. I coughed and gasped, peering through watery eyes for my route of escape. *Finally*, I could make out the bottom steps again, but Miss Price had been right...it *was* too late. Painfully cold air was creeping up my back, and my skin felt like it was blistering with frost bite. Then, there came the sound of a door groaning slowly open somewhere behind me.

The darkness wrapped itself around my body, dragging me backwards and slamming me into a tiny space...the coat closet. I watched, terrified, as the door swept gently closed. Grabbing for the knob, I twisted frantically to no avail. It wouldn't open. There was no lock on the door, but something was holding it shut.

"Lily?" William's muffled calls came from the stairs, but I couldn't answer him. I was suffocating in silence while the Incubus took shape, became more substantial. It was a mass of hands and arms moving in serpentine motion across my body. Again and again I tried screaming, but the sound had no more volume than my own breath.

In darkness he'll take you.

Some vile part of the creature slipped across my lips, and I bit down hard, making it hiss and coil around my thigh with painful force.

In darkness he'll take you.

My assaulter raked its nails sharply down the skin of my arms, and I used the pain to sweep all my emotion to the surface, willing myself to illuminate the tiny prison.

Please, God. Please, God. Please, God. Please … .

At first I thought I was imagining it, the pale glowing, but the bastard loosened its grip on my throat enough that I could call out before it shoved an icy hand in my mouth, trying to stifle me again. By now, though, there was shouting and footsteps tearing down the stairs. Someone bashed at the door, and it splintered at the knob, allowing a thin stream of light in. The Incubus growled and fell away, cowering into the shadow behind me. Then, the door swung open, and I squinted into the sudden brightness as William grabbed me and pulled me out.

Everyone stared, terrified. I could only imagine what I looked like.

"Oh, Lily." William held me around the waist, trying to look me in the eye. "Shit. Lily … ."

My skin was crawling, and I felt like I was going to be sick. "I need to sit," I managed to sputter. William helped me over to the bottom step, and I collapsed.

"Is it still in there?" Christian asked, eying the closet. I nodded, and as I did, the creature poked its head around the door frame, no doubt intending to flee. It halted when it saw us, its face visible for the first time. Several tongues slid out of its mouth and lapped at the air in every direction. It looked crazed, its bulbous eyes blinking almost constantly. One moment it appeared to have two arms, then three, then countless, all blurring together. It left a trail of glistening muck as it inched across the wall.

"Jesus," Christian grimaced. He shot his arm out quickly and closed his fist around nothing.

The Incubus began to convulse, its tongues lagging limply over its lips. Its neck narrowed and twisted grotesquely.

"Do it," Christian ordered. With a nearly imperceptible movement, Anna and Clara blasted a ray of searing heat at the Incubus. Its writhing stopped, and it seemed to solidify, turn to stone. Clara exhaled, and the remains of the creature fell to the floor in a pile of ashes.

We all watched in horror until William's hushed voice broke the silence. "Lily. Lily, I'm so sorry," he said. "I'm so sorry."

"It's okay," I said, finding my voice.

"Like hell it is!" Christian roared. "*Goddamn it,* Maddox, you do a fuck up job of just about everything, don't you!"

"Christian, don't." I shook my head weakly. My arms throbbed where the Incubus had scratched me, and I wondered if I was bleeding. Hopefully it wouldn't soak through my sleeves. That was the last thing Christian needed to see.

"It was a fucking diversion!" Christian continued. "It *wanted* her left alone. You might as well have wrapped her up in a bow and presented her to him yourself!" He shook with anger.

"I didn't realize." William turned to face Anna. "I thought it was attacking you."

"Don't concern yourself with my sister!" Christian bellowed. "I don't see what the fuck good you'd have done even if it *had* been attacking her!"

To my astonishment, William didn't fight back. Instead, I felt the pain of his remorse radiating powerfully.

"We should never have brought him," Christian concluded.

"Keep your feelings to yourself," Clara cut in.

The timing and direction of Christian's outburst was completely unforgivable, and the trauma of my attack took a back seat to my increasing anger. I went to ball up my fists, and realized that William had been holding my hand. He pulled away immediately, mistaking the gesture for hostility. Mortified, I slid my arm discretely between us and rested my hand over his. He glanced at me sideways, surprised, then smiled ever so slightly. Why had I hated him again?

"We can sort all this out later," Anna said. "Let's just go. Lily doesn't look so good."

"I'm fine," I lied.

"Don't make light of it, Lily! This is inexcusable!" Christian said.

My pulse raced. "Christian, no more," I warned, my voice pinched. He ignored me.

"Abram and his weakness for hopeless cases," he said. "He's a fool to have chosen you, Maddox. You're useless to her."

"Say another word, Christian!" I challenged him, standing up suddenly. "Say one more word and see what happens."

He fell silent, his eyes wide. "God, Lily. He nearly got you killed…or worse!"

"He did not! It wasn't anyone's fault!" I snapped.

"Lily," Christian spoke, shaking his head. "You don't honestly believe that?"

"Of course I do."

"Then you're crazy. He should never have left you."

"He *didn't* leave me! I dropped something but I was right behind him. I was on my way upstairs, okay? I was only alone for a minute, but it all happened too fast. Now, back off. Let's just find Miss Price and cross her over."

"Lily, you can't be serious," Anna said. "We don't have to do this tonight."

"Yes, we do."

William looked down at me. "Lily," he shook his head. "We can come back anoth—"

"Don't deny me this," I implored, searching the room for a willing face. It was hardly fair, this approach. As if they'd have the heart to refuse after what had happened. I felt a twinge of remorse—but not a very big one. Something positive had to come of all this.

Clara caved first. "All right, love, a crossover you shall have," she said. "Miss Price?" she called. Everyone glanced around expectantly. "Miss Price, do show yourself. We're all *very* tired and the Incubus is dead." She paused for a moment, her eyes resting on the stairs. "I know you're there, dear," Clara urged kindly.

"I told her not to come back," said Miss Price, misting into view.

"Yes, we realize that, but we *had* to come back, you see," Clara explained.

"And you've killed him. He's gone," she responded, dazed.

"Yes. You *were* watching, weren't you?"

Miss Price nodded.

"Well, then, you've no need to be here anymore, not in this way," Clara concluded.

"I suppose not," said Miss Price. "But … I don't remember where I was before."

"It's very simple dear," Clara promised. "You'll have to trust me."

Miss Price nodded again.

"Splendid. Then let's begin." Clara took a few steps toward the ghost and stopped. They stared at each other for the longest time. Was she even blinking?

I looked at Anna, who smiled at me. "It's happening," she said.

"It is?" I asked.

"Yes. It's a good deal more internal than anything else. A casual observer wouldn't have the slightest clue what was going on."

A moment more passed, and Miss Price blended outward, as if the particles of her form were dispersing into the atmosphere. Clara seemed to come to, gasping quickly and blinking.

"Well, there you have it, dear." She turned to me.

"Uhm…wow …. That was …."

She laughed at me. "Utterly boring from where you're sitting, I'll bet," she finished.

"Yes." I nodded. "But I'm sure I was missing something."

"Indeed," she said. "Don't worry, though. Soon enough it will be time for you to practice this, and then you'll understand."

"I look forward to it. Maybe when…," I began, shaking off a wave of lightheadedness. "When …." I began again, and then the room went black.

❧

I mustn't have been out very long. When I came to, I was lying on the sofa, and Christian was seated on the floor by my side like a golden retriever.

"Where is everyone?" I questioned groggily.

"They've just gone to the car," he said, lifting his head at the sound of my voice.

"We should go."

"No, please. Wait just a minute," he said, all traces of anger gone from him. "Forgive me, Lily. I've made this so much worse for you."

I stared at him. "Yes," I agreed.

"Do you hate me?"

"Probably not." I sighed.

"Good. Because I couldn't live with myself if you did," he said. "What can I do to make it up to you?"

"Apologize."

"I'm sorry. Really I am," he swore.

"No, Christian. Not to me."

He narrowed his eyes. "Lily, what are you playing at?

"I mean it. I want you to apologize to him," I said, ready for battle again.

"For God's sake. You don't know what you're defending."

"I'll bet I do," I shot back.

"No, you don't."

"You'd be surprised how much I know, Christian."

"Then you're aware that poor William isn't human? You know what he is?" he said defiantly, hoping to shock me.

"Yes," I nodded.

His expression fell. "How? Who told you? How long have you known?"

"Long enough."

"And it doesn't bother you?" he asked, disgusted.

"I don't think it does. Not anymore."

"You're making a mistake, trusting him."

"Well, if I am, then it's *my* mistake. Let me make it."

He sat back. "Lily. Please. You promised."

"That was before I knew what I was promising. I've been ill-informed, Christian," I scolded him.

"I didn't want to scare you … and you're so damned obstinate! No need to test the limits of your curiosity," he said.

"Yeah, well, I can take on more than you think."

He raised an eyebrow. "Are you certain about that? Because there was a passed out Sentient on the couch just a moment ago that suggested otherwise."

"That's different," I said.

"How so?"

"Trust me." I shivered. "Some things you can't just brush off."

He sighed, looking at me warmly, and then, in a typical display of Christian-like emotion, grabbed me around the shoulders and held me tight. I winced, my arms still throbbing, but said nothing.

"I'm really rather fond of you, Lily," he whispered, his voice breaking. "Don't get hurt."

"Christian," I said, chuckling awkwardly. "Get a grip. I'm fine." Though I was anything but.

He let go. "All of this is only going to make me loathe him more," he cautioned. "I'll try to get it under control, but your insistence on fighting my protection only serves to worry me further."

I shrugged.

"And apologizing isn't an option for me," he added.

"Then, I am officially pissed off at you," I said.

"Fine. But you don't hate me …." He smiled brightly, the same kind smile that had comforted me the first time we'd met.

"No." I sighed.

Ten

*T*he car ride back to the house was mercifully quiet. Everyone seemed to know better than to talk to me about what had happened, and they certainly didn't dare bicker. I had no intention of discussing anything once we got home either, though Christian was chomping at the bit to throw another bitch-fit. There was no verbalizing what had happened, what *was* happening to me. I couldn't understand it, but I wanted out of the car, out of my skin.

"I'll check on you later?" Christian caught me as I slunk away toward my bedroom.

"I'll be fine," I called back. All I really wanted was to hide.

The first line of business was a shower. I unbuttoned my shirt and cringed as I peeled it off my arms to find dried blood caked into the sleeves. Four deep scratches ran the length of my left arm, and five on my right. I frowned. They were crimson at the centers but black along the edges, as if part of the skin had died away. My stomach twisted and heaved, and I sat down quickly on the bed, fighting the urge to cry. I failed. Tears trickled down my face, and I wiped them away. The action was pointless as more rushed to replace them.

Funny, no matter how scalding hot I made the shower, it wasn't enough. The feeling that the Incubus had left behind, the sensation of my skin coming to life with vermin, worsened my weeping. I scrubbed ferociously at my flesh, and the pain served as a small distraction for a while. Only after the water had turned intolerably cold did I shut it off.

How would I treat the wounds without anyone noticing? I searched through my medicine cabinet for bandages. There were only small ones; no gauze, no tape, no antiseptic gel. What self-respecting Sentient would need those things anyway? Only I was inexperienced enough to let myself get hurt.

I closed the cabinet and avoided my reflection. What should I do with myself now? Something mundane. Leaving the bathroom to put on pajamas, I chose something sleeveless that wouldn't rub against my arms, then considered what my next mindless action would be.

A television would have been perfect—some background noise to numb my senses. But my bedroom didn't have one and I certainly didn't want to go to the living room. I sat on the edge of my bed.

Rufus wound himself around my feet and then hopped into my lap, purring. I pulled him closer, scratching under his chin. If I were in Scranton right now, I'd be curled up with a book or working late at the store. It was *those kinds of* practices that seemed like the fantasies nowadays. Unpacking bottles of Jack Daniels, restocking shelves, calling a last minute vendor. Had life really been so bad before? I set Rufus on the bed and grabbed my cell phone.

"Hello, my Grandpa," I said.

"Lily! I was just thinking about you, honey."

"Were you? Something good?"

"Ah, you know you're perfect in every way."

"You're completely full of it, but don't stop. I need the encouragement."

"Uh-oh. Why's that, kiddo? Trouble with the job?"

I nearly started crying again, but that was out of the question. "I guess you could say that," I said, inserting a feeble chuckle.

"Who's giving you hell? Name names and I'll kick their asses," he offered. "I can take down a man twice my size!"

My laughter was real this time. "It's not anyone here," I said. "Let's just say the clients are a bitch."

"Beggars being choosers?"

"Eh. The occasional hostile job site. It's fine," I said, vague as usual.

"So, when are you coming home to visit?"

"Soon, I hope. I might bring a guest or two with me when I do," I said.

"Well, good. It'll be nice to meet the people who have made my Lily so happy."

Connie shouted in the background, "Ask her if she's found herself a man yet!"

I sighed. "Tell her I have not. But … ."

"But?" Frank's voice rose inquiringly.

"Well, there is more potential for that out here."

"Hm. That ought to keep her happy for a while," he said.

Someone knocked on my door.

"I have to go, Grandpa. I have a guest."

"All right then. Love ya, honey."

"I love you, too. Night."

Wrapping a sweater around my shoulders, I made a face at the door. The last thing I wanted right now was to see or be seen by others, and Christian's neediness was getting tedious. He was worse than a woman sometimes.

I yanked the door open. "Chris … oh."

"I won't stay. I just wanted to apologize again … properly," William said.

"Stop apologizing, William. It wasn't your fault." Rufus twisted himself between my feet, and I scooted him to the side.

"No." He looked me in the eye. "Christian was right. They could have handled it. I should have waited for you. I should have known better."

"For the love of God, William, it all happened in less than a minute! I was the idiot who decided to play Suzie Homemaker instead of coming when you told me to. This was my fault. Rufus, *quit* it!" The cat stood on his hind legs, pawing at my thighs until I moved to the side.

"Unbelievable." William frowned. "As if you have anything to be ashamed of."

Didn't I? Then why did I feel so disgustingly awful. I dropped my head, pretending to look at Rufus again. He swooshed his tail excitedly.

"Lily, … what happened back there?" he said.

No. Please don't ask.

"What? You were there," I said.

"You know what I mean. You're … not the same."

"I am, too." I laughed. Miserable Sentients.

"Your energy is off, Lily." His eyes narrowed.

"No. It's on. It's completely on," I lied.

He sighed and reached forward to touch me. I gasped and flinched back.

"Like hell it is," he said.

"William, close the door," I demanded in a whisper.

He did so quietly. "Don't think I'm not aware that this thing hurt you, Lily. You haven't looked one of us in the eye since we left the mansion. I know what an Incubus can do."

"And what if you do?" I argued. "Why even bring it up? Just let me get over it."

"It doesn't necessarily work that way. This wasn't a human attack."

"No kidding," I bit back. "You would know."

His expression changed, and there was no denying the surprise, the hurt.

"William. God," I moaned. "I'm *sorry*. I didn't mean it. Just please don't ask me anything else. Rufus, no!"

But it was too late. The little traitor had made a running hurdle for my arms and I caught him, clinging precariously to my chest. My sweater lay at my feet.

William's jaw dropped. "Lily. Oh my God. What did it do to you?"

"Don't look at me," I said, mortified, and dropped Rufus as I scrambled for the sweater. William beat me to it, catching my wrists. I turned my head so that I couldn't see his face. "Just don't touch me. Please, I can't stand it." I slipped to my knees, crying, and William knelt over me.

"Lily. Lillian, don't do that," he said. "I can help you. *Please* let me help you."

I shook my head, shuddering with every sob. I was going to throw up. He was touching something foul. He would catch my disease.

"I'm disgusting," I said. "I'm so repulsive. Just let me die." The words shocked even me, pouring forth of their own accord.

"Lily." His face was twisted in pain. "I'm not leaving you this way. You have to trust me just this once. After that you can hate my guts. Do you hear me?" He took my face in his hands, forcing me to look at him. I just nodded, not really knowing what I was agreeing to. Who cared? If it meant he would stop touching me, I'd go along with it.

"Don't move, okay? Just stay still no matter what happens."

I nodded again, and he pressed his hands to the wounds on my arms. The pain was agonizing at first. I had to squeeze my eyes shut and grit my teeth together to keep from screaming. But then it started to fade, and every inch of flesh, muscle, and bone from my hands to my shoulders was pleasantly on fire. The heat cleansed, purified. I hoped it would burn me to bits, leave nothing behind.

William was deep in concentration now, his breaths coming short and quick while mine slowed and steadied. Then my state of mind altered. I felt strong, invincible, and much more importantly, I felt beautifully and wonderfully good. He let go of my arms, flexing his hands and laying them in his lap, holding on to the fabric of his jeans.

"Are you okay?" he puffed.

I looked at my arms and then at William, smiling in amazement. They were perfect. The nail marks were gone. "William," I breathed. "You fixed me."

He nodded, smiling weakly.

I laughed. "I can't believe you can *do* that! That's the most amazing thing I've ever seen, ever felt!"

"Better than repelling?" he smirked.

"Ha. *So* much better! Anna said you could heal but … I guess I needed to see it to believe it."

"Well, I haven't had much use for it lately."

"That's good, right?"

"Yeah. It is. I guess. Though, other than my jaunts to vampire land, I'm feeling pretty unhelpful these days."

"Well, you've helped me," I said. "William … I don't know how to thank you."

"No need. It was my fault to begin with. This was the least I could do."

"Now don't start that again," I complained. "I mean it. No more about it."

"Fine."

"I just have one more little favor to ask of you, though, … not that you haven't done enough already."

"Name it."

"Don't say anything to anyone, okay? I don't want them to know that, that … well, I just don't want them to know what happened."

"Okay. I promise under one condition."

"What?"

"Don't lie to me, okay? Always tell me the truth."

I took a deep breath. "Okay."

I stood up, invigorated, and offered William a hand. He took it and pulled himself up, teetering a bit before standing up straight.

"Your hands are shaking. Your … everything is shaking." I frowned. Now that I was paying attention, he was looking even more washed out than normal.

"It's just what happens." He shrugged. "Always has to be balance in the universe, Lily. This is how things even themselves out."

"It weakens you."

"Yes."

"For how long?"

"It depends. But for something like this I should be fine in a few days."

I looked at him with a mixture of sympathy and admiration, and opened my mouth to speak when someone knocked on the door.

"Lily, it's me," Christian said from the hall.

I sighed and grumbled, ignoring it.

"Lily, please open up?"

I scowled. "One minute, Christian, I'll be right there."

William shrugged apologetically and took a step for the door.

"William!" I whispered quickly. He stopped and raised an eyebrow. "I …." Just *do* it, woman! Grow some fucking balls.

I pushed all thoughts aside and took a quick step forward, wrapping my arms around his neck, hugging him tightly. "Thank you," I said, then kissed his cheek.

He went stiff for a second, but I stubbornly held him until he relaxed and sighed, hugging me back. "You're welcome, Lily."

"Lillian, … are you alive in there?" Christian's voice rang from the hall.

I rolled my eyes and released William.

"And you let *him* get away with calling you that? Unfair," William moped.

"Don't worry. He'll get his," I promised.

He grinned wickedly. "Can I watch?"

"Goodnight, William."

"Night." He chuckled, then pulled open the door and stepped out, nodding at Christian as he passed.

Christian narrowed his eyes suspiciously. "What was *he* doing here?"

"Checking on me. Apparently it's the thing to do."

"And why wouldn't you answer the door?"

"I was giving William a piece of my mind." I smiled.

"Oh. Well. Are you all right? Mum seemed convinced that you weren't, but, you … certainly look like you're okay."

"I am."

"Good. Then, I'll let you get some rest."

"Thanks, Christian."

He didn't move, just stared at me for a second longer, an unnamed question in his eyes. It passed. "All right then. Good night," he said.

"Night." I smiled and shut the door.

Eleven

Christian was relentless. If Anna and I went to dinner, he came with us. If I needed to run to the drug store, he'd develop a sudden need for lip balm. For nearly three months, Christian served as the most constant guard dog companion a girl could ever ask for … and it was beyond what I could tolerate even a moment longer.

The only time I could traverse beyond the house without Christian sniffing me out was during training sessions, and I don't know what my sanity would have done without them—or without my teacher, for that matter. After the incident with the Incubus, William had upped the defensive ante, hard-core. Every trick of the trade he could teach me, I learned. And when I'd had enough, when I was sick to death of all the techniques and energy-control and exhaustive means of protection, he'd invariably tell me to suck it up, holding that in order for me to most effectively help others, it was my duty to defend myself like a pro. The man was like a Sentient personal trainer. He was unrelenting, and most surprisingly of all, he was more my friend than I could ever have imagined.

So, naturally, I wondered if he'd caught on to my well-nurtured thoughts of escaping. Lucky for me, Clara and Anna hadn't. They were surprised that I'd turned down the chance to see a poltergeist, but they could hardly disbelieve my excuse. After all, wasn't I always ready to participate? Hadn't I jumped at the chance to watch Clara crossover a few members of the posthumous population of an asylum in Virginia? And just last week we'd taken a jaunt to the local monastery to investigate the source of some inexplicable singing coming from an empty bedroom. Presently, my housemates had no reason to disbelieve that my complaint of a headache was anything less than genuine.

Day was edging close to its end, and orange light glowed in through all the windows. As Christian and Paul drove off with half the house, I strolled happily along the back corridor toward the French doors. My first stop: the grounds.

"Lily?" I turned around. William was walking up behind me. "I thought you were in bed, suffering horribly."

I shrugged. "Maybe not *horribly*," I said.

"Right. And what is this? Headed straight for the outside world, unchaperoned? Is this an outright act of mutiny, Lily? Christian would be aghast." He shook his head in mock dismay.

I sighed. "Fine, I'm escaping him for a while. Just don't say anything, okay? There's no need for him to follow me *everywhere*. It's been months. I'm able to, at the very least, recognize danger before it has the chance to recognize me."

"I agree," he said. "And I think you'd be fine without him traipsing around the place after you like a body guard. Besides, it's doubtful that there's much real danger for you on the grounds, anyway."

"Thank you."

He nodded. "But …."

"But?"

"But, I wonder, are you completely opposed to the idea of company? For a little while, anyway?"

I narrowed my eyes. "You're not going to pull a Christian on me, are you?"

"No." He chuckled. "And we wouldn't even have to talk. I mean, as long as we're both headed in the same direction, I just thought …." He paused, shaking his head. "In fact, forget it, never mind. It's totally understandable that you'd want to be alone."

I considered this. Had I wanted to be alone? Or did I simply want to free myself of certain … baggage? Ah, well, if he proved to be annoying, I'd give him the boot. Besides, and I allowed this observation only an instant of acknowledgment, he was unnaturally beautiful in this light. There could be worse company.

"You know? I don't think I'd mind," I said.

"All right, then. Let's go." He took several long strides toward the door and opened it for me.

Gallantry, how amusing. "Nice," I said, stepping outside.

"What?" he scoffed. "Are you one of those women who hate chivalry? Because if you are, we could go back and you could open the door yourself."

"Jesus." I laughed, despite his perturbed appearance. "I meant it, you idiot. It was nice. You're not winning any brownie points here, William."

"Oh." He dropped his eyes. "Sorry."

I shook my head, smiling. "Honestly, lighten up!" I elbowed his arm.

He smiled faintly and we walked down the path, parting around the fountain, and meeting again on the other side. A sweet wind wafted through the trees and across the water, then lapped at my face. This was nice—the first real peaceful moment since … since … I couldn't even remember anymore. And William was true to his word. There was no need for incessant chatter. We reached the usual end of the path, the grouping of trees where the two of us had so often trained. To my surprise, he walked a few feet in and waited.

"Should we really be navigating pathless woods at night, William?" I asked, instinctively afraid.

"Should we not?" he responded, smiling playfully. "Come on. I'll walk ahead, and you try and sense me in the dark."

"Isn't it dangerous? I mean, I don't … I don't like the dark, William." I blushed, ashamed. As much as my capabilities had been honed, I found my guts to be lacking after everything that had happened. I was starting to wonder if I wasn't simply *afraid* of being alone, afraid of my own shadow.

"Lily, still don't trust me?"

"I … it's not a matter of trust; it's just common sense."

"That it would be," he said, "if, in fact, your argument wasn't so flawed."

"What are you talking about?" I asked, weakly feigning annoyance.

"Come on, Lily, feel for yourself. Where are you safe?"

I sighed dramatically. "You and the feelings."

"My God, it's no wonder you never go anywhere! Yes, *feel*."

"Uhm, *I'm* sorry, but what is *that* supposed to mean, exactly? I don't go anywhere alone because no one will let me."

"Bullshit. You don't go anywhere alone because you've lost your nerve. Christian is just a crutch."

I opened my mouth with the intention of telling him off, but then realized he was right.

"Fucking hell," I muttered to myself before sighing. "Okay. So, I'll feel for your energy."

He nodded, and I looked intently at him in a reluctant attempt to feel something.

"You're looking," he sang, disapprovingly.

"Huh? Oh. Right, sorry. Shall I close my eyes then?"

He smiled. "If you need to."

I shut my eyes. "And what am I aiming for? What will you feel like?"

"Me," he said.

"What?" I opened my eyes again, and he was gone. I groaned. I hated it when he did this, but I especially hated it now. "William. Come on. Where are you?" I rolled my eyes. The night was too quiet as I stood at the path's end. I wished for some traffic noise, some loud music. But everything was still, and William was nowhere to be seen.

What was worse, the world was a foreign place to me now. Monsters and creatures of fearsome power did exist, and this was the first time I'd had to face this knowledge on my own. An ache of abandonment swept through me.

"William?" I whimpered. "Please, don't leave me out here alone, okay? Seriously," I spoke in a whisper.

Despite its former beauty, the path leading back to the house seemed long and sinister as the glow of moonlight set shadows against it. I turned toward the woods again.

"Ugh, I *hate* the woods." I pouted. Wiping away a few tears, I took a step into the unknown. How could he do this to me? It was too much, too soon. I would never forgive him for this. I walked forward unsteadily until the outermost line of trees was behind me. Just a few feet more and I'd be fully immersed in the darkness. I steadied my breathing. What a wretched excuse for a Sentient I was. What a pathetic, terrified little girl. And no one was going to redeem me but me. So, I kept my eyes open and relaxed every muscle, every nerve.

"What's safe?" I shuddered, my voice as small as a child's.

Safe. The word was a mantra. Then I felt it. It was the comfort of a like source. It was so many things, and the most important of these was safe. It was safe. The sensation coursed through me again, like a wave. *Turn left.* I walked slowly, waiting for the warmth to return.

Keep walking. Don't stop walking.

Again it flowed through me, stronger this time, tugging at my center with force. I struggled to remain relaxed because anytime I tensed, it faded. I walked more quickly now, pushing tree limbs aside, finally locked onto the energy's ebbing supply. Tears stained my cheeks, but it was relief that drew them forth. With a gasp, I crashed full force into something.

"You found me." His voice was soft.

I began to cry and he wrapped his arms around my shoulders, pressing me against his chest tightly. I shook violently and clung to him.

"Shh, Lily, shh. It's okay. You're fine, you're safe. You've been protected for too long. You've forgotten yourself."

I lifted my head, trying to make out his face in the darkness. At first, there was superb contentment, and then ... .

"How the hell could you *do* that to me?!" I punched at his chest with my fists. "I was so afraid! How could you leave me alone? What if there'd been ... " and my words were lost in an ocean of weeping.

"Lily." He chuckled tenderly. "I never left you. I was never more than twenty feet ahead of you at any given time! You weren't alone. And, hey ... ." He lifted my face from his shirt. "You did it." He smiled. "You'll always be able to find your way." He bent and placed a soft kiss on my forehead. "Or, at least, you'll always be able to find me."

Benign as this gesture was, the old questions nagged at me. Should I feel ashamed? Revolted? But relief won over every objection, and I accepted his comfort. He rested his chin on the top of my head and a while passed. My breathing slowed and the shaking ended. "I won't do that again," he promised.

I sniffled. "You always say that and then you go and do something even worse." I frowned.

"You're right." He laughed.

"Hmph," I sniffed, still clinging to him.

"Lily?"

"What?"

"What did I feel like? My energy? I've never asked anyone before. Is it cold?"

"Cold?" I thought for a moment. The irony of the situation coaxed a slight smile from me. "No. Not cold. Warm." *It's like being held*, I thought.

I felt his low laughter against my face as it vibrated in his chest.

"Let's go back now?" I pleaded.

"Sure." He lifted his chin and looked down at me. "Lily," he said. The tone of the word was not a question, but his expression was. He brushed my cheek with the back of his hand, and my flesh warmed immediately. I stiffened. *Not Good.* He was my trainer. He was only half-human, he was … *so* fucking close I could feel the heat radiating off his skin.

"William," I cautioned.

"What?" He frowned.

"Back to the house."

"The house?"

"Yes. You know … the oversized box in which we live?"

I was hit with the smallest burst of frustration before he sighed. "Okay. Come on," he said. Taking my hand he led me out of the woods.

Twelve

*H*ad I really agreed to cook dinner tonight? What in the name of hell was I thinking? Who could compete with Clara's cooking? My best laid plans were sure to be a calamity.

Anna and I had gone out shopping the day before and decided on a lark that the menu for the evening would be vegetable lasagna. And now I stood, musing over my ingredients and feeling daunted.

Where was the right opening? I turned the package of frozen vegetables over, examining it ruefully. "Hmph." I ripped it at the side, a few pieces flopping out onto the counter. Someone snickered, and I turned to see William behind me.

"Honestly, Lily, no need to torture it. There *is* a prescribed method for opening these things." He took the package from me and tore it across a perforation.

"Well, there are also prescribed methods for entering a room. Must you always be stealthy like the ninja?"

"Like the ninja," he repeated, smirking. "I'm *that* good, huh?'

"Come to think of it, you never announce yourself. Just, poof, and 'Oh, look, William's here.'"

"Hmm. I'm impressed with myself now." He beamed, picking up the spilled cauliflower and plunking it onto a dish.

"How would Anna put it? Cheeky, that's what you are." I smiled.

"Oh, humor me. Christian can't miser away the entire bulk of ego in this house."

I laughed. "No, but he does keep an ever replenishing stock."

"*Lillian*," he said, amazed. "Sullying the name of Saint Christian? Are you ill?" He laid his hand on my cheek.

"Shut up." I blushed. "I never said he was perfect."

"Mm. Glad to hear it."

"Just mind yourself and hand me the Alfredo sauce," I scolded.

"*So demanding.*" He shook his head, half-smiling. "Ask nicely."

I looked at him angelically, speaking in dulcet tones. "Please, William, please hand me the sauce before I repel your ass out the window."

He backed up a pace. "Works for me," he said, handing over the jar. I attempted to open the lid, but it wouldn't budge. Were the stars aligned to make me look like a fool today? I struggled harder, willing him not to notice.

"You can throw me across the forest but you can't open a lid?" he mused, grinning and crossing his arms.

"It's not the same."

"No?" he chuckled.

"Not at all. I'm not angry at the Alfredo sauce."

"Not yet, but when you finally pry that thing off and it explodes all over you, will you be angry with it then?"

I scowled and thrust the jar at him. Of course, he opened it with ease and handed it back.

"Are you done with me now?" he complained, still smiling. "Honestly. You take, take, take," he teased dramatically, edging toward the basement door.

"*William*," I warned.

He opened the door and stood next to it. "You're welcome," he said and ducked down the stairs.

"That's right! Run!" I laughed after him as Anna pranced into the kitchen, a bottle of wine in each hand.

"What was *that* all about?"

I chuckled. "Nothing."

"How's it going with the dinner?"

"Don't ask."

"Lily, darling," she sang. "Don't fret a thing. It shall be magnificent beyond their wildest imaginings."

"Yeah, I'm sure .... Oh shit, *shit*," I cried out as the pasta noodles foamed over. I grabbed the pot hastily off the stove, scalding myself.

"Whoa, relax!" she laughed.

"No! Nothing's working!" I rushed the pot to the sink, my hands shaking.

Anna hoisted herself up to sit on the counter and studied me carefully.

"Lillian Hunt." She shook her head slowly. "You're in love."

My face ignited into flames. "Have you escaped from an institution recently?" I said.

"Irrelevant." She giggled. "You *are*! I can feel it!"

"Guh, Anna. Feel, feel, feel. Can't you guys get through one day without sniffing around for a mystery?"

"What would be the fun in that?" She sulked.

"Anyway, I refuse to discuss such a ridiculous speculation any further. Moving on."

"Fine. But I've got my eye on you, Lily." She grinned in excitement.

"Pasta strainer, please," I ordered, jutting my hand out.

"Pasta strainer," she repeated, handing it to me.

❧

Essentially an infant to this world, the routine of training had become something of a security blanket. There was so little that I could count on, so little that I could predict, and every victory gained through these exercises increased my sense of empowerment, while offering a protected atmosphere. That's why it unnerved me when William knocked on my door, preempting the expected trek to the woods.

"Hi," I said, clearly surprised.

"Afternoon." He smiled. "So we've been doing the defensive stuff for a while," he said.

"Right."

"And you can sense me coming with little effort."

"Correct."

"Well, it's time to move on to something more complicated. I have to admit that this aspect of your instruction seems more fitted to Clara's guidance than mine, but Abram insists."

"What aspect?" I asked. "And what's with the escort service?"

"It's just that I don't need the seclusion of the trees for this. Matter of fact, we'll have to be pretty comfortable." His brows scrounged together thoughtfully. "Would you mind if we used your room?"

"My … room?" I sputtered. "Why?"

"It's either yours or mine." He shrugged. "It's got to be uninterrupted. Private."

I studied him. "And the woods wouldn't work?"

"I suppose they would—if you didn't mind sitting on the ground, unmoving, in the heat of day, for X amount of time," he pressed. "Hope you have sunscreen," he paused, "and bug repellent."

I laughed a little. "Why would that be the case?"

"Because we'd be locked in."

"We'd … be what?"

"We'd be in a state of vulnerability. Once we began, it could be raining barbells on us and we wouldn't know it."

"Okay, so indoors it is. But why the privacy?"

"Because we don't want any external sources of interference to conflict with the process."

"What *is* the process?"

"You're a pathcrosser *and* an empath. That is one volatile combination. The most difficult interactions for you to handle will be internal. You've seen Clara at work. You've seen her cross spirits over. She looks like she's in a trance, doesn't she?"

"Yes."

"Well, in a way she is. See …." He stopped, glancing behind him as Ginny tugged at his shirt. "Uh … hey there." He smiled. "Where did you come from?"

"Outside! Whatcha doin'?" she asked.

"Talking to Lily," he said. "What are *you* doing?"

"Nothing, just collecting." She beamed. "I'm bored. Lily, you wanna see something?"

I laughed cautiously. "What?"

"Look!" She lifted a hand from behind her back to reveal the tiny, limp form of a bird. "It's a baby! I think it fell out of a tree," she explained, concerned.

"Ginny … I …." I breathed. I had to do something, take it from her, distract her before she realized.

"You wanna hold it?" she offered.

"I'll …."

"How 'bout you, William? You want ….oh!" she cried, suddenly. "Why isn't it moving? It was moving when I found it!" Her face was heartbreakingly sad. "I tried not to hold it too hard." She frowned deeply. Yes, it was definitely dead.

William sighed. "I think it's okay, though, Ginny. See? Look, it just needs to be woken up a little." He reached down and took the bird from her hand, laying it gingerly in his open palm. Lifting it up to his face, he placed three fingers along its tiny body.

"Hey, little bird, wake up!" he whispered. A few seconds passed before its fragile frame expanded with an intake of air, and then it was breathing again, quick and steady. It fluttered its featherless wings, lifted its head, blinking blindly at nothing.

"Oh, it *is* okay!" Ginny exclaimed.

"Yes." William grinned warmly. "But you'll have to take care of it from now on. Be *so* gentle with it, Ginny, okay?" He handed it back to her.

"I will," she swore, her face glowing with pleasure. "I'll keep it safe! I'll take it to Grandma; she'll help me!" She took off down the hall before gasping, then slowing down. "I'm being very careful!" she called back, and then she was gone.

I turned my awe-struck gaze on William. "That bird … it was dead," I said. He nodded.

"You brought it back to life." Even as the words left my mouth I couldn't believe them. "You actually … you—"

"Lily, please don't make a big thing out of this," he said.

"Well, why not?! I mean, I'm…you're … just…come on." Pulling him into my room, I closed the door and locked it behind us. No small surprise, his hands were trembling.

"Why did you do it?" I asked.

"Honestly, Lily. Wouldn't you have?"

"Yes." I smiled. Amazing.

"Come sit down," he said. "Let me finish my thought from before—about Clara."

"Okay."

We sat next to each other on the bed and began again. "What happens to Clara is typical of your kind. You'll have to make contact with the essence of a soul, not just its astral form. This is something that will happen to you automatically, a state you'll enter into with no explanations necessary. But once you're there, sharing the same mental space with it, that's when things get tricky."

"This sounds hard. Can't we just run around in circles? Ginny swears by it," I said.

"Funny, Lily. And it *is* hard. That's why we're doing it here first. You need to experience it in a restricted setting."

"Experience the trance thing?"

"If you want to call it that. But really, it's connecting soul to soul. I couldn't do this with just anyone. You're the only one who can make it happen. *You're* the pathcrosser."

"Fascinating," I mused. "So this is under *my* control only?"

"Correct."

"That's awfully trusting of you, William. Are there any risks?"

"In all fairness, not really, other than exhaustion. But you ought to be used to that by now."

"And you said that it can't be interrupted once begun? How do we end it?"

"No, it can be stopped whenever you choose. What I meant was that you'll be oblivious to anything happening outside, in the physical world."

"Well, I'm confused. What about the external influences thing? You said that we had to be somewhere private. What's the point of that if I won't hear or see anything around me?"

"We *have* to start out this way, Lily. Because you'll be super sensitive to energies the whole time. Anyone walking past, any other spirit in the vicinity can throw you off. That's why it's so much harder to do in the real situation. At times, you'll have to battle to keep your target locked in place. Do you understand? These spirits don't necessarily want to move on, and they'll try to push you away using any means possible."

"All right. So what is the object of this exercise? What are you teaching me?"

"I'm not teaching you anything. You're teaching yourself this time—to hold me hostage, so to speak."

I raised my eyebrows. "Oh?"

"You need to hold on to my energy. Don't let me break away, no matter how I struggle. No matter what happens."

"And you're certain I'll know how to do this?"

"Yes," he said with confidence.

Now this was amusing. I'd be holding William prisoner ... in my bedroom. I nearly laughed, then caught myself.

"And what is so funny?"

"Oh, just remembered a joke."

"Mhm." He seemed unconvinced. "Anyway, shall we start?"

"Sure."

"All right, turn to face me, then." I scooted further up the bed and sat with my legs criss-crossed, facing him, as directed. "You can find me, right? You reme mber what I feel like?"

I knew what he was saying. His energy was recognizable to me now, just as a voice or a face would be. "Yes."

"Okay. Now draw it into yourself." He closed his eyes.

I narrowed one eye suspiciously. "Are you sure you know what you're doing?"

"I'm just following Clara's instructions." He smiled. "She said you'd get it."

"Uhm ... 'kay." I closed my eyes and waited for the surge of his energy to wash over me. Again I was taken aback by its warmth, and in the safety of this room, its ability to make me feel so extraordinarily happy. "Now what?" I smiled.

"I don't know, Lily. This is your territory," he said quietly.

I sighed, aggravated, and squeezed my eyes even more tightly shut. "Do you really expect me to—"

"Are you losing my energy?" he admonished. "Lily, concentrate and relax!" I could hear the scowl in his voice. He was right. I loosened up and drew him forward again.

What was I supposed to be doing? How would I know if I was doing it right? Then I remembered something. Anna had shared a vision with me once. Hadn't she effectively pulled me into her mind?

"William, open your eyes," I ordered.

"What? Why?"

"Because, you have to. Just do it."

He did as I told him, lifting an eyebrow. "So demanding."

I smiled. "That's right. The shoe's on the other foot, isn't it?"

"Touché." He smirked. "But don't get carried away."

I leaned in. "Too late. Focus, William."

"I *am*," he complained.

"No, I mean look *right* at me. Lock your eyes on mine and don't look away."

"Yes, ma'am," he said, half-smiling.

How had Anna done this again? I let my arms rest in my lap and felt for William's energy, drawing it in until it penetrated my own. And all the while our gaze remained perfectly adjoined. Maybe if I just kept this up I might actually … .

William took a sharp intake of breath and seemed to propel forward into me. It was almost painful, but then the fullness of his energy settled into place and we were facing each other again … light ebbing from our forms, and the rest of the world in complete darkness.

"Lily," he thought. "You did it!" His lips weren't moving, but I heard him nonetheless.

"I know."

"Clara insisted you'd figure it out. How did you manage it?"

"I had a little help from Anna."

"I see. I'm going to try and pull back now, okay? Don't let me!"

"I'll try not to."

A feeling of lightness grew in strength as he moved away. I was a cup being emptied, and I fought to hold him, keep him with me. In a rush, the lost energy poured back in, and I sighed with relief.

"Nicely done," he thought.

"Thank you. Same to you. Will it always be like this? I mean, will they always try to get away?"

"No. Some of them will stay with you willingly and listen to what you have to say. But others *will* try to escape. Shall we do it again?"

"Okay."

Then he withdrew with some force, sending me lurching forward with the loss of it. I had to steady myself before calling him back, fighting the tide of his spirit as it sought to return to its source. Once I was convinced he'd given up, a swell of intense sadness overtook me.

"Lily, I'm testing you in the worst possible way now, I'm sorry. But remember that they'll use any means to get away, and putting you off your guard via emotional manipulation is one of them. Push the pain aside and keep me here."

The urge to cry was unbearable, and memories, immobilizing memories, cropped up into view. Every thought of despair I'd ever had threatened to dislodge my hold, and it was nearly impossible to care that William was withdrawing, siphoning away like sand. With every ounce of determination I had, I struggled to regain him. Crying tearlessly, I felt trickles of him returning, though resisting with all he had.

Then, the sorrow subsided, to be replaced by blissful happiness, concentrated affection. The lights around us intensified. "I'm no match for you. You can have me." He laughed.

"I win, then?"

"Yes."

"That was awful, William."

"I can only imagine. I'm sorry, Lily. I didn't want to."

"I know. Can we retire this for now?"

"If you'd like," he thought.

"Definitely. You can go, I promise."

"Are you sure?"

"Yes."

I was catapulted forward as he left me, the breath ripped from my lungs with the weight of emptiness. Then we were sitting again on my bed, still facing each other. Neither of us had moved at all. And I felt unbearably cold. The absence of William's energy left an awful void.

I shuddered, and before I could think it through, I'd thrown my arms around him, buried my face in his neck. He sat perfectly still for a moment, undoubtedly trying to understand what was happening. Then he closed his arms around me, stroking my hair, kissing the top of my head. "Lily," he said, disarmed. "What's the matter?"

"I don't know," I cried. "Just don't let go."

"I…won't," he said. He brushed my hair aside, stroking my face and jaw with the back of his hand. I tried not to let the usual doubts rear their head just yet. I needed more time to do whatever it was I was doing. What *was* I doing?

"Lily, please," he whispered against my head. "What's wrong?"

"I felt …." Another shiver ran through me. "Alone."

"I had no idea," he crooned in my ear. "Clara never mentioned this as an after effect. I'm so sorry, Lily. I think maybe she should take over from here. I'm not sure if I'm the best option anymore."

I raised my head to look at him. His expression was heavy with worry and guilt. "No." I lowered my eyes and shook my head.

"No?" he asked, befuddled.

"No. She doesn't have to do that. I don't know that it would help. I've done this once before, sort of, with Anna, and the experience was hard, but, I didn't feel this way afterward."

"So, what are you saying? What do you think is wrong?"

"It's just you."

His eyes darkened. "Me?"

"Yes, you. I mean, well, it's not the way it sounds."

"No? Then what way is it?"

"I meant …." I couldn't look at him and say it. I couldn't even *say* it.

"Just tell me, Lily," he said, holding me away from him. "Did I feel off to you? Did I feel … *wrong* to you? *Tell* me."

"*No*, William," I pleaded, forcing myself to face him. A ball of fear raged in my stomach. Was I about to say something anarchic, something mutinous? No. Son of a bitch. The truth is never wrong.

Reaching up I took hold of both sides of his face and looked him in the eyes. His expression immediately softened. "There is *nothing* wrong with your soul," I said, holding his gaze.

He shut his eyes and shook his head between my hands.

"Nothing," I insisted. "William, listen to me!"

He opened his eyes again and I continued. "You have to understand why I'm torn, why I've been afraid around you. To a certain degree, I still am!"

"Wow." He let out a bitter laugh. "That's fantastic, Lily."

"Isn't it fair that I should be confused?" I defended. "Can't I have more time for all of this to become real? Normal? Just when I think I understand the rules, someone throws me a curve ball! William …." But he refused eye-contact. "William Maddox?" I repeated, arching my neck to the side in an attempt to make him face me.

He granted me the favor, but there was no feeling in his eyes. "Don't trust me," he said. "Don't waste another minute feeling one way or the other about me. I give up, Lily."

The very idea made my heart explode. "Please don't," I begged. "Please."

"*Why not?*"

"Because I don't want you to. I …." For the love of God, speak up!

He ground his teeth together. "So…is this how it's always going to be? Do you have *any* desire, *any* intention of saying what you really mean?"

"Yes," I promised.

"Then start now! Tell me the truth, damn it. What was wrong with me?"

"Nothing! I meant it. There was nothing wrong with your energy. It was good! It was perfect."

He scoffed.

"Don't react that way if you really want the truth!" I snapped. He was still scowling, but his jaw relaxed. I went on. "It's just that you feel painfully good to me. I felt it in the woods, and just now … I was drowning in it. And then it was gone. So, I was afraid." It was so hard to look at him. I was horribly embarrassed by my feeble choice of words. Then, I felt his hand on my cheek. I peeked and he was smiling.

"I don't make you feel horrible, frightened, repulsed?" he asked.

"No. Nothing like that."

"And you're saying I felt good to you?"

"Yes. I am." My face was burning hot.

"Wow. That took guts." He smirked.

"William, God, don't do this to me, not now." I laid my head in my hands.

"I'm sorry." He laughed. "Lily, please?" He took my hands away from my face. "You are a strange, impossible woman. I'll never understand you."

"Yeah, well, join the club."

"Hm. And are you feeling better now?"

I was and I wasn't. The initially frightening solitude had faded, but a yearning remained. I sighed. "Well enough, I guess."

"How very convincing."

I shrugged. "I'm not going to lie. I promised I wouldn't."

William took my hand. "We certainly can't merge all the time." He chuckled. "But …." He moved around behind me and pulled me into his arms. For a moment I froze, a final note of indecision playing itself out, but the heat of his energy was an overwhelming comfort and I lay back against his body, sighing.

He held his arms over mine, and rested his chin on my head. "This is a perplexing sort of relationship we have, isn't it?" he whispered.

I breathed deeply, laying my head sideways so my face rested against his shoulder. "Very."

"You know, for someone who isn't entirely sure they trust me, you really act like you do."

"Well, forgive the remains of my stubborn loyalty, William."

"To Christian?"

"Mm." I nodded.

"Why? I know he retrieved you. I know he saved your life, but that doesn't entitle him to total lifetime control."

"No, of course not. But he's just so reactionary. And he *means* well …."

"Yes, I know."

"Plus, every time I think of what he's been through, I just can't help feeling guilty whenever I let myself get too close to you. It's not even personal, William. It's just like I said … a bizarre sense of allegiance."

"Right. And does *this* make you feel guilty?" He alluded to our present condition.

"Somewhat."

"But not guilty enough to kick my ass out of your bed," he laughed in my ear.

"No." I smiled as his breath tickled my skin. "The old loyalties are wearing away."

"Ah, I see. Explain why that is, exactly."

"Because I'm happy with you, William. I've tried not to be, but I can't help myself," I complained. I was finding it much easier to speak candidly when we both faced straight ahead.

"Flattering, as usual."

I laughed quietly. A few seconds passed in comfortable silence before William leaned his head forward to lay his cheek against mine in yet another courageous breach of boundary. I decided it was acceptable, even reciprocating the pressure, and wondered how many of these margins I was willing to tromp on with him.

"Lily?" he breathed into my ear. The sensation was ridiculous.

"What?" I squeaked.

"You feel just as good to me."

"I do?" Hold on…where had my voice gone?

"Mmm." He rubbed his nose lightly against my jaw.

"That's nice." My breathing was becoming labored.

"Lily?" he asked again.

"Yes?"

"I'm so glad you came here."

Such simple words, but their significance was immeasurable. One thing was finally clear. He was, in my opinion, no longer one to be looked down upon. In fact, my realization of William's character made the very idea seem preposterous. It was *I* who didn't deserve *his* trust.

In a rush of fondness, I swiveled around and hugged him tightly and he rested his head on my shoulder, a role reversal if ever there was one.

"I'm sorry I've been unfair," I whispered. "And forgive my being a coward. But I'm getting braver." I was feeling *very* brave right now, in fact. There was just so much I wanted to try. I placed a cautious kiss in his hair—it smelled like rosewood—then another. He lifted his head, and the smallest smile played across his face. I brushed a lock of black hair away from his forehead before kissing it, then his nose, one cheek, and the other. All this he took with great patience, smiling kindly at the innocent offering. When I seemed quite finished, he laughed.

"You can be so pleasant when you want to be, Lillian."

I made a face. "Don't."

"What?" he asked, fighting back a smile.

"Nice try. But if *anyone* should know better than to call me Li—"

"Shut up, Lily." He smirked. Then his lips grazed my forehead, and I felt the skin beneath blazing to life. A chord in my heart exploded as I realized he was mimicking what I'd just done. My cheeks ignited, then the tip of my nose. Finally we were eye to eye, both of us taking in quick, shallow breaths. I waited for more, I expected more, but he simply lingered, his lips a single excruciating inch away from mine.

"Your move," he said, his voice hushed and broken.

I could never have resisted, but the moment was sullied by what I imagined to be the most obnoxious sound I'd ever heard.

Someone was knocking on my door.

I fumbled to regain composure, and standing up, I wobbled unsteadily across the floor. I looked back at him repentantly, and opened the door. It was Christian and Anna.

"Hey," Christian smiled. "We're going to the cinema. I wanted to see if you'd like to join … oh … I didn't realize you were training." He pursed his lips unhappily, noting William. "A rather unusual setting, I might add."

"We're practicing a soul merge. The idea was to *not* be disturbed," William said, disgruntled.

"Oh." Christian frowned. "Well, I'm sorry then, Lily. I didn't realize." He glanced back and forth between William and me. "Are you all right?" he asked me.

"Yes. I'm fine." My voice was pinched, but I tried to smile.

"Well, then." He threw William a warning look. "Are you going to be much longer?"

"I don't know," I said weakly.

"Oh, come on, take a break!" Anna begged.

"You go on, Lily," William said, getting up from the bed. "We can continue this later."

I sighed. "Okay."

"Good girl, Lil!" Anna said, slinging her arm over my shoulder. "All work and no play, you know? Would you like to come, William?"

Christian bristled and William laughed quietly. "I think I'll pass this time. Thanks."

A feeling of resentment swept over me. Why shouldn't he join us? What would Christian do if I insisted that be the case? But I could see William was uncomfortable, and this was probably not the best time for a standoff.

"So, we'll just finish up here and I'll be out in a second, okay?" I said.

"Sure!" Anna turned on her heal to leave, but Christian lagged in the doorway, glowering at William for a moment before following after her. I closed the door and laughed.

"That was amusing." William smiled.

"Yeah. Exactly the word I'd have chosen." I leaned back against the door, breathing out with relief. William walked over and rested a hand on the wood beside my head. I smiled up at him, my heart beating in unnatural rhythm. He leaned in, the corner of his mouth turned upward, and whispered in my ear.

"Let's meet in the woods tonight, Lily... I just thought of a vitally important lesson we need to go over."

I had a mini stroke, and then nodded. "What time?"

"Wait till it's dark." He chuckled.

"Right." I gulped and prayed for an ounce of decorum. How inconvenient. My hormones were hosting an orgy. *This* would make for some dignified behavior.

Thirteen

"So, your first soul merge," Christian pondered, putting his foot down on the break to let an overzealous car pass.

"Yep." I said.

"Tell me about it!" Anna requested, animated as usual.

"Uhm, well, I mean, it's nothing you wouldn't know already." I laughed, working to sound unaffected.

"Sure it is! Each soul is unique, Lily. Each experience different. What was it like?"

"Yes, Lily," Christian chimed in. "Tell us what William's *soul* felt like." The derision in his voice was inescapable.

"Well, considering I've never …." I thought carefully before proceeding, "I've never joined souls with anyone, I guess it was fine."

Christian huffed. "You're right. If you think anything about him feels fine then you *are* sorely inexperienced."

Anna's nostrils flared. "How many souls have *you* crossed over that you'd be the expert on how it's supposed to feel?"

"That's completely beside the point."

"Oh, is it? Do tell me from where you've gained such an expert knowledge of something you'll never fully understand or be able to do yourself!? I'm terribly curious," she goaded.

"Fuck off, Anna." He sighed.

"Guys, come on. Let's not do this," I implored. I was already feeling nauseous with nerves, and Christian's erratic driving coupled with the tense atmosphere was making it worse.

Anna smiled. "You're right, you're right. I'm sorry. Let's drop the whole thing and enjoy our evening then." We both looked at Christian.

"Yes, fine. Sorry," he muttered. "By the way, Anna. Abram mentioned that some of the Northwest members are coming into town."

"Really? When?" She leaned forward in her seat.

"I think he said in a few weeks."

"And, did he say who all, I mean, how many were coming?"

Christian smirked. "Something about the Rushes, Chris and Laura Polmieri, Wendell, too, obviously."

"I see," she said, looking disappointed.

He laughed to himself. "Oh, and I almost forgot. Katrina as well." His smile was more prominent now.

"She is?"

"Yes. And word on the street is that Katrina didn't want to come unless you were here."

Anna suppressed a smile, and the energy she was giving off was reminiscent of my own at the present moment. A bell rang in my head.

"Anna." I smiled wickedly. "*Who* is Katrina?"

A crimson pool settled into her cheeks and a grin broke through her seldom seen reserve. "Ugh, God." She threw Christian a vengeful glare. "She's a Sentient from Northern California."

"*And?*" I pressed.

"And nothing. We're just kind of friends."

"Oh, *right.*" Christian laughed.

"Christian, please!" Anna looked horrified.

"What, Anna?" I asked. "Is she, I mean are you two … you know?"

"What?" Anna grew more perturbed.

"Come on, Anna, she won't care," Christian scolded.

"I won't!" I swore. "Really, I won't."

Anna paused briefly, deciding whether or not to risk the confession, then settled back into her seat. "I guess I sort of have a thing for her," she sighed.

I giggled. "I can't believe you never said anything to me!"

"Well, the topic rarely lends itself to easy conversation." She smiled. "It doesn't bother you?"

"Are you out of your mind? No fucking way!" I said, beaming. "I realize that Sentients have a much more limited social circle, but still. I was beginning to wonder if you had any interest in dating at all."

"Oh, you're one to talk!" she ribbed. "Oi, Christian, where's the queue of potential men for Lily begin again?" She arched her neck about, looking out the windows for effect.

"Ah, I've filtered through the lot, and I don't know that any of them would be good enough for her." He smiled. He had *such* potential for being charming. If only it wasn't dwarfed by the enormous chip on his shoulder

The movie was forgettable, and my mind too full of distractions. The only real entertainment came in the form of bits of info Anna whispered to me about the Northwest Sentients.

"They usually join up with us a few times a year," she said. "Abram and Wendell—that's their Seer—have been friends for a long time."

"And how close are you and Katrina?" I dared to ask.

"We…it's complicated. I'll talk to you about it later when we're alone," she said.

"Okay," I whispered back, disappointed. There went a perfectly good diversion, though I had to admit that a movie was the safest of activities for the evening. At least this way I wasn't forced to pull off a facade of normal behavior. My mind was nearly non-functional knowing that William and I had…had done *what* exactly? More importantly, what were we *going* to do? My stomach lurched. I felt like a traitor, sitting between Christian and Anna, and all the while anticipating a cozy reunion with a vampire.

Even after stopping for sushi, Anna, Christian, and I made it back to the house by five o'clock. It was late summer now, and we had a good four hours of daylight left to go. This was going to be torture.

"Lily." Anna grabbed my arm discretely and I followed her to her room. We sat on the thick, soft rug and leaned back against the side of her bed.

"We first met five years ago," she began, "when Trina and her father, Ty, came to Vancouver to help with the rebellion," she began. I straightened up and nodded, giving her my undivided attention. "And we were both kind of thrown together, you know? The only two girls in the bunch. So," she shrugged, "it was inevitable that we'd get to know each other. But what was difficult was that she was involved with someone else at the time, someone from Sydney. I mean, they hadn't seen each other for months, but still. And while she was with us, the girl kind of gave Katrina the boot, told her it wasn't working out and left her high and dry when things were really getting tough for everyone. I can't pretend I was upset about this, since I had all but fallen for her the moment I saw her, but she wasn't in a way to reciprocate any advances, and so I kept my feelings to myself."

"Of course," I said.

"Well, we'd spent weeks together and we became really close. The night before she left, we just sort of ended up kissing," she said.

"Nice. Okay."

"Yeah, and it was brilliant; it was too perfect. But then she had to leave, and that was that."

"All right. And have you seen her since?"

"Yes. I … ." She burst into laughter.

"What?" I joined in the giggling.

"I should certainly say so." She raised her eyebrows meaningfully and my jaw dropped.

"Oh … my" I smiled.

"Mhm. It was only a week. She came to Atlanta last summer and I'd half worried that the old feelings wouldn't be there anymore. Well, they were."

"This must be so hard, Anna. I don't know how you could make it work."

"I know." She frowned. "She's been so devoted to caring for her dad. It's not like there was any other option *but* for her to return to California."

"What's wrong with her father?"

"What *was* wrong," she corrected. "He's passed over now."

"Oh, no. What happened?"

"Heart failure. Vancouver was his last battle. It took too much out of him."

"Poor Katrina." I sighed. "First she loses a girlfriend, then her father."

"Yes. And her mother was never much help. Her parents were divorced for more than twenty years when her father passed. She's not very close to her mum."

"I see."

"Well, that's it then," said Anna. "Who knows? Maybe she's met someone else by now."

"Maybe not." I smiled, and then winked.

"Maybe not," she said. "And what of Lily's love life? Any juicy history there?"

"Ha! No. All completely uneventful."

"Oh, come on, then. There must be something. What's the most serious relationship you've ever been in?"

"You mean the *only* relationship I've ever been in. Before Scott, I'd dated a few times and nothing ever came of it."

"So you met Scott and knew it was meant to be, then."

I snorted. "No, Anna. More like I met Scott and said 'All right, I give up. I'll just settle for this one.'"

She gasped and laughed loudly. "Oh, dear. That's dreadful."

"No." I shook my head. "We wasted three years of each other's lives before we finally said enough is enough. I'd become totally unresponsive to him. We just had nothing in common, and he did nothing for me."

"Mhm. And so it doesn't sound like it was a very difficult break up."

"It wasn't and it was. I mean, no one wants to be alone, and I think he was in love with me. But I couldn't pretend forever that there was something there that wasn't. All the while I was convinced that I'd never find anyone that I really wanted, who could really make me happy. So, really, I should have been desperate to keep Scott close. But I wasn't. I was actually resigned to living alone forever."

"How depressing," she moaned.

"I know!" I agreed. "But you have to understand it from my perspective. There was something missing in every single man I'd ever met, and I couldn't put my finger on it. Well, as it turns out, there wasn't anything wrong with these guys; it's just that I was sorting through the wrong rack."

Anna shook her head in confusion.

"I was looking for something while having no concept of its existence, do you understand? I must have wanted a Sentient."

"No matter how I try, I can't completely relate, Lil. Sentients are all I've ever really known. I guess that's what Abram meant when you first came here. That your experiences would be just as alien to us as ours are to you."

"Yep."

"And what of now?"

"Er… now?"

"Sure. With William, I mean."

"Anna! Don't start this again," I said, lying immediately.

"Oh, you *are* bad at hiding things!" she squealed. "Tell me, come on!"

"No, Anna."

"Argh! Why not? So *stubborn*. Nevertheless, whatever it is, I'm all for it."

I raised an eyebrow. "You are?" I asked guardedly.

"Ah-ha, then it's true!" she squeaked. "Does he know?"

"No!" I hushed her frantically. "I mean, there's nothing *to* know."

She glared at me, disappointed and skeptical. "If you're worried about my dear brother, don't be, Lily," she said. "This wouldn't be the first secret I've kept from him and it won't be the last. I can promise you that!"

"Anna." I sighed. I wanted to tell her what was happening, wanted to spill everything—my confusion, my fear, my shame, my excitement. But I had yet to admit half of those things to myself. Already a part of me flirted with the urge to renege on my evening plans. I wasn't afraid of William anymore, but I *was* afraid of myself when with him. And not so deep down I knew that to go to him would be the end of my indecision—it would be the decision, itself.

"Where are you, Lily?" Anna mused.

"All over the place," I admitted, mindlessly fingering the hem of my shirt.

"I'll say. Your energy is making me dizzy."

"Sorry." I shrugged.

Anna sighed. "Lil, remember when you first came here? When I showed you my family's past? I swore I would repay you. and I damn well meant it. Now is the time. Tell me what you're thinking, no matter what it is. You can't carry it all alone, remember?"

I swallowed. What a cumbersome thing to ask of her. The bond it forged would be akin to treachery in Christian's eyes. Wasn't it enough that I would soon be wavering on the edge of his hatred? Could I ask the same of his flesh and blood?

"Anna, I love you very much. But some things can't be said."

I expected the wrath of an angry Viking, but instead, to my great dismay, she bent forward, pulled me into her arms and began to cry.

"Oh, Lily, you are *too* good. But it would hurt me irrevocably if you kept this to yourself," she said. "You *must* tell me." This was manipulation at its best. Years as a Sentient had polished her flair for emotional control, and though she'd never tried using it on me before, I was fairly certain that she was now. The waves of her pain, whether genuine or convincingly contrived, washed through me. It was now that I hated being an empath the most.

"God, Anna, not … fair," I sobbed with her.

"Too bad," she wept.

"Okay, fine, fine, I'll tell you," I whimpered, my voice still ripe with her emotion.

"Promise?" Her shoulders shook with each sob.

"Yes, yes, just please, stop crying." I stroked her hair.

"Good," she sniffled, then sat up again, wiping her eyes clear of tears and smiling.

"Oh, Anna, that was wrong in every way!" I said, angry and impressed in the same breath.

"What? I meant it!" She huffed. "Now you promised."

"*Fine*! Shit. You're dangerous."

"Only to the bad guys!" she chirped, happy again.

"Yeah, I'm not sold on that idea." I rolled my eyes. "But anyway …."

"Yes?"

I sighed deeply. "Anyway, something … some … thing …."

"Something?" she repeated, making encouraging hand motions.

"Something has … changed." I gulped. "Something with William and me."

"Naturally," she said, nodding me on.

"Well, what do you mean naturally?"

"Oh, do let's not drag this on, *please*," she moaned, her accent more pronounced when frustrated (a trait she and Christian seemed to share).

"Right," I snapped. "Fine, well, I don't know. He and I are just … we get along … really well. I mean, too well! Unreasonably well. We, we seem to …." I struggled for the right words.

"Connect? Make each other happy? Fit perfectly? Both enjoy cross stitch? For bleeding Christ's sake, Lily, speak your mind!" she beseeched.

I giggled. "Yes. All of those! Eh, except the cross stitch. I'm hopeless at crafts."

She smiled. "Thank the fuck," she sighed. "So, have you two … you know?"

"Are you nuts?" I spouted. "No! I mean, how would that even work? Can vampires … erm …."

"Have sex?" She finished my thought with minimal delicacy. "Frankly, I had a rather seedy conversation about that once with Delbert Stone, one of Christian's friends from London. He'd said that as vampires are living beings and blood flows through their veins, they can perform most human functions. Come to think about it, their abilities in sensory control are naturally so much more fine-tuned than ours. I mean, they're built to detect what you're feeling and either dispel or glorify it. The experience is not only mental but physical … as you were unfortunate enough to have learned in Pennsylvania. That's how they trap their prey. One would theorize that they'd be buggering brilliant in bed."

"Huh," I said, trying to appear only mildly interested. "Where do the stories begin, you know, about vampires being reanimated corpses, dead men walking? I mean, William feels just like anyone else. It's absurd."

"Sheer ignorance." She shrugged. "Mum holds that William is more human than he is vampire now, anyway. Especially aging as he is."

"How *is* that happening, anyway?" I asked.

"It's not complicated. Beings with souls age, Lily, … they *must*. The very essence of the soul is constant transformation. One can't remain stagnant while in possession of it. Age is inevitable. And so, as William has a soul …."

"Right." I smiled. This all seemed too damn easy. Wonders like these made for precarious ideas where William and I were concerned. Surely there was a catch. There was always a catch.

"Yes, I reckon it *is* a miracle of sorts," Anna said. "Unfortunately, it takes a hell of a lot more than a working birthday to convince most Sentients of William's place here." She frowned. "The whole thing has made Abram a bit of a black sheep in the Worldwide Society, I'm afraid."

"The Worldwide Society?"

"Yes. It's an assembly that gathers in Edinburgh every few years to evaluate its Seers from region to region. You didn't suppose the Sentient world had no rules or structure, did you?"

"Well, I'd assumed there must be some infrastructure. What do they do?"

"They judge the effectiveness of each group and handle the dispensation of funds. Let me tell you that the last time those old codgers got together, things were touchy for Abram, at best. We've lost a good deal of support from them since letting William in."

And there was the catch, like clockwork. Here I sat, wet behind the ears, no name, no reputation and no blood connections. So why should fate deem it necessary that I fall for the very thing that could ruin me right out of the box? Maybe I was more like my mother than I thought.

"If it weren't for Thomas…," Anna continued, then paused. "Lil? Lily, you're doing it again." She snapped her fingers in front of my eyes.

"Oh, sorry."

"Bless your heart." She giggled. "So much happening so fast," she said.

"You have no idea."

"So you two haven't slept together. What *have* you done then?"

"We've…we've been affectionate," I said, thinking truthfully about the whole uncanny bond for the first time. "I mean, extremely affectionate, but…we've never really even kissed."

She laughed. "A bit odd, but it sounds lovely! Still, I have to wonder. William? Affectionate?"

"Huh! I know, right? It's bizarre. He's just not at all what you'd expect."

She narrowed her eyes. "And what do you mean you've never *really* even kissed?"

Such an irritating penchant for observation, I thought.

"It was more William's idea of a training strategy." I smirked.

"I *am* sorry but…what?" She frowned, uncomprehending.

"It was a while ago. Remember when Christian was so excited because I'd repelled William?"

"Bloody hell, you repelled him because he *kissed* you?" she howled with laughter.

"Yes." I sniggered. "He was too brazen. I wasn't prepared for that."

"And…are you prepared now?" she asked, becoming very quiet, very serious.

The concept was staggering. "I think I am."

❧

The rest of the evening was spent watching a baseball game with most of the house joining in. Clara and Ophelia were absent—they were early to bed types. Thomas had been gone for days to Virginia to dredge out a phony Sentient, and William would be rolling around at his usual pace, I was certain.

His presence was nearly always the most unassuming, and it was rare for him to announce his arrival.

It always surprised me how much Abram participated in these sorts of activities. But he did, with relish. Board games, for instance, were of particular enjoyment to him.

"It is a shame to see him go." Abram shook his head.

"Thank you!" Demetre bellowed. "He's their MVP! Knuckleheads. Why *wouldn't* they up his salary? They won't be taking another World Series for years," he complained.

"You got that right, old man," Paul said. "Of course, it was pure luck that they won it last year."

"I'm warning you, boy." Demetre scowled.

Paul smirked and downed half his bottle of Heineken.

"Not to interrupt a sentimental moment or anything …." I turned to Paul. "But I've been wanting to ask you something for a while."

"Oh, yeah? Well, the answer is thirteen." He offered up a crooked smile.

"What?" I asked, perplexed.

"My shoe size, right?" he winked.

I sighed and rolled my eyes. "Thanks for the revelation. But really, what's with the muscle shirts? Surely you own *something* with sleeves."

"Ohh, the wound." He pretended to double over in pain. Christian patted him on the back. "I own 'em," Paul said, recovering quickly. "Matter of fact, I have *quite* the array of fashionable attire. But I'd be doing the world a grave injustice if I denied the female population its rightful view of my well-chiseled physique."

"Oh, Lord God," Demetre groaned. Christian gagged on a pretzel.

"The boy does have a point," Abram intervened jovially. "Still, in all, you don't want to wear them out with too much of a good thing," he suggested.

"Huh. Maybe not," Paul conceded.

By nine o'clock people were beginning to fade. Paul had put away enough beer that he was now snoring blissfully next to me, his head back and an empty bottle still dangling precariously from his fingers. Demetre flipped through the stations, settling on a program about the nocturnal life of house mice.

Abram had left as soon as the game ended, retreating to his study as he always did when darkness fell. Darkness. I glanced over toward William, not certain at what point he'd come in. He was leaning forward in an armchair, half-heartedly flipping through the pages of a women's magazine.

Christian stood up and stretched. "I'm done. Four a.m. comes early."

"Bleh. Ungodly hour." Anna grimaced. "Why did you agree to go with them anyway?"

"Because, our dear mother asked me to," he said.

"Where are you going so early?" I asked.

"With Mum and Ophelia," said Anna, "to visit an old friend. We all know Mum won't drive in the dark."

"Ah. 'Night, then," I said to Christian.

"Night," he called back, leaving the room.

I waited almost patiently, sitting on the floor, sorting through a stack of catalogs and wondering how long it would take Christian to fall asleep. Ten minutes passed, and Paul awoke enough to drag himself to bed. Demetre and Anna remained. Somehow she'd become wrapped up in the mating habits of Asian elephants and was now coiled tightly in a ball on the sofa next to him.

My heart leaped into my throat as I heard William lay his magazine down. A moment passed and I knew when I looked over he would be gone. I was right. I listened intently for the faintest sound, the tiniest creek of the distant French doors. An eternal minute later, I heard them. The sound was so small that you'd have to be listening with all your strength to ever hear it. Only my ears were so attuned this evening.

I let another moment pass, flipping through a few more pages with great effort to seem interested. Then, my hands trembling, I set the catalog down and swallowed hard. When had I last been so nervous? Even during my first day here I was more relaxed. I forced my respirations to steady and stood up slowly.

Anna smiled, still watching the TV screen. "Going to bed now, Lily?"

"Ehn, maybe," I said.

I walked out of the room with deliberate ease, even stopping to stretch my arms above my head. Once I'd crossed the reception hall, however, I soared down the bedroom hallway. Rounding the corner to the back foyer I slowed down and stopped. The glass doors stared back at me like a secret passageway, moonlight filtering in and adding to the effect. I swallowed again, my heart pounding. What an exhilarating emotion this was. Exhilarating and terrifying. Nothing had ever made me feel so overwhelmed, so ethereal. Of all the new mysteries in my life, this was the most wrenching. Everything would change now, I knew. But—hadn't it once already? I was better at embracing change than I'd ever realized. It was just William, I could tell myself. But it wasn't anymore. It wasn't *just* William. It was *my* William, and tonight would reveal that.

Walking tremulously toward them, I opened the doors, and the night air hit me with exaggerated force. Everything meant something, every scent—the green, the jasmine. Every rustle and soothing breeze was intensified. I would memorize this night.

I stared down the path as it disappeared around the distant corner, the entrance to the woods … *our* woods, yet unseen. Then I danced forward, joy surging through my veins, past the fountain, down the crystal path and further still. Turning the corner, I faced the tree line. He should be there, but where? I walked quickly until I reached the perimeter, breathed in deeply, and stepped inside. Something glowed ahead. I moved toward it, grasping tree trunks and pushing myself along. Then, in a small opening, I saw him. He sat on a blanket and a fire burned in front of him, warm and low. He smiled, and it was stunning.

"You came," he said.

I stood, glued in place, and nodded. "Did you think I wouldn't?"

"Well … ." He shrugged.

"And … you did this?"

He gave me a wry smile. "No, Lily. It was a woodland fairy."

"You know, I don't think it's wise for you to say such things where no one can hear you scream," I teased, taking a seat beside him. The fire glowed across his features. A beautiful ghost.

He smirked. "You're in a good mood," he said, examining me. "And I'm awfully suspicious about the whole thing. It seems too easy. There's always supposed to be a fight with you. It's the rule."

I laughed at him. "Oh, be fair. I'm not *that* bad."

"You? Not that bad?" he said. "Lily, I've still got bruises to present as evidence if necessary."

On the whole, a comment like this would have raised Cain, but I was incapable of feeling angry with him tonight. Something had changed, something had clicked inside of me the moment I saw those doors.

"Well, I'm not currently experiencing any violent urges," I said plainly.

"Good." He swallowed. We stared into the fire, its warmth—or his—wafting through me. I closed my eyes, leaning my head on my shoulder so my hair draped down my arm.

"I want so badly to just let go." I opened my eyes again, watching the flames.

"Let go of what?" he asked.

"Fear. To feel like there's no room for anything else but happiness."

William rested his hand over mine.

"What if it ends?" I asked, horror-stricken.

"If what ends?" William shook his head. "You're being very cryptic this evening." He sighed.

"What if this life is one huge nervous breakdown? And what about you? I mean, we were taught in Kindergarten that vampires didn't exist, William."

"They should update their curriculum," he replied with a chuckle; then he lifted my hand to his face. "I'm real. Feel for yourself."

I ran my fingers along his cheek and down his neck.

"I think this must be another one of your endowments, Lily," he said.

"What?"

"Touching. You're very good at it."

I laughed. "To make up for the abuse," I said.

"Mm," he agreed.

"It's easy with you though, William," I admitted.

"Really?"

I nodded. "Yes," I said, running my palm across his forehead and into his hair. "You lend yourself well to it."

He smiled and then bent forward, whispering in my ear. "Lily?"

"Hm?"

"Do you intend to get any closer, or is arm's length the new black?"

I scoffed. "Well, how much closer can we get?" I asked, before feeling tremendously naive.

"Don't you remember where we left off?" He gave me an impish smile.

"Yes?" I said, scrambling for control.

"Great, saves me the recap," he continued.

"You can recap … if you want to." I breathed across his lips.

He chuckled low, just a fraction from my mouth. "No, Lily."

The man was merciless. Why couldn't he just let me be the coy, simpering female? What a pain in the ass he was. Ah, well. It was useless to fight the inevitable. I could taste his breath on my tongue, and my body took over, shoving all reserve out the window. Leaning forward, I gingerly brushed my lips to his, but the delicacy was short-lived. He'd apparently had all he could stand of my reservation. Pulling me against him, he parted my lips, his tongue seeking contact with my own, and began to drink me in. The kiss was urgent, almost frantic, and I'd have been overwhelmed were I not busy simmering in a pool on the ground. It seemed that there was no room for air, no wasted space allowed where some part of us could be touching. In fact, when I'd pulled away—only for a moment—William drew me back.

"Not yet," he pleaded, and then found my mouth again. I slid my fingers into his hair and wrapped them thoroughly around every strand, answering his need until my lungs threatened to burst.

"God," I broke away slightly, managing to laugh. But he shook his head against my lips, the kiss never ending, and pressed me harder to him. Even in my daze, even with every cell and every nerve seeking to implode upon itself, I grasped that it must have been so long, so very long, since he'd really been loved by another human being. Tears streamed down my cheeks, soaking both our faces, flavoring our kisses with salt. Finally, he broke the embrace, but only for lack of breath. I rose to my knees and wrapped my arms around his shoulders, pulling his head to my chest.

"You have to know by now," I whispered. "I trust you more than anyone."

Then at once, to my wonder and elation, I felt him sob against my skin, his humanity unequivocal. I held him this way for a long time, until his heart had emptied itself of its torment. Then I lay back, bringing him with me. He sank into my chest while I stroked his face, combed through his hair with my fingers, and before long, in a haze of contentment, we slept.

෭

"Lily," said a gentle voice in my ear. "Lily, wake up. You'll be eaten alive out here." William kissed my temple, nuzzling me awake.

I blinked in the darkness, still disoriented. Where was I? The split-second amnesia passed and I shot up quickly. "Oh, *shit*. Do you have a key?"

"Yes." He chuckled, pulling me off the ground and into his arms.

"Do you think anyone noticed?" I asked, ashamed of the question.

"Doubtful," he said. "Why? The fear setting in now?"

"No ... yes," I said.

"And you care what he thinks?"

"Yes." I sighed. "I know full well he's unreasonable, and I have to resist the urge to rip him a new one half the time, but he's like my family."

He lowered his lips to my forehead, kissing me softly. "We'll take it as it comes. It's not like we have to issue some kind of public statement or anything. It's our life, not theirs."

I nodded, dropping my gaze.

"And besides …." He slipped a finger under my chin, tilting my face upward. "I kind of like this sneaking around business."

"Do you?"

"Mmm." He leaned in to kiss me and met with air as I dodged him playfully.

"Better work on those reflexes, Maddox." I smiled.

He laughed and walked us forward, backing me into a tree. "Behave," he ordered.

I raised an eyebrow. "Make me."

He flashed a wicked grin. "There are some things vampires are better at than humans, Lillian," he warned.

"Oh, yeah? Name one."

"Biting," he said, roughly.

My head spun as he bent down and caught my lower lip between his teeth. Unholy hell. Only the waning strands of my pride—and the threat of daybreak—could save me now.

"You are *not* playing fair," I rasped.

He ignored me and began a slow decent toward my right ear, nipping it before carrying the torturous motion down my neck and around to the other side. I closed my eyes and dug my fingers into his shoulders, fighting for every breath.

"Now." He raised his lips to mine, hovering, and his words were slurred as he peppered my mouth with hints of contact. "Are you … going to … behave?"

I gasped and nodded.

"Good girl."

And I praised Jesus, Buddha, Krishna, Allah, Santa Claus, and Oprah all at once as he kissed me, pressing my body into the wood, leaving me absolutely incapable of standing on my own two feet. I'm not sure what nature of vocalizations I was making, but William seemed appreciative, increasing the eagerness of every movement in response to them. And this was just a goddamn kiss.

I felt myself fading, my legs going limp, and so did he. Breaking the embrace he caught me before I could slip too far.

"I was right," I concluded. "You *are* evil."

"And *you* are one delicious human." William smiled.

I held my breath, but I was unable to subdue the impending fit of laughter. It was a peculiar response, I had to admit. But the whole of my experience in this place, this life, had been so utterly incredible that my body sought release. It was either laugh or keel over and die.

William gawked at me; then he shook his head, laughing quietly at my burst of madness.

"Should I be offended?" He eyed me furtively.

"No." I giggled.

"Hm. Because I may be out of practice, but I didn't think my technique was *that* rusty."

"There is definitely nothing wrong with your technique, William."

He smirked. "Really? You don't think it requires a bit more practical application?"

I laughed shakily. "Oh, I don't know how much more practical application I can handle for one night without getting entirely carried away."

"And would that be so bad, Lily?" he purred against my mouth.

Inching my hand toward his chest I slid a few fingers between the buttons of his shirt and gripped the fabric, tugging him closer. "Absolutely not bad. When the time and place are right." I sighed. "But how *will* I pass for normal from now on?"

He snorted. "When did you ever pass for normal?"

"Mind yourself, or you'll be thirty feet in the air."

"Uh-oh." He smiled. "I almost forgot about that."

This would be a juggling act, keeping my feelings a secret. How would I manage it in the light of day? I imagined myself disregarding the draw of his eyes, teasing and beseeching in the same moment, or the way his hair fell carelessly about his forehead, or the temptation to hold him close. The idea that no one would notice was utterly simple-minded.

"It would be awfully obvious if we just started hanging around together all the time." I frowned.

He shrugged. "You underestimate my flair for subtlety. And there's always training," he said.

"We'll get nothing accomplished," I ribbed.

"Nonsense!" He feigned indignation. "I am a professional."

I grinned. "It's not you I'm worried about."

Fourteen

Today's the day!" Clara sang from the main hall as I braided Ginny's hair on the couch.

"The day?"

"Yes!" She walked in and stood behind us. "The big adventure. Peachtree Retirement Home, to be precise."

I kept braiding Ginny's hair, but cast a confused smile in Clara's direction.

"Retirement home. That *does* sound exciting," I said.

Clara frowned. "Anna has been rubbing off on you, Lily."

I laughed. "Sorry. Okay, what are we doing at a retirement home?"

"Not we, dear. *You.*"

"Me? What am I going to do?"

"A crossover," she said, pleased.

"A what?" I gaped. "Am I ready for that?"

"Yes. I'm sure you are."

"Whoa. Okay." I let go of Ginny's hair.

"Are you done?" Ginny hopped.

"Oh, uhm … almost," I said, grabbing her hair again and hurrying to finish. "Just … a few more strands and … all right. You're done!"

"Thanks! I'm gonna go play with Rufus, okay?" She slipped off the couch and ran out of the room.

Clara took Ginny's place next to me. "Anxious, love?"

"I don't know." I shrugged. "Maybe a little."

"Well, you have nothing to fear. William tells me you're quite efficient at holding his energy."

"Yeah, but that's William." I sighed. "He isn't hostile."

"Well, you didn't think I'd force a difficult soul on you your first time, did you? I'll make sure the spirit is reasonable before offering them to you."

"I'm grateful." I smiled.

"Always my pleasure." She looked at me warmly and placed her hand over mine. "Pardon my being forward, but there's something I wanted to ask you about."

"Sure."

"Lily, do bear in mind that I consider you one of my own. And so, entertaining certain mothering tendencies as I'm prone to do," she laughed at herself, "it would be negligible of me not to notice that you're simply dripping with happiness lately."

I smiled cautiously. "Am I?"

"Absolutely. And moreover, it seems to be quite a bit more pronounced when you're in—or have just *been* in—the company of a certain Sentient?" She raised an eyebrow, smirking.

"I … I don't know," I stammered, then blushed, looking down at Clara's lovely hands.

"Oh, now I've embarrassed you!" she said. "Lily, you must forgive me. I really had no right to say anything, but I couldn't help myself! I first noticed it in the few days after the Incubus attack. I'd expected you to be a wreck. I thought we'd have to do a whole mental wash. But that wasn't the case. And now, well … you're radiant! I'll admit I tried to finagle the information out of Anna just this morning, but the stubborn girl won't say a word to me, and that is simply not like her. Not that I don't understand why; it's just terribly silly of her to think that I wouldn't notice!" She patted my hand.

"I suppose so," I said, uncomfortably.

"Lillian … " She touched my cheek. "I won't say anything to Christian. I promise."

"Thank you." I breathed.

"But, I would ask you to be careful. With William."

"Ugh, Clara, not you too. He'd never hurt me; I know he wouldn't."

"No, no, you misunderstand me. I didn't mean it that way. I meant be careful with William's *heart*. There are few women who would be willing to love someone in his situation, and his chances at happiness are fractional compared to ours. Do be certain that your intentions are as strong as his before letting things escalate further."

Though her words delivered an initial sting, they also pleased me. She was trying to protect William.

"I will."

"As I imagined you would. Anna, you can stop eavesdropping now, dear," she said.

"Oh. Well, bugger." Anna stepped into the room.

I laughed at her. "You're shameless."

"Yes, quite!" she chirped. "Isn't it wonderful? Think of all the juicy tidbits I could tell you about."

"Well, you'd hardly be telling me anything I don't already know," I said.

"Now don't burst my bubble," she chastised. "I happen to be in the know about a lot more than you realize. I have connections."

"Right. And who might these connections be?" Clara asked, her hands on her waist.

"If you really want to know," Anna said scandalously, crossing quickly to the couch to squeeze in between us. "When our visitors arrive next week, it would be advisable not to get on Theo Rush's nerves. He's been having issues with his endowment lately."

"What sort of issues?" Clara asked

"You remember he can move things, right?"

"Yes."

"Well, when they visited Sydney a few weeks ago, he came into contact with a Blitzer." She widened her eyes.

"Oh, heavens! How dreadful," Clara moaned.

"I know. And ever since then, he's been all shorted out. He's been plucking things up and dropping them here and there, knocking everything over, pushing furniture about, tipping pictures off the walls, etcetera, etcetera."

"Sounds hilarious." I giggled. "Oops, was that inappropriate?"

"I hope not, because I couldn't stop laughing when Katrina told me," Anna said.

"And what the heck is a Blitzer, anyway?" I asked.

"It's a bewildering spirit," Clara explained. "It protects itself from attack by disorienting its pursuer mentally."

"Brutal," I said. "How long will he be all messed up?"

"Who knows? It happened to my husband once, and he wasn't right for months."

"Oh, I remember that!" Anna tittered. "Every time he tried to strangle a vampire, he'd choke himself!"

"Yes. Your brother had to sharpen his abilities rather quickly that year, I'm afraid," said Clara. "And how is Elaine handling her husband's befuddlement?"

"Oh, you know her." Anna threw her hands up. "She's giving him a time of it, bless him."

"Well, we shall be as delicate as possible about the whole issue then… even if he is incapable of delicacy himself at the present time," Clara concluded, chuckling at her last few words.

"So you see, my beautiful ladies," Anna said, wrapping her arms around both of us and pulling us close. "You mustn't hold my thirst for knowledge against me. It comes in handy."

"Keep telling yourself that, dear." Clara pinched her cheek. "But you're still a meddlesome little snot."

"Hmph!" Anna huffed. "I shall go and talk to Abram, then. He appreciates me." She stood up and went to leave, pausing in the archway to toss me a grin as William walked in.

"Time for a bit of lunch," Clara said, squeezing my hand.

William halted, mid-pace, to watch Clara leave, an eyebrow raised. "Have I done something wrong already? It's not even noon."

"No," I said. "They just … had things to do."

"Ah-ha." He sounded unconvinced, staring dubiously at me a little longer before smiling. "Did you sleep well last night?"

"Sure." I blushed.

"Hm. Well, I didn't."

"No?"

"Uh-uh." He stood behind the couch and leaned down, resting his arms on the back so that his head was next to mine.

"Why not?"

"I don't know. I had the craziest dream," he mused.

"Ha. Well, Sentients *do* have a lot of dreams."

"True, but this one was very vivid," he whispered in my ear, and my skin prickled.

"Was it?"

"Mmm." He brushed my hair to the side and moved his mouth to my neck. "Do you ever have dreams like that, Lily?"

Ooof. "Sometimes," I said, my voice wavering.

He laughed against my skin and stood up as the sound of a car engine fractured the moment. Seconds later Paul and Demetre walked in the house, arguing animatedly.

"Because I don't think it's appropriate!" Demetre barked.

"What? It could be fun, just us guys. Come on! You don't know what you're missing," Paul said, throwing his keys on the table by the front door.

"DePrimo, there is a lady present." Demetre glanced in my direction.

"And there would be a *lot* of ladies present if we do what I'm proposing." Paul nodded, pleased with himself.

"No way. Go peddle it elsewhere, boy," Demetre said, leaving Paul standing in the middle of the room alone.

"Huh." He shrugged. "Hey, William, would you—"

"No, thanks," William said quickly.

Paul let out a conquered sigh, and then perked up again. "I wonder … ," he began, taking off down the bedroom hallway.

"I'd like to pretend I don't have the slightest idea what he's up to … but I'm afraid I have a few." I laid my head back.

"Lillian." William tsked, sitting next to me. "You mustn't entertain those kinds of thoughts. They'll sully your innocence."

"Innocence?" I laughed.

"Yes. Hold on … ." He held a hand to his chest in mock horror. "Don't tell me you aren't innocent?"

"Well, it depends on what you mean by that," I said.

"You're over complicating this, Miss Hunt, but according to traditional sensibilities it means pure of thought and action."

"Pure? Are we talking filtered water or refined liquor?"

"Which do you prefer?"

I considered this. "Both, depending on the occasion."

"Hm. So your brand of purity is completely circumstantial," he teased me.

I laughed out loud. "Yes?"

"I see. Well, I *am* curious to know which occasions usurp your efforts at sainthood."

I cast him a wry smile. "You *would* be."

"What? Still convinced I'll use things against you?"

"Without a doubt."

"Smart," he said, an unholy edge to his tone. "The natives seem preoccupied. Think it's safe for you to venture a few inches closer?"

"At your own risk."

"Good thing I'm so daring then." He held out an arm.

I listened intently before moving. Things *were* awfully quiet. I hoped Anna wasn't snooping at the door again. With as lithe a motion as possible, I bridged the distance between us, leaning back against his arm.

"Better," he said.

"Is it?"

"It is."

"Why is that?" I asked distractedly, keeping a cautious ear open.

"Isn't it obvious?" He dipped his head and kissed my hair.

I smiled and tried to relax my body, realizing I'd been holding myself rigidly.

"Lily." He peered at me. "You are really truly nervous about this, aren't you?"

"A little," I admitted.

"A little? No, not a little." He sighed. "Hey …." He touched my face to get my full attention. "Do you regret what happened last night?"

I felt immediately remorseful as I realized the impression I was giving him. "No!" I said more loudly than I'd intended.

"No?" he urged.

"No," I spoke quietly. "I don't regret it. I can't function for thinking about it," I admitted.

He chuckled. "Good. You had me worried there for a minute."

"I'm sorry, William."

"It's okay," he said, but the fall in his expression left me uncertain.

I reached up to trace the lines of his face, pushing a lock of hair away from his eyes. I loved the strength of his jaw, the combination of gentle eyes and masculine structure.

"I don't regret it," I repeated.

He smiled, and as I slid my arm around his neck, he held my face with his free hand. This should have been one of those William moments that propelled me into oblivion, but instead he narrowed his eyes in aggravation. "Christian's coming," he said.

I pulled my arm away from him and moved to the other side of the sofa.

"How do you know?" I mouthed.

"Vampire thing." He sighed.

Sure enough, Christian emerged from the side hall, Paul on his heels.

"I'm not interested!" Christian grumbled.

"Well, this is just un-American," Paul goaded.

"Handy for me that I am *not* American." Christian swerved to a stop in the living room.

"Where are all the real men among Sentients?" Paul rallied. "Will no one go with me to see Cotton Candy Mandy?"

William choked on nothing, and what I'd hoped would be a quelled giggle on my part turned into full blown, rolling laughter. "What the hell, Paul?" I gasped.

"She's an exotic dancer! The best in the business, if you ask me. She's coming to Savannah at the end of the month, and I can't convince any of these schmucks to go with me. This is a once in a lifetime entertainment opportunity, people! We could make a night of it, stay in a fancy hotel."

"I'll go," Anna said, appearing in the doorway.

"*What?*" Christian blared, appalled.

"I want to go. I'll bring Katrina," she said to Paul.

"Well, *all right.*" Paul nodded, grinning smarmily. "Even better." He put his arm around Anna's shoulder, and she promptly dislodged it.

"Hands off."

"Anna, please tell me you're joking," Christian scoffed.

"Oh, Christian, sod off, you hopeless prude," she said, dismissing him.

William smiled approvingly.

"But you have no idea what sort of people hang about those places!" Christian argued.

"The horny male type, I'd suspect," said Anna. "And if you're so worried, then you should come with us!"

"Not fair," he said.

"Well? It makes sense. Join us. Just for a laugh!"

"Yeah, man, I'm telling you," Paul encouraged. "You'll come home with a smile on your face."

Christian sighed. "Jesus. Fine. But only as long as you're going," he said to Anna.

"Wicked!" Anna smiled.

"While we're recruiting …." Paul looked at me. "Lily, I don't suppose you'd—"

"Nope!" I said.

"Hmph. At least one of us is sensible," Christian mumbled. "So, are you excited to cross over your first astral, Lily?" he asked, changing topics.

"Sure." I smiled pleasantly while my stomach roiled.

"I look forward to seeing it," he said. Ugh. An audience.

"Lunch!" Clara called from the kitchen.

"Mmm. Food. I love you, Clara!" Paul called back, rubbing his stomach.

"Then you can do the dishes! Now come along while it's hot!"

Everyone filtered out of the room with the exception of Anna, who lagged behind.

"Cotton Candy Mandy should work out swimmingly for *all* parties." Anna winked at me and walked away.

Had she just single-handedly pulled off one of the most brilliant acts of scheming I'd ever seen? While Paul and his group of strip club attendees were out plugging dollar bills into some girl's g-string, William and I would have an entire night together … Christian-free. What an evil, unscrupulous character Anna was. I loved her so.

"Are you coming today?" I asked William.

"Do you want me to?"

"Yes, please."

"Well, then, I am," he said.

"Thanks." I smiled. "Somehow I don't think it will be the same as what we've practiced, though."

"Probably not. But just think about it, Lily. Once you've done this, you'll be, you know, official."

"Huh." I grinned proudly. "You're right."

"You always seem so surprised when that happens." He sighed.

"Yeah, sorry about that." I patted his knee.

"You are positively cruel," he admonished.

"I make up for it."

"Go eat." He nudged my shoulder with his own. "You'll need the energy."

The Peachtree Retirement Facility was far nicer than I'd expected. It didn't appear to be the kind of place where astrals hung around looking to be rescued—unless they were particularly attached to the extensive collection of video games.

"Ooo, virtual pinochle," Christian said, browsing the selection. "Because everyone knows how physically taxing the real thing can be."

"It probably is when Lily's playing," Anna complained.

"Oh, do try and focus." Clara hurried us along to the nurses' desk.

"Good afternoon, Clara!" the pretty young nurse greeted her.

"Afternoon, Rochelle." Clara smiled brightly.

"Here to see Mrs. Spanglin?"

"Yes, in fact we are. Is she in?" Clara asked.

"Actually, our hairdresser just took her for a spruce up. She should be back in a little while, though, if you want to wait."

"Thank you, that would be fine," Clara said.

"Okay, then, you folks have a nice visit!" Rochelle called after us.

We turned a corner and entered a bright hallway, the walls creamy yellow with a daisy border. Each door was crisp white. They were really trying hard to fight the stereotype, that's for sure. I'd seen my share of nursing homes in Pennsylvania, many of which had gray or green walls, worn out rugs, and smelled of stale urine. This place smelled like lemons. Or was it limes?

The sixth door on the left was Mrs. Spanglin's. Clara turned the knob, and I suddenly felt like a trespasser. "So, who is Mrs. Spanglin?" I asked, stepping inside.

"Ophelia's cousin," Clara said. "We've visited her several times since we came here. Mrs. Spanglin is not the reason I've brought you, though, Lily."

"I'd assumed as much."

"It's her roommate that's of concern."

"*Oh*," I said, catching on.

Mrs. Spanglin's room was very nice, albeit a little overdone with the pastels. Her walls were painted sky blue and her bed was made up with a buttercup yellow comforter and white bedposts. A creamy, oversized armchair took up a far corner, and an entertainment bureau, complete with essential media playing devices, stood against the wall in front of the bed.

"So, Mum? I've been thinking about retiring," Anna said.

I laughed. "No kidding. I can only imagine how much this place costs."

"You shouldn't try, dear. Ghosts are scary enough," Clara said.

William chuckled discretely behind me. I hadn't even heard him come in. He'd driven his own car, as usual.

It was definitely awkward with our personalities mixed together again, and this time in such close proximity. Christian did his best to ignore William's presence altogether, and William, as usual, played right along. He'd only bite when bitten.

What interested me more were their chosen stations in the room. William held back a little, while Christian stood close to my left. It was still assumed by all that this was the natural order of things, but it didn't *feel* natural anymore. I had to wrestle the urge to take a step back.

"Have you all noticed anything yet?" Clara asked.

"I think I've found her," Anna announced.

"Who? Where?" I swung my head around, but saw nothing.

"She hasn't really formed yet," Anna said. "And might not unless you do something about it."

"But how do you know where she is?" I asked.

"Well, she's formed a *bit*." Anna nodded to the arm chair. I peered closely, still seeing nothing. Approaching the chair, I examined it again. The area was generally colder than where I'd come from and my breaths came out in smoky puffs. Something was there all right, even if I *couldn't* see it yet.

"Christian, pull down the blinds, will you?" Clara said. He did as she asked, and the room went dark. I looked at the chair again, letting my eyes refocus in the lack of light. What I saw was beautiful. It was a shimmering, wisping cloud of the palest light possible, but it was there. I gasped.

"Aaand she's spotted her." Christian grinned.

I smiled. "Well, I mean, it's a her? It doesn't, she's not … ."

"She's appeared to me twice before," Clara said. "But I wanted to save her for you."

I sat down on the foot of the bed. "So, what do I do now?" I said, still watching the chair.

"Talk to her," Clara said.

"What's her name?" I asked.

"Don't know, I'm afraid. You might ask *her* that."

I was self-conscious, and though I knew all this was real, some part of me still felt stupid, sitting here talking to a chair in front of everyone.

Ah, well, I thought. *Here goes nothing.*

"Uhm …." I snuck a peripheral peek at my observers. All but one wore expressions of anticipation. William just smiled warmly. I blushed a little, and then regrouped.

"Hi," I said to the chair, glancing back at everyone. This was ridiculous. Did they all have to watch? William seemed to sense my discomfort and let his gaze fall to his shoes.

One down. Better than nothing. I just needed some courage and a little more faith.

"So…I'm Lily," I said. "Would you mind making yourself just a little more visible? I'm new at this, and…well, it would be really nice of you."

The shimmering mist simply billowed delicately. I sighed. "Please?"

Nothing. This was so embarrassing.

"Try telling her about yourself, Lily. Tell her something about your life," Clara urged.

"Okay." I thought for a moment. "I'm assuming you're from here," I said. "So you probably never really saw much snow, but when I was little, it snowed so much that we'd get an entire week off school. It was great! Until we realized that our summer vacation wouldn't begin until July."

The mist turned to fog. I kept talking.

"Well, regardless, those snow days were the only good part of winter in Scranton. Otherwise, it was frigid and gray and dark. And I hated it. I was really alone." I could feel my eyes welling up. "See, my mom left us when I was a baby, and my dad, he died of cancer when I was little. So, Frank and Connie, my grandparents, raised me. I used to take care of their store, before I came here. We sold some really interesting stuff."

The fog was starting to take on a shape, undefined, but getting there.

"They're really something, my grandparents. I miss them." I considered for a moment. "And my friend Kate." I stopped. This wasn't a subject I'd planned to talk about, but the silver mist in front of me was developing very human features, and I wasn't about to quit now. She seemed to like the personal stuff.

"Kate and I were best friends from childhood. She was the closest thing to a sister I've ever had. But … she couldn't handle the changes in my life. So, that didn't end so well." I looked down at my knees.

"That doesn't seem like a very nice friend," said a soft voice in front of me.

My mouth fell open. The sweet face of an old woman looked pitifully upon me. "Why didn't it end well, darling?"

My words caught in my throat as I tried to answer. I heard the happy sighs of Clara and Anna in the background. I beamed. "Well, I couldn't tell her what I was, you know? I mean, for the longest time I had no idea, anyway! And so when I came here, she couldn't accept it. She felt betrayed."

"My goodness. What on earth couldn't she accept? You're not a homosexual, are you, darling?" The old woman smiled pityingly. I choked back laughter. Anna and Clara giggled. I was glad the men couldn't hear her end of the conversation.

"No! No, no, no. No." I laughed, shaking my head. "I think that would have been easier for her to deal with. The truth is, I can help people who have died and don't know how to get where they need to go. Kind of lead them in the right direction, you know?"

"People who have died?" She puzzled over my words.

"That's right. You know? I can help them to the afterlife. Or, at least, I hope I can." I frowned at my own uncertainty.

"Well, that *does* seem a little far-fetched," the old woman said.

I laughed. "Not so far-fetched."

"You seem like a nice girl, though," she said. "So, I'll ask you."

"Ask me what?"

"Have you seen my Luther? I've lost him."

"Luther. Is that your husband?"

"Yes. Yes, he is. Do you know him?"

"I'm afraid I don't. What's *your* name?"

"Bonnie Pooltower," she said.

"Nice to meet you, Mrs. Pooltower. I'm sorry I don't know Luther, but I'm willing to bet I can get you to where he is."

"Really? Oh, that would wonderful of you," she said distantly.

"I'll need you to really pay attention, though, okay? I mean, look me right in the eyes so I can help you. You'll have to trust me. Can you do that?" I spoke as respectfully as possible.

"How will this help me find Luther?" she said. Detached spirit or not, this woman was no dummy.

"Well," I began. This *had* seemed too easy. "It's hard to explain. But it's worth a try, right?"

She looked confused, but shrugged. "If you say so."

So I locked eyes with her and worked to draw her in. Surprisingly, where I expected to be inundated by cold, her energy was, in fact, pleasantly warm. William was right. The visual astral presence was not the true essence of a soul.

I had to work much harder with Mrs. Pooltower than I had with William. He knew what I was doing…*she* didn't, and her cooperativeness waned as she sensed the change in her being. She looked afraid now.

"Don't be scared. I won't hurt you," I whispered as slow, irregular waves flowed toward me. Before long, the expected darkness set the backdrop, our light the only illumination.

"Well, what on earth?" she thought.

"Incredible, huh?" I responded.

"What have you done to me, exactly? Where are we?"

"In a place where I can make you understand," I thought back.

"Well, someone should, and quickly."

"You're a spirit, Bonnie. You've been haunting the bedroom of a rest home. Didn't you realize that you'd died?"

She gasped. "No! I mean, I can only remember being terribly mixed-up all the time. It was just like being lost in a dream. Are you an angel?"

I laughed in my head. "No. I'm just a human, but I can do some helpful things. You asked me before, about Luther. Do you remember that?"

"Luther? Oh, my poor Luther," she said, her sadness washing over me. "I lost him in 2000. After that, I kept falling, forgetting. My children put me in a retirement home. When did I die?"

"I don't know, I'm sorry. But you don't have to suffer, Bonnie. Your soul is meant to move on."

"Will I be with my husband?"

"In one way or another, I'd say yes."

"Then how do I get there?"

This part Clara had explained. Sometimes you just needed to point out the obvious.

"It's very dark around here, isn't it?" I thought to her.

"Yes. It is."

"It's a good thing. It makes that light over there really easy to spot."

Her energy shifted its direction. "Oh," she thought, mystified. "How could I have missed it? It's *breathtaking.*"

Of course, I couldn't see the light. It was only for her eyes. But as long as she could find it, that's all that mattered. "Just walk right into it, Mrs. Pooltower. It's for you."

"My God. Are you sure?"

"Absolutely."

"And that's it? It's that simple."

"Always has been," I said.

"Oh, darling. Thank you!" And then, in a new experience for the both of us, her light flashed brilliant white, and I thought I'd be incinerated before I found myself on the foot of the bed in Mrs. Spanglin's room, staring at a truly empty chair.

Laughter and cries of happiness filled the room as arms pressed around me and kisses landed on my head and cheeks.

"Lily, you did it!" Anna squeezed me a little too hard. "Absolutely fantastic!"

"I'm so proud of you, dear," Clara gushed. "You have no idea."

"You were perfect," Christian said, smiling tenderly before sitting by my side. "Just perfect." He rested his hand on my back. I looked at William. He'd crossed the room with the rest of them, but remained safely out of the circle. There was something in his gaze that seemed off. Despite his attempt at a quick smile, I knew he was hurt. His should have been the first and most important acknowledgment. He had, after all, been the one to show me what I was capable of.

"I couldn't have done this without your help," I said, clearly speaking to William. "In fact, there's a lot I couldn't have done without your help."

Christian's hand fell from my back, his stature stiffening.

William allowed me a real smile. "It's all you, Lily. You just need somebody to urge you on, that's all."

"Well, you guys are the reason I am where I'm meant to be," I said, looking at them all in turn. "I love you all."

Christian's expression softened, and he rested his hand over mine. "Things weren't half as interesting before you came along," he said.

"Glad to keep you awake."

"We should celebrate!" Anna said. "Why don't we go out and do something fun? Lily, you decide!"

I considered my options. "I think I have an idea."

❧

I'd demanded that William come with us, and even went so far as to insist on riding with him to ensure his presence. This didn't sit well with Christian, of course, but I was determined, so he backed off.

"Is this really the best idea you could come up with?" William complained as he drove.

"What? It'll be fun!"

"Will it, now? I have my reservations …."

"Just ignore him. He's the only one with the problem."

"Yeah, well, he's vocal enough for everyone."

"William …." I frowned, as we slowed at a yellow light and came to a stop. "If you weren't coming, I wouldn't enjoy myself."

"That's crazy, Lily."

"It is *not*. I…William … God."

"What?"

I clenched my fists. "Pull over."

"No."

"Pull … over."

"Lily, they'll wonder—"

"We'll tell them we got stuck in traffic! This won't take long."

He sighed, but then he pulled off into the parking lot of a pet supply store. "What is it?" He looked at me.

"You can't avoid being around me just because Christian is, you know," I said.

"I know," he grumbled. "I thought I'd be fine, but … it's surprisingly frustrating, watching him touch you without the luxury of saying anything. And worse, not being the first one to grab you up and kiss you back there …." He laughed bitterly. "Well, it was more difficult than I thought it would be. I suppose I'll just need to work on flipping the switch in my mind between night and day. I'm sorry, Lily."

Once again I mentally kicked myself. Why *wouldn't* this be bothering him? It was bothering me and I wasn't despised by Christian—yet.

"*I'm* sorry," I said. "I'm sorry things are the way they are right now. I know it's not fair to you."

He stared at the storefront.

"William, please. Forgive me."

He laid his head back on his headrest. "I'm not angry with you, Lily," he said finally. "It's okay. I really am happy for you. And I'll try to enjoy myself, I promise." He turned and smiled at me, stroking my face quickly with the palm of his hand. "Now, let's get going before Christian comes looking for us."

The Pirate's Cove Adventure Mini Golf course in Duluth was just as predictable as every other mini golf course I'd ever seen—which was the beauty of it. Something conventional, a distinctly non-astral distraction. People rarely died playing putt-putt golf. It was perfect.

"What took you so long?" Christian grumbled as we approached the game booth.

"Traffic," I lied flippantly.

"Oh. Well, it wasn't bad for us."

I shrugged. "The roads like you, Christian."

We paid for our game and picked out some balls and appropriate sized clubs according to height. William's and Christian's were considerably longer than the rest of ours, and I felt a new surge of camaraderie with Anna and Clara. It was nice not being the shortest one in a group all the time.

"So, are you actually any good at this or do you just enjoy embarrassing yourself?" Anna asked.

"I could never really figure that out," I said. "One game I might slaughter the opposition, the next I end up with the worst score on the card. Maybe I just like to smack things with sticks."

She laughed. "I have those days."

"Well, regardless, I'm feeling lucky. I think I might win," I said.

Christian raised an eyebrow. "We'll see."

"Be polite, dear," Clara smiled.

"No, no, it's too late," I said. "Now it's on."

"I don't know. My dad and I used to play a *lot*. I'm pretty good, Lily," Christian warned.

"Put your money where your mouth is."

He laughed. "Are you always this competitive?"

"*Yes*," said William and Anna in unison.

I looked around, aghast. "Traitors."

"Hey, it's every man for himself," Anna defended.

"You know." I smiled as adorably as I could. "You could all just let me win, as I *am* the guest of honor."

They stood still for a moment, silent and blank faced.

"Pff! Dream on," Anna said as William snorted.

I scowled. "Wouldn't want to lose by forfeit anyway," I mumbled as they started down a hole.

The first three holes went quite well. My score was one under par. But hole four was a doozey, and I was the last one to go. Christian and William lagged behind, while Anna and Clara watched from the end. There was a hill to make it over, and then once you'd managed that, a series of jutting stones to navigate. I could choose to try and straight shoot it, or throw in some strategy, pinging the ball off the stones at just the right point. I stood, eyes narrowed, deciding on a method of action.

"You know, if you just hold the club a little bit closer and don't tilt the tip forward so much, you'd have an easier time of aiming," Christian suggested.

I threw him a look. "Advice? I don't remember asking for any advice."

"No, but you want to win, don't you?"

I ignored him.

"Come on, Lily, seriously, give it a try."

I held the club closer and fidgeted with the angle.

"Nope, almost, but look …." Christian swooped in, wrapping his arms around mine from behind. "Just like this." He adjusted my club. "Now swing."

I took a shot, and the ball bounded over the hill and disappeared.

"Lily! Hole in one!" Anna squealed from the bottom of the hill.

"See?" Christian smiled and kissed me on the cheek lightly before letting go and walking down to his ball.

I was terrified to look at William. I couldn't do it. Oh Lord, I hoped he hadn't seen it. But I knew he had. I stood completely still, afraid to move for a moment, then turned around slowly. William was still there.

"He's only going to keep getting bolder with you," he said. I couldn't remember the last time he'd looked this perturbed.

"I don't know why," I huffed.

"Don't you?" He raised his eyebrows, his sudden smile filled with frustration.

I said nothing. I was a giraffe. If I just closed my eyes, the lions wouldn't see me.

"Let's go, Lily." He walked on.

Afraid of Christian stepping in again, I played each shot with every bit of skill I could dredge up and, as a consequence, we managed to make it through the rest of the game with little occurrence. By the second to last hole, my score was better than ever. Still, I wasn't in the clear yet—there was that blasted final hole to tackle, and it would tap me dry. It had a water feature and nothing on the sides to keep the ball from plunking into the artificially blue depths.

I'd watched everyone fail miserably. Anna lost her ball completely and had to get a new one. William was the only one to actually stay out of the water.

My plan was to give it a quick hard whack as straight as I could, try to bypass the obstacles—but it failed. The ball flew up in the air and pelted against the fake cave side, dropping with a splash into the stream. I could see it being carried into the cave. "Crap!" I cringed and chased after it. William followed.

"Where are you going?" Christian asked.

"To get my ball," I called back but kept moving.

"I'll come!" he offered, eyeing William unhappily.

"Oh Jesus, Christian," Anna whined loudly. "It doesn't take more than two people to find a ball. Finish your hole so I can!"

Her complaint must have worked, because Christian didn't follow. The lights in the cave were dim, but the water beds were lit from below and glowed turquoise. A fake waterfall trickled down the middle wall. Where was that damn ball? I looked around, searching the pool.

William had followed along behind me, double checking what I'd already passed.

"Are you mad at me?" I said, only pretending to look now.

"No. Of course not."

"But you're angry that I made you come."

"Actually, I'm glad you made me come. It's helped me see a few things more clearly with regards to Mr. Wright."

"Like what?" I asked.

He scoffed at the question.

"Never mind, it doesn't matter," I said.

"It matters, Lily."

"Well, then, *tell* me," I insisted.

"Think hard. This is your specialty, Lily. You figure it out. And quickly, please, before things get even more complicated."

His words struck a blow and I was hurt, but I tried not to show it. Turning to look for my ball again, I wiped away the descending tears as quickly as they appeared. If my vision hadn't been skewed, I would have seen the wet patch and bypassed it. But, as fate would have it, I didn't and slipped backwards. William caught me mid-air, saving me from a quick and thorough soaking.

He held on for a moment, letting me steady myself, then let go.

"Lily, what's the hold up?" Anna shouted down the wet path. "Haven't you found it yet?"

"Not yet," I said, casually. "I think it's a lost cause. I'll keep looking a minute more. Just go on and play the last hole without me."

"Fine. You'll still win anyway. But hurry up! I can't stall him forever, you know," she said and then left.

William sighed. "I'm ruining the game for you."

"No. It's not ruined." I stared to the side, hoping he wouldn't see the stupid tears.

"Lily, were you crying?"

"No," I said defensively.

"Shit. Lily, you were."

"Just forget it."

"I don't think so," he said sharply.

"William," I snapped. "Let it go!"

"No!"

I glared at him in exasperation, and then sighed, dropping my eyes.

"Hey," he spoke quietly, reaching into his pocket. "I found your ball."

I looked up and he was smiling cautiously, holding it up.

"When?" I asked.

"When we first came in here," he admitted.

"Why didn't you tell me?" I laughed.

"To buy myself some time."

"For what?"

"To congratulate you."

He lowered his head quickly and covered my mouth with his, and once I realized what was happening, I grabbed a hold of his hair, crushing him closer. If Christian had walked in now, he'd have to pry us apart with a crowbar and dynamite.

William tore his lips away. "So, how was … *God*, fuck it," he whispered, diving back in to kiss me again. I laughed against his lips.

"William," I spoke when I could. "We really … need to get … back … ."

He nodded but held my face in his hands, prolonging the last few seconds of the kiss before breaking away a fraction at a time. Soon only our foreheads rested together.

"Bear with me, Lily," he recovered. "I've been waiting to do that all day."

I smiled. "Remind me to put things off till the last moment more often."

"Pitiless." He chuckled, pulling me out of the cave.

We released hands once we reached the exit, and rejoined our group at the end of the course.

"Well?" Christian said, looking at me expectantly.

"Well what?"

"The ball?"

"Oh! Uhm, yeah, just found it."

"After all that? You were in there for like five minutes, Lily!"

I shrugged. "We were being thorough."

William coughed to cover a laugh.

"What's his problem?" Christian sneered.

"Cave air," I said. Anna giggled.

"Well, are we all going to stand here and discuss missing balls or can we get a bite to eat?" Clara asked.

"I trust Maddox won't be needing to join us for that part?" Christian stared defiantly in my direction. I opened my mouth to argue, but William was already shaking his head to stop me.

"Nope. I am good." William grinned, cheerfully. "Thanks for the beat down, Lily. Ladies." He nodded at Clara and Anna, smirking at Christian as he passed.

"What the hell is he so happy about?" Christian asked, watching William leave.

Clara smirked at me. "Indian food then?" she said.

❧

To be enthralled again was a chilling prospect. But where better could I pull off such a practice than in the company of my trainer? Christian would have wrung my neck. He would have positively set the forest on fire if he'd known my plans for today's session. Thus, I was keeping it to myself.

Of course, there were *other* reasons to maintain a kind of quiet air around training anymore. The most appealing of which met me half way down the path on my way to the woods.

"Afternoon, Ms. Hunt." William matched my stride as I stared straight ahead, suppressing a smile with all my might. I had to think subtle. We were still within eyeshot of the house, after all.

"Afternoon," I offered.

"Ready to reveal the big mystery?"

"I suppose it's safe now," I said, leaving the path behind and grazing my hands across the first of several tree trunks. "I want you to enthrall me, William." I stopped, turning to gage his reaction.

He cocked an eyebrow. "You want me to what?" he laughed.

"Enthrall me," I said, and then I blushed. Why did it sound so much like a come on? For that matter, just being in William's presence was becoming one massive unspoken suggestion. It was maddening.

"Oh, *really*." He smiled, crossing his arms.

"Really," I nodded. "I want to see if I can break free. Teach me to fight it, William."

"It's not easy, you know. You might not be able to at first," he cautioned.

"So, then we'll do it again and again and again. Until I can," I assured him.

"All right. But," he began, his brows furrowing. "I … I don't …."

"You don't what?"

"I don't like this, Lily. I don't relish the idea of enthralling you. I haven't put it into play since my change, and I'd hoped not to ever again, frankly."

"Oh," I said and glanced at the forest floor. What was I thinking, asking him to do this? Wasn't I really asking him to teach me how to fight *him*? In effect, mocking his attempts to be human? I hoped he hadn't taken it that way.

"You know," I said, stepping closer to him. "This was a lousy idea. There are other ways I could learn. Let's go over those."

He thought for a moment. "Nope. You've got a point. This could be a valuable lesson for you. Come on." He took me by the arm and we cut further into the trees, stopping when we'd reached a small opening.

"Okay. Stand still," he ordered, then placed his hands on my shoulders. "What do you notice first?" He stared at me intently.

"Your eyes," I whispered.

"What about them?" he asked.

"They're amazing," I said.

"They're … *Lily*," he half-scolded. "I mean it." He tried to look stern, but a smile broke through and his face lit up. Oh, this was going to be harder than I'd expected. I was going all shmoopy. This was our first bit of defensive training since we'd made our feelings known, and it was already hell to focus on the task at hand

"Uhm …." I chewed my lip, concentrating on his face. "You're not blinking," I said.

"Right. That's true. If you can get me to blink, or distract me somehow, that may give you a necessary instant to repel me. But with my being so close, it will be pretty damned hard."

"Okay. So … are vampires ticklish?" I asked.

He laughed. "I'm afraid not."

"Hm. Scratch that, then." I sighed.

"Are you?" he asked.

"Am I what?"

"Ticklish." He raised an eyebrow.

"Considerably," I admitted.

"Figured," he said. "Empaths are incredibly responsive … in every way." He smirked, suggestively.

I pressed my lips together and smiled, looking to the side. "*Any*way," I went on. "Back to the enthralling …. How about if I ask you a serious question?"

"Okay." His shit-eating grin broadened briefly before the teacher returned. "What's that?"

"How are vampires able to do it? How does enthralling work?"

"I don't know," William began, "other than to say that some animals are fashioned with venom, some razor sharp teeth, others claws. Since vampires retain intellect, their minds are their primary hunting mechanism."

"It would sound almost natural if it weren't so completely …."

"Unnatural?" he finished my thought.

"Right, exactly." I nodded. "So … can we go again?"

"Sure," he said, then exhaled through his nose and held me firmly. Every muscle of my body went limp at once. While my legs were as heavy as anvils, my mind was light, empty. I stared at him happily. I felt fantastic! High as a kite. Higher, in fact. William was even more handsome than normal. Was he always this good looking? Oh, well, who cared? I didn't. In fact, there was a remarkable absence of caring going on. William sighed sternly.

"Lillian." He scowled, releasing me. My body felt normal at once.

"Mmm?" I smiled, senselessly.

"Did you even try?"

"Try what?" I breathed.

"Try to fight me off? Remember? The whole point of this little exercise?"

"Oh. Oh, right. Sorry. Got distracted."

"By my eyes, right?" he teased.

"Well, you *are* kind of making it difficult for me to concentrate," I complained.

"Am I? How so?" he asked.

"I don't know. I mean, we're all alone out here, and you're all … you know, and I'm having a difficult time with the focus, right now. I feel like we need an ice breaker."

"I'm all 'you know'?" he taunted. "What exactly *is* 'you know'? 'Cause I'm just trying to do my job here, Lily," he pestered, but his eyes flashed playfully.

"Fuck, William, you're … well, come on! You know!" I threw up my hands, flustered.

"I have *no* clue what you're getting at," he said. "But for the sake of successful instruction, what would you suggest as an ice breaker?"

"Uuh … tell me a joke?" I shrugged.

He laughed at me. "A joke? Not a problem. I can do that," he said, leaning his head down and pressing his lips to my ear. "Knock knock," he whispered. Goose bumps spread along my arms and across my chest.

"Wh … who's there?" I giggled, breathing quickly.

He chuckled before answering. "Who do you *want* to be there, Lily?" he whispered.

"Okay … not helping!" I lamented, gripping the sides of my shirt so hard I felt the hem rip a little.

He grinned as he straightened up again. "At least let me get to the punchline," he said.

Before I could tell him to spare me, he'd grabbed me around the waist and pulled me into his arms, kissing me with no small force. My toes were curling. My toes were mother-fucking curling! It was a mother-fucking toe-curling kiss.

As a matter of fact, every part of my body was curling, throbbing, pulsing, or otherwise threatening to cave in. And his hands were wandering, down my spine, up my back, into my hair. His tongue had easily coaxed mine out of hiding, and, much to my arousal, it was William making the noises now. Who in the hell needed a goddamn training session anyway? He pulled away, working to breathe.

"I'm sorry, but no one would laugh at that joke, William," I barely said. "That wasn't in the least way funny."

"All right," he panted, pressing his forehead to mine. "True. But the ice is shattered to pieces now, right?" He smiled with his eyes closed.

"Melted, in fact." I laughed.

"Perfect." He ran his hand along my neck. "Then we can go on?"

"Oh, absolutely. Please, go on." I beamed woozily.

"I meant with the enthralling." He laughed.

"Ah. The enthralling." I sighed. "Well, it *was* my idea, so fine. Enthrall away."

He stepped back and this time took my hand in his. Again, my body split in half, my legs nailed to the earth, my head floating pleasantly above it. I attempted to speak, to say something about how beautiful it all was, but nothing came out. My goodness, but life was blissful perfection. Everything was ideal. Still, I couldn't help feeling like there was something, some small little sliver of something I was supposed to be doing. What was it again? I sighed inwardly, tapping at the tree of my memory for a bit of recognition. William would know. I should ask him. Then ....

"Oh," I said, and the fog began to lift. "Wait … William?" My hand slipped from his and I could see again.

"I'm here." He smiled. "You actually let go of me. That's extraordinary, Lily. I thought perhaps you'd become cognizant for an instant, but not that."

"It was easier this time, though," I explained. "When I was with Lolial, I only managed to make noise. It did seem to distract him for a second, but I couldn't move an inch."

"You were able to break Lolial's concentration?" William looked utterly stunned.

"Ehn, well, only for a few seconds. I mean, I still couldn't move or anything."

"Lily," he spoke softly, shaking his head. "Time has an opposite effect on vampires than it does on humans. The older a vampire gets, the stronger his abilities, the more unbreakable his grasp. Do you realize how old Lolial was?"

I shook my head.

"He was four hundred years old, Lillian. You threw off a four-hundred-year-old vampire." He smiled on, looking incredibly proud.

"I did?" I asked.

"Yes! Shit." He gazed at me. "You're insane."

"I am not!" I grumbled.

"In a good way!" He laughed.

"How can one be mentally off balance in a good way?" I glared at him.

"I meant insanely gifted. You're too much. More than anyone deserves," he said, and his smile faded.

"William, you're mistaking me for someone else. I'm annoying and judgmental, remember?" I took his hand.

"That's right." His smile returned, but weakly. "I remember you."

Fifteen

"Anna, stop cleaning!" I ordered, pulling a worn sponge from her hand and tossing it in the sink as I passed.

"Do that one more time and I'll get the vacuum out!" she threatened, grabbing it up again. I paused, watching her scrub madly at the kitchen counters. The Sentients from California would arrive today and Anna hadn't slept a wink the night before. *She* hadn't slept, and so, in turn, I hadn't either. Neither had Christian or Clara, as Anna flitted between our three rooms in various states of distress.

"What if she sees me, realizes how dull I am, and can't remember why she fell for me to begin with?!" she'd lamented, working the strings of my comforter into tattered strands.

"Impossible, Anna my love," I'd assured her, yawning. "You are perfectly wonderful and anything but plain."

"But you *have* to say that," she'd protested. "Because you love me."

"No," I corrected her. "I have to say that because I am far too tired to lie."

Elaine and Theo Rush, Chris and Laura Polmieri, Katrina Winguard, and Wendell Russettman, their Seer, were slated to arrive in less than an hour. The house had been cleaned thoroughly and repeatedly, yet Anna continued to bear down with savage hostility upon its surfaces. If they didn't get here soon, I'd have to hide the Spic and Span.

Christian trudged into the kitchen, dragging some chairs behind him.

"Still cleaning?" He shook his head, stacking the chairs next to the table. He grabbed an orange from the counter.

"Don't eat those!" Anna snapped and stole the fruit from his hand. "I had them arranged perfectly!"

"But I'm starving." Christian frowned. "You wouldn't let us eat breakfast, after all."

"I gave you the option of going out to eat," she reminded him.

"I was too busy fetching things for you!" he argued.

"Well, don't you have an arm you can gnaw on? Go and get the rest of the chairs, Christian."

"You are maniacal!" he groaned, storming out of the room.

"Anna." I sighed, wearily.

"*What?*" She glared, arms akimbo.

"Don't you think you're acting just ever so slightly … fractionally … nearly imperceptible amounts of tyrannical?"

She huffed. "Certainly not!"

I stared at her a moment longer.

"All right, perhaps a *little*," she acknowledged. "But someone has to keep things in order!"

I looked at her beseechingly. "Let the boy eat. One less citrus fruit won't throw the whole house in disarray."

"*Fine,* then." She gave in, handing me an orange. "But a nice specimen of manhood he is, going all puny at one lost meal," she grumbled.

I shook my head and went outside to find her brother.

"Hey!" I waved the orange at Christian as he pulled extra seats from the storage shed.

"You're an angel!" He dropped the chairs, taking the fruit from me and sitting on the ground. "Join me?"

"Sure." I settled onto the lawn next to him. I was wearing shorts and the blades of grass poked at my thighs.

"Wonder how many bugs are crawling against my legs right now." I squirmed.

"Lucky bugs." He flung a piece of orange peel behind him.

"Christian! That was such a guy-ish thing to say." I laughed.

He raised an eyebrow. "Have I ever given the impression I was anything else?"

"Well, no. It's just that sometimes I forget, you know? Because you're Christian."

"I see." He nodded, his face falling. "And so, you rarely look at me as a man then—strictly as Christian?"

"I … huh?" I puzzled.

He sighed and smiled. "Nothing, Lil, have some orange."

"I don't want any … ."

"Have some bloody orange, Lil, please!" He laughed exasperatedly.

"Right, taking some orange now." I rolled my eyes. "What is *with* you people today? I mean, Anna's in love, what's your excuse?"

He gagged on a bite of fruit, his eyes watering.

"Are you okay?" I asked, leaning over to smack him between the shoulders.

"Good, fantastic." He coughed, red in the face.

"Do you need a drink?"

"No!" He shook his head, lifting a hand; then he jumped up and grabbed two arm-loads of folding chairs. "Break's over," he said, rushing toward the back porch.

"Uhm … okaaay." I ran up behind him. "Let me help you with those."

"Not necessary. I've got them, thanks." He shot down the bedroom hallway and around the corner. I gave up on following him and slowed to a stop in the middle of the reception hall.

"What's with Golden Boy?" Paul looked up from reading a sports magazine on the couch.

I sighed. "I'm not positive, but I think I've insulted his masculinity."

"Hm. Those Brits are sensitive guys." He snorted.

"I guess so," I said.

"Now *my* masculinity is completely intact. I could probably give him some pointers," he offered in all seriousness.

I laughed. "I'm sure you could, Paul."

Something broke with a glassy splatter in the kitchen.

"Oh, no!" I heard Anna's dread-ridden cry as she rushed out into the hall. "I'm not ready!" She looked at me, horrified.

"Ready for what?" I asked.

"They're here!" Her voice was so shrill it could have split an atom.

"They are?" Then the doorbell rang. "Oh. Wow. So they are."

"Lily, hide me!" She squealed, grabbing my hand.

I giggled. "Are you nuts, Anna? No!"

"Ugh, I'm going to die, I know I am." Her face was twisted with apprehension.

"Annelise, get a grip!" I demanded.

"Okay." She breathed deeply for a moment. "Okay."

"You," I began, looking at her with complete concentration, "are so, so very beautiful. Don't answer that!" I stopped Paul as he went for the front door. He peered at me oddly but backed away. "There is nothing about you that this girl could have lost interest in. And my guess is she's been just as terrified as you," I told her.

"Can't open it yet," Paul informed Demetre, Ophelia, and Thomas as they entered the room.

I went on. "Imagine what it took for Katrina to travel all this way, the hours of anticipation. She didn't have a house to clean. She's probably suffering more than you are. And here we are, making the poor thing wait outside!"

Anna smiled.

"Now, *you* get the door," I finished. By now, everyone in the house was waiting impatiently. Anna nodded, then took a few quick steps forward and opened the door bravely.

It was easy to pick out the Polmieris and Rushes based on what I'd been told, all four being middle-aged. Laura and Chris Polmieri were an eclectic looking pair. Chris, were it not for the ratty jeans, could have been a college professor in his dress shirt and tie, while Laura wore a long billowing skirt and ruffled blouse, the collar cluttered with layers of beads. Her salt and pepper hair reached the small of her back.

The Rushes were considerably shorter than their counterparts, and dressed more conventionally in jeans and T-shirts. Elaine and Theo couldn't have been more contradictory in their physical appearance. Theo was a pale, plump man, balding and jolly faced, and his wife looked to be of Native American decent, with chocolate brown hair and bronze skin. She had an exquisite figure for her age.

You'd think I'd have been used to an array of people by now, but for a Seer, Wendell was a surprise. He wore his long white hair in a ponytail and was sporting the most colorful Hawaiian shirt I'd ever seen—my mind conjured hippies at a luau.

Still, the inner spotlight was placed most ceremoniously upon Katrina Winguard. There was certainly no mistaking who *she* was. You only had to look for the excessively beautiful green eyes and head of red glossy curls staring lovingly at Anna. Talk about useless worrying.

"Anna." She smiled. "You look amazing."

I couldn't help mimicking their expressions. The vibes passing between them were incredibly strong.

"I've … missed you." Anna blushed. Well, this was uncomfortable—touching—but uncomfortable.

Katrina squealed quickly before leaping forward and enfolding Anna in a massive hug. Everyone laughed. I wiped away a few stray tears.

"Well, come in, come in!" Abram broke out, grinning. He'd been waiting good-naturedly by my side the whole time.

The group stepped inside and greeted everyone with embraces and pats on the back. I stood by, watching happily. Christian laughed as Chris made a joke, and I was glad to see his ego wasn't too badly bruised. William had joined us, undetected as usual, and was observing the scene with a cautious smile. We shared an understanding glance. I didn't know a single one of our guests, and he felt like the perpetual interloper.

"And this is our Lillian," Abram introduced me proudly.

"Ah, the pathcrosser!" Chris smiled.

Laura took my hand. "Yes! Finally we can put a face with the name."

"Oh, Wendell," Elaine spoke. "It's like stepping back in time."

Wendell nodded. "She even has her smile."

Elaine continued to stare at me in astonishment. "My God. You look *so* much like your mother," she said.

"I do?" I spoke for the first time.

"Yes! Oh, Theo, look at her!" She touched my face, her eyes watering.

Theo stepped forward. "Well, now. How about that."

"I'm Elaine Rush." She took my hand. "Your mom and I were close friends."

"You were?" I asked.

"Yes. I was her maid of honor, you know!"

"No. I didn't know that," I said with a twinge of melancholy.

"And this is my husband, Theodore."

He extended his hand, and I went to take it when a jolt sent me slamming backward into the front door. I slid down to the floor, dazed. William laughed out loud.

"Lily!" Christian rushed over to me. "It's not funny, Maddox," he hissed.

Elaine groaned and Theo looked mortified. "Oh, Lillian, I am *so* sorry!" he said as he bent to help me.

"Wait!" Elaine shouted. "Don't touch her. Don't … touch … *any*thing!" she reprimanded. Theo looked affronted, but stayed put nonetheless.

Christian pulled me to my feet, holding me around the waist.

"Uhm," I began, my body aching. "What just happened?"

"My fool of a husband repelled you," Elaine said, glaring at him.

My jaw dropped. "Oh." I giggled slightly, remembering Theo's condition. "It's no big deal. I was overdue for one of those, anyway." I made a face at William, who chuckled quietly in the corner.

"Good-natured of you," Laura laughed. "We haven't tolerated it quite so well, have we, folks?" She shared a knowing expression with her group.

"Yes, well, I'm sure there are a few things Wendell and I can come up with to help," Abram offered. "We'll find a way to speed the process of recovery along, not to worry."

Theo looked relieved.

"How about something to eat?" Clara suggested. "Let's have some dinner while Christian brings your things in."

Christian peered at her, and she smiled sweetly. I felt bad for him. He just couldn't seem to beg his way to a lump of stale bread. He released me and slumped, browbeaten, out to their cars. Everyone made for the kitchen and William strolled up behind me.

"Not so pleasant, is it?" he smirked.

"Zip it, William," I sang, smiling.

"Oh, no way. You'll be hearing about this for *months*," he said.

"Bite me," I said, turning to leave.

He grabbed my arm and touched his lips to my ear. "Tempting. But now's not the time."

Oh, Lord have mercy. Where was a dark corner I could drag him into? I looked around to ensure the room was empty before thrusting him against the wall and kissing him a bit too enthusiastically. The action took him off guard, so much so that he barely had a chance to respond before I dashed out of the hall and into the kitchen.

Sixteen

So, an actual cemetery?" Katrina balked, fanning herself with her hand. We sat on the top step of the back porch, watching Paul, Demetre, Chris, Theo, and Christian play horseshoes. Paul was winning and did the occasional touchdown dance for what he perceived to be our benefit.

"Yes!" Anna swore. "It's at the Mount Lorna chapel in Ruthersville, South Carolina."

"Where is Ruthersville?" I asked.

"Western edge of the state," Anna said. "I've been doing some research."

"Before you launch your seminar on topography, why would Abram want us to go there?" Katrina questioned. "You know as well as I do that cemeteries are rarely haunted. They're a waste of time."

"This one is different," Anna insisted. "I'm telling you. He says it's a big deal."

"Ghosts … in a cemetery … ." Katrina shook her head.

"I didn't say ghosts," Anna went on. "It could be anything. And who knows if the astral is even attached to the cemetery? It could be the church, or even the grounds."

"Hm. Well, who all is going?" Katrina asked.

"The pathcrossers, obviously," Anna said. "So, Mum, me, Lily. We'll have to bring a combatant, of course. Probably Paul or my brother."

"Elaine would do it!" Katrina smiled.

"Ooh, good idea!" Anna said.

"Wait, Elaine's a combatant?" I said, astonished.

"And a damn good one, too," Katrina boasted. "Maybe we can make a whole thing out of it," she said. "We can leave the men behind and escape to Ruthersville for the night."

"Somehow I doubt Ruthersville has much to escape to," I said.

"No matter. She has a point," Anna said. "It would be fun to spend a little quality time with just us females."

The idea may have been appealing to them, but it was a rare chance for William and I to be alone together and I was feeling deprived right about now. I frowned.

"Oh. You don't want to go?" Katrina asked.

"What? Of course I do," I said.

"No … you clearly do *not*," she argued.

"Why would you say that?" I laughed apprehensively.

"Because you thought so," she answered, a look of remorse on her face.

"I'm sorry?"

Anna pursed her lips and winced. "Oops. Lily, I'm afraid I've neglected to tell you something."

Katrina nodded in agreement. "But it should really be me who tells her," she said.

"All right," Anna said. "You'd better do it then."

"Uhm …." Katrina turned to me. "My endowment … I can, I'm …."

Anna gave her an encouraging smile.

"I can hear people's thoughts," Katrina blurted out, then closed one eye, watching me from the other.

I must have turned red, because she rushed to damage control.

"But only when I need to!" she said quickly. "I mean, I try to block them out. I do a good job of it! But, things do kind of fall out of people's heads a little too loudly sometimes," she offered with a sulk.

I thought as quietly as I could for a moment. "Huh," I said, finally. "So … what exactly did you hear, then?"

She hesitated. "You really want me to say? Exactly as I heard it?"

"I'm not sure." I squirmed. "But go ahead anyway."

"Okay. Well, you'd rather be with William."

"Shit," I said, wrapping my hands around my head to protect my brain.

"It's okay!" She smiled. "Anna told me about you two."

I was tempted to give Anna a scathing look, but there was no point. If she and Katrina were this close *and* Katrina was a mind reader, what did I expect? You had to learn to give up a certain level of privacy as a Sentient.

"Just don't say anything to anyone," I begged. "You have to understand, this is *not* uncomplicated. Christian would turn green and bust through his clothing," I said.

"I know, believe me. I can hear his thoughts sometimes too, Lily." Katrina sighed. "And I realize, maybe more than you do, how hard that would make things."

More than I did? Doubtful. But still, I appreciated her sentiment. "Thanks." I smiled. "I'm glad you—"

There was a sickening thud and my expression of gratitude was interrupted as Paul shouted, "Man down!" We jumped up and took the stairs two at a time to find Christian on his back with his hands over his head.

"What happened?" Anna questioned, looking down at her brother.

"He got hit in the head with the horseshoe," Demetre mumbled as Theo looked on guiltily.

I knelt next to him, prying his hands away from his head. Sure enough, there was a welt.

"Oh, Christian." I tried not to laugh. "Are you dead?"

He looked up at me and frowned. "Not yet. But I feel a bit woozy at the moment," he said.

"I would imagine so," I giggled.

"Are you here to rescue me?" He smiled.

"Of course. I owe you one, don't I?"

He laughed feebly.

"Come on. I'll help you up." I offered my hand. He took it, and Demetre and Paul grabbed both of his arms, lifting him with no effort at all.

"You should get inside and put some ice on that head," Demetre said.

"Will you be my nurse, Lily?" Christian chuckled, wobbling in place.

"No problem. Come on," I said.

❧

"Too cold!" Christian flinched, grabbing my hand as I sat beside him, resting the homemade ice pack against his forehead.

"I realize it's cold, you whiner, but that's the whole point. The cold keeps the swelling down. You don't want to end up with a concussion, do you?" I scolded.

He sighed and let me hold it in place.

"So what happened?" I asked, already knowing the answer.

"Theo's toss ran a bit rampant." He smiled.

"Ah. Yes. Figured as much." I sniggered. "Poor Theo."

"Poor *Theo*?" Christian raised an eyebrow and then flinched in pain. "Uhm, *I'm* the one with the war wound here, and you pity *him*?"

I laughed. "I'm sorry. Let me start again. Poor, poor Christian."

"That's better. God, this really does throb badly," he complained.

I frowned. "I would make it better if I could," I said.

He looked at me and the corner of his mouth lifted a bit. He pulled my hand and the ice pack down and lowered his head. Did he honestly want me to kiss it? I laughed out loud.

"You are a big baby, Christian." I snorted.

"I insist. You wouldn't want me to die, now, would you?"

I smirked. "I could call your mother for you."

"She's not you. You said you owed me one. You're not a welcher, are you?"

"So this will equal things out, then? We'll be square after that?" I narrowed my eyes, doubtfully.

He grinned broadly. "Perhaps."

I didn't trust where this was going, but I also didn't want to make something out of nothing. So, leaned in and kissed his forehead anyway. He lifted his eyes to mine and I knew that expression. It was the same look he'd given me the day I told him I'd repelled William. I stared out the kitchen door. There was no way I could deal with this right now. I'd just have to figure out how to run away without hurting him irrevocably.

"Lily." He sighed. "Will you stop studying the exit and look at me?"

I shook my head. "I'm going back outside," I said.

"No. Lily. Really, look at me."

"What is it, Christian?" I said, sitting back. He threw the ice on the table and leaned forward. I clung to the back of my chair. Shit. Shit. I would have to flee.

But it was too late. His arms were awkward but powerful as he reached for me. "Why are you keeping your distance? Are you afraid of me?"

"No, of course not!" I said.

"Then why have you shut me out?"

"Christian. Let me go. Don't do this." I shook my head, trying to twist myself free of him.

"I have to. I have to." His voice was shaky, uncertain. "Please, Lily. You can sense things, for Christ's sake! Surely you know how I feel by now!"

"Please *don't*," I cried.

"Why not?" His face looked pained.

"Because I don't feel the same way about you," I said.

"How would you know that?" he asked. "How could you possibly know that? You've never even given it a chance!"

"I just do," I said.

"Well, that's no kind of answer," he seethed, and I had no hope of thwarting what came next. As he kissed me, it was torture. I could feel his need, his pain, his release, his fear, all wrapped up in this one action. Worse were the tears. As often as Christian had portrayed the man of men, he lost the battle here. Everything he'd stored up until now—tried to keep from me—came pouring out and I had to endure it all. It's not that it was horrible, but it couldn't compare to the torrent of adoration that William induced with just a single look.

He broke away, breathing heavily. I was inundated with his emotions and knew that my present state would not allow for sound judgment. I took a few deep breaths and sat as far back as I could, clearing my head. "Why did you have to do that?" I asked sadly.

"I couldn't help it," he said.

"I wish you could have. I can't change how I feel. This is not going to happen."

"Why?" he raised his voice. "What's wrong with this, Lily? We make perfect sense!"

"You'd *think* so, but that's kind of the problem, isn't it? Everything in your head is so damned black and white! For a Sentient, you're the most shortsighted man I've ever met. I don't reciprocate and what's infuriating is that I can't tell you why!"

"What the hell does that mean?"

I stood up. "It means … don't forget your ice," I said, and left the kitchen without looking back.

☙

William sat on my bed, watching me pack. "Women are insane," he said, picking up my hairdryer and plunking it into the duffel bag.

"That doesn't go there, William." I took it out and laid it on the dresser.

He shrugged. "Sorry," he said, turning his attention to a dress I'd laid out. "But I don't get why you need a battalion's worth of paraphernalia for a two-day trip." He reached into my bag. "I mean come on, Lily. A back massager?"

I blushed. "Out of the bag!" I grabbed the object hastily, shoving it back into the sack and zipping it closed.

"Anyway," I changed the subject. "Women like to feel prepared. What if we run into the Prince of Wales and he invites us all to a cocktail party? Would you really want me to attend such an event sporting khakis and frizzy hair?"

"I can see your dilemma." He rolled his eyes. "Because the royal family has built up frequent flyer miles with all their trips to South Carolina."

I laughed and threw a shoe at his head, but his reflexes were impeccable. He ducked with seconds to spare, catching the shoe before it hit the wall.

"That was uncalled for." He frowned, examining the offending object. "You wear a size nine?"

"So I have big feet," I said. "Hand it over."

"*Oh,* no. I don't think you should get this back so easily. I think I'll keep it for a while."

"William, it goes with the dress!" I complained, crossing the room and snatching at the footwear.

"Is this the same dress you plan to wear to the imperial ball of Ruthersville?" He sniggered, holding the shoe at bay.

"Yes!" I pouted. "Give me my shoe!"

"It's yours if you can take it from me." He chuckled, leaning further back onto my bed.

"Oh, if they only knew the real you."

"Who is the real me, Lily?" He smiled.

I dodged for his hand, and he caught me, pushing me down hard onto my back. He tossed the shoe off to the side and kissed me indecently.

I groaned into his mouth before breaking away. "I love Paul."

He narrowed his eyes. "Paul?"

"When is it they're supposed to go to Savannah?" I asked.

"Oh," he said roughly. "Yes. God bless Paul."

He let his hands wander down to my hips and pulled me tight against him before his mouth found my neck. "So ...." he murmured, enticingly. "How much longer do you think we can carry on like this before we both repel each other off the ceiling?"

"Not much longer. Good thing I leave in half an hour." But the words were a lie. It wasn't a good thing to be leaving William. He would retreat to his lonely world once I was gone.

After a prolonged kiss to my shoulder, he rolled off me and sat up. "You should finish packing, anyway."

I lay on my back, completely limp. "Sure. I'll get right on that."

"Come on. Up. The royal family is waiting." He tossed me my shoe.

I sat up. "What will you do while I'm gone?" I asked.

"Same thing I did before you came here," he said. "Ignore Christian."

I laughed at first, then a shot of reality smacked me in the chest and I fell silent, feeling queasy.

"Are you all right?" William asked.

"Yeah. Just, do me a little favor, will you, William?"

"Of course."

"Keep out of his way while I'm gone. Christian's in a rare mood."

"What else is new?" He peered at me. "But why now?"

"He's in love with me, I think." The words were hard to say, but even harder to hear.

William went rigid, and then he sighed deeply. "Took you a while, Lily. I was beginning to think he'd have to kiss you to get the point across."

I felt the wave of shame coming on but couldn't quell it. I began to cry.

William rounded on me, taking my shoulders in his hands. "He did … he kissed you, didn't he?

Fuck. Why couldn't I keep my reactions to myself?

"Only a little," I sobbed. "I'm sorry."

"Well, what happened? How did you handle it?"

"I … I … told him it was impossible. Told him it would never happen."

"And how did he respond?"

"Stubbornly." I sniffled.

William sank down beside me in defeat. "He can have everything. He can have his human status and his vanity and his perfection, but he can't have you." He kissed my forehead. "Not you."

"No. Never," I pledged.

Seventeen

Katrina belted out the lines to "Livin' on a Prayer" with gusto, and I winced, snorting with laughter. She was gloriously and unimaginably off key, and I had been seated next to her for the past two hours. How had this happened? Anna and her road-trip mix CDs, that's how.

"Come on, Lily! Sing the next one!" Katrina jostled my shoulder.

"Uhm, still just listening, thanks!" I shouted over the noise.

"All right, fine. We'll give it a rest." Anna laughed, turning the volume down on the radio. "I am so *psyched*, ladies!"

Clara and Elaine had decided to take their own vehicle, mercifully for them, while Anna, Katrina, and I gave my car a good work out. I had survived interpretations of songs by every eighties hair-metal and punk band known to man. As far as I could tell, I'd lost the will to live somewhere between Stockbridge and Greensboro.

"Ruthersville, ten miles!" Katrina beamed.

"Someone please remind me to kiss the ground once we arrive," I teased.

"Spoil sport!" Anna stuck her tongue out.

❧

I set my bag on the motel floor.

Anna had been the driving force behind our choice of lodging, opting for the "whole Ruthersville experience." And as these places went, the Rebel Lodge was a blast from the past. The bed was made up with a pea-green comforter covered in orange flowers, and the carpet was mustard yellow. The air smelled like old smoke and wet dog.

I frowned at the lamp on the lone end table. The shade was missing.

"Groovy," I sighed. Still, who could beat twenty bucks a night? I'd just have to wear two pairs of pajamas to sleep.

Pulling the blanket tentatively back, I half expected it to stick to the bed. It seemed supple enough, and bonus—nothing crawled out from under it. So far so good.

This was the first time I'd been away from the house in months. It was the first time I'd been completely free of Christian. The feeling was surreal and I got an idea.

Dumping the contents of my purse onto the bed I grabbed my cell phone and dialed a number I'd never called before.

"Hello?"

"Hi." I smiled into the phone.

"Lily?" William chuckled.

"Mhm," I said.

"Wow. You called me."

"Yep. Didn't you think I would?"

"Well, it's just … no one *ever* calls me," he said.

"Oh." I pouted on his behalf. "William, that is pitiful."

"I'll survive."

"Guess where I am?" I leaned back against the headboard, hugging a pillow.

"I'd venture to say—and I'm really hazarding a guess here—but Ruthersville?"

"Bingo."

"Meet any princes yet?"

"Mhm. But he's a hundred miles away in Landsfield, Georgia."

William laughed. "Ah, Lily. You're nicer from out of state."

"I am nice in general, thank you very much!" I griped.

"Actually, I like this," he began. "You sound really sexy over the phone."

"Oh, yeah?"

"Mhm. Like, full on adult-entertainment sexy."

I laughed. "Ah-ha. Well, it's a good thing that I'm completely alone then, isn't it? Or I'd have a scandal on my hands."

"Alone? No Anna?"

"Nope."

"No Katrina?"

"Uh-uh."

"You're all by yourself?"

"Yep." I grinned.

"Nice. You must be giddy."

"Completely! I don't know what to do with myself!"

"So you called me?"

"I miss you," I said.

"Really?"

"Of course." I laughed. "I miss you terribly."

"I … I miss you, too," he said, sounding genuinely mystified by the whole interaction. "So when do you go to visit the Chapel?"

"Shortly."

"It could be fun. Don't be afraid to get your hands dirty," he said.

"Will do." I glanced at the alarm clock beside my bed. I was supposed to meet the girls in the main vestibule in ten minutes.

"I guess I have to go," I complained.

"If you must. But I like this phone call thing. Let's repeat it?"

"Of course." A sinful thought crossed my mind. "Hey, William? One more thing," I crooned into the mouth-piece.

"Yes?"

"That back massager?"

He hesitated and I could hear the smile in his voice. "Yes?"

"You do realize that has nothing to do with my back," I whispered seductively. There was dead silence before he swallowed hard on the other end.

"Bye, William." I smirked.

"Uh-huh," he breathed.

❧

We arrived at the Mount Lorna Chapel in under five minutes. Nothing in Ruthersville took more time than that to navigate. The building looked like an old school house, white-washed and complete with bell hitch and cross on top. The surrounding area was overgrown with long dried grass and you could barely make out the headstones of the cemetery in back.

The plan was to meet a Mrs. Bridgit Cavanaugh at the front of the building around seven p.m., but she was nowhere to be found.

"What's she look like?" I asked Clara as we stomped over crabgrass, trying to get to the windows along the side of the building.

"I couldn't say. She sounded like an older woman, though," Clara said.

Katrina swatted at a cloud of gnats. "If I were them, I'd be more concerned with skunks and termites than anything otherworldly," she grumbled.

"Just keep moving." Anna sighed, squashing a weed underfoot. "And do *not* look over—too late," Anna groaned at the sound of Katrina's screeching. She'd spotted the hornet's nest under the gutter.

"Elaine?" Clara called for our lone combatant.

"I'm here!" Elaine responded from around front. "Just keeping an eye out for our host!"

I strained to see through the murky glass of an old window. The lights were off in the building and the interior was dark.

"I guess she's running late." I shrugged. "I'm going back."

Elaine was seated on the porch landing of the chapel, her hand shielding her eyes from the dusky sun's glare. "There's only one route leading to this place. When she's even remotely close, we'll see her," she said.

I crossed my arms, peering down the narrow road.

"Here comes somebody." Elaine stood up and we watched as a tiny speck of a vehicle crested the hill and neared at perilous speed. "How the hell fast is she going?" she said.

The dilapidated car was indeed traveling at maximum velocity, kicking up clouds of dirt behind it. The closer it came, the more certain I was that it would not stop, and I watched in horror.

"Holy crap," I said. The car did not slow down, but rather pulled to a swerving, screeching halt in front of the chapel. Dust spread out behind it and billowed up toward us. I coughed and waved at the air in front of me. Clara and the girls ran around front, staring wildly.

The driver's side door opened. A tiny woman in her sixties, at the youngest, hopped out and slammed the door shut with massive force. In a netted hat and blue and white flower-print dress that landed below her knees, she looked like she could have been anyone's grandmother.

"I'm here, goddamn it!" she cursed.

Or not.

"Damned hoodlums blocked my progress!" She bounded toward us, waving a cane in the air. "I'll tell you that's the last time I let them near my car without runnin' em' all down!"

"Uhm. I'm sorry," I said.

"Goddamn skate boarding ruffians think they own this town! Do you know what one of them did to me on my way here?"

I smiled sympathetically. "No. What?"

"I was at a red light listening to my cassettes, when he hopped that damned thing right up on the hood of my car! Nicked the damned paint job! Little pisser! Hope he skates into a pile of shit!"

I gawked and Elaine stood up quickly. "I'm Elaine Rush. You must be Bridgit Cavanaugh." She extended her hand.

"And y'all are the folks come to get rid of my little problem?"

"That's right," Clara piped in.

"You don't look like those psychic ghost busters on TV." Mrs. Cavanaugh squinted.

"That's because we're not." Elaine chuckled. "We're the real deal."

"Well, I hope so. Between the pests downtown and the pests around here, I'm about to bust out the rifle."

"Oh, now we wouldn't want that to happen," Clara spoke soothingly. "Why don't you show us around? Tell us a little more about your problem."

"All righty, then. Move aside, move aside." Mrs. Cavanaugh cut through the middle of us and jingled a key impatiently in the lock. The double doors clicked and she pushed them open; then she flipped on a light switch.

"Just look at that!" She pointed angrily. Everything was a shambles. Hymnals were strewn across the room with abandon, torn pages scattered here and there. Chairs lay in senseless heaps, pointing in every direction.

"Oh, my goodness," Clara said.

"You got that right!" Bridgit barked. "Look at this mess! Every morning I clean it up and by the next one it's back to this again! I am *old*. My bones are a crumblin', my back aches, I fart when I walk, I don't *got* no more teeth! I get tired just gnawing on a chicken leg!" She rounded on Elaine. "Now, what can you do for me?"

"Might I suggest euthanasia?" Katrina mumbled in my ear. Anna's face went an unnatural shade of purple. I could only imagine what great exertion she was putting forth not to laugh. Katrina's lips were pressed into a tight, straight line. I kept my hand over my mouth, just in case.

"Erm, why don't you let us have the run of the place for the night," Elaine suggested. "I'll bet by morning we'll have figured the whole thing out."

"You do and I'll give you my prosthetic!" Bridgit promised.

"Oh, well, that's very…kind of you," Clara said. "But you can keep all your limbs, Mrs. Cavanaugh. We're just happy to help."

"Happy to have ya, then! I'll leave you folks alone." She backed out the front doors. "See you in the morning!"

Mrs. Cavanaugh was fast for someone with crumbling or otherwise artificial body parts. Before we knew it, she was speeding down the street again, the sound of screaming brakes fading into the distance.

I cleared my throat, and Anna and Katrina collapsed with laughter.

"That was an experience." Elaine smiled.

"That was too fantastic!" Anna giggled through her tears.

"She's something, all right." Clara shook her head. "So, where do we begin?"

"Might as well start out easy," Elaine said. "Who knows? Maybe we can punch this job out in an hour and go out for drinks afterwards."

"Amen," Katrina said.

"Girls, why don't you try and draw it out?" Clara said to Anna and me.

"We're on it," Anna said, excitedly. I knew the drill well enough by now. As a pathcrosser, you only had to linger patiently before your light became irresistible to a spirit. They would show themselves one way or another. I took one side of the chapel and Anna took the other. Standing perfectly still, I waited.

Five minutes passed and my feet began to ache, but I didn't move and neither did Anna. Ten minutes passed and we looked at each other, sharing bored expressions.

"Stubborn," Anna commented.

"Mhm," I grunted.

Clara and Elaine had gone around back with Katrina to inspect the gravestones and everything was perfectly quiet. There was only a fraction of the sunlight we'd had when we first arrived, and this was just the time for your mind to play tricks on you. More than once Anna and I would think we saw something, a shadow or a streak of light out of the corner of our eyes, but nothing made its presence blatantly known.

After half an hour of this and several shifts in position to ease the discomfort of standing still for so long, I was ready to give up and join the others outside. But my bout of disillusionment was not destined to last much longer.

"Lily," Anna whispered. "Lily, there's something circling you." She remained still.

I gulped. "There is? What?" I whispered back.

"It's not human," she said.

I could feel the hair on the back of my neck begin to rise and something cold shot across the front of me. I froze, not breathing. It returned, breezing across my face quickly before prickling the skin on my back. She was right. It was circling me. The astral picked up speed, blowing around me so that my hair flew out from my head.

The room was filled with the sound of rushing breath. My head was spinning and I was losing my sense of balance. This was the time to put what I'd learned with William to use. Taking a deep breath inward, I gathered my fear into the pit of my stomach and used it as ammunition, blasting the pent-up energy outward. The rushing breaths faded into silence and the room went quiet.

"What the bloody hell?" Anna said.

"I do *not* know," I answered. "But I didn't like it."

"Well, I think we've found the source of the problem." Anna rolled her eyes.

"Yeah. Definitely."

"Let's see if we can harness it," Anna suggested. This aspect I was not comfortable with yet. Detecting was one thing, or crossing over an astral spirit, but wrestling with something sinister was still not my preference.

"Don't you think we should get Elaine in on this?" I asked nervously.

"Good idea," Anna whispered. "I'll be right back."

"Anna, wait! Don't .... Shit," I whimpered.

A few seconds in and something whirred past my head. I jumped back, looking all around me. "God, Anna, hurry up!" I squealed.

Then the wind began again and cavernous breaths coursed through the room in sudden gusts. It was all I could do to keep standing.

"Lily!" Clara was running for me. The wind died immediately, and I stared at her wide-eyed. "Lily, it's a dark astral. Has it spoken to you?"

"No!" I caught my breath. "Why?"

"Have you spoken to it? Engaged with it at all? This is important, Lily," she spoke urgently.

"No, I didn't. I couldn't."

"Good. This bastard needs to be bound and expelled, so don't engage it. Elaine, your expertise, please?"

Elaine nodded quickly and eyed up the room. "It won't come back with us here," she said. "We'll have to leave her alone again."

"*What?*" I cried.

"We'll be right there, right outside the door, Lily. I promise. The moment he shows himself, I'll be on him."

If Christian were here he'd have objected vehemently. But he wasn't. And if I really meant it when I claimed to want independence from his watchful eye, I had to prove it to myself first.

"Okay. All right." I nodded, and then shooed them out and waited.

Nothing was happening. Everything felt normal. Maybe we'd scared it away.

"Come on, you asshole," I whispered. "You're afraid now, aren't you?" I goaded. Then I scolded myself, remembering Clara's warning about engaging. My hands were shaking and I dug my nails into my palms.

Something exhaled across my neck. I resisted the urge to breathe too quickly and tightened every muscle, trying not to move. A long, low growling wind built in front of me and mounted into a laugh. The last time I was this afraid, I was being fondled by an Incubus. Where was Elaine?!

The laughing ceased and a new sound began—a bizarrely evolving grunt like a snorting bull.

Beautiful, I thought.

The room fell silent again, and then ... .

"Lillian," it sang in a deep rattle. "Lillian." It laughed.

I could have died. It was saying my name. It knew my name.

"Shit, Clara!"

Elaine rushed into the room with everyone close behind. She threw her arms forward, grasping for something. The laughing continued until she found what she was looking for.

"Got you, you nasty little asshole!" Elaine said.

The spirit scraped against the floor, the walls, struggling to free itself of her hold.

"Free me!" It choked out a snarl.

"Fat chance," Clara shouted. "You need to leave this place. Recede into the earth or we'll kill you," she said.

The spirit seemed to find this idea amusing, cackling uproariously.

"He's not cooperating," Clara told Elaine, so our combatant tightened her fists. The spirit screamed—the ugliness of the sound unbearable.

"Why have you left your plane?" Clara demanded. "You know you don't belong here."

"I go with the darkness," it snarled. "I followed the old woman here. She has seen pain."

A parasite. I remembered what Christian had told me once. This spirit was the offspring of suffering.

"Fine," Clara spoke, calmly. "Since you're so determined to stay, we have no choice but to put an end to you," she said.

It screamed again and Elaine struggled for footing before falling backward, gasping. A howling wind swelled around the chapel and wound itself into a dark funnel in the center of the room. We huddled together, shielding ourselves from flying chairs as the vortex moved in a line toward the open doors of the church. It was trying to escape, but luck was not on its side. The moment it came into contact with outside air, it disintegrated, dropping the chapel's contents into a heap on the ground out front. We huddled together as remnant debris rained down over our heads. No one spoke for a moment while we caught our breath.

"I suppose the old lady will expect us to clean this up," Anna sighed.

❧

Our waitress stuck a pen behind her ear and chomped loudly on a wad of gum. "Would you gals like separate checks?"

"Yes," I began as Clara said the opposite.

"This one's on me, dear. Consider it a reward. The chapel *was* in perfect order this morning, after all," Clara announced brightly over a bite of fried potato.

"Yep. It was free and clear," Elaine nodded. "I think we chased it out, ladies."

"Thank goodness for that. It was a real bitch." Katrina scowled.

"I have to thank you, Lily, for your courage back there." Elaine smiled. "You really took a shot for us."

"Glad to be helpful." I sipped on my orange juice. "But how is it that I always end up being the luring device in these situations?"

Anna laughed. "You're right, Lil. That role does seem to fall on you a lot. But you can't help being so appealing. It really comes in handy."

"How lucky for me." I chuckled.

"William seems to appreciate it," Katrina muttered over her scrambled eggs. I ignored her.

"How goes it with William, dear?" Clara asked. And the subject was officially unavoidable.

"Fine." I smiled a little, then a little more.

"Hm. Someone's smitten." Elaine grinned at me. I avoided eye contact.

"She's been thinking about him all weekend," Katrina blurted out, then covered her mouth. "Not that I heard much!"

If she wanted to read my thoughts, let her read this. I smirked and vividly flipped Katrina the bird in my head. She gasped and exploded with laughter.

"What did I miss?" Anna complained.

"Nothing," I sang.

"I refuse to be left out!" Anna frowned. Katrina leaned in and whispered in her ear.

Anna's mouth and eyes shot open. "Lillian. I am aghast!" She giggled.

Clara turned to Elaine. "I have no idea what they're getting on about, do you?"

Elaine shook her head. "Nope. I'm completely lost."

"My darlings, it is simply bad manners to read minds at the table," Clara admonished.

"Sorry, Clara." I laughed. "I accept full responsibility."

"As well you should," Anna said. "One must only use their Sentiently powers for good."

"Exactly," Katrina continued the teasing. "You should use your powers for good—not evil. Just think of all the people who don't even *have* an endowment."

Elaine perked up. "That reminds me. I talked to Nicole. She says hi."

"Oh, poor Nick," Katrina moaned. "I wish she'd come with us. She needs a break." She sighed.

"Who's Nicole?" I asked.

"She's Duncan and Rita's daughter, out west," Anna explained. "A non-Sentient."

"Living among Sentients," Elaine spoke the words significantly.

"I assume Duncan is being his usual douche-bag self?" Katrina said.

"She didn't mention," Elaine answered. "But you know how Nick is. The girl doesn't complain."

"Asshole," Katrina muttered. "She can't help not having an endowment. I can't stand the guy."

"So, not all Sentients are honorable characters, then," I surmised.

Elaine laughed. "No way! Just having an endowment doesn't guarantee a good nature."

"That's right," Clara added. "And not having one hardly discounts it."

I thought of Christian, then Frank, and knew this theory was true.

❦

Clara and Elaine had decided there was no sense in paying for another night of luxury accommodations in Ruthersville when we had finished the job a day early. Of course, I was thrilled to be going back, but Anna was devastated. She'd pouted and whined for two hours straight, complaining about the tedium of it all. It was apparently harder for life-long Sentients to get used to a bout of stability the likes of which our group had recently known. While Abram had obviously struggled to give them as much in the way of normalcy as possible, they had conditioned themselves for change.

"There's always your trip to Savannah," I reminded her cheerfully as we pulled our overnight bags out of the trunk. Lord knows *I* hadn't forgotten. I'd been counting down the days till Cotton Candy Mandy would put William and me out of our misery.

"That's true," she acknowledged, but sighed forlornly. I laughed and shook my head. There was no way her mood was rubbing off on me today.

"Welcome back!" Thomas beamed as I grabbed a soda from the fridge.

"Thanks! Where is everyone?" I asked.

"They're wrapped in a heated game of pool," he said. "Downstairs."

"Fun," I replied. My treks to the basement were few, but I liked the idea of being so close to William's room. I had yet to find an excuse to see inside it.

I opened the basement door and snuck down a few stairs with Anna on my tail, stopping short of the bottom step. She narrowed her eyebrows at my hesitation and I hushed her.

"Make your damn move, Maddox," Christian grumbled.

"I like to be precise," William shot back. "Paul, remind me why you asked him to join?"

I peeked around the stair rail.

"You're getting as bad as me," Anna whispered.

Christian hunched over the pool table, scowling. "I could give a damn about your accuracy, Maddox. Just hit the ball so I can carry on with beating you."

"I don't know," I said, hopping off the bottom step. "His practices really came in handy for me this weekend."

"You're home early!" Christian grinned. He moved as if to approach me, then hesitated, changing his mind. Obviously he knew better than to press his luck after the other day.

"How'd it go?" William asked.

"Well enough, considering the swirling vortex of death," I said.

"Pardon me?" He chuckled.

"It was a really dark astral," Anna said. "And it was all over Lily. Would probably have attached itself to her if given the chance."

"I should have gone!" Christian said.

"Don't flatter yourself. I was fine!" I insisted. "Who's winning?"

"I am," William said. "And I knew you would be, Lily."

I smiled at him. "Can I watch?"

"Why don't you join?" William asked, standing his cue stick on the floor and folding his hands over it.

I considered, and then I laughed. "No, I really don't think so."

"Uh-oh, have we hit upon a game you can't win?" he taunted.

I shrugged. "Everybody's got a weakness."

"You should be careful about revealing an Achilles' heel in certain company," Christian said curtly.

"Why, Christian?" I snapped. "Can't you be trusted?"

William's eyes widened and he smiled cautiously. Christian gaped at me like I'd grown a set of horns.

"And what's with Paul?" I complained. "He looks like someone's smashed his toy."

Paul grumbled incoherently in the corner.

"He's upset because our little trip to 'Pervert City' has been called off," Christian recovered. "Abram is sending the combatants to Florida to handle a possession."

"Oh," I said. "You mean … ."

"Bloody *fantastic*," Anna moaned. There would be no living with her now.

"That's right," Paul blurted, miserably. "No sexy ladies! No Savannah, no wild weekend."

Shit! But wait. The combatants were going to Florida. William wasn't a combatant. Hope sprang eternal.

"Don't worry, Paul," I offered. "There are plenty of other strippers in the sea."

"Yeah, but this was …."

"I know, I know. Cotton Candy Mandy," I said. "So who's Abram sending?"

"Me, Paul, Elaine," Christian began. "And Maddox," he glanced to the side.

"William? Why?" I said, only barely concealing my disappointment.

"In case anyone gets hurt, Lily." William sighed.

"Oh," I slumped.

Christian rolled his eyes. "Pointless if you ask me. We haven't needed him yet."

I clenched my fists and Anna peeked at me warily.

"Don't you ever get tired of being such a painstaking asshole?" I peered at Christian and he looked sincerely shocked.

"Honestly, Lily." He shook his head. "I know you've got a soft spot for fuck-ups and all, but no need to overreact."

"Enough." I ground my teeth together. My anger was mounting, and I feared that if I didn't hold the particles of my body together, they would fly apart, tearing into him like shrapnel.

"No problem," Christian said and he turned to William, glaring at him scathingly. William returned the gesture.

"Uhm … is the game over, then?" Paul asked weakly.

"It's over," Christian said and threw his cue stick on the table. "Lil, come on." He turned to me. "Don't be this way."

"You're behaving like an arrogant prick!" I chastised. "And you know what else? There are a lot of people out there who think that *I'm* a fuck-up. My family thinks I'm insane, my best friend hates me! I don't know *what* I'm doing half the time. Don't I belong on your list of undesirables?"

"Lily, please." Christian looked horrified. "I would never think that way about you. You *know* how I feel. What's happened to you? How could you ever put yourself in the same category as him?"

"With little effort!" I fumed. "*You're* the fool, Christian, and yet you treat me like a stupid, clueless, weak little girl. I won't keep protecting you forever!"

"Protecting *me?*" He laughed. "Protecting me from what?"

I glanced at William, who looked as if he would spear Christian with his cue stick.

"Figure it out," I demanded.

Christian seemed to register nothing. Either he was dumb as a rock or completely in denial. Incensed, I headed for the stairs. "And *do* not follow me."

*"Hatred does not cease by hatred, but only by love;
this is the eternal rule."*
-Buddha

Eighteen

I stood at the center of a web of dark halls, staring down the passage straight ahead, and all manner of images flashed into my peripheral view. One of the tunnels became a room from my old apartment; another, a wooded trail. I could barely glance at them fast enough to catch the vision before it flickered out of sight. Rufus jumped across my feet, and I gasped as he disappeared down a lightless corridor.

"Rufus?" I called after him.

"*Rufus?*" An echo bounced around me.

"Rufus, come here," I whispered desperately, peering into the pitch black, but I couldn't bring myself to wander after him. I was too afraid of what I'd find ... or what would find me.

"Lily."

I swung around. "Grandpa?"

He glared at me. "How did I miss it before?" he asked.

"What?"

"You're no good. You're just no good."

"Grandpa ...."

"Don't bother coming home. We can't stand the sight of you."

"You don't mean this," I replied, dazed. He laughed at me in a voice that was not his own, then flickered like a hologram and disappeared. When I woke, I was crying.

Months had gone by without a disturbing dream, but lately I was breaking records. In fact, I'd counted four nightmares this week. The phenomenon left me out of sorts, and I wasn't the only one suffering the consequences. William had returned from fighting off evil in Florida, only to be greeted by a tired, jumpy, aggravated female.

"Give up, Lily." William chuckled, leaning back in the chair behind Abram's desk.

"I used to do this all the time!" I complained. "I'll *make* it fit."

Abram's study had finally gotten to me. I'd been dying to straighten the book shelves for months and he'd graciously agreed, so long as I didn't dust them off. Abram was fond of the dust.

"If I switch the book on Masonry to the bottom shelf, I can fit the atlases right ... *here*." I stretched, teetering questionably.

"And if you attempt those acrobatics again, you'll fall off that ladder and break your neck." He frowned.

"What? I'm being careful."

"I don't doubt your dexterity, Lily. It's the integrity of that death trap that concerns me."

I switched out a dictionary for a book on Alexander the Great. "You're starting to sound like Christian."

"One day I'll shock you and run to your rescue." He smirked.

"That day has repeated itself regularly since I met you," I said. "Rescuing doesn't have to be physical, William."

He smiled and got up from Abram's chair, walking around the desk to stand behind me.

"It works both ways." He sighed. Wrapping his arms around my waist, he pulled me off the ladder.

"But I'm so close to being done!" I admonished. "Look. A half dozen books at *most*."

"Forget the books, Lily," he whispered against my ear. I closed my eyes. "You've been filling every spare moment with trivial tasks." He kissed the nape of my neck. "What are you trying to avoid?"

I spoke, but barely. "Nothing. Things."

"Things?" he repeated, sliding his hands down to my hips. "What kinds of things?"

"Uhm." I gulped. "Stuff."

"Mm? You're not avoiding *me*, are you?"

"Are you joking?" I asked him. "I steal every moment with you that I can."

"No, Lily. You know what I mean." He moved his mouth to the flesh of my shoulder.

"Well, anything further would require that we have more than thirty minutes alone together at any given time." I scowled. "Unless … there's always the woods."

"Lillian, we are not … consummating things … in the dirt surrounded by a swarm of mosquitoes," he scolded.

"Agreed. Itchy does not equal sexy." I sighed.

"You know, my room is nice. What's wrong with my room?" he asked. As if I hadn't thought about it … repeatedly. But what were the chances of me sneaking in and out of the basement undetected? There were, to name a few, a mind reader, three empaths, and an energy finder dwelling within these walls. Not to mention a bitter combatant whose watch had become ever more vigilant in the last few months, despite my increased abilities.

"I'm scared," I said sadly.

"Don't say that," he responded, sounding hurt. "You'll never be safer with anyone than you are with me."

"You don't understand." I turned to face him, kissing him softly. "I'm not afraid of you. I'm scared of what will happen if Christian finds out. I'm not worried about protecting him anymore. I just won't risk him hurting you."

"I can take care of myself, Lily."

"You'd better! You *have* to! Look, I don't think you get it. My ability, my confidence in this world, is pathetic without you. If anything ever happened—"

"Stop it," he ordered, grimacing. "It's completely twisted that you feel that way, Lily. It's an insult to everything I've been trying to teach you. You will *always* have everything you need to hold your own, with or without me," he said. "And in my defense, I've been around a tad longer than Christian. He can fight. He can kill. But anger doesn't equal strength. Anyone can react on instinct; anyone can feel first and think after. That doesn't make him stronger than me. And just because I take his outbursts in stride, that hardly means I'm not every bit as powerful as he is and then some, all right?"

I nodded.

He fanned his fingers across my cheek. "One day soon you'll lose the last of that persistent fear, I know it. And when you do …." He paused and leaned down, kissing me deeply. I responded well, my body melting in his arms before he pulled away.

"Hey … don't stop." I pouted. "Why are you stopping?"

"And when you do …." He smiled, holding me away from him. "You'll know where to find me." He was nearly out the door before my brain kicked in.

"Where are you going?" I complained.

He grinned. "To help Abram and Wendell with Theo. We're going to try and reset his batteries."

"Oh. How long will that take?" I moped on.

He shrugged. "Might be a while." He raised an eyebrow. "Why? Is there something you need?"

"Well … no," I whined.

"Enjoy those books, then." He nodded at the shelves and walked away.

Oh, he was *so* smug. Since when did *he* play hard to get? It was irresistible, and if I had any qualms left, they were scurrying away like rats.

ℇ

"Watch the windows!" Elaine yelled at her husband as a paperweight thumped against the house's siding. For two days, Theo had practiced reaching for various objects we'd laid on the picnic table out back. He'd progressed successfully from rubber bands, to rubber balls, to wooden blocks, and now he was attempting the hefty stuff.

"I feel like a fool," he grumped, laying a cautious finger over a casserole dish.

"Well, you have to admit you're making progress," Elaine said. "I don't know what you did for him, William, but this is the first time I've felt safe letting him anywhere near a stapler."

Abram chuckled. "They'll take a tad more time to completely diminish, but the effects are definitely wearing off. Just remember not to touch anything too hastily, Theo," he warned. "Your mind reacts first, after all."

"I know." Theo sighed. "And I'm sorry to wear you out, son." He frowned at William, who had spent the better part of the last few days attempting to loosen the grasp of poor Theo's befuddlement. As was to be expected, our resident healer was looking a little worn out.

I sat cross legged on the lawn and observed William taking in the warm September air. He was trying not to let it show, but I could make out the subtle shaking, the confirmation of his efforts with Theo. Christian had planted himself pointedly between us and was watching Theo repel a Tupperware container.

"Why don't you get some rest?" I leaned around Christian to address William.

He shook his head. "I'm fine."

"But you can barely keep your eyes open!"

He shrugged, glancing at Christian just long enough for me to make out the shade of resentment. Unwavering restraint had long since ceased to be tolerable for William, and I knew he longed to be free of it. A rush of adrenaline set my pulse racing. How, I wondered, would Christian respond to a slight act of revolution?

I got up from the ground and crossed in front of Christian, settling down next to William, who smiled in the smallest way. Sliding my hand behind his arm, I pulled him toward me until the sides of our heads rested together. Christian narrowed his eyes, but said nothing.

"If you're going to push yourself so hard, you should at least allow time for recuperation," I advised, quietly.

"I don't know," William whispered in my ear. "I might jump off a cliff if I thought you'd respond this way."

Christian strained to hear what we were saying, a murderous look on his face.

"This is daring, Lily," William continued. "He's about to have a seizure trying to figure this out."

"Let him," I said.

❧

The status of the Pennsylvania vampires had become the topic of choice lately, and I dreaded every moment of it.

"What if we just ambushed the creeps?" Paul sat on the couch, dangling a shoe lace in front of Rufus.

"Bad idea." Wendell shook his head. "They'll be waiting for you to do just that. There are only a few reliable tricks you'll have up your sleeves and the best of them is the element of surprise."

"And if past experience is any indication," Thomas added, "we should try to isolate the core. The rest always scatter after that. As it stands in Philadelphia, their number is one substantial cell. It's too dangerous."

Rufus flipped onto his back happily, pawing at Paul's shoelace with abandon.

"So, we wait for them to make a move, then?" Christian asked.

"Precisely," Abram said. "Once they've begun to form smaller groups, we'll take action upon the strongest one."

"But why?" Christian argued. "Why let them spread out? If Wendell's people come with us, we—"

"No, Christian," Abram stopped him there. "I see no need to involve Wendell's group at this time. We will do away with them one cell at a time, as they are too much of a threat to us en masse, and I won't have my Sentients taking that kind of risk."

Christian sat back in the arm chair and sighed unhappily.

"But we'll absolutely help if needed," Wendell assured Christian.

"We know," Abram said. "And thank you."

"I agree with Abram," Katrina added, her head resting on Anna's shoulder. "These battles have taken too much from us already. We have to be smart about this."

Anna kissed the top of her girlfriend's head. "Yes," she agreed. "Let's please think about ourselves for once."

I grabbed Rufus into a hug and tried petting him, but he had other plans. Squiggling to free himself, he darted away toward William.

"Careful, William!" Anna began. "He's got a mean streak."

But Rufus had already plopped himself into William's lap and was purring contentedly.

Brilliant cat, I thought, smiling.

"He never lets *me* pet him like that," Anna protested dramatically. "And to think I gave him my last bite of pot roast!"

"Your mom does ridiculous things with a pot roast," Katrina gushed. "I swear I can't even smell what she's cooking without salivating all over myself."

Paul licked his lips. "Same here. You know how I feel about Clara in the kitchen," he said.

"Tonight's *was* an exceptional meal," Abram agreed.

"Hm." Christian nodded. "For those of us who can partake, that is. Have you eaten yet, Maddox?" He leered at William and the room fell silent.

William shot him a look, but said nothing, scratching under Rufus's chin.

"What? Haven't made your way to the basement yet?" Christian goaded. "Were you waiting for the rest of us to rush off to bed so you could have your little fix?"

"Christian," Abram warned, but something wicked was burning in Christian's eyes now, a desperate hope.

"Don't start anything, Christian," I spoke calmly.

"Oh, *hell*, Lily," he said. "Come *on*! You can't honestly be okay with it?!"

"Okay with what?" I said.

"*Wait* a moment. Wait just one moment. Do you mean to tell me he's actually left that bit out?!" Christian glared at William. "She has *no* idea? How convenient." He laughed.

"Don't," William said.

"But why not? You've got her so fucking convinced of your normalcy it makes me sick! This is just *exactly* what she needs to hear."

"You'll say no more," Abram ordered, standing up. I looked back and forth between Christian and our Seer, wondering if even Abram could stop him now.

Christian dug his fingers into the arm of his chair, biting his tongue, and William stood up slowly, dislodging Rufus from his lap and setting him on the chair.

"William, you don't have to go anywhere." I stood up with him.

"I'm sorry, Lily," he said.

I reached for his hand. "You have nothing to be sorry for."

He looked at Christian. "It should be me who tells her. Please. Just let me tell her."

"Go for it, Maddox," Christian said.

"It won't matter, William," I swore.

He opened his mouth to speak, then dropped his eyes. "Damn it." He shook his head, letting go of my hand.

"Don't be a coward, Maddox," Christian demanded. "Tell her, or I will."

William looked at me again and his eyes were pleading. "Not here. Not like this."

"It's okay. Whatever it is … I trust you," I said.

Anger amplified his energy as he turned his gaze back to Christian. "I'll show her tonight," he said bitterly.

Nineteen

I was convinced William had changed his mind. He'd been gone for hours, and it was nearly midnight now. I waited in my room, trying to imagine what he might show me. Christian's enigmatic revelation hadn't shocked me as much as he'd hoped. I knew William had to eat *something*, but I'd never broached the topic, knowing he would do so when the time was right. You had to hand it to Christian. The man had a knack for pushing William and I together and there was no doubt in my mind that whatever I learned wouldn't change how I felt about him.

It was quarter to one when William finally knocked on my door.

"I thought you weren't coming," I said.

He smiled tiredly. "But you're still awake."

"And I would have stayed awake."

"Lily." He held my face in his hand. "Come on before I lose my nerve."

I followed him down to the basement.

"This way." He sighed, leading me across the game room and around a corner.

"So, that isn't just a utility closet?" I remarked, and peered down a tiny hall. Its walls were hung with pictures of men on a fishing boat holding up a fruitful line, and there was a closet at the end.

William opened the door and a blast of cool air swept out and around us. Reaching in, he flipped a switch to light things up. It didn't help much. The overhead bulb was weak and bare, but I could make out a water heater and furnace. We *were* in a utility room, but it was bigger than I'd anticipated. I looked at William. "Well?" I urged.

He stepped inside and I followed. To our right was a refrigerator. William paused in front of it and then opened the door. In theory, it looked just like the inside of a refrigerator should, with four metal racks and a crisper at the bottom. But there were no milk cartons or heads of lettuce. Instead, each rack housed clusters of neatly arranged vials containing a luminescent blue liquid.

I snorted. "Okay, so…this is it? This is the big deal? Christian thought I'd freak out over this? God, bring on the voodoo dolls and dead animals."

William snickered. "So delicate."

"Seriously, William. Just tell me what this is."

He picked up a glowing vile and held it in his palm, allowing me to examine it more closely. The liquid inside was thicker than water, coating the sides as he tipped it back and forth. There was no denying what it reminded me of.

"You know I'll never hurt a human again," he said, looking at me very seriously.

"I know that."

"But biologically, I have to have some derivative of human blood in my system to survive."

I nodded.

"For this to make sense, you'd have to understand the essentials of how a normal vampire feeds and what happens when someone is turned," he said. "Do you know anything about that?"

"Only what you've taught me or Christian's told me…and we both know that latter part isn't much."

"So, I'll start from the beginning," he said.

"Please do."

"It's pretty macabre, Lily."

"I'm hearty. Let me have it"

"All right. Then, you should understand why they drink blood to begin with," he said. "The thing is, when a vampire bites a human, its intention is to take in their essence. Vampires have no soul, so there's a constant hunger for one. Human blood is as close as they come to it. But human blood doesn't last long in its pure form outside the body, so drinking it only sates their need for a short time before the emptiness sets in again."

"So, vampires drink blood to replicate the feeling of a soul," I summed it up.

"Yes."

"Okay. But, before you go on, I have another question … about turning. How does it happen?"

"It happens in two stages. First, enough blood is drained from the body so that the victim is barely hanging on and then…." He looked at me apologetically before continuing. "And then the victim is given vampire's blood to replace what's been lost."

"Given?"

"Fed. Then, after it cycles through the system, there's no going back. The process is equivalent to death, since the soul leaves the body, but vampire blood keeps the flesh animated, the mind functioning. It sustains its own kind of life. The thing is, that sort of birth is not generated from the Source. It's purely organic, empty of light energy. So the knowledge of good is not there. All that's left is insatiable hunger and thirst."

I thought back to the vision that Anna had shown me, the image of Christian's gun. Why had his father insisted that Christian shoot him when he was already turning?

"But, Christian shot his father," I began. "I don't understand."

"They found him in time, before the change was complete. His soul must still have been intact, but he knew what was coming."

"So they *can* be killed like you or I…."

"Only if you catch it in time."

"God," I said.

"I'm so sorry. Sorry you have to hear any of this," he said.

"I'm sorry you had to experience it. But, William, if a soul can't survive in a vampire's body, how are you possible?" I asked.

"I said human blood can't survive. A soul can endure nearly anything," he answered. "The real problem lies in getting the damn thing back in once it's gone."

"Oh."

"And since I have a soul, the hunger for one is null. I don't want human blood."

"But how do you survive then?"

He paused, weighing his words. "If I can't drink what flows through your veins, I need to nourish what flows through mine. The blood in my body is aging, Lily, and *this*," he lifted the vial again, "is relatively fresh vampire blood. Keeping it cold preserves just enough remnant human cells to slowly replace what keeps me alive."

"So, why don't you just go through a blood bank? Drink what's been donated? You still wouldn't be killing anyone that way."

"I have no right to that blood, Lily. This body took enough of it in the last few decades. Besides, at least I know this stuff equals a dead vampire."

"Okay. And where in the hell does it come from?"

"Abram gets it for me."

"How? How does he pull that off?" I laughed.

"Think about it. Sentients battle vampires all over the world, right?"

"So I'm told."

"And Abram has connections nearly everywhere in the Society. He has his confiscators, so to speak. As silly as it sounds, it's packed in ice and shipped to us—it *is* organic matter, after all. Remember how combatants do away with vampires?"

"They break their necks, right?" I answered, like a good little student. "Via a psychic hold, since it's unsafe to come too near one."

"So their blood is rarely lost," William added.

"Ah-ha." I caught on. Taking the vial from between his fingers, I held it up to the light. "Why is it blue?"

"Wow, now you're just getting way too technical."

"I want to understand this. Come on."

"Fine, Lily." He laughed. "Because in humans, corpuscles are required to color the blood red. Young red blood cells mature, then they become the adult form in the bone marrow. That increases the production of hemoglobin, which is the red pigment in blood mixed with protein. You still with me?"

"Uuhh." I blinked. "Sort of. Keep going."

"Okay. So the reason human blood doesn't last long in vampires is because vampires, biologically, *don't* age, don't physically mature, and so they can't sustain the re-growth of new blood cells or the formation of hemoglobin. Therefore, vampire blood remains blue."

"And the glowing?"

"It's bioluminescence.

"Wait... like, the same thing that happens to fish at the bottom of the ocean?"

"Exactly. Vampires have been living in the dark for so long, in underground caves, in sewers, coal mines, hidden away from the light, that they've evolved an adaptation."

"Shit. Which is why their eyes are kind of black?"

"Exactly. No light. Pupils are almost always dilated."

"Huh. My goodness. This is fascinating."

"You mean disturbing?"

"That too. Okay, so, refocusing, you're drinking vampire blood. What's Christian's problem? Aren't you even more vital as a Sentient now, thinning the vampire population?"

He looked distressed. "*No.* Any blood coursing through their veins is, essentially, the result of a stolen human life. Doesn't that upset you? You don't resent me for that?"

I was beyond judging him. The darkness of his past was not his choosing.

"No, William. I'm not upset. And I don't resent you," I said as I reached up to touch his face, cupping his cheek.

He shut his eyes and placed his hand over mine. "Why do you think Christian despises me?" he sighed. "In his mind, the only honorable option would have been to let myself die."

"He's a damaged child," I said.

"And yet he holds more credibility in most eyes than I ever will," he said. "Sometimes I'm still amazed that you trust me. How is that possible?"

"Well," I began, "you wouldn't ease up on me for a moment. You were pushy, relentless, impossible. Unlike Christian, you refuse to fight my battles for me, even when I'm scared shitless. You understand that I don't need a hero—I just need some guts. You've always had faith in me, so, it's only natural that I should return the favor."

"That doesn't mean I'd let anything happen to you, please believe that," he said.

"I know," I assured him.

"I'd die first," he said, stepping closer to me.

"No dying!" I scolded. "Who else would put up with me half as well?"

He laughed. "You are definitely a bully."

"I am not," I grumbled. "I just get a little carried away. Sometimes my feelings kind of throw me off guard."

"Yet, ironically, I'm always the one getting *thrown*, Lily." He frowned.

"Eh…well, this is the truth."

"Mhm. You're a safety violation and you need a warning label."

"I have one. It says 'don't piss off the empath.'" I smiled, coyly. "And I seem to remember expressing that sentiment on more than one occasion. You had plenty of warning."

"Yes, I recall something now." The corner of his mouth turned up, and he lowered his face to mine, pausing a breath away. "What was it you said? I think it was 'never,' wasn't it?"

"Never?" I swallowed.

"Mhm." He sighed, forlornly. "Such a shame. But, as I'm exceptionally accommodating…." He shrugged and put the vile back, and then he turned to walk away.

"Rule change!" I called after him.

He stopped on a dime, turning his head back, and a slow grin worked its way across his face. "I'm sorry?"

"I made the rules; I can break them. The aforementioned 'never' bylaw shall now be known as the 'always' bylaw…er…something."

"Is that right?" His eyes were thoughtful.

"Yes."

He returned to me, taking both of my hands. "I like that rule," he said seriously. "It's a good rule."

"I think so," I said.

"Lily?"

"Hmm?"

"If Christian was here, standing right in this room…would you let me kiss you?" he asked.

"Might be a little awkward." I smirked.

"I mean it. Would you let me kiss you, out in the open, with the knowledge that he would actually see us?" he demanded.

Would I?

Yes. I would. "If he saw us, so be it. In fact, kiss me right now. He knows we're down here."

"Be certain what you ask for," he said. "I might get carried away this time."

"I want you to," I said, my heart pounding. He took a few quick breaths and lunged for me.

There was something new in this kiss, something feral. I liked it. And somehow—though it was beyond my capacity to know when—he'd managed to work us into the doorway, yet another act of rebelliousness. Leaning me into the frame, he deepened the contact, pressing himself wholly against me.

"I'm always secretly afraid," he whispered against my mouth, "that it's wrong for me to want you this much."

"I hope not," I answered. "Because I'm not about to discourage you."

"And I'm not about to stop," he said, pulling me up so that my legs wrapped around his waist. He continued his assault, biting my shoulder, my neck before tracing a line back up to my lips with his tongue. "God, sweetheart, I…." He paused at my mouth again, out of breath.

"You…yes?" I panted. He didn't answer, just appraised me, uncertainly.

"William, what?"

He smiled weakly and laid his forehead against mine. "I want to tell you, but I don't want to scare you," he whispered.

"Well, now, let's think about this. I've recovered from death-hold via soul sucker, molestation by a perverted demon, and unwanted attention from various creepy black things. I'm pretty sure you can throw most anything at me now."

He nodded, smiling for an instant longer, and then his expression faded into something sober. "You *know* I'm in love with you, right? I mean, even beyond that. I just…I love you."

I stared blankly, waiting for my head and heart to catch up. Despite everything that had unfolded between us, it was a shock to hear William say the words first. Wasn't I supposed to be the emotional one? The lag in my response distressed him.

He set me down. "Should I not have said that?"

"Yes, you should have." I hid my face in his chest and began to cry.

"Don't cry, sweetheart. I shouldn't have sprung that on you. You don't have to say a thing. I'm begging you, please, don't cry."

This was the beginning of the end for me, I knew it. His embrace was far too perfectly fitted to mine. "I won't cry anymore," I promised.

"Good." He tilted my face upward and kissed my cheeks. The words were there. They were *right* there, dangling in front of me—but so was Clara's request. Was I strong enough to choose this road? There would be such an outcry from certain Sentients, Christian most of all, and all our lives we'd be forced to endure a certain level of exclusion. And yet, William deserved to be loved. Should he suffer alone because of my insecurities? I'd do better than tell him. I'd *show* him.

"William," I began, shakily, "take me to your room."

He watched me, mulling over my request. "I need for you to be positive of what you want. There's no pressure here. If you're not sure you love me, then I'll wait until you are."

I took his face in my hands. "Take me to your room … please."

"Not until you're sure."

So it would always be with William. He may have been the master of provocation, but he'd never rob me of an opportunity to make up my own mind. In the end, my choices would always be my choices.

I laughed exasperatedly, staring up at him. "How is it possible that you *still* drive me crazy?"

"Considerable skill on my part." He cracked a smile, but the worry in his eyes was undeniable.

"So, this is up to me," I said.

"It's always been up to you, Lily."

I couldn't stand it. How could he be so exasperating and so wonderful in the same instant? If it was time for a flood, I might as well open those gates all the way. "All right, William. You want to know how I feel? The truth is, I'd give it all up, the sentience, the endowments, and I'd go back to Scranton and work in that damned store and stock fucking Pez dispensers for the rest of my life if it meant that I could still be with you until I die."

He stared at me. "That's the last thing I'd want you to do," he said.

"I know!" I smiled. "That's just it! How could I help but love you? I'm yours, because I choose to be."

"So … you love me," he finalized.

"*William*!" I laughed. "Without question I love you. I'm *in* love with you. Everything! *All* of it!"

His face was pure joy. "Then you own me. I'll give you anything you want."

"I *want* to go to your room!"

"*Thank* God," he moaned, lifting me up and carrying me across the basement to his bedroom door. He pushed it open and flipped on the light switch.

I looked around. "Whoa, no fair. You totally lucked out with this room. It's the biggest by far," I commented. Even the king-sized bed at its center seemed dwarfed in comparison. "And whose decorating job? Anna's?" I asked.

"No. The walls were already this color, but the rest is me."

"*William*," I said. "I am impressed!" The room was a dedication to Zen masters everywhere. Someone had painted the walls a muted green and William ran with it, placing a bamboo rug under his bed and various leaf prints on the walls. I smiled at the mental image of him hanging art.

"Were you gay in a past life?" I peered at him.

"Don't be mean." He frowned, setting me down. "I needed *somewhere* to escape to. Besides, straight men can have good taste, too, you know."

"Of course I do. And it's great! I swear. Wait, do I smell…patchouli?" I laughed.

"Cut it out, Lily," he warned.

"I'm simply observing." I shrugged. "I like your room." And I meant it.

"It's a good thing, because I don't think we could get away with this in yours." He smiled, strolling forward and pulling me into his arms.

"What *are* you doing?" I said, mimicking a southern belle.

"Trying to determine the nature of your purity at the moment."

"Oh," I said meaningfully. "How's that?"

"Well, are you feeling like a mountain spring or Triple Black?" he asked.

"How about a mountain stream filled with Triple Black?"

"Whoa. That's a lot of alcohol."

I burst out laughing. "You know, I'm still not exactly sure what the hell you mean by that," I said.

"Don't worry," he said, his voice low as he brushed his lips against mine. "I'll clarify."

He kissed me again, slowly this time, and seemed perfectly happy to do so. It was the sweetest kind of suffering, but I was losing patience. Instinctively, I grabbed hold of the back of his head and intensified things.

"Wow." He broke away, smiling. "Eager?"

"Not at all," I whispered.

"Liar." He took hold of my wrists and locked them behind my back, then returned to torturing me. His mouth brushed feather light against my shoulders, my neck, my jaw, and I did my best to keep my legs from folding under me, since collapsing would have really ruined the moment.

"Having trouble … standing …." I gasped.

He laughed quietly and backed me against the bed, laying me down on the foot of it. My hands immediately shot up to his face.

"Uh-uh," he scolded, pressing them into either side of me on the comforter.

"William," I complained. "Why are you trying to kill me?"

"Don't exaggerate," he said, dragging his teeth down the front of my neck.

"I'm … uhm, God," I croaked.

"You're what?" he asked, sucking on the flesh of my collar bone.

"Not … exaggerating." I was struggling for air now.

He snorted, and then raised his face to mine. "Lillian, let's establish a few points here. For one, it's been a long time since I've done this, so I'm not rushing through it …."

"Right," I caught my breath. "Wasn't thinking about that."

"And for another, will you let me lead?"

"Fine."

"Good girl. Now, I'll let go of your hands if you'll promise to match my pace," he offered.

"Okay," I whimpered, gathering up my discipline.

I wound my arms around his neck as he traced my lips with the tip of his tongue. Then, the bastard proceeded to kiss every part of me he could manage with my clothes still on. Excruciating, that's what this was. Naturally, I was more than a little relieved when he sat me up, placing my hands on the button of his shirt.

"So we get to take the clothes *off* now, William?"

"Unless you'd prefer I do this mentally." He smirked. "Because I could—"

"Not particularly," I interrupted, unfastening buttons. Yes. It may not have been decades for me, but as far as I was concerned, this was as good as my first time. Making love in the past had been a chore, a pretense. This was real.

I pushed the fabric of his shirt aside, taking him in. He was so pale and smooth. The muscles of his chest and torso were well-defined and there wasn't an inch of fat on him. No surprise, considering his diet. I ran my hands from his belt line up to his neck and covered his mouth with mine. He responded by searching for the hem of my shirt. I broke away, allowing him to pull it over my head.

He stared at me.

"You're sure?" he said finally. I didn't answer, just took his hands and led them behind my back to the strap of my bra. He hesitated again, looking at me strangely, and then unclasped the hooks. I shrugged out of it enough that he could slide it down my arms before I tossed it to the side.

He slid his shirt the rest of the way off and I lay back, holding my arms out. The look in his eyes was almost unbearable as he lowered himself over me, resting his chest against mine.

"What is it?" I asked him.

He inhaled slowly, taking a tendril of my hair between his fingers and playing with it.

"Lily. I don't know if I deserve this," he said softly. "Maybe you should reconsider."

So that was it.

"You pick a hell of a time to have reservations," I said.

"I'm sorry. It's just that you could have anyone. Someone who's good all the way through."

"William." I laughed. "Do you know what I see when I look at you?"

"A crash test dummy?" He smirked.

"Ugh! I am being so serious right now, so shut up and listen."

"I'm all ears."

I sighed. "What I see, what you *are*, is a man who had his life ripped away from him in the most unimaginable way, just because he was trying to do some-thing so very good. And, even after the darkness took you, you still struggled to find the light again. I don't think I'd have it in me to do the same."

"Yes, you would," he said, quickly.

"Don't be so certain," I argued. "But regardless, I've wasted valuable time being insufferable, conceited, proud, judgmental. And, as it turns out, I'm the one who doesn't deserve you. *You* reconsider."

"Never."

"Then it's settled. We both deserve to annoy the living shit out of each other for the rest of our lives."

He chuckled, and then his laughter grew in strength until it was shaking us both. "You are truly perfect for me."

"That's what I'm saying! Now ...." I caught his face with my hand. "Stop stalling. Or have you forgotten how this works?"

William raised an eyebrow. "That's dangerous, Lily."

I grinned, biting my bottom lip. "As usual, I am stricken with terror."

"I keep forgetting how out of the loop you are when it comes to vampire capabilities." He grinned.

"Is that a threat?"

"It's a fact."

The breath was knocked out of me as a surge of pleasurable heat swelled from the tips of my toes up through my thighs. I gasped, staring at William wide-eyed.

"What the hell was that?" I breathed heavily, squirming under him.

"Foreplay," he said.

"I see. Well, I don't know that it's completely fair," I said, scowling.

"Why not?" he complained.

"Because, you shouldn't be allowed to use the vampirey manipulation stuff in bed."

"*Why not?*" he persisted. "I can't use it anywhere else."

I thought about this. Surely I could come up with one good reason.

"Well, for one thing … it kind of makes for an uneven playing field, don't you think? I mean, I can't compete with that!"

"Is that what this is? A contest?"

"I …." I stuttered, thinking hard. Wasn't it always? "No?"

"Good," he said. "Because I would completely win."

"Oh, you are so … *nnngghh.*" I gripped the back of his head, my fingers clenching his hair as another searing ball of who knows what swelled from my thighs to—God help me—my center and upward still. This was not something I'd felt before, but holy fucking shit, it was good.

"Now, you were saying?" he whispered huskily against my ear.

"William. God. What are you doing to me?"

"Just moving my energy … here … like this," he whispered, hovering a hand above my knee. I shook with the sensation, the tingling, then pulsing of an unseen force. "And here …." He slid his fingers up, up ….

"I … I see," I panted. "That's really … ," more panting, "impressive," I said, the last word delivered in a shaky whimper.

He paused and burrowed his face into my neck. "And here," he began, his hand pausing an inch above the heat between my legs. "You feel me, Lily?" he asked in a voice so uncharacteristically deep and rough, it singed me through to the bone.

I swallowed, paralyzed, unable to moan, unable to speak. The feeling from his suspended touch was such that it locked me down, stunned, and all the while he watched my face through half-lidded eyes, breathing as if he'd run a marathon. He broke the floating contact long enough for me to catch my breath.

"Oh … fuck," I gasped. "Aren't you going to run out of energy?"

"Never." He slid his hand along my arm, over my stomach.

"If you keep doing that I'll be useless," I swore.

"Angel," he whispered in my ear. "Humor me. You have no idea how incredible this is," he groaned. "I never thought I'd have a chance to use any of this constructively. And God, just the sight of you …."

"Whoa, now. Hold on. So, I'm your guinea pig?"

He shrugged, smiling.

"William!"

"All right, fine. I'll show some mercy."

I nodded, lifting my head to kiss him again. Really, he didn't need to do much more than that. I'd never felt so powerfully attracted to anyone in my life. He could have read from a Rolodex at this point and I'd have lost it. He lowered his head, dragging his lips between my breasts.

"Are you … being a vampire again?" I rasped.

"No, Lily," he whispered, smiling against my skin. "This is all human. And … Jesus, you taste amazing, you know that?"

I didn't know whether to laugh or cry. So I did both, as usual.

"Empaths," he teased, burning his way down to my stomach. Gripping the snap on my jeans he went to unfasten them.

"Wait!" I stopped him.

"Do I have to?" His voice was rough.

"Yes."

"Why?"

"It's my turn." I slid out from under him, pushing him down onto his back.

"Your turn?" he repeated.

"That's right. You think you wrote the rulebook on foreplay?"

He looked amused. "Go for it."

"No problem." I eyed him up. The time for retribution was at hand. I dipped my head to his abdomen, stopping at his navel, and nipped my way up the full length of his torso.

"Hmm," he breathed out, his eyes closing as he laid his head back. "This is nice, Lily. But I'm still *very* much in control," he concluded, stubbornly.

I ignored his statement, grinning as I settled myself over him, pressing my hips into his. Oh my. He wasn't as cool as he let on, was he? Riding a shiver of anticipation at the feel of his erection, I ground myself into him once, twice.

"*Uuh*, God." His eyes shot open and his hands went for my ass, holding me there. "Shit, Lily," he laughed, unsteadily. "You're really cutting to the chase."

"I don't know what you mean," I taunted him with doe eyes.

"No?" he said. I should have seen it coming, but I was too wrapped up in feeling proud of myself. The next thing I knew I was on my back again, whimpering helplessly. William ran his hand quite determinedly between my legs, over my stomach and breasts, extraordinary fiery bursts traveling beneath his open palm. Pausing, he brushed his thumb lightly over a nipple before bending to take it in his mouth.

"Oh, *pleeease*."

"That's right, beautiful." He blew across the moistened skin. "You have to let me win sometimes," he said.

I twisted my hands into the blankets, trying to speak. "*Mean*," I whined.

"Consider it tough love," he said, letting up on the blazing torment long enough to unzip my jeans. Slipping my hand between us, I proceeded to follow his lead, tugging at his belt. Before long, we'd flung the bothersome attire on the floor and I sighed with relief.

"Boxers. Thank God."

He laughed. "You have an issue with briefs?"

"Absolutely," I admitted. "I could never love a briefs man."

"I'll keep that in mind. But in the mean time …." He grabbed hold of my leg and wrapped it around his waist and I gasped at the contact. His length pressed into the flesh of my stomach and he wrapped an arm behind me, pulling me into a kiss that was nowhere near gentle anymore.

"Lily…" he groaned, his mouth wide against mine.

"Yes," I encouraged.

He shuddered. "I need to be inside of you."

I raked my fingernails down his back, urging him on, and he entered me slowly, shaking as he filled me completely, pausing to plant soft kisses on my face before withdrawing.

"I love you so much, Lillian," he said, filling me again. "So much."

I wanted to respond in kind but was afraid that—for the zillionth time in a row—I'd start crying. So I sought his mouth instead, kissing him deeply.

"So," he managed between kisses. "You really thought you had the upper hand there for a minute, didn't you?"

I laughed. "I can take control of the situation any time I want."

"Denial … not your forte," he said.

I ordered myself to say something clever. But no. Goddamn you, William Maddox! Typical of him to thwart my efforts at comeuppance. I groaned against his shoulder, gripping down with my teeth. Was there any area in which he didn't qualify as Mr. Know It All? Hell, who even cared anymore? As I rocked against him, I was rapidly approaching the point where comprehensible thought was impossible. And watching William's face wasn't helping. He looked on the verge of tears. I could feel how this, yet another milestone in human reconnection, affected him. I draped my arms over his shoulders and looked into his eyes.

"Just this once," I said. "You win."

He smiled weakly, but his usual impish edge was replaced with an unmistakable expression of relief.

"Uugh, *shit*," he moaned, squeezing his eyes closed. "You feel *so* much better than I imagined," he said, and his movements increased in speed and force, the muscles in his shoulders tensing beautifully.

"You imagined?"

"Every day." He pressed his forehead to my cheek, his breaths hot against my face. "Fuck, Lily. I've needed you for so long."

My heart broke. It took guts for a man to admit he needed a woman, and with that kind of honesty on the line, I wasn't about to fail him. "I love you, William," I told him. "I love you and I'm not going anywhere," I repeated, arching upward to meet his lips, his desire, to take him in, body and soul. Holding on for dear life, I was overcome with the perfect nearness of him, the ache of human solitude nearly conquered.

William's lightline came alive and was totally exposed, pulsing its blue illumination in rhythm with the motion of our bodies. With each beat he brought me closer to where he was until we both stopped breathing. It was hard to comprehend what was happening, only that I'd lost track of where he ended and I began. A force intense and electric passed between us, and I realized that my own light was completely enmeshed with his. The charge concentrated where our bodies met and seemed to explode outward, filling my senses beyond their capacity. We held each other tightly, both of us trembling.

"Is this happening?" I gasped. William shook his head, his face hidden in my neck. A moment passed before he collapsed against my chest, winded and smiling.

"Unbelievable," he said.

Twenty

Theo reached across the table for a grapefruit, and it shot ahead of him. He hissed and dodged forward, catching it with a satisfied huff.

"Can someone hand me a knife?" he asked.

"No!" Katrina and Elaine shouted in alarm.

He glowered at them.

"So, did he show you?" Christian asked me. Theo dropped his grapefruit and everyone tensed.

"Let us enjoy our breakfast, please," I said.

"I'm just asking," he said casually. "A simple yes or no would suffice."

"He did," I answered.

"And?"

"And nothing," I said. "It doesn't bother me."

Christian sat back in his chair, examining me. "It doesn't bother you at all?"

"Not at all." I found myself smiling.

He narrowed his eyes and shook his head, flipping his fork around between his fingers.

"Lily, just be careful. Be sure your opinions are your own," he said civilly.

"What does that mean?" I asked him, working to sound unaffected. If he was willing to behave himself, so was I.

"Remember what he's capable of," he said.

"My mind will always be my own, Christian. Don't worry."

He nodded.

"Where is William this morning?" I asked no one in particular.

"He's with Wendell and Abram," answered Clara.

"Mm," I said.

"They've been in there all morning," Katrina added. "I don't know if I like it very much."

"Why not?" I asked.

"Wendell has been trying to keep it to himself," she sighed. "And I've *tried* not to read any of his thoughts but, sometimes they just slip out."

"Slip out? About what?" I asked.

"*Craaap,*" she moaned in frustration. "I don't think I ought to say anything just yet. Truth be told, I may be completely confusing everything. Let's just wait, okay? Sorry I even said anything."

"I hate it when she does that." Anna sighed.

"I think I've lost my appetite," I said, frowning over my French toast.

"Not like you brought one with you this morning, anyway," Christian remarked. "You haven't actually *eaten* anything. Just pushed it around in circles."

"Huh?" I looked down at my plate. So I hadn't. "Very observant of you, Christian."

"I have my moments." He flashed a grin. "Don't stress... or if you *must* stress, give me your leftovers."

I sighed and pushed the plate in his direction.

Anna peered at me strangely, and then shared the expression with Katrina. It was time for me to exit before a certain Californian knew too much.

"Time to feed Rufus," I lied, grabbing a section of newspaper to take with me.

"That's not the crosswords, is it?" Christian shouted after me.

"No, Christian!" I waved the evidence in the air as I left the room.

Ah, the power of four walls and a closed door. They almost had the ability to make your mind your own again. Spreading the paper out across my bed, I browsed the recommended local events section. I giggled, imagining that "Cotton Candy Mandy" would probably not make the list. Then, somehow, the article transformed into a feature devoted to William Maddox, as did the editorial section, political cartoons and want ads. *Especially* the want ads.

This was no use.

I flung the paper to the side and lay back. Now would've been a good time to have Kate around... if only she didn't hate me.

"Lil? Open up!" Katrina knocked.

Fuck. This was one battle I could not win.

"Hello, ladies, miss me already?" I smiled, letting Anna and her now everpresent sidekick enter my room.

"Devastatingly," Anna cried.

"Besides, you've got the goods and we want some dishing." Katrina grinned.

"I have *no* clue what you guys are talking ab—" I stopped as Katrina crossed her arms and cocked an eyebrow at me. "Come on! I thought you were trying not to read other people's thoughts!" I whined.

"*Oh, wow.* So there *is* something good to tell! You're amazing, Anna!" Trina turned to dote on her girlfriend.

"What just happened?" I frowned.

"Been teaching her how to wheedle information without the mind-reading." Anna smiled proudly.

I put my finger to my temple and shot my head. "Positively medieval behavior, Anna."

"Oh, now. Let's not lose sight of the ball, shall we? Fill us in!" Anna closed the door quickly and popped onto the floor.

"On what?" I maintained my innocence.

"On what William is like in bed, of course!"

"Are you crazy? I'm not telling you, I mean, there's nothing to…shit." *Dammit, Annelise!*

Katrina beamed at Anna before joining her on the floor. They were two peas in a pod: one a master of cunning, and the other of conning. I sat on the bed, staring at them woefully.

"Lord, Anna. I'm glad you're happy, but the two of you together are a force of nature," I complained.

"And speaking of forces of nature…." Anna raised and lowered her eyebrows mischievously. "Quit stalling with the good bits!"

"Ugh! How did you know?" I glared.

Anna smiled. "William's energy was hard to tell apart from yours this morning," she explained.

"Do you think anyone else noticed?" I panicked.

The girls exchanged looks. "Not everyone…" Katrina said. I flushed head to toe.

"Not my brother, anyway," Anna comforted. "Combatants can't usually detect the intricacies of emotion in an aura."

I nodded, breathing again.

"So, was my theory right, then?" Anna asked. "Was he, you know, gifted?"

I couldn't stop the corner of my mouth from lifting. "You could say that," I admitted.

"Oooh, I *knew* this would be good." Anna bounced. "So, was he nice? Was he vocal?"

"Too far!" I said. "I'm not getting that personal."

"You can't tell us if he was nice?" Trina asked.

"Well, no, I mean that's fine, I guess. He was more than nice. He was William."

They stared at me blank-faced. "What does that mean, exactly, Lily?" Trina began. "You're the only one of us besides Clara who seems to read the guy well."

I smiled, dreamily. "He was stubborn in the best ways, and tender, and evil, and perfect."

Katrina sighed deeply, reflecting my glow. "Oh, Lily ...."

Anna interrupted the shared moment. "Wait, wait, wait ... screw the sappiness. Evil? What exactly do you mean by that?"

The girl didn't miss a beat.

"I mean, you were right. He ...." I laughed to myself, undoubtedly blushing. "He, uhm ...." I bit my lip.

"How good *was* he?" Anna said, suddenly at a whole new level of interest.

"I actually had to make him promise to knock it off so I'd have a fighting chance at dignity," I admitted.

Both girls' mouths fell open.

"Damn." Trina gaped.

"*Anyway*," I moved along. "That wasn't even the most amazing part. It was the end."

"The *end*? You were glad when it was over?" Anna made a face at me.

"No! Okay, definitely not. I mean, when we were ... you know...."

They looked on, clueless. I scowled.

"Oh!" Comprehension dawned on Anna's face. "Right! The best part!" she sang.

"But that's the point!" I said. "It wasn't. I mean, sure there was the—granted above average—physical pleasure, but something more, too. Something better."

Anna lifted to her knees. "*What*, Lily?"

I sighed. "I can't understand it, but our light, our light just … came together. I mean, it merged. For a long moment, it felt like we weren't two people anymore. Just one. I know it sounds horribly sappy, but it was real."

"God, Lily." Trina smiled. "Sounds like a fated blend."

"A who?" Anna looked at her, confused.

"It's only a theory," Trina continued. "My mom told me about it once. Of course, she *is* the queen of knowing everything and understanding nothing, but … I remember her mentioning fated blends. She said that some souls are bonded so closely from one life to the next that their greatest comfort is to join, to blend together."

"What for?" Anna asked.

"No idea. Who knows if the theory is even true? We *are* talking about my mother, after all."

I was in awe. This hadn't been the first time I'd experienced the fulfillment of linking souls with William. "You know," I said, "I love him, Anna."

"Well, I knew that all along!" Anna bragged. "Even if you *were* completely deluding yourself into thinking otherwise."

"Wouldn't you be?" I challenged. "William is the most controversial straw I could have drawn. Christian would string me up!"

"Don't be absurd!" Anna barked with laughter. "My brother would throw himself into a herd of stampeding elephants to keep you safe. He would have a huge messy fit about you and William, but he'd never hurt you."

I frowned. "But would he hate me?"

"At first … maybe. But not forever, Lily. I don't think he could if he wanted to. He might go after William, though," she admitted.

"He'd have to get through me first," I vowed.

Katrina whistled. "Man. You are hard-core passionate about Maddox, Lily. That's really funny."

"Why is it funny?" I asked, glaring defensively.

"Well, I mean, I'm not claiming to be any kind of expert in the field, but William has always seemed so …."

"Go on …."

"Aloof? Hands-offish?"

"He's not like that once you get to know him," I clarified.

"Does he talk?"

"Ha! *Yes.* But he's just more selective than most people about his subject matter. He observes and *then* gives an opinion," I said.

"The most vocal of which are nearly always prompted by my brother," Anna said. "William spends a lot of energy deflecting Christian's jabs. It's a wonder he has any left to be with you, Lily."

There had been a time, thanks to me, when William was forced to deflect attacks from two directions. "I can't believe he was so patient with me." I stared out a window. "You have no idea how horrible I was, Anna."

"Oh, Lily, he obviously forgives you."

"Yes, but why? Why did he put up with me like that? I cut him down in the worst way. He just refused to give up on me, even when he had every right to."

There was movement in the hallway and footsteps. I perked up. "They're done talking."

The three of us sat still, listening hard until the footsteps faded out of earshot.

"Did you get anything, Trina?" I asked.

"What? You mean thoughts?"

"Yes."

"*Now* you want me to?" She put a hand on her hip.

I frowned.

"Fine." She sighed. "They're going to gather everyone."

"Well, *come* on, then," Anna prompted, jumping up.

We made our way as far as the reception hall. Everyone else was there already.

Christian stood next to Clara with one arm around her shoulders. Anna joined them and Trina followed, waving me along. I shook my head, pausing where one room met the next.

"Ah, good, we're all together," Abram said, standing next to Wendell in the living room archway. The group radiated a dynamic of preparedness. Demetre and Ophelia were off to one side, Ginny fidgeting peacefully between them. Paul hunched with his hands in his pockets next to Thomas, whose arms were crossed. The Polmieris and the Rushes waited together, off to my right in the corner.

Only one person stood alone. William watched Abram from in front of the hall window. The crisp white of his shirt, rolled up at the arms, stood out in the dark room. He looked stunning there—guarded, and if I was not mistaken, worried, but stunning.

"Good morning, everyone," Abram began. "I trust you can all conjecture why we're here?"

Some nodded soberly, while others waited for Abram to continue.

"In the past months, my Sentients have enjoyed an idyllic cycle of peace. We've boasted as stable a home as any such group could ask for. But, as you all know, our enemy does not sit idly by. The coven of vampires we drove from Vancouver, the same that dwelt in Philadelphia these eight months, is once again on the move. They have regained their strength and their numbers, split into lesser concentrations, and are headed north. And so, we must ready ourselves. In under a month's time, when we know where their leaders are positioned, we will move on."

Nothing could have prepared me for this, even the months I'd spent here, even knowing what I knew now. This life wasn't a game; it wasn't a trip to Oz. It was real.

"I will also add," Abram continued, "that one in our number will take their leave sooner still. I have asked William to go ahead of us, to learn, if he can, of the central coven's condition and whereabouts."

I froze, locking eyes with William. He looked at me only briefly before watching Abram again.

Our Seer went on. "The latest report comes from our friend and Sentient reconnoiter, Hensel Utterbach. Hensel has spent the last month traveling through our areas of concern and reports that the loss of Lolial has, evidently, caused some confusion among their ranks. Hensel could not, however, safely determine the root location of their leaders. This is where Mr. Maddox will come in. It is likely he would recognize their more prominent figures, since many of them belonged to the same group he penetrated in his protection of Lillian. He will be departing in two weeks time. I trust that he will be as invaluable to us as he has always been."

Someone scoffed to my right—unquestionably Christian. I ignored him.

"I am truly sorry." Abram sighed, sadly. "But we will rebuild and regroup again. We are, after all, family. Now, let's enjoy this day while we are all together!"

Everyone began to move, mingle, and chatter—this was a usual transition for them—while the world felt as if it had dropped from under me. I leaned against the wall, battling tears. William crossed the room and stood beside me, watching me silently for a moment.

"Lily?" he started.

A thick snake coiled itself around my lungs and squeezed. "This is bad."

William frowned. "Yes. But at least we still have a few weeks before I leave. Everyone will join back up in a month, anyway. It'll be all right."

"But you're going to have to be with them, to talk to them…and what if something happens? You'll be all alone out there!" I whispered, terrified.

He smiled. "Well, it wouldn't be the first time."

"That doesn't make it any better," I said. "This isn't fair."

"Lily, I have no choice. I have to go. We have to keep tabs on them. It's our job to weaken them."

And now those beasts were moving north. North. Toward those I'd left behind.

Everything felt boxed in, airtight. Christian's gaze oscillated repeatedly in our direction, and the room's noise grew steadily in volume. I felt the color leaving my face.

"I have to get some air," I begged.

William noted my panic and nodded quickly, following me. I slid behind the Rushes, lost in conversation about the casualties of the Vancouver battle, and William trailed close behind me. Anna noticed me leaving first, then Christian caught on at the last second, but we were already out the door.

I booked it to the passenger side of William's car.

"Where are we going?" William asked as we walked.

"I don't care! Anywhere."

He studied me. "Okay."

"Wait!" Christian was running down the front porch steps toward us. "Are you okay?"

"Fuck," I muttered. "I'm fine, Christian!"

He stopped a few feet short of me, peering at the keys in William's hand.

"Where are you going?"

"I have no idea," William admitted.

"Why are you going, then?" Christian said.

"Why do you *always* need to know?" I asked.

"Because you look like you're going to throw up, that's why!"

"Then let me get out of here for a little bit, okay?"

"All right. Then let me take you!" he insisted, disregarding any efforts at pretense of meaning.

"No!"

"Why the hell not?" He stared at me.

I could just say it. I could just blurt it out. Because I loved William, because he was mine. Because I needed him now.

"Because I asked William," I said.

"So? Change your mind! Ask me instead." He snapped his head toward William. "Tell her, Maddox."

"It's up to her." William stood his ground. "She's not a child."

Christian gritted his teeth, laughing out of his nose. "I don't know what kind of fucked up games you're playing with her, vampire. I don't know how you're screwing with her head …."

I bristled. "You need to *stop*—"

"But I'll *damned* well find out, though," he said over me, then he turned and headed back to the house.

I exhaled.

"Get in the car, Lily," William ordered, stiffly.

I did as he told me, and barely had my door closed before we were past the property line and driving at considerable speed. William's fists tightened and loosened around the steering wheel. He swerved off the main road onto a country lane, passing the few homes on this route until there were only wheat fields. Then he slowed down and pulled over onto the shoulder, crushing some dried stalks under his tires.

I stared at him, thought about speaking, but looked out my window instead.

"I hate him sometimes," he said finally.

"I know. Me too."

"I'll always be this *thing*, won't I?" he said. "I'll never measure up. And if it was only Christian, it would be one thing. But it's not. It's the majority of the Society. It's a huge faction of my own community that wants me dead."

"William." I went to touch him and he winced. He got out of the car, slamming the door behind him. This was the first time I'd really seen William angry on any level close to Christian's fury. It was intimidating, but I slid off my seat and followed him anyway.

He walked around the car to the other side and leaned against the back door, staring into the field. What could I say? There wasn't a single worthy thought in my head. I had no idea what he was going through.

He sighed. "I was supposed to be helping you," he said. "I'm sorry, Lily."

"Oh, screw it," I said. "I'm okay now."

We stood in silence again.

"I'm sorry, William." I made a feeble attempt at comfort.

"This sick role I have to play … I can't stand it. Do you think I relish pretending to be one of them again?"

My energy was obviously causing William's walls to fail. He was probably saying more than he'd intended, but I made no effort to stop him, just followed as he stormed toward the field, cutting into the golden waves.

"Where are we going?" I asked, trudging along.

"I don't know." He paused suddenly, looking at me. "But what if we don't stop? What if we keep walking? We could keep walking, Lily. Or driving."

It was tempting. But how would he survive? And how would we be safe? And, more than anything else, how could I live with myself if I ran away from my own life? "No. You know we couldn't." I sighed.

"You're right." He stomped onward. "Because I've got years of absolution to work out."

"William, slow down!" I begged, the heat of the sun bearing down on me. He veered to the right, ripping up strands of wheat as he went, flinging them off to the side. We were nearing a large magnolia tree that was growing along the line where the field ended and a grassy plain began. Finally, some shade! "Hey, I mean it, stop!" I ordered, grabbing his shoulder.

He jerked around, staring at me. "Why?"

"Because I'm tired, William!"

At first he glared at me. Then his anger turned to sadness, then despair. It was the most frightening expression I'd ever seen on someone I loved. How dare I say *I* was tired? What a joke. My life was a joy ride compared to his.

"God … I'm so sorry," I said quickly. "And I'll follow you to Scandinavia if you want me to. I adore you, William. *I'll* be your fucking absolution," I said.

He remained silent for an infinite moment, the light gone from his eyes. Then the sky flipped upside down as he flung himself at me, kissing me quickly and nearly toppling me over. It was overwhelming. He was angry and relieved and a million other things, and if he kept kissing me like this I'd have to combust in a wheat field.

He broke away, allowing me some air. "Everything is wrong without you," he said.

"If you really want to leave, I'll come with you."

He shook his head. "No, you're right. We can't escape this life. And I have to go where I'm needed. It's my job and I'll get over it. Just, let me … touch you." He dropped to his knees, pulling me with him and I leaned in to kiss him again. It occurred to me that we were—for once—really, actually alone. I took hold of his hands, urging them to roam freely.

"Is this okay? Here?" he asked, breathing coarsely against my mouth.

"Yes. Here works. Anywhere works," I answered.

We didn't bother taking all our clothes off. It was so much more effective just to lose the apparel requiring removal. I climbed into his lap and settled over his arousal, taking the length of him into me with a broken gasp as he guided me with his hand and a raw new intensity. After only a few moments we were out of breath and saturated with sweat.

It was all happening so fast. My body seared from the tips of my toes to the end of every hair. A mounting whimper worked its way out of my chest and into the open, and I pressed my lips together, trying to be reverent, clinging to an asinine shred of modesty.

"Don't, Lillian," William growled. "I want to hear you."

Modesty was overrated anyway.

I opened my mouth and instinctively cried out, falling limp into his arms with the force of my climax.

"God … *perfect*," he muttered and laid me down on the ground, assaulting my lips as he moved inside of me. I whispered how I wanted him, how I loved the way he felt, and with a drawn out moan, he found his release, the roughness of his kiss slowing into something more tender. When we finally parted, he breathed above me, invigorated.

"Am I absolved now?" he chuckled.

"Not quite." I smiled lazily. "It's like Hail Marys. You'll have to repeat the assignment several more times before the redeeming business kicks in."

"Then we better get cracking. I've only got a few weeks," he said smiling.

Twenty-One

*H*ow do you squeeze every last ounce of potential out of a day, an hour, when the passage of time is your worst enemy? I knew the answer to this question quite well, and in the face of panic and malice, William's room had become our late-night haven.

We sat on the floor, leaning against the foot of his bed. His television was on, but neither of us were watching. Instead, I stroked his face with my thumb.

"You're pretty," I said.

He smiled warmly. "So are you."

"And I'm rather fond of you," I added.

"I know. It's a nice change from the days of you hating my guts."

I shrugged a shoulder. He kissed my forehead. "That reminds me. I've wanted to ask you something for a while," he said.

"What's that?"

"When, exactly, did you fall in love with me?"

I thought back. "After the Incubus. When you healed me."

"Huh. You hugged me. I wasn't expecting that."

"And *you* were a tad unresponsive," I said.

"I was afraid to move. I thought you might let go."

I sighed, snuggling closer against him. "I thought I'd freaked you out."

"No, Lily. Every kind word you allowed me, even the suggestion of a smile, made me hope. Though, I was prepared for you to fall in love with Christian. It made more sense. He *is* the knight-in-shining-armor type."

"My hero preferences are far less prosaic than you give me credit for," I said.

"I realized that after a while."

"Good. And how about you? What on earth put it in your head to fall in love with me? You're a glutton for punishment, William."

"I must be." He laughed. "It was probably the first time you repelled me."

"What?" I giggled.

"Yes. I have a weakness for strong women."

"Very progressive of you."

"Or maybe your first morning here. When you choked on your cereal," he said.

I laughed. "Oh, that was awful. You were very thoughtful, though."

"I couldn't help myself. You were so beautiful," he said, smiling. Then his face fell. "So how much longer can we drag this out before you have to make an exit?"

"We have time. Unless you want me to go." I pouted.

His arms tightened around me. "What do you think?"

I sighed deeply, feeling horrible. There was no reason for me to hide this anymore. A huge part of my life was William and a true Sentient would embrace that boldly. I tilted my head up to look at him. "William? It's time we announced ourselves," I said.

He widened his eyes. "You know what you're saying, right? This is guaranteed not to end well with certain parties."

"And that will always be the case for us, won't it? We have to start somewhere."

"Hmm." He reached down and twined our fingers together, then lifted my hand to his face, kissing my wrist. "What will we tell them?"

"Well, the truth. I'll just say 'William and I are….'" I hesitated. "In love? Dating? A couple?" I scratched my head. All my options played out flat or cheesy.

"Courting?" He smirked. "Involved?"

I made a face. "Bleh, none of those. We need a thesaurus."

"An item?" He chuckled, kissing my forehead. "Lovers?" He kissed my cheek.

"Oh, really, that's just painful," I said.

"What about …." He kissed me gently and looked me in the eye, his gaze soft. "Engaged?"

A split second passed before the word sunk in. Oh my Lord. Jesus, Mary, and Joseph say something....

"Lily?" His voice broke, but he didn't look away. "I'm an idiot. Scratch that from your memory. God, I screwed everything up, didn't I?"

"Please...one minute...." I begged, and then I waited. Where was the panic? With the reality of William's suggestion gestating and as heavy an issue as it should have been, where was the panic? Hadn't I put off every other man I'd known? How did I understand that this was right? A million thoughts flashed through my head at a million miles a second. Abram had done it. He'd locked us together. He knew. What did he know? I had to talk to him. Now.

"William—"

"Really," he interrupted. "I love you. Never say yes and I'll be happy enough just to have you with me."

"Would you listen to me?" I laughed, hopping off the bed. "I have to talk to Abram. I'll be right back."

"Okay...." He sat up immediately and rested his head in his hands, pitifully. Returning to him, I pried his hands free, letting him rest against me instead.

"Don't worry, okay?" I said. "I love you, William. Just give me a few minutes." I lifted his face and kissed him quickly, then ran upstairs.

It was midnight. Abram had said that there was no bad time for me to talk to him. Did I dare test that theory? What were the chances of him being in his study at this hour?

My joy at seeing the lights glowing under the door was overwhelming. I knocked and Abram opened it without delay.

"Come in, Lily. I was waiting for you."

I smiled back, tears turning his light into an amber blur.

❧

"How long have you known?" I asked, watching Abram.

"For longer than you've been Lillian Hunt to this world," he said.

"What *are* you?"

"Only a man...who happens to see overlapping generations, the wider span of time."

"And *what* do you see, about William and me?"

"You're willing to receive this now?"

"Desperately."

"Then I shall gladly tell you. You see, William was not born in your time, Lily, though he was meant to be, nor were you born in his, though *you* were meant to be. Souls progress to the next life at varying rates, depending upon their willingness to move on, their state of mind at death. Sometimes, a soul is not reborn immediately, but lags behind. You, as a pathcrosser, should know this well."

I nodded.

"Understand that the spirit must live many lives in succession in order to gather the knowledge of a whole being. Your spirit possesses everything needed for perfection from the moment of its very first birth, but in the human form, you cannot comprehend your full potential without repeated trials.

"With each new life, we come across the same core group, the same union of souls. This is why Sentients are so often born of Sentients, you see. I cannot say what caused the timing to misalign for you and Mr. Maddox, but I *can* say that the universe was aware of your bond, and it was working in flawless perfection to bring you together."

"That's why …." I barely breathed.

"That's right, Lily. One of you had to suffer the greater cost for the purpose of joining again. But William would do it repeatedly, a thousand times over, I'm certain, if he knew why it had to happen."

"He doesn't know, then?" I lifted a hand to my heart. "You've never told him?"

"No, Lily. I thought it would be best coming from you."

Even without Abram telling him, William clearly understood that much. It was always supposed to come from me.

"You know," Abram began again, "it can be terribly lonely, this Sentient's life."

I nodded. "I remember Christian saying that to me the very first day I met him."

"Yes. It's true. One often believes it best to choose the higher path over the companionship of another. But, this circumstance draws to mind a point which Seers might forget too easily."

"What's that?"

"That love *is* the higher path."

I smiled at him. "Oh, Abram. I have to tell you … he's asked me to marry him."

He nodded. "Congratulations. That is assuming you'll say yes?"

"Of course I will. I love him."

"Quite obviously." He grinned happily.

"And … I have to go now."

"Indeed. Before the boy loses his mind."

I laughed, and then hugged him tightly. "Thank you. Thank you."

"Ah, Lily. There will be trials," he said, taking my hand. "You must be strong for him."

"I know."

"Then you have my blessing for all your days." He released me. "Go!" He smiled on.

And I ran.

○

I stood in the doorway for a moment as William glanced up at me with wary eyes. He hadn't moved from his place on the bed.

"I'm back," I whispered, walking over to kneel at his feet.

"I know. I see you."

I took his hands and kissed them, holding them in both of mine.

"You've always pushed me too close to the edge and then left me hanging there to choose. It's not fair, William."

He stared at me, then lowered his face. "I'm so sorry, Lily."

"It's not fair," I went on. "But it was a small, insignificant price I've paid to reach this place. Trivial, compared to the price you've paid."

He looked up at me again.

"All this time, you've thought the universe abandoned you," I said. "Left you unwantable."

He held my hands more firmly as they began to shake.

"You've suffered a long time, William. And it's so unmerited that it's cruel."

"Lily, why are you saying all of this?" he pleaded at last.

"Please. Just let me," I said.

He waited.

"Abram says…he says you were turned because your soul was trying to catch up, trying to realign your timing."

"Timing?"

I gazed at him and my heart ached. "For us."

The look in his eyes was perplexing. Why couldn't I read his mood?

"William. Do you understand what I'm saying? You were turned to bide your time. You were waiting for me."

He lowered his hand to my arm. "Then I'm not cursed anymore, I don't deserve to die…."

"No!" I leaped up. "*No.*" I kissed every inch of his face. "You are a miraculous man, a beautiful man."

He came alive. "We're *for* each other," he said, taking my face in his hands. "We're intended."

"*Yes.*" I smiled.

He stared in astonishment. "And you'll marry me?"

I sat in his lap, wrapping my arms around his shoulders. "If my soul is lucky enough, then I will. Every time around."

Better that my bones were made of steel as he crushed me in a suffocating embrace.

ᦇ

"Big news? What kind of big news? I'll tell ya, kid, you keep me young." Frank chuckled into the phone.

"Uhm… *well*, it's of a rather shocking nature," I admitted.

"Again, this is becoming the norm with you, kiddo," he teased.

"Okay, I'll give you that one. But, really, I think you ought to get Grandma on the other line for this. She'll appreciate it. Trust me."

"All right then. Connie!" he shouted. She didn't answer. "Oh, Christ, she probably doesn't have her hearing aids in. One second…."

A full minute went by before he returned to the phone. "Okay. She's on," he said.

"Hi, Grandma." I smiled.

"Hi, Lily. Frank says you have news. You're not pregnant are you?"

"*What*? No, I am not!" I laughed.

"Well, what is it?" she asked. "Are you married?"

"Hey," Frank broke in. "What did I say about laying off the man stuff, Con?"

I smirked. "Ooh, I don't know about that," I said.

"What? Why?!" Connie said, excitedly. "Have you met someone?"

"Erm, yes?" I cringed.

"Well, is it serious?" she squawked.

"Yes," I said.

"How serious?"

"We're … he asked me to marry him, Grandma."

"Praise God!! How the hell much longer did I have to wait? But, hold on … how long have you known this boy?"

"Ever since I moved here."

"And you're just mentioning him *now*? I've spent countless sleepless nights praying for you to find yourself a—"

"Now, Connie," Frank said quickly. "I'm sure she had her reasons for not saying anyth—"

"Oh, put a sock in it, old man!" she barked. "Lillian Hunt, you're lucky you're in Georgia or I'd swat your behind. I don't care *how* old you are."

I sighed. "You know, Grandma, they have workshops for people with anger management issues."

She fell silent. "What?" she asked.

"Never mind. Anyway, you may just get the chance to inflict some damage soon enough. We're coming to Pennsylvania."

"You are?!" Frank said. "When?"

"A few weeks. There's a project we need to work on. We'll be there for a while, I think."

"It's about time!" he said. "I've missed your face."

"I've missed you, too. And you'll get to meet my William."

"William, is it?" Connie sniffed. "Do you hear that Frank? He's *her* William, and we're only now learning his name! Does he come with a last name or will you reveal that *after* the wedding?"

"Maddox," I said. "His last name is Maddox."

"Lillian Maddox," Frank said. "Has a nice ring to it, don't you think?"

"I do," I said.

"And you really love this guy, huh?" he asked.

"Ugh, God, so much." I swooned.

"Haha! My Lillian's in love. I knew it would happen one day, on your own time," he said.

"Well, I'm glad one of us did," I said. "And, Grandma, I didn't say anything because I didn't want to get your hopes up until I knew for certain what the outcome would be … because I love you so," I added.

She huffed, and then sighed. "Well, so long as I get great-grandbabies," she said.

Problematic. There was no explaining this one to her. What would I say? "I'm sorry, Gram, but William can't make babies on account of he's a vampire and he has no sperm"? No, that would never do, so I cleared my throat and bypassed the issue.

"Promise you won't scare him," I said.

"Nonsense. I'll be a saint," she retorted.

William had faced down every kind of horror this world had to offer, but he had yet to meet Connie Hunt.

❧

"This is a bright day in the history of my Sentients." Abram sat with William and me in his study. "Be brave. No matter what happens, know that you are right and good and I am exceedingly proud."

William smiled at me and took my hand.

"I've anticipated this moment since you joined us, Lillian," Abram went on. "Though I must admit you had me concerned. You were far more obstinate than I'd expected you to be."

"You have no idea," William said dryly.

"And you gave the boy a terrible time," Abram teased, smiling.

I gaped, trying not to laugh. "In all fairness, Abram, he gave it *right* back," I said.

"This is good," Abram said. "You two will never grow tired of each other."

I laughed, glancing at William. "No. Not possible," I said. William smiled into his lap.

"And Mr. Maddox?" Abram fixed his eyes on William. "Now that you've got her, I trust you'll endeavor to keep her?"

William looked at me. "If I have to let her repel me across the continent," he said. I smirked at him.

"On that note, then, shall we go?" Abram got up from his chair. I sighed nervously, squeezing William's hand.

The three of us walked to the reception hall where everyone was already waiting. A swarm of nerves threatened to kick my legs out from under me, but I fought them back.

Abram led us to the center of the room and paused. "Say what must be said," he told us, stepping aside.

Already it was William and I versus the world. Every face was on us. Some were smiling—Anna and Katrina— while others simply gawked curiously. William and I had done such a thorough job of concealing our affections that this would undoubtedly come as a shock to many. Still, only one person's expression suggested any sign of dismay. I looked away from Christian. As spiteful as he had become, it would pain me to hurt him.

"Lily," William whispered, wrenching me from my daze. I scanned the room once more, summoning my strength, and then took William's hand. Katrina gasped. She had undoubtedly captured the purpose for our gathering. Anna peered at her, but she kept quiet.

"William leaves tomorrow," I began. "But before he does, there's something I need to say."

Abram nodded.

"We're …." I faltered, my whole body shaking.

"I'll tell them." William gazed at me affectionately.

"No. I think… I think it has to be me," I said. And my words felt true. This was my stand to take. He'd carried us both for long enough.

"I've been afraid," I said to them, my voice breaking, "to tell you the truth." A tear rolled down my face, and I wiped it away quickly. "About who I am, who I love. But, I can't be afraid anymore."

Elaine and Clara looked on sympathetically. But Christian shifted, shaking his head, his eyes wide with alarm.

"William leaves tomorrow, and I won't let that happen before telling you all … we're engaged," I said finally.

"Oh, Lily!" Anna squealed and ran for me, flinging her arms around me and beaming wildly. "I *knew* it!"

"No, *I* knew it," Katrina corrected her.

"Well, *I* didn't know it!" Paul complained. "Way to leave me out of the loop."

"Don't feel bad, kid," Demetre said. "I didn't know squat."

Thomas patted William on the back. "Congratulations, son. You certainly do keep a low profile about these sorts of things, don't you?"

William laughed and lifted an eyebrow. "If you say so."

"He's not that sneaky," I said. "He's just exceptionally good at following directions." William looked at me and winked, then bent down to kiss my cheek.

Perhaps that was the straw that broke the camel's back, or maybe my reluctance to so much as peek at Christian had hidden the danger all along. But in an instant, William was thrown back against the wall and something was choking him.

"Christian!" I screamed, running to William's side. "Stop it! Stop!"

Christian disregarded my pleas, standing rigidly in place with his arm outstretched. William battled for air, writhing and gasping on the floor.

"Son, please!" Clara cried. "For the love of God, no more!"

Abram edged closer to Christian's side. "Christian, think about what you're doing. You're not a murderer," he spoke to him calmly.

Christian sneered. "No. *He* is." He tightened his hold on the air and William convulsed, his eyes rolling back in his head.

I turned to face Christian, a tidal wave of anger searching for its quickest escape. With no effort, it clawed its way free of my flesh and I drove my energy outward. Christian lifted in the air and smashed against the hall window, shattering it loudly.

At last, William took the first of several jagged breaths. I slunk down the wall to kiss his face, holding his head to my chest. "I'm so sorry," I whispered. His chest rose and fell arduously, but he reached his arms around me, pulling me closer.

"I'm not a monster …." He breathed against me.

"We know you're not." I buried my face in his hair, crying.

Clara stood in the center of it all, completely torn, and I felt the agony of her dilemma. Should she come to our aid, or the aid of her own son, now sobbing silently in a mess of broken glass?

Anna sensed the moment and went to her brother, kneeling down beside him. "Why did you do it?"

"Don't." Christian shook his head, pushing himself up. Blood soaked through the back of his shirt and stained his hands. "Don't talk to me. You *knew*. You, all of you *knew*!" He looked at his mother and Katrina.

"Christian, we didn't know how to tell you," Clara said.

"You're my mother!" he moaned. "My flesh and blood. You knew this was happening and you kept it from me?"

"We knew it would make you upset," Clara said.

"*Upset*?" Christian began, shooting Anna an enraged glare. "You can't even begin to imagine. You're all insane! How can you stand by and watch this… this repulsive game play out? He'll never be one of us! He's a fucking spawn, a fucking cold blooded parasite! He only survives as long as the enemy does!"

"You've lost all perspective," Abram said. "Your father did not turn at William's hand. And the man we know as William is not the creature you despise. That creature died the moment his soul returned."

"Leave my father out of this!" Christian said.

"But how can we," Abram began, "when your entire mode of existence has been built upon his death?"

"You're damn right it has!" Christian rounded on William. "Why shouldn't he suffer alone? Why shouldn't he pay for what's happened? You always say it, Abram, the universe demands balance. And if Maddox *has* a purpose, it's to even the score."

"Christian," I broke my silence. "There's no getting over what happened to your father. But if you ever try this again," I spoke slowly, deliberately, "I can't even formulate in words what I'll do to you."

"Would you kill me, Lily?" Christian responded, his tone a mix of amusement and disgust. "Don't waste your energy. You already have."

I wanted to hate him so badly. But even now, there was no way. "How could you *say* that?" I asked him. "You believe I'd actually *want* to hurt you? Christian, if there had been a way to make everyone happy—"

"But there wasn't, Lillian," Abram interjected. "If you *had* attempted such a feat, you would have never lasted a week here. And one day, Mr. Wright will realize that misery does not attract company."

For once Christian had nothing more to say. He reached in his pocket, feeling for something, and pulled out his car keys. Stepping to the coat rack, he grabbed his jacket and slipped it on, wincing.

"Where are you going?" Clara asked.

"What does it matter," Christian said lifelessly. He opened the front door and went to leave, then halted, turning half way round to face William. "If anything ever happens to her, if you ever harm her in any way, if you ever *think* about harming her, I'll destroy you," he said, slamming the door behind him.

I pulled my sweater tightly around me as I walked William to his car. An early autumn chill was in the air and a misty curtain hung low over the trees. Christian hadn't come home the night before, and everyone was still asleep, tired from waiting for his return. William opened his trunk and slid a large suitcase in. I handed him a leather satchel and he tossed it on top. We exchanged doleful looks.

"Lily," he sighed. In mere minutes he would be leaving me, and the course he would follow was nothing short of deadly.

"So, I know I can't call you," I said. "We can't have your cell phone ringing in the middle of a dangerous encounter. That would really blow your cover." I tried to laugh, but it all fell apart as the tears began. He immediately pulled me to him, enveloping me in warmth.

"I have to hear your voice. I'll call *you*," he promised. I clung with desperate hands to his shirt, trying in vain to smother my sobs against his shoulder.

"Lily, please … you're killing me, sweetheart," he begged. "It makes this so much harder. You have no idea." His embrace was so all-encompassing, and I felt like a little girl, clutching a savior for strength. Though it took everything I had, I clenched my teeth together, held my breath, willed the tears to stop, and then nodded against him.

"Angel, let me see your face," he said, kissing the top of my head.

I took a few deep breaths, shuddered, and lifted my eyes to him.

"It's only a couple of weeks," he said, resting his forehead against mine. "We'll be together so soon. It will be like I never went away."

I sniffled. "I know. I just love you."

He shook his head. "It's a miracle, you know…to go from a speck of intolerable nothing to this."

"Nothing?" I laughed, appalled. "From the beginning, the only thing I couldn't tolerate about you was how *impossible* you were to ignore. You were some kind of lighthouse to me, William. You were everything I needed."

"I understand how you feel," he whispered. "If you'd never come here ... well, I don't even want to think about it."

I considered his words and laughed, realizing how we sounded. "When did we become so sappy?"

"Lillian ... don't go there." He grinned. "I can still whip your ass into shape when necessary."

"Then get your game back on, Maddox. I'll expect to be relentlessly worked over in fourteen days."

"Just remember that you asked for it." He smirked. "And I won't tolerate any whining."

"Same goes for you."

"Please." He rolled his eyes.

"William?"

"Hmm."

"Kiss me goodbye now. And make it impressive. I have issues with my short term memory."

He smiled again, and then lifted me in the air, kissing me forcefully. Two weeks was, after all, a whole half of a month. After several failed attempts at breaking the embrace, we finally tore ourselves apart.

"I think I'd better go before I'm physically incapable of doing so," he said hoarsely.

"I guess so."

William released me. "I love you," he said.

"I love you, too. So don't do anything stupid. I'm warning you."

"I will try to act in accordance with your standards of intelligence, Lillian." He winked and opened his car door.

"Good," I sighed.

"Goodbye, Ms. Hunt."

"Goodbye, Secret Agent Man."

He smiled and closed the door, and I watched him drive away into the Georgia mist.

Twenty-Two

Abram stood in front of the house, his eyes gray and alien. My fellow Sentients waited in a stern line across the porch behind him.

"I'm sorry this wasn't meant to be, Lillian. We're all very disappointed," he said.

"But why?" I implored. "What have I done? Tell me what I did wrong and give me another chance!"

"No more chances," Christian said, stepping in front of Abram. "You had yours, and you wrecked it." He threw my bags on the ground.

"No. No." I shook my head, terrified. "Please don't send me back. I don't belong there. There's nowhere else I could possibly be. Abram, *please*."

"Leave, Lily. And take your *freak* with you," Christian snarled, pointing behind me.

I turned around to see William, face down in the dirt.

"What did you do?" My voice was trembling. "*What did you do*!" I wept, running to where William lay and falling over him. I turned him over, and his eyes were wide open, caked with mud.

When I woke, tears had dripped all the way down to my neck and every inch of my night shirt was drenched in sweat. I buried my head in my pillow and wailed with anger. What the hell was wrong with me lately? These dreams were grotesque.

"Lillian," someone whispered, and I froze, sweeping my eyes across the room.

Then air blew cool on my face, and I shot straight up to see grainy, gray smoke spreading across the foot of my bed. I pulled my feet closer to me and watched in alarm.

"*Okay*," I said. "What are you? And don't just slink around my bed like a weasel, you bastard."

The smoke hissed, then seemed to bubble upward.

"That's it? You're just going to blob around like a tar pit?"

"Lillian ... Hunt," it wheezed.

"That would be me," I responded impatiently. I'd be damned if I was going allow William's blood, sweat, and tears to go to waste. He'd expect me to show some pluck.

"Get out of my room before I squash you like a bug," I said, feeling a tad more fearless than logic would advise.

It retreated and slid down the side of my bed, across the floor. I got up and watched it flow underneath my door and out into the hall. I cracked the door open, peeking out of my room, but the smoke was gone.

"Fucking stupid ghosts," I grumbled.

❧

Day five of William's departure crept upon me, and the tone of the house was dire. Clara carried out a constant vigil by the phone in hopes that Christian would call. He hadn't. Anna and Abram tried to comfort her, but it was no use. Christian hadn't come home, hadn't phoned in days, and the guilt was overwhelming. Somehow I thought I should talk to Clara, but what could I say? So I said nothing, barely came out of my room, and ate in silence. I was too afraid to even look at her. Anna was the only one I dared interact with, and that was at her insistence. Every day she'd force her way into my room, and she always had the same thing to say.

"No one is angry with you, Lily. I don't know what we could have done about my brother. Maybe we should have told him from the beginning, but how? He'll turn up; he always does."

But no matter how many variations on the argument she chose to use, I could only contemplate my fingers as they wore out the hem of my shirt. There was certainly no making eye contact. That was impossible. Whatever Abram believed about the relevance of my decisions in regard to William, it was beyond me to use that as a mechanism for happiness when so many others were suffering. When Christian was home safe and sound, maybe I'd consider not hating myself so much.

Even worse, I'd only spoken to William once since he'd left for Pennsylvania. My fears escalated with every night that went by not knowing if he was in danger, not hearing his voice. I had behaved myself and not called him, but he had promised to call me in return … and he hadn't. Abram assured me that this was normal, that William was likely establishing some trust with the enemy, and that took time. But, regardless, every night I went to bed frightened and ardently willing the universe to keep him safe.

Ironically, one of the few escapes I had was the woods, and I visited them every day, rain or shine. They were a connector, a bonding place between my soul and William's, and they served as a frequent reminder of my silver lining—my provoker, my royal pain in the ass, and the best thing that had ever happened to me. If William didn't call me soon, I would hunt him down and tie him up.

"Lily." Paul waved his hand in front of my eyes. "Lily Lily bo-Billy, heads up!"

I blinked and focused. "What?"

"I said, do you want some pie?" He offered the dessert across the table.

"Oh. No. Thanks," I said, staring blindly at my plate.

"It's good pie," he urged.

"I'm … full," I murmured.

"But, you haven't eaten anything yet." Katrina sighed.

"I haven't?" I looked down at my food. There was a mutilated leg of lamb, a crumbled roll, and a mound of shredded green beans. I'd evidently tormented my food, but not eaten it.

"Lily, dear, please put something into your system," Clara said, concerned. Until now we hadn't spoken to each other much, and I'd assumed she was angry. But the look on her face suggested nothing of hostility, only maternal concern.

"I'm sorry. I wasn't paying attention," I admitted.

"I noticed. We've all noticed. Lily, you don't look well." She frowned. "William isn't even going to recognize you at this rate."

I cringed inwardly at her speaking his name. Didn't she hate him? Didn't she blame him for the gravity of her son's pain? Or had I underestimated her goodness, her forgiveness, her understanding?

"I'll eat." I smiled faintly and forked a piece of lamb.

She nodded in approval. "That's better."

"Any word from Pennsylvania?" Demetre asked Abram.

"No. Nothing yet," Abram responded. "But William is wise. He'll make contact soon enough."

Ginny laid her hand on my arm. "Lily?"

"Yes?" I looked down at her.

"May *I* have your pie?"

I chuckled a bit. "You can. If Ophelia says it's okay."

"I suppose so," Ophelia agreed. "If you promise not to wake us all up at midnight again."

"I was playing elephant! Elephants are *loud*, Grandma," she huffed in exasperation.

"Yeah, well, maybe it would be better to play elephant during the day, monkey," Demetre suggested.

"I'm not a monkey, Grandpa. I'm an elephant!" Ginny corrected him.

I smiled. "But you see, elephants sleep at night. So if you're going to *really* be a *real* elephant, you have to do things just like they do," I said.

"Oh," Ginny responded thoughtfully. "Okay." And that settled it.

Paul went to steal a forkful of Demetre's pie, then stopped, craning his head to see out the kitchen window.

Clara stood up. "Who is it?" she asked, eagerly.

"I don't know. I can't see," he answered.

"Well, let me through, then!" Anna jumped up and pushed behind his chair to get a better view. "Mum … it's him."

"Oh, thank heavens!" Clara sighed, placing a hand on her stomach as my heart leaped into my throat. I was both relieved and anxious. One missing man found, one to go.

The front door opened, and we all waited as the sound of Christian's footsteps neared the kitchen. He stopped in the doorway. The last week had taken something from him; he looked like death warmed over. There were dark circles under his eyes, and his skin looked sallow. At some point he had bought new clothes, but they were plain. His normally sharp, trendy attire had been replaced by a wrinkled T-shirt and jeans, and his frame was thinner. How could he have lost weight in such a short time?

"Hi, Mum," he said.

"Christian." Clara went to him instantly, hugging him to her. His face reflected pain and she drew back.

"It's all right. I'm just still … healing," he said, looking away from her.

"Oh. Yes," she acknowledged.

How could I have forgotten? When Christian left he was bleeding and wounded … and I had caused it. Common sense reminded me that I'd had no choice … that I'd *had* to repel Christian to save William's life. But again, I felt powerful remorse.

"Do you want to eat, dear?" Clara asked him.

"No." He glanced at the table, looking away the moment his eyes fell on me. "No, I'm not hungry."

"All right."

"I'm tired. I'll just to go to bed," he told her. Then he kissed her on the forehead and left the kitchen. Clara looked as if the weight of the world had been lifted from her shoulders, and I sighed with relief. Christian could hate me all he wanted. At least he was home with his family where he belonged.

⁓

We'd reached day eleven, and there was still no word from William. Though the atmosphere had lightened since Christian's return, he was hardly himself. Anna's jokes fell on deaf ears, and Clara's attempts to engage him in conversation solicited only minimal responses. If Christian was in a room, I steered clear of it. No doubt my presence would only pour salt in the wound.

Ophelia's room, with the fan of photo albums spread across her bed, served as a wonderful escape from the possibility of running into Christian. I'd avoided him thus far. Surely the world offered countless other time-consuming activities to conceal my existence.

"And this is my Uncle Rinaldo," Ophelia said, pointing to a black and white photo of a potbellied man with oversized teeth.

"He was … uh … ," I began.

"Ugly as sin, don't I know it," Ophelia laughed. "But his wife was beautiful … see?" She pointed to a curvaceous blond woman in a figure hugging dress.

"Whoa, how did he land her?" I peered at the photograph.

"Sheer luck … and money." She laughed again.

"Ah. Money." I nodded.

"Money isn't everything, though," she added. "When I met Demetre, he had nothing. He was a farmer from Tennessee. But, oh, how I loved him. It wouldn't have mattered what he did for a living."

I grinned, and it was the first real smile I'd experienced in days.

"How did you deal with him being a Sentient?" I asked her.

"It was hard at first," she admitted. "You see, Demetre thought he could somehow live one way and another at the same time."

"You mean, he thought he could be a farmer and a Sentient?"

"Yes. But it didn't work out. His energy was too strong and things found us. They would gravitate to us, just as they did *you* before you came here, Lily. And we had our family to think about. For years he tried to practice as a Sentient on a smaller scale, doing random tasks for Abram while manning the farm, but once Caroline was born, well, things changed."

"Caroline? Ginny's mother?"

"Yes. Here, see?" She flopped the photo album closed and opened a new one. It was full of pictures of a beautiful little brown-haired baby. The pictures progressed through childhood and teen years until Ophelia settled on a page with a lovely young woman.

"Ophelia, she was beautiful," I said.

"She was. And Demetre realized that she needed to be raised in a place where the danger was driven back. So, before she was a teenager, we joined Abram's group."

"I see. Did she marry a Sentient?"

"Mhm. Joshua Logan. He was a good boy. But the two of them always acted like they were invincible when they weren't." She stared at the photo album, clearly upset with the memories it evoked. "As a Sentient's wife and mother you fear losing your family to the dangers of the job, but I couldn't have foreseen them dying in such an *un*-Sentient-like accident."

"So they weren't killed by vampires?".

"No." She shook her head. "No. They were caught in an ice storm on the highway. Their car careened across the median into opposing traffic. They were killed instantly."

I rubbed Ophelia's back as she blotted her eyes with her sleeve.

"But the miracle," she went on, "is that Ginny survived. She was in the car, and she escaped without a scratch."

"Ophelia," I said, amazed. "I can't wait to see if she has an endowment."

"Neither can I. Though Demetre would probably be happier if she could live a normal life forever."

"Hm. The grass is always greener." I sighed. "Before I came here, I longed for more. And now, I realize the price you pay for it."

"Yes. But I want you to know that you have such a gift, Lily. Not just as a pathcrosser, but as a human being. You intrinsically understand how to love, how to handle people. So please, don't let one bad experience ruin who you are. Stay open. Don't become jaded."

"I hope not to," I said.

"Good. Hope is everything." She smiled.

"Ophelia? Are you in there?" Anna knocked and called from the hall.

"Yes, honey, come on in," Ophelia answered.

"There you bloody are, Lily!" Anna said. "Didn't you hear the phone ring?"

"No!" I hopped off the bed.

"Well, you'd better go take your call then. Abram's got it in the kitchen."

"I'll be back," I told Ophelia.

"Don't worry about me! You go on. These old pictures aren't going anywhere," she said.

You'd have thought I'd never spoken to him before. You'd have thought I was in high school. I was actually shaking. Love was insane.

"I'll prepare them … " I caught the tail end of Abram's conversation. "We'll only need a few more days before the move." Abram noticed me and waved me closer.

"Yes. He is," he went on, then listened. "Very well, considering the circumstances." I could guess what he was referring to.

"She is, in fact. Shall I put her on?"

My heart leaped out of my head and blew a hole through the ceiling.

"All right, Mr. Maddox, we'll see you soon." He patted my shoulder and handed me the phone. I sat down at the table. *Come up with something brilliant for a first line,* I thought.

"William?" I asked instead.

I could sense him smiling through the phone. "Hello, Lily."

"Thank God you're alive!"

He laughed. Jesus how I'd missed that voice.

"Yep. Quite alive," he said. "I haven't been able to return to the hotel for days, though. I just got back about an hour ago, half-expecting to find my phone clogged with voicemails. You didn't call me once … it was a little depressing."

"Well, I know the rules. I didn't want to get you killed."

"Appreciate that. I love you, Lillian."

"I love *you*. Oh, William where the hell have you been? I've been really freaked out."

"I can imagine. I'm sorry, baby. It's been extremely … tricky."

"Baby? Did you just call me baby?" I giggled.

"I did. Is this an issue?"

"No. I like it," I said. "Can I call *you* baby?"

"You can call me anything you want, Lily."

"Same here."

"Well, then. I can think of something I'd *really* like to call you," he spoke smoothly into the phone, and goose bumps spread across my arms.

"What's that?" I sighed.

"Mrs. Maddox."

Ugh. Melting piles of ooze. That's what I was. I was in danger of woefully losing my edge with him.

"It's not fair, William."

"What's not fair, my Lily?"

"The way you've connived me into being nice to you," I said.

"Oh, please. There was no conniving involved. The problem is that I'm dead sexy and you couldn't resist me."

"Ugh, be quiet." I laughed.

"If you insist."

"No! Don't be quiet. Please talk to me. I love you, damn it."

He sniggered. "Lily, my absence is making you bi-polar."

"No more than usual. But I'll admit that I'm miserable. Everything is weird. I mean, even my dreams."

"Your dreams?"

"Yes. I don't know. I just wish I could hurry up and get to you."

"That sounds like a plan. I'll be here."

"Where exactly *is* here? Where are you?"

There was silence on his end, and I thought I'd lost him.

"William? Can you hear me?" I asked.

"Yes." He exhaled slowly. "This is the part I wanted to avoid, but I knew I could only put it off for so long."

"What? William … seriously, where are you?"

"I'm in Wilkes-Barre."

"Wilk…. Why are you *there*? You're only half an hour from my home town."

"Because, Lily. Their strongest faction is here."

His words were momentarily incomprehensible. Vampires couldn't be that close to my grandparents. There was no way that was possible.

"Please don't tell me that," I begged. "Please don't say that."

"Lily, I'm sorry, sweetheart. They're hiding in the coal mines."

"Shit, William, *no*."

"Hey, it'll be all right," he soothed me. "We're all going to convene on this place and send them away, dragging their limbs behind them, okay? Do you believe me?"

"Yes," I whimpered.

"You'd better. I've seen the condition they're in. And it's not all that impressive. Since Lolial is dead, they've sort of taken turns leading and their hierarchy is naive. Dangerously reckless—but naive."

"So, what does that mean?"

"It means that they have no strong head, no genuine alpha male. And their haphazard leadership is made up of fools who are ready to stab each other in the back at every turn. We'll weed them out and fuck them up."

"William … you're so vicious," I teased. "It's turning me on."

"*Really?*" His voice turned to honey. "Well, then, remind me to snap a few necks in your company."

"Hope there's a hotel room nearby."

He laughed. "You know, you're not the only one who's been having dreams."

"No? Have you been dreaming?"

"I have."

"What sort of dreams?"

"Uh … well, they primarily involve you … and me," he said.

I raised an eyebrow. "I see. And are these good dreams or bad dreams?"

"They're good *because* they're bad, Lily."

"Oh ...." I stammered. "Wow. Well, I leave for Pennsylvania in three days. How many hours is that?"

"Seventy-two," he answered immediately.

"Seventy two," I grumbled. "I like the sound of three days better."

"So do I."

"I love you, William. I miss you. Thanks for not getting hurt."

"My pleasure, believe me, though, your obsession with me injuring myself is a bit disconcerting. And I love you, too. With all my heart."

"My God. You are *completely* pussy whipped," I said.

He laughed loudly. "You're just asking for trouble, aren't you, Lillian?"

"What?" I asked innocently.

"Three days, angel. And watch out, that's all the warning you're going to get."

"Bring it on."

❧

Night fell upon our last evening in the house, and everyone was cloistered away in their own spaces. Each possession was packed and bagged up, as were all the memories that came with them. How lucky I was to have started out in this place. Knowing the Sentient lifestyle, it could just as easily have been a hotel room.

Walking the grounds in the thick of night wasn't something I would have believed myself capable of just months before, but tonight I'd been intent on it. It was the best place I could come up with to clear my head and evade Christian.

Tossing a handful of pebbles into the pond, I listened as they scattered across the surface of the water. The moon was new, and heavy shadows concealed the trees. At this hour, the air was cold enough to require that I not venture too far before getting chilled, so I stopped just short of the fountain and turned back toward the house.

Something blocked the path.

A column of charcoal mist bobbed shapelessly above the concrete. I walked on the grass to the left, thinking I could circumvent it, but the form moved with me. As I stepped to the right, it did the same. I sighed and crossed my arms, peering at it.

"Fine," I muttered. "I'll have to *make* you move."

Taking a brave step toward it, I prepared to repel using the only emotion I could feel at the moment ... fear. In response to my efforts, the misty column tightened and darkened and shot a hazy gray line outward and through me. I fell backward, banging my head on concrete as a sharp pain ripped across my chest. Pushing through it, I scrambled up quickly and faced it again. In the time that elapsed between my falling and recovering, it had closed the space between us by a good ten feet.

I narrowed my eyes. "You've been following me, haven't you?"

"I know you," it answered.

"Good for you. And what do you want?"

"Are you afraid?" it asked.

"No," I lied.

"Yes, you are." It cackled. "I smell it."

"Are you the reason I've been having the dreams? Are you causing my nightmares?"

It said nothing.

"You are, aren't you? Get out of my way!" I seethed.

"Lillian," it sang, drawing the word out.

"My name again? *Ugh*, you are *so* redundant." I barged forward, infuriated, prepared to send it flying, but it dispersed on its own. At last, my path was clear to the house, and I took it with some speed. Daring a look behind me, I barreled through the back door and right into Christian.

He caught me before I fell backward. "What's wrong?" he asked, glancing outside apprehensively.

Had he actually spoken? I panicked, wanting to tell him the truth. But for the love of God, I should have been able to handle this myself, right? After all the training, all the practice, could I chance losing even more respect in Christian's eyes over my inability to vanish a stinking gray cloud? I made up my mind to keep my mouth shut and mumbled a quick "nothing" before heading for my room. I made it as far as the door.

"Lily, wait! Please," he said, and I stopped. He halted right in front of me. "Will you never speak to me again?" He sighed. "Will you ignore me forever?"

I shook my head. "Christian, I wasn't ignoring you. It's just.... I was staying away because ... you hate me." I teared up.

"No!" He looked at me remorsefully and laid his hands on my shoulders. "No, never. Not possible, Lily," he swore.

"But, you said—"

"Forget that. Forget it. I'm sorry I hurt you. No matter how I feel about … about him, I can't bear to hurt you."

"God, Christian," I cried and took hold of him, hugging him tightly.

"Lily," he whispered. "Can we talk in your room?"

I nodded.

We sat on the floor and rested our heads against my bed. For a while we both stared through the blackness, until our eyes attuned themselves to the dark. Then he spoke.

"I've loved you from the moment I met you, Lily."

"God." I laid my face on my knees.

"Really," he continued. "You were so damned stubborn. And your endless barrage of questions … I didn't stand a chance. You had me wrapped around your little finger. I'd have done anything for you."

"Christian," I whispered. "You don't have to say this."

"I want to. I *have* to say it."

I waited and he went on. "There was hope in the beginning. I thought I stood a chance with you. But everything changed. You were with him more and more and then *defending* him, for Christ's sake. I didn't like it, not one little bit. And I don't just mean because he's a vampire. I didn't like it because I knew I was losing you to him. I missed you and worried about you all the time, and I hated him even more for it. I felt betrayed."

"I knew you did," I said regretfully. "And I tried hating him. I tried insulting him. I was impossible, horrible. I hoped he'd hate *me*, mistreat *me*, give me a reason not to care about him. But he didn't. He was patient and always knew what was best. The worst part was the whole stupid empath thing! I had no choice but to know that the feelings coming off him were human. That was the most annoying part. I'd expected something foreign, but that wasn't the case."

"But how can you be certain, Lily? How can you be so sure that he wasn't just manipulating you?" he pressed.

"Because he's *gone*. He's been gone for two weeks, and my feelings have only gotten stronger. I love him even now. *Especially* now."

He narrowed his eyes, shaking his head. "You don't know what I would give for you to love me like that. I'd go find myself a fucking vampire, get *myself* turned if I had to," he whispered.

"Christian." I couldn't help giggling. "That would *not* be a good idea."

He sighed. "Perhaps not. But I can't help it," he said, turning to me. "Why him? Why *not* me? What does he have that I don't?"

I thought about this. The answer came naturally. "He carries some inexplicable part of me in him," I answered.

"I don't understand."

"I don't completely understand myself."

"But he isn't human. Doesn't that affect you at all?"

"He's more human than you give him credit for."

"But I can't get past his means of survival. If nothing else, that's impossible for me to ignore."

I laid my head back against the bed again. "Sometimes I wish things had ended up differently. That it *had* been you I'd fallen in love with. It would have made things so much easier on everyone."

"Hmm," Christian agreed.

Swift, grim realization ripped at my heart. "Except William," I added. And that alternative was unacceptable.

"How does he treat you?" Christian asked gravely.

"Would it do any good if I said incredibly well?"

"Yes. It would reduce my ardent desire to break his neck to a mere inclination."

"Nice," I grumbled.

"Well, what did you expect, Lillian? Did you think I would be happy about this? I'm not. Not even close. But I can't hate you. I tried. The most aggressive action I can think of is to just … grab you up and kiss you. But that didn't work the first time."

"No, and it wouldn't work any subsequent times, either," I warned.

"I know. It doesn't mean I don't want to, though."

"Christian … I'm engaged."

"Right. And how the hell did Maddox pull *that* off? Bloody freak."

"Christian!"

"Sorry. Sorry, Lily. I'll keep it to myself."

I reached over and felt for his hand. "Thank you for not detesting me. I love you very much … in a sisterly way."

He sniggered. "Someday, Lily. You never know. Maybe he'll fuck up colossally or you'll realize how stunningly handsome I am."

"You know, William's no slouch in that area," I countered.

"Right. If you like the tall, lanky, ghostly type."

"I do."

He shrugged. "There's no accounting for taste."

"Maybe you can't see it right now, but I am giving you *such* a dirty look."

"I can imagine it," he said, and I barely made out the smile on his face.

"So. Tomorrow we leave," I said.

"Mm."

"I'm sad."

"I'm sorry," he said. "I think we all are."

I sighed. "Thank you for bringing me here. For retrieving me. My life was missing a vital element before you came along and dragged me to Georgia."

"Mine, too."

Amazing. Hadn't I met this Christian once? I could have fallen in love with this version. But the universe had other plans for me.

"By the way, Lil, your powers of repelling are ridiculously good," he complained.

I blushed. "Shit, Christian." I quelled a laugh. "Oh, man, I am so sorry—but hold on a moment—no, I'm *not*!" I seethed, remembering the reason behind the repelling. "I can't believe you! Don't you *ever* touch him again. I mean it!"

"Relax, Lily. I learned my lesson. You love the freak. Got it."

"God, stop calling him that!"

"Fine. I'll strictly call him that behind your back, all right?"

I scowled. "Christian, if there's anything you need to understand right now it's that I love him with every fiber of my being. And if anything ever happened to him …." My voice was shaking, so I left it at that.

"Lily, I won't try to hurt him again. You have my word. As long as he doesn't harm you, I'll back off, I promise."

I nodded, sniffling.

"Now," he said. "It's late and we leave early. We should get to bed."

"Okay," I said, getting up from the floor.

"One thing, though, before I go."

"What?"

"If he wasn't in the whole cosmic picture … if it had just been you and me … could you have loved me?"

"Yes," I said simply.

"So I'm not … you don't think that I'm … I'm …."

And there it was, the self-loathing buried under all that anger, blasting from him like a backdraft.

"No. Not even close," I told him.

Twenty-Three

My car. My beloved car. How it had longed to *really* be driven. Six months had passed with only minimal use, and now it soared down the highway, with the aid of my leaden foot, like a bat out of hell. CCR sang their souls out on my CD player. I was free. It was a surreal experience, driving to Pennsylvania alone. If only Rufus hadn't yowled from his back seat carrier the entire second half of the trip.

The Northwest Sentients had stayed behind at Abram's request, understanding that they need only follow if our group was unable to complete the task successfully. In doing this, we would maintain a reserve. Only Katrina would be joining us in Wilkes-Barre.

I was halfway round the Pennsylvania turnpike when reality smashed down my door. This time last year I'd accepted that there wasn't any real rhyme or reason to my unhappiness, that there wasn't a man alive I could trust or relate to. And so it was completely natural that I should have been proven wrong by a vampire. A vampire. My fiancé was a vampire.

What in the name of God?

I yanked my steering wheel to the side and pulled onto the shoulder of the highway. My brakes squealed in protest as the tires kicked up dust and pebbles in a cloud, and Rufus's carrier smacked against the door. He growled at me.

"Sorry!" I said, laying my head on my arms. "Holy *shit*," I spoke into the steering wheel.

Squeezing my eyes shut, I tried to process it all in my head. Then, after a moment, I opened them again. I wasn't sleeping. I wasn't sleeping? Maybe I was in a mental facility tied down to a bed and plastered with sedatives. Was I comatose and living out my life in dreams? I cranked open my window and cold air whipped my hair against my face. No. I was on the side of the highway somewhere close to Wilkes-Barre having a panic attack. And it was all real. The house in Georgia, Christian, Anna, Clara, Abram, the dreams, the miracles, and William. He was real, too.

I didn't know how the hell it had happened or why I should deserve it, but my circumstances were real. And as frightening as things had been, I had no desire to trade any of it. After all, life wasn't life without some healthy risk involved. I took the car out of park and resumed driving.

Wilkes-Barre was a lot like Scranton. Residential streets were hilly, cluttered, winding, and narrow, with cars parked disturbingly close to each other. Crossing the Market Street Bridge made me nervous. I already disliked heights, but the drop into the Susquehanna River made the whole experience that much more exciting.

With as many as were in our party, this adventure would get expensive, and our funding was hardly limitless. Abram's plan had been to reserve rooms for a few weeks until we'd gotten the vampire situation under control. After that, a musician named Edmund Post—indebted to Abram, of course—had a split Victorian in Philadelphia he was happy to rent. If I'd learned *anything*, it was that Abram always knew someone, always had a plan. He'd done a lot of favors in his lifetime, and they consistently paid off.

My cell phone rang as I rounded the corner onto Saint Paul Street. A Gothic-looking church sprawled across a quarter of a block, and I felt for my phone while gawking at it. Only in this neck of the woods would you see a two-hundred-year-old cathedral next to a gas station.

"Hello?" I answered.

"Lily? Where are you?" Anna asked.

"I'm in the city, sweat pea. Less than ten minutes from you."

"What took you so long? We've been here for an hour!"

"I took the scenic route. It's been a while since my car and I had this much quality time together."

"Well, now you have, so floor it. Oh! And I saw the strangest thing on my way here," she added.

"Yeah? Which strange thing was that?"

"Well, I could have sworn I saw a priest coming out of a pub!"

I laughed out loud. "I wouldn't be surprised. Have you seen William yet?" I asked.

"Yes. He's in room seven-A. He's been talking with Abram since we got here," she informed me. "By the way, Lily, *you're* in seven-B … compliments of Abram."

I grinned and bit the corner of my bottom lip. "Okay, then," I said.

"I'll also mention that he's looking especially handsome today, as boys go," Anna said.

"And why are you telling me this?" I smirked.

"Just to heighten your anticipation…and get you here quicker. Really, Lily, come on. Where are you now?"

"I'm just passing Chester Street Elementary. I'm less than a mile from you."

"Wicked! I'll stand out front."

And she meant business. Anna waited in the circle drive of the main hotel entrance and barely let me park before opening my door.

"Come on, then, out. Get some circulation going in those legs," she prodded.

"Jeez, Anna. Give me a minute to recover. I just drove, like, eight hundred miles."

"Oh, cry me a river," she scoffed, pulling the latch to open my trunk and disappearing behind my car.

"Fuck, she's impossible," I muttered to myself.

"I heard that!" she said.

"Where's Katrina?" I asked, getting out of the car to join her.

"She's scoping out potential dinner locales. This place is full of Italian restaurants! And what is Old Forge style pizza? A lovely old lady told us we had to have some."

"It's only the best pizza in the world. I'll pick up a few boxes when I go to see my grandparents."

"Fantastic!" She swung my largest bag over her shoulder and raced toward the hotel. Was it just me or was she even more over-stimulated than usual? This had to be a testament to how bored senseless Anna must have been by the time we'd left Atlanta.

I grabbed Rufus's carrier and met her at 7B. She had already laid the bag on the ground and was leaning against the building.

"Have you been snorting pixie sticks again?" I frowned at her.

"No. I'm just invigorated, Lily! It's a new place, a new life. I like change!" she exclaimed, sliding my key card through the sensor.

"I've noticed."

"Well? Don't you?"

"Yes. But these aren't exactly ideal circumstances." I flung my suitcase on the sofa. "And I tend to get attached easily. Although, this place is *nice*," I conceded, noting my surroundings.

"I know! We all get our own little suites. Mine is exactly like yours."

I looked around. Immediately off the entrance was a small living space with a couch and television as well as a kitchenette. The bedroom and bathroom were through shuttered doors to my left. Abram obviously wanted us to feel as much at home as possible.

"I suppose we'll be in and out of each other's spaces like usual," she smiled. "It would get awfully lonely otherwise."

Yes. I could see that happening. The initial excitement of a hotel room wore off pretty quickly before cabin fever set in. We'd be room hopping in no time.

"So, where's your brother?" I asked.

"With the guys. They're brushing up on their poker skills in hope of taking you on." She grinned.

"Huh! They're on *my* turf now," I bragged. "My radar's locked into the homing beacon. They don't stand a chance."

"What's the homing beacon?" She giggled.

"Ground zero. The place where it all began!" I called, heading for the bathroom. "I need a minute. I want to brush my teeth."

"No problem. I'll just follow you!"

"Great!" I joked.

"So, how much do your grandparents know about us?" she spoke outside the door.

"As much as they can handle. Which isn't much at all. As far as they're concerned, we're like a civic organization. We're traveling do-gooders."

"Ah. Mysterious. I like it!"

"You would."

Anna was waiting faithfully by the door when I'd finished in the bathroom.

"What *would* you do with yourself if I'd never been retrieved?" I sighed, squeezing her against me.

"Absolutely die of the most hideous case of tedium anyone has ever seen," she said.

We both snorted.

I slumped onto the couch. "Do you think Abram is done with my fiancé now?"

"I certainly hope so," Anna said. "You should have seen William's face when he discovered you weren't here yet. Pi-ti-ful," she stressed.

I smiled, irrepressibly giddy.

"Oh, my word, you are simply hopeless." She shook her head. "When you love, you love hard. You're a lot like Christian in that way, you know," she added.

"Yeah, I do."

"Well, let's go see then."

The girl just moved too fast for me, it was that simple. By the time I made it outside, she was already standing with her arms crossed, tapping her foot impatiently. She nodded toward Abram and Thomas, who were rapt in conversation at the end of the hotel sidewalk.

"Looks like the meeting's over," she said, grinning.

"Anna," I whispered. "My inclination is to shriek and hop, but I'll resist. Such a response would reflect poorly on my level of maturity."

"Fuck that!" she blurted. "It wouldn't stop me."

"Yes, well, the world can only handle one raging lunatic at a time," I said. She nodded. "This is true."

"How 'bout if I just knock on his door?"

"That could work."

"All right, then. Sorry to abandon you."

"Ah, think nothing of it. I shall go hunt down my own sexy beast. Of course, she'll probably know I'm looking for her already. Can't seem to spring a bloody thing on her." She scowled.

I nodded sympathetically. "Damned mind readers."

"Hmph. Good thing she's got nice tits. Later, Lily." She grinned and gave William's door an evil glance before jogging off.

I smiled at 7A through pursed lips. Was it normal to be this excited at this age? I hoped so, because there was no suppressing my high.

I raised my hand to knock and the door swung open. Anna was right. He was irrationally handsome in a blue shirt—the first few buttons undone at the top—that may have started the day tucked in, but now hung halfway out of his belt line. His hair framed the sides of his forehead in uneven waves. If there was anything the man was good at, it was making exhausted look incredible.

I took him in, grinning. "That's a relief. You've saved me from the tiresome act of knocking. How can I ever thank you?"

He smirked and that was it. I propelled myself forward and into his arms, our mouths instantly locking in a frenzied kiss, my hands grasping his collar, his shirt, his hair, his anything.

He broke away first. "Are you real?"

"Yes, I think I am," I said, out of breath and frowning at the loss of his lips.

"I was beginning to worry that you were just a figment of my imagination. That I'd dreamed you up," he teased as he gripped me more tightly.

"Hm. Maybe you'd better check to make sure I'm not a mirage, then."

"I think I'd better. For my sanity's sake," he agreed.

I nodded. "Or we could just stand out here all night and freeze to death while you decide whether or not to call a therapist."

He chuckled. "You *are* real," he said, then pulled me into his room, kicking the door shut.

Walls were beautiful, especially when William had you pressed against one. And doors, doors were beautiful, too. In fact, I think we visited every solid surface available as he kissed me senseless, leading us closer to the object of utmost interest.

"Bedroom," I gasped against his mouth and he nodded quickly. We'd just made it to his bed before his hands and lips were everywhere.

"I've missed you," he said.

"Same here. Don't leave me anymore. It's intolerable."

"It was two weeks." He plied my neck with kisses. "Did you really miss me that much?"

I nodded, unbuckling his belt. "Didn't you miss *me* that much?"

He shook his head. "More," he insisted, nuzzling my face before returning to my lips.

"Clothes...are...infuriating," I breathed.

William laughed at me. "You're right; clothes are Satan." He tugged at the button of my blouse. It wouldn't cooperate, so he ripped it instead.

I giggled. "You sure know how to back up an opinion."

"Aah, angel," he whispered in my ear, and I outright moaned. "How could I have forgotten how incredible this is?"

I lifted my head to look at him. "Gross negligence on your part. Now please remember … quickly."

"Don't worry. It's coming back to me." His hand wandered between my legs.

"Oh, God." I scrambled to retrieve some brain function. If he were to try any vampire funny business right now I'd be lost to the world, and I wanted to be aware of every moment. "Supposing," I whimpered, "I told you to skip the workup? Would you be offended if I said there was no need for that right now?"

"Whatever you want."

"You're a saint," I said.

I wrapped my legs around him in invitation and he took me at once. Again, I felt every molecule of his energy pass through me. Again, I lost all sense of where and who I was, spiraling dizzily in what felt like mid-air.

"What is this? Have we … *shit* … figured it out yet?" I smiled blissfully as he drove deeper into me.

"No … but who cares?" he groaned.

"Well, keep up the good work," I cheered him on.

"Glad to … oblige …."

I'd had enough orgasms in my life, and to define the culmination of this event as such would be missing the mark altogether. Whatever happened when William and I were together was beyond my ability to understand. If no biological reaction ever came of it, there'd still be so much to feel. Nevertheless, our climax was swift and shocking. Maybe I said something, maybe I made a sound, but the only memory I have is of William's face. I could never doubt he loved me; his eyes shone with it.

He dropped on his back, pulling me with him. Weeks of torturous nightmares and the loss of his presence stirred up absurdly strong emotions in me, and I let him hold me as I cried.

"Lily? Haven't those tear ducts run dry yet?" He chuckled.

"Don't laugh. I'd be ripped apart from the inside out if I ever lost you," I said.

"That will never happen. Never."

"Just hold me," I whispered, thoroughly twisting my limbs around him.

Sure there were vampires in the city, but I had my priorities. First line of business, take William to Scranton. Once again, I savored being behind the wheel.

"You know, your taste in music is pretty reasonable." William squinted at my Lynyrd Skynyrd collection. "It almost makes up for your driving. How'd you get into this stuff?"

"My dad listened to it. It calms my nerves. And don't talk smack on my driving, William," I retorted.

"So, you had issues with your nerves *before* you joined us?"

"Ha! Yes. Give it a few minutes and you'll understand why."

"You keep dropping these warnings, Lily. What exactly am I in for?"

"Uh," I fumbled. "Connie's just … kind of … different."

"Different?" William glanced at me sideways.

"Well, a little outspoken. She blurts before she thinks."

"Uh-huh, so that's where you get it from."

"Oh, you will be *so* sorry you said that," I teased. "Believe me, I will look like an etiquette coach after today. Anything merely creepy or otherwise fearsome you have ever encountered will pale in comparison to meeting this woman."

"Wow," he said. "You really know how to paint a pretty picture. And you lived with her?"

"I love her. You get used to the crazy."

"Ah. Again, an outlook I can appreciate."

I gawked. "Damn, Maddox, you certainly are making up for lost time, aren't you?"

"Just setting the mood." He shrugged. "I've always liked you slightly miffed with me. Turns me on."

"Vampires," I snickered.

"Humans," he retorted.

I smiled happily, and his hand crept across the seat and found mine.

"William?" I asked.

"Hm?"

"It's just occurred to me that you're about to meet my family, and you'll *very* likely be answering questions *I* have yet learn the answers to. Enlighten me."

"Okay. What would you like to know?"

"Uhmm…. Where were you born?"

"In Scotland. My parents were both from there."

"Really? Where's your accent?"

"Sorry to disappoint you, Lily." He grinned. "We moved to America when I was six months old."

"Not disappointed," I told him. "So, was either of your parents a Sentient?"

"No."

"What were their names?"

He smiled thoughtfully. "Cora and Andrew. They passed away after I was turned. I wasn't there when either of them died."

I squeezed his hand. "I'm sorry."

"I am, too. I regret it every day."

"You regret a lot of things. I can feel it."

"It's just that I can remember … this mind retains the memories of being an animal, Lily. I remember every single one of the people I killed. And even though I realize that it wasn't me—that my actual self resided elsewhere—those memories aren't erased with the restoration of a soul."

I recalled how Anna had told me that he'd wanted to die. He'd begged to die.

Without tearing my eyes from the road, I lifted our joined hands and kissed the back of his. "I wish someone would come up with a better phrase than 'I love you,'" I said. "That's nowhere near strong enough."

He smiled and his lightline burst into view, blazing with happiness.

"So, I have another question for you," I said.

"Yes?"

"Do you have a middle name?"

"I do."

"Well, what is it?" I asked excitedly.

He laughed at my enthusiasm. "David."

"William David Maddox," I announced. "What a good combination."

"You don't think it's boring? Too traditional?"

"No! It's strong. It stands the test of time."

"Appropriate," he said.

"Where did you grow up?"

"Arizona, a generation after the Dust Bowl. My parents settled near some family, and they were horribly poor."

"And how did you learn you were a Sentient?"

"Kind of a long story, but as I said, economically and agriculturally things were a disaster, and my parents planned to move out east to find a good job and earn some money. But that wasn't meant to be."

"Of course not," I chimed in. "What did the fates have in store for you, Mr. Maddox?"

"Well, a stranger came along, an old woman named Magdalena. She informed my parents that I was gifted, that she wanted to teach me, to take me into her group and educate me. In turn, she would ensure that my father found a good job right there in Arizona."

"She was a Sentient?" I asked.

"She was a Seer."

"Oh! Your Seer was female?"

"Yes."

"That's fantastic."

"She was exceptional," he added, smiling.

"Wow. So then how did you meet Abram?"

"Fast forward a bunch of years, my group was helping to exterminate some vampires in Kansas and Abram happened to be visiting at the time."

"Ironic."

"If you still believe in irony," he joked.

There was something else I'd wanted to ask him, and now seemed like the proper time for it. "What happened?" I began. "How were you turned?"

He paused, his brow furrowing as he searched for the memory. "Some nearby vampires learned what my endowment was, learned that I could heal, and they put a target on my head. The very first time I left the safety of Magdalena's group to visit my parents, I never made it back."

"Oh, William. So they just took you? How?"

"I was grabbing a pile of firewood, I think … from the back of my parent's house. And that's all I know. I don't remember the turn, only what happened after."

"What *did* happen after?"

"Well, they weren't anticipating a troubled child, but that's what they got. As it turned out, I had a former Sentient's soul hovering around and nudging me relentlessly toward Abram. The more I fed, the more miserable I became. So, I started refusing the replenishment of blood, and as a result, my endowment—

which stems from human energy—became useless to them. Naturally, they were insanely pissed off and not at *all* fond of me. That's when I went to Abram."

"Couldn't Magdalena help you?"

"She'd died."

"And Abram brought you back." I squeezed his hand.

"And Abram brought me back."

"Remind me to buy that man a storeroom full of syrup."

He laughed loudly. "Will do."

❧

"Kind of cramped around here, isn't it?" William noted the cars parked halfway into the middle of Bellmont Avenue. I pulled into a tiny space across the street from my grandparents' house.

"Yep," I said. "The claustrophobia really kicks in during the cold season. Funny, but even with all the people, it gets lonely."

"You won't be lonely this year. Or any year after that." William brushed my face with his fingers, and I shuddered, my skin tingling pleasantly.

"William, did you just ... ?"

"What?" He smirked. I cocked my head to the side and glared. "Fine," he conceded. "Perhaps I used a marginal amount of vampire."

"That's what I thought," I said. "And I'm not complaining. I just don't want to be left in the dark. So, are you ready?"

"Bring on the apocalypse. I'm not afraid."

"You say that now." I frowned.

"Have a little faith in me, Lillian. Now, let's go."

I got out of the car and stared at my childhood home.

"My father built this house," I told William, and he took it in.

It was impossible not to feel close to Dad here. Not when he'd set every brick and painted every board with the sweat of his own brow. Talk about ghosts.

"I don't pretend to know much about carpentry," William began, laying his hand on the small of my back, "but it looks like your father knew what he was doing."

"He did. He was amazing," I agreed.

"It's in the genes," he offered.

"Way to hustle with the charm." I smirked. "I think I like you a little."

He kissed me gently. "Same here … now quit stalling." And he pulled me across the street.

I scowled at the door.

"Are you going to ring the bell or shall I?" he asked.

"No, I'll do it."

"Okay …." he conceded.

A few seconds passed.

"Lillian!"

"Fine!" I rang the doorbell. *Please let Frank answer,* I thought.

The door opened, and I knew that God existed.

"Well, if it isn't the most handsome man in the world," I said.

"Lily, look at you!" Frank grinned from ear to ear, stepping outside and shutting the door behind him. "You look so good, baby doll!" He drew me into his arms, and I lost it.

"Grandpa … I've … missed you … so … much … ," I managed to say between sobs.

"Oh, honey, don't cry now. Not over me," he said, rubbing my back.

I sniffled and held both of his hands, smiling through my tears. "You've gotten shorter," I said.

"And you've gotten even more beautiful, kiddo," he said. "I assume this is why?" He winked at William.

I laughed. "A big part of it," I agreed. "Grandpa, this is William. William, Frank."

William reached out to shake Frank's hand. "She talks about you a *lot*," he said.

"I wish I could say the same for you, son." Frank pulled him into a hug. "But the girl can be a bit shady with the details."

"Hmph," William grunted. "Yeah, she's a tough one to crack—but worth the wait." He gazed at me.

"So, now that we've all established how inconceivably difficult I am, shall we go inside?" I asked.

"Uh … well," Frank began, his eyes darting to William then back to me. "I wanted to catch you two a little early, give you a chance to prepare yourselves."

"Prepare ourselves?" I questioned uneasily. "*What* has she done, Grandpa?"

"Well ...." He shrugged. "She got a little excited when I told her you two were coming, so she ... she invited a few people over."

"A few people? Who? How many are a few?"

"Just the girls."

"The girls?! Ugh, no, not that! *Please* tell me you're joking," I pleaded.

William cleared his throat. "Lil? Clue me in?"

"Oh, God, William." I cringed and sighed. "The equivalent of the old lady mafia is what they are."

"Hm. Okay." He laughed. "Am I going to be tortured? Are there baseball bats involved here?"

"Erm, not exactly," Frank said. "More like cross-examined under a microscope."

William raised an eyebrow, but smiled nonetheless.

"I tried to warn you." I wrapped my arms around him from the side and moped as repentantly as possible.

"Lily." He kissed my forehead, chuckling. "Do I still end up with you when it's all over?"

"I hope so."

"Then I'll recover," he said. Frank beamed. William had apparently won *his* approval. Now on to the lion's den.

The sound of hen-like chatter carried into the living room as I laid our jackets over the back of the sofa. Frank was first to the kitchen, poking his head in. "Connie? Company."

Several excited female voices grew in volume, and my grandmother spoke over them.

"Is that our Lily?" she asked.

"Well, who else would it be, woman? Get off your duff and come see for yourself," Frank answered gruffly.

I shook my head. Ah, home sweet home.

"Lillian Hunt!" Connie exclaimed, crossing the room with half the neighborhood at her heels. "I'd clock you if I wasn't so damned happy to see you!" She pinched my cheeks and hugged me tightly.

"Hello, Grandma." I blushed. "I missed you as well."

"Evidently not enough to come home sooner! Haven't I taught you better than that?"

"I'm sorry, Gram. Things have been a little … crazy. But I'm here now, right?"

"Yeah, yeah, well, this is the boy, then?" She grinned gleefully at William.

"Yep. This is William."

"Are you Catholic, William?" she asked, and I groaned.

"Well, actually, I was raised Presbyterian," William spoke for the first time. Connie's cronies whispered to each other. It wouldn't have surprised me if someone was taking notes.

"Presby … well, I suppose that's close enough. Besides, you can always convert," she declared.

William's jaw dropped, but he recuperated quickly. "I'm sure that would be a possibility." He smiled at her, clearly amused.

"William," I cut in. "These are some of Connie's old friends. Martha Picatto, Eleanor O'Malley, Delores Cryzinsky—my old piano teacher."

"Don't forget about me!" said the loudest of the women.

"And, of course, my Aunt Carlotta." I had not forgotten about her. I had simply chosen to ignore her for as long as possible. Carlotta had never passed up an opportunity to speak ill of my mother, and as a result, had never ranked high up on my or my father's list of family favorites. In fact, only Connie liked her. The rest of us tolerated the woman only as long as she made dinner. No one could cook like Carlotta.

"Lillian, the boy looks like you've been starving him!" Carlotta scowled, turning to William. "I guess by now you've figured out that Lily is an unfortunate cook," she told him as I gaped on. "If I remember correctly, her mother wasn't very talented in the kitchen, either. But I'd be happy to give the girl a few lessons, if it would help put some meat on those bones."

"Carlotta, let up on the kid," Frank scolded. "How could she learn to cook when you were always hogging our stove?"

She ignored the remark and spoke to William again. "I made manicotti. You eat up, and I'll send some home with you." She shuffled off into the kitchen.

William's expression was strained. He was trying not to laugh.

"Well, let's eat then," Connie said to the group.

"Uhm ...." I looked at William, who smiled calmly. "I just need a minute to ask William something."

"All right, but hurry up before it gets cold," Connie muttered. "You know how sensitive your aunt is about her cooking."

"No problem." I waited for the room to empty. "Fuck," I whispered to William. "What do we do about the eating?!"

William shrugged. "I can handle it. It won't do me a bit of good nutritionally, but I can eat the stuff. It won't kill me. Might make me sick, though," he admitted.

"Oh, God, my poor William." I slipped my arms around his neck. "You don't have to do this. It's not worth it. Let's just say you've got a stomach virus or something."

"Lily, Lily," he said, then he bent to kiss me. Even here, with my grandparents in the next room, I was completely drowning in the comfort of his energy. He broke away. "I'd do anything for you. And if it means eating your Aunt Carlotta's manicotti, then I'll suck it up ... or swallow it, more appropriately."

I giggled. "You're insane."

"Pots and kettles."

It was an odd thing, watching William eat. Just the mechanics of it were fascinating. There he was, holding a fork, then putting the food in his mouth, then chewing it, then—most amazingly—swallowing it. At any moment I expected him to gag, choke, or black out. But he stayed with it until the end, even making a point of sopping up the sauce with a bit of bread. Carlotta was pleased.

"There. You see now?" she commented, satisfied. "You feed him like this more often, and he won't look like an escapee from a refugee camp!"

"Uh, yeah. Thanks." I smiled nervously, an eye always on William.

"So when's the wedding?" Delores asked.

"We haven't decided yet," I answered.

"Hmph. Well, you ought to hurry up and pick a date," Connie ordered. "The sooner you two get married, the sooner I get some great-grandbabies. I don't have much longer, you know."

William choked on the glass of lemonade he was braving a sip from.

"What do you do for a living, William?" Connie asked. "Children need to be supported, after all."

"I help to rehabilitate our staff," he said. "I'm a physical therapist, of sorts."

"Hm. They make good money," Carlotta said.

"Yes, my nephew is a physical therapist, and he makes over fifty-thousand a year," Martha commented.

"How much do you make?" Carlotta dared to ask William.

Frank scoffed. "You're being nosy."

Carlotta shot him a look but changed her approach, returning to William. "Then I assume you can take care of her?"

"We can take care of each other," I snapped. "End of topic."

"My goodness, Lillian, you certainly do have your mother's temperament. It's a shame she didn't stick around longer so you could learn by example how *not* to behave," she said huffily. "Though it looks like you've already inherited her knack for running off." She shook her head.

"Carlotta…." Frank stood up.

"Oh, now, she knows I'm speaking out of the goodness of my heart." She smiled at me. "I'm sure you would act less irrationally if only you weren't *always* so overly sensitive."

I tried to prove her wrong, but my eyes were already watering. William shifted his gaze toward her, and Carlotta's lemonade spilled into her lap.

"Oh, Christ!" she exclaimed, standing up quickly. Connie rushed to get a hand towel and blotted at her sister's pants. "I can do it!" Carlotta grabbed the towel from her.

"Maybe we should call it a night," William suggested. "It's getting kind of late."

I stood up. "Good idea."

"But what about dessert?" Connie prompted.

"Next time, Gram. Thanks for dinner, Aunt Carlotta. Ladies, good to see you all."

Frank and Connie followed us out of the kitchen.

"You two come by again when there's less of a crowd," Frank said, handing me my jacket.

"A wall of lava couldn't keep me away, Grandpa."

I turned to Connie. "Really, Grandma…Aunt Carlotta? What are you trying to do?"

"Well, I just thought she'd ... ," Connie began. "Hell, I'm sorry, honey. She won't be on the guest list next time. And William, I'm glad to see Lily's not alone anymore. You watch over her."

"I promise," he said.

☙

"Ugh, that was horrible!" I groaned, turning the key in the ignition.

"Actually, it wasn't so bad, my love. I'm pretty sure it was worse for you than me."

I sighed. "Why is she allowed to parade around pretending to be a human when, in fact, she's a gigantic flappy-mouthed instrument of torment?!"

William laughed. "Goes to show that being human doesn't guarantee likability. And the world needs people like her, Lily. They make the rest of us look civilized," he explained.

"Good point. So, you really took a crack at the whole eating thing. How are you faring?"

"So far, so good," he said.

"And how often have you tried human food?"

"A few times."

"What have you eaten?"

"Some bread once. And then a few bites of steak."

"A few bites of steak? So you've never downed a plate full of sauce covered, cheese filled pasta before?"

"Nope. Can't say that I have."

"Well, what happened those other times?" I asked.

"With the steak I was okay. The protein is similar enough to blood for me to digest in small amounts. But the bread I didn't do so well with."

"What happened?"

"Hm. Remember that stomach virus idea you liked so much?"

"Yes," I said, my tone miserably knowing.

"Give it an hour and you'll likely get your wish."

I sped the rest of the way to Wilkes-Barre.

Twenty-Four

*L*eroy's Tavern was jammed with people. There was no chance of being seated quickly.

"We estimate a forty-five minute wait," the hostess told us at the door.

"Oh, dear," Abram said.

Paul groaned. "I am *starving*. Maybe we should just order pizza."

"I'm game," Christian said.

"No!" Anna protested. "Lily says they have the best waffle fries in the universe. I will *not* be deprived of the best waffle fries in the universe!"

I frowned. "Forty-five minutes is an awfully long time to wait, though, Anna."

William smiled at the hostess. "Are you absolutely sure there isn't an opening that you may have overlooked somehow?"

She stared at him, expressionless, her eyes suddenly blank. A few seconds went by, and she seemed to snap out of it. "Uhm … you can have table fifteen. Carlos has almost finished bussing it. Uh … Ashley, would you take them to fifteen, please?" she said to a nearby waitress.

The girl looked confused. "But I thought—"

"You were wrong," the hostess corrected her.

"Ooookay, then." The waitress smiled at us. "Follow me."

I took hold of William's arm, slowing him down so that we walked behind the group.

"So, that was suave." I smirked.

He grinned and shrugged.

"And absolutely no chance of supernatural abilities being involved whatsoever," I added sardonically.

"Lily, I am insulted," he replied. "I'll be right back."

I watched as he weaved through the dark restaurant toward the men's room. He'd never been here before, so how he knew exactly where to go I couldn't understand. Still, William was a vampire, and there were undoubtedly many more fascinating tricks up his sleeve.

"What are we talking in terms of numbers?" Paul asked, popping a fry in his mouth before he turned to ogle a passing waitress.

"Their group is more than a hundred strong. But the core appears to be made up of seven members," Abram explained. "That shall be our focus. William has said they are immature, and we know the weak tend to scatter when their leaders are conquered."

"He's also said they're dangerously angry," I reminded Abram. "That's got to add something in the risk area."

"Indeed," Abram agreed. "And I will bear that in mind." He motioned for us to gather nearer so that he could speak in a hushed voice. "Tomorrow, we'll take the mine from the east entrance. That appears to be the least frequented area. But for now ...." He raised his voice again. "I should like to try some more of this spinach dip ... delicious."

"Where *is* Mister Incognito Double Agent, anyway?" Anna asked.

"He's in the men's room," I muttered, sipping my water awkwardly.

"*Again?*" she whispered, peering at me. "Lily, did you knock him up?"

"And there goes the beverage!" Paul laughed as ice water jetted out of my nose. "Classic, every time."

"For all the drinks you people make me waste, I'm getting really thirsty," I grumbled.

The waitress returned to the table and set a beer in front of Paul. "Are you sure I can't get you some black ale? It's our house specialty," she asked Christian for the second time.

"No, thanks," Christian said. "But she'll have another water, please." He nodded at me.

"Okay." The waitress frowned. "But if you need anything, don't hesitate to ask!" She flipped her hair and moved on.

"Goodness. Looks like you've got plans for the evening." Anna nudged her brother.

"She's not my type," he said immediately.

"Oh, come *on*, you idiot. She's kind of ditzy, true, but how long has it been? You need to get laid, Christian." She sighed.

"I'll second that!" Paul raised his beer.

"Yes. A bit of frivolity would do you well," Abram added.

Christian and I gawked at Abram, but no one else seemed fazed.

William returned to the table and took a seat next to me, fidgeting with a salad fork. I put my hand on his back and leaned into his ear.

"Will you ever forgive me?"

"It's questionable," he said.

"Please?" I begged, kissing his cheek.

He snorted. "You think it'll be that easy?" I looked at him imploringly and he sighed. "Why can't I say no to you? You're nothing but trouble."

"Thank you," I said, then raised an eyebrow. "And in all fairness, it *was* your idea to eat."

"True," he said, resting his elbow on the table and laying his head in his hand.

"I can't believe you're not better yet," I muttered, and Anna perked up, so I whispered in his ear again. "It's been twenty-four hours."

"Well, apparently your Aunt's cooking is as lethal as her personality. How do humans digest that stuff without exploding like a hand grenade?" he complained.

"Practice, William. They start us young. It's like the Olympics."

His eyes narrowed. "Hm. It's time you redefined your concept of competitive sports."

"Italian food *is* a competitive sport around here," I informed him. "But I really am sorry. How can I make it up to you?"

His expression turned sinful. "I can think of a few ways."

"You know, for a vampire, you're kind of a pervert," I whispered.

"Only for you, Lily."

Anna glared at us. "How about letting us in on the secret?"

"That's right," Katrina added. "Enough of the whispering. It's rude."

"No secret," I said. "We were just discussing sports."

"Sports? You?" Paul scoffed.

"What? I like sports." I scowled.

"Right," he said.

"Okay, focus people," I redirected. "Don't we have evil to conquer? Shouldn't there be more strategizing? Let's not lose sight of what's important here."

"Oh, *ab*solutely," Anna goaded. "It's a good thing you came along, just in case we'd forgotten about the whole vamp—eh—work thing."

"Yes, thank you for the passionate call to arms, Lily." Abram chuckled.

I made a face at them, and then laughed at myself.

"And are you feeling quite better, William?" Anna asked, and I kicked her in the leg.

"Uhm … fine. Thank you," he said.

"Were you unwell?" Abram asked.

"Just a little under the weather. Don't worry," William mumbled.

"Too bad we haven't got a healer to heal our healer," Katrina commented.

"This is completely true," Anna agreed. "I mean what *would* we do if…." She paused, looking away from me. "You know, without him?"

She may have cut and run, but I knew what she was thinking. *If anything ever happened to him.* Better she didn't say it.

"Trying to do away with me, Anna?" William crossed his arms.

"Definitely not," she answered. "It's simply a statement of your irreplaceability."

"I see," he said.

"Here, here. To William and his brave work for our Society." Abram raised his glass.

The rest of our group did the same, with the exception of Christian, who rested his hand beside his glass instead. Maybe it was just me, but he appeared to be working out a very difficult equation in his head.

"So, Lily says the little buggers are angry," Anna spoke to William. "More than usual?"

"A bit," William said. "They're nursing a grudge at present. About Lolial."

"I see." She looked at her brother nervously.

"Then it's best we not let it slip which one of us completed the task, so to speak," Abram proposed.

"To hell with that!" Christian scoffed. "Go on and tell them. Let them know who laid that bastard out."

"Don't be a hero," Anna said.

"Too late," I added, smiling. "He's already saved my butt."

"Mhm," Christian said, drolly. "And you were remarkably ungrateful."

"I was a little shaken up," I said.

He rolled his eyes. "Do you know that she actually refused to budge? She stood there in the middle of the bloody woods with her bloody arms crossed and wouldn't move," he complained. "I had to pick her up and carry her."

William eyed Christian disapprovingly. "So I was right. You *did* manhandle her," he challenged.

"Only a little, Maddox," Christian said with a sneer. "And she seemed to be enjoying it."

"*Please*," I said. "That's because someone was being all shiny with the lights and the glowing. Ignorance is bliss for only so long, Christian."

"There's nothing wrong with a little healthy mood alteration," Christian said.

William stared at him. "There's nothing wrong with letting her feel the way she feels, either. And you accuse *me* of mind control."

Christian opened his mouth to respond, and I glared at him. To my surprise, it worked, and he settled for crumbling his napkin into a tight ball.

"Abram, will we all be going tomorrow?" Anna intercepted quickly.

"Yes," Abram said.

"Even Lily?"

"Without a doubt. By now, there should be no question of her abilities."

Christian shook his head. "With our typical clients, yes. But this?"

"Believe me," William muttered, half-smiling. "She knows how to handle a vampire."

I blushed.

"I'm starting to lose my patience," Anna said. "Mum and Demetre have been gone for hours. Do you think they got lost?"

"I should have gone with them," Christian complained. "Who knows what sort of wild goose chase Maddox has sent them on."

"My directions were highly accurate," William commented, sitting back in his chair.

Anna turned to Abram. "Well, do you think they could have been spotted?" she asked. "What if they've had a run in with any of them?"

"No, no. This is new territory for us. I'm certain they are simply being meticulous," Abram assured her.

"What's to know?" I shrugged. "They're coal mines. They're wet, dark, drippy. Occasionally a rock falls on your head."

"You've been in one?" Anna asked.

"Well, naturally. I did grow up here. We have tours … they make you wear a hard hat," I informed them proudly.

"Tours? Of … coal mines … ?" William peered at me oddly.

"Of … *yes,* of coal mines. Is that so abnormal?"

"Kind of creepy," Anna said.

"Hm," I mused aloud. "You know, now that you mention it, I guess it is." Half the table nodded.

"Well, you should all be used to creepy by now, anyway," I declared.

"Mum!" Anna stood up and waved Clara and Demetre to our table. "Where have you been? I've been wigging out."

"We've been observing. Watching the exits," Clara indicated, pulling an extra seat to the end of the table.

"Did you have a hard time finding the place?" Christian asked.

"Not at all," Clara replied. "William's directions were perfect."

William smirked at Christian, who rolled his eyes.

"What, if anything, have you two gathered, then?" Christian continued.

"Well, for one thing," Demetre began in a low voice, "they ignore the east entrance. It's too exposed."

"Yes. It should be quite accessible for us," Clara agreed. "But they don't hesitate to pop out of the other entrances. The area is *not* safe for park goers anymore."

"Brave," Paul said. "They come out a lot? In broad daylight?"

"Yes," said Clara. "And, not surprisingly, there have been several disappearances that local police are hard pressed to explain."

"Are there any woods nearby?" Paul asked.

"It's in the middle of a state park, dear … so, yes."

"Good," Paul said. "Is there any chance we could drive them out and into the woods? We always have an easier time that way."

William shook his head. "Doubtful. They like this place. Better than the sewers, I think."

Anyone eavesdropping on the quiet tones of our conversation would likely have thought we were about to take out a nest full of field mice.

"The mine channel is completely closed off to the public," William explained. "No one's been inside it for decades."

"How far down does it go?" Anna inquired.

"A hundred feet or so. There's a steep descent that the mine cars used to use, and you can't see into it. We'll need lights."

"Do *they* use flashlights?" I asked William, somewhat amused at the thought.

"No, love," William said. "They can see in the dark better than they can in the light."

"Oh. Really? Do you see better in the dark?"

"Yes, actually," he acknowledged.

"Hm. That would explain some things." I gave him a dirty look. "So, they've already got an unfair advantage. Do you guys really cart flashlights around with you during something like this?"

"Lillian, Lillian." Anna snorted. "Do you think we're amateurs? We don't use flashlights. We use ourselves!"

"Ooh. That's right," I said, giggling. "Sometimes I take for granted what a gleaming bunch of oddballs you are. But…what should *I* do? I'm not exactly up to par, light-wise."

"Ours should be sufficient should you have difficulty," Abram said. "Stay close to us, and you'll be fine."

"Okay, then." I slid my hand under the table and rested it on William's, and he wove our fingers together.

The cleavage-baring waitress returned to our table, and I could have *sworn* even more of her boobs were hanging out. She lifted a glass of dark-looking beer, and Paul went to take it, only to be bypassed completely on her way to Christian.

"I'm sorry, but I don't think I ordered this," Christian said.

"It's on me." She flashed him a grin. "That is *such* a cute accent you've got, by the way. You're not from around here, are you?"

"No." Christian smiled politely.

"Where are you from?" She cocked her head to the side, twisting a length of her hair.

"London," Christian answered.

"Oh, wow! That's in England, right?"

"Why, yes. Yes, it is," Christian said.

I bit my tongue. *Don't laugh, don't laugh.*

"Cool. I just love that country," she gushed.

"Oh? Have you ever been?" Anna chipped in.

"Been what?" the waitress asked.

"To England," Anna said.

"Oh! No. But I've seen it on TV."

"Well, you should be quite the expert, then." Anna smiled.

That was it. My reserve could only hold for so long. I coughed and choked the laughter back, shielding the side of my face with my hand.

"Is she okay?" The waitress squinted at me.

"Don't be alarmed." William leaned toward her, whispering dramatically. "She hasn't taken her medicine yet."

Her face went white, and her mouth fell open, and I collapsed on the table in what she must have perceived as fits of sobbing.

"Well … I'm just, I'm going to go get your bill," she stammered, backing away.

William chuckled and put his arm around me, pulling me close.

"Why do you guys *do* this to me? It's embarrassing," I lamented, wiping tears from my face.

"Because, my friend," Anna began, "it's so very blazing easy!"

She was right. This was the happiest I'd been in a long time. If only Christian didn't keep looking at me the way he did, things would have been perfect. But there was no ignoring the grief in his eyes every time William so much as smiled at me too long. Christian seemed to have moved from furious jealousy to mourning. I could handle the jealousy better.

≈

My perpetual tendency to deny the unpleasant was catching up with me. While William joined everyone in discussions of combat, I watched mind-numbing television in my suite, trying like mad to hedge off the impending dread. The rest of Abram's Sentients were treating this venture like an annoying bout of spring cleaning, but I had yet to become indifferent to the process.

It was easier when I wasn't alone. So I'd spent as much time with people as I could, even watching cartoons with Ginny for a while. Now, only Abram, William the emissary, and the combatants remained awake. It's not like I *had* to be alone. I'd tried observing their conversation. But that's when the worry began, and now it was spiraling out of control.

I turned off the television and flung the damn remote on the couch. Pointless drivel. Even if it *did* succeed in distracting me, its ultimate consequence would be the deterioration of my brain. Such a thing couldn't possibly up your A game when fighting the forces of evil.

Grabbing a book, I committed what Abram would have considered a cardinal sin and ripped out one of the blank pages from the back. I pulled out a stool from the table and began drawing.

If you'd asked Frank, he'd tell you I was Picasso, but he was highly biased—I was well below mediocre. Picturing William, I sketched the lines of his jaw, the raven locks of hair that brushed his forehead. There was something in his eyes, though, that I had no way of capturing. My frustration level mounted with each failed attempt. Several erases and retries later I dropped the pencil.

"I wonder," I said, staring at it with all my might. It didn't move, so I pictured Aunt Carlotta. The pencil shot straight up and stuck in the ceiling.

"Ooops." I giggled, climbing up on the table to pull it out. The hole was clean enough that no one would notice. I looked down at the floor and immediately regretted it. The room swam around me, and I had to put my hand on the wall and close my eyes. Such was my reaction to heights, even four feet from safety. Perhaps if I opened only *one* eye and left the other one firmly shut, I could get down without a 911 call. Barely peeking, I lowered myself onto the table. My plan was working. As I swung my feet off the side, the doorknob to my suite began rattling.

"Anna?" I laughed.

The rattling stopped, and I hopped off the table, crossing to the window and opening the blinds. No one was there, so I closed them. It was probably a drunken wedding party attendant.

The knob rattled again, and then someone banged loudly on the door.

"Anna, will you *knock* it off!" I pulled the door open to see absolutely no one standing there.

Stepping outside, I looked left and right down the walkway. The suite windows were all in darkness with the exception of Abram's, and it was doubtful anyone from that party would be the culprit. I turned to go inside, and a loud, rushing wind swept behind me. For a moment everything was calm; then the breeze picked up again, this time to my right, at the furthest end of the walkway. I couldn't see it at first, but I could hear it, moving leaves and dirt and sweeping closer to where I stood. I could have pretended that it was just a normal autumn bluster, but what was the point? My skin was prickling away, and I knew what that meant. The swell of air stopped just beside me and dry leaves floated softly to the asphalt.

"Make your move," I whispered. "You know you want to."

A deep, low rumble of icy energy swirled at my feet and rose slowly until it was circling me completely. This was familiar. I hated it when things were familiar. Rarely did anything good come of it.

"Did you really follow me all the way from Georgia?" I asked.

It laughed as I stood trapped in its wake, unsure of whether to move or not. Son of a bitch. Why hadn't I caught this earlier?

"You're from the chapel, aren't you? You gutsy little slime ball."

It growled again and snapped at my face before pulling away, then formed its normal smoky mass in front of me.

"We didn't vanquish you at all…," I murmured to myself.

The air began to wheeze. "I like you…," it rasped. "So much to feel."

"*That's* right. You like pain … allow me to accommodate," I snarled, repelling it across the parking lot. The creature broke apart as it slammed against a jeep, then reformed itself, squealing angrily. A rush of light poured onto the sidewalk as Abram's door opened, and the astral ceased its return and shot into the air, out of view. It would be back, but at least I knew what I was dealing with.

As the men filtered out of Abram's suite, I kept a cautious eye on the darkness. How could I get rid of this thing? I wasn't a combatant. Could I dispel a dark astral?

"Aren't you cold?" William noticed me standing there, jacketless.

"Freezing," I said, my teeth chattering.

"Well, come inside, then?" he suggested, tugging me toward shelter.

"Okay." I hesitated at the door, peering one last time into the parking lot.

"Lily? What are you looking for?" he chuckled.

I shook my head. "Just getting some fresh air."

He narrowed his eyes and closed the door. "Well, enough with the oxygen for now. You're blue."

"Am I?" I asked distractedly.

"Mhm ... Lily?" He bent down so our eyes locked together.

I smiled. "Hello, William Maddox."

"Hi, angel." He smirked. "Just noticing you had company?"

"Sorry," I laughed softly, still shivering.

William searched the room for something and spotted the quilt Connie had made for me balled up on the sofa. He picked it up and wrapped it around my shoulders. "Come on," he said, pulling me to the couch and into his lap.

"Where is my Lily?" he whispered in my ear. "Has she been abducted by aliens? Are you really just an android?"

I giggled. "I am not an android."

"This is good." He kissed my neck. "Androids are boring as hell. I mean, they're far less contrary, but you can't have a decent conversation with them."

"I am *not* contrary," I argued.

He snorted. "No?"

I laughed. "I'm spirited."

"Oh, sure," he said. "Spirited. And apparently delusional as well."

"William." I turned to face him. "You're really past due for a good repelling, and I've gotten *so* much better since last time."

"Have you?" He grinned. "I'd like to see that."

"I ...." Shit. What was I going to say again? It should have been effortless, the perfect comeback. But all cerebral connectors were non-functional. His eyes were too beautiful, too exasperatingly distracting. No wonder I couldn't draw them.

"I love you," I breathed. *Oh, Jesus H. Christ. That* wasn't it.

"Aw, Lillian, you've gone soft," he said and bent to kiss me. I definitely wasn't cold anymore. Not with my hands buried in his hair, his mouth warm and wet against mine. Where had he learned to kiss this way, anyway? It was indecent. I pulled away.

"You know, now that I've had time to reflect," I said, "it was decades before I came along. You really *shouldn't* be so good at this."

"I'm just doing ... " he brushed his lips against mine, "....what comes naturally." He kissed me again.

"Well, it's a total loss that more vampires don't follow your lead."

"No, it's not," he said. "Then I'd have competition, and you wouldn't want me."

"Wrong," I said.

He smiled. "You mean you're not just using me for my superhuman mind?"

"Nope. It's all about your body."

"That's a relief," he said.

I chuckled, then sighed, remembering tomorrow. "What are we really up against here?" I asked seriously.

He shrugged. "Same old thing. We go in, hold the bad guys at bay while the combatants do away with them."

"You make it sound so easy!" I said.

"Well, this is how it's always been, Lily. You saw what happened with Christian and me. If I was a normal vampire, he could have easily killed me. A combatant's grasp is nearly impossible to overcome."

"But you said you could defend yourself," I said. "Why didn't you? Why didn't you fight back?"

"Lily, if he attacks me, people understand. If I hurt him, I've ruined our chances at living within our own Society. Fighting back was the option of last resort."

William was right. As long as he was a vampire, any action taken against a human would be considered aggressive, regardless of its justifiability.

"That's fucked up," I complained.

William took my hand. "Don't worry about that right now, okay? All I'm really trying to express is that Paul and Christian are well equipped. The bigger threat falls on regular Sentients, because they keep the coven back. And unfortunately, combatants can only kill two at a time."

"Two hands," I said.

"Exactly."

"We need to retrieve some combatant octopi."

He laughed loudly. "Now, how could Abram have made such a careless oversight? It's obvious he needs to consult with you in the future before making any major decisions."

"Thank you, William. I've been telling him that from day one."

He raised an eyebrow. "I'll bet you have."

"Listen," I threatened, "I may be sickeningly in love with you, I may even want to screw you silly, but I am *nervous* as hell, and I'll have no more of your back talk this evening."

"Sounds like a plan." He grinned.

"It does?" I asked, cautious of his eager cooperation.

He flipped me suddenly onto the cushions and hovered over me. "Conveniently for you," he began, nibbling his way down my neck, "there's a traumatic pasta episode you've promised to make up to me, and it needn't involve a single syllable … though, I *do* prefer it when you're loud, Lillian."

Twenty-Five

I watched Demetre from a distance as he surveyed an old outline of the mine's interior. He would have it committed to memory in no time—which was helpful—because getting lost down there was not an option. Abram had chosen midday. Waiting until nightfall would have been foolish when our enemy functioned best at that hour.

The battered coal-wash machines remained, rusted, crumbling icons of a harsher past. Countless lives were lost to these mines, and they were the ideal site for a mass haunting. I'd remembered the stories from my childhood about how my own great-grandparents had been coal rats. In their time, labor laws were nonexistent and even children had been sacrificed to the greed of mining tyrants. As a result, the enduring energy hanging over the area was like a pall—mournful and dreary. Even the fiery foliage surrounding us, picturesque as it was, did little to bolster the atmosphere.

"Why do they keep this stuff up?" Anna asked me, peering at the decaying machinery.

"Local government makes a good part of their revenue via history hungry tourists," I said. "This is commonplace."

"Hm. A hundred years isn't that long ago. Americans have such a fixation with recent history."

"This country is an infant, Anna. Unless you're talking about Native American burial grounds, recent history is all we have."

"True. Oops, there's our signal." Anna nodded to Demetre as he waved to us from the mouth of the east entrance. "Are you ready?"

My heart raced and my breathing sped up. "No clue."

"Well, there's only one way to find out. Just do what comes naturally!" she said, chipper as usual.

"What comes naturally?" I repeated nervously as we walked toward the others. "It feels *natural* to run in the opposite direction."

"Then do what comes boldly, instead."

I nodded. "Boldly. Okay. Wait. Where's William?" I looked around, worried.

"He's gone ahead to make sure they haven't sensed us," Clara said. "He'll be waiting at the start of the slope if the coast is clear."

And if he isn't? I thought. Vampires were masterful at Sentient detection. It was a wonder they hadn't suspected us yet.

"How is it that we can stand out here like this?" I asked. "Why aren't they all over us by now?"

"Because the same device that hides them from the world is often their undoing," Abram noted. "The earth acts as an effective barrier where the exposure of our energy is concerned…and these mines run deep."

"A unique upper hand in one regard," Thomas said. "Unfortunately, the barrier works both ways. I can't seem to get a hold on where *they* are, either. Thus, Mr. Maddox is our scout."

I sighed deeply. The idea of William as a plant made me sick. Demetre misunderstood the gesture and patted my back a tad too roughly, nearly knocking me over.

"I admire your spunk, kid. But don't be too disappointed," he said. "Once we're in there … they'll know it."

"You got that right," Paul agreed.

Disappointed? Were these people crazy?

Katrina leaned into my ear. "Yes, they are," she said, and I laughed to myself.

"Stay close at all times, Lily," Christian added sternly, and then repeated, "at *all* times."

"Yeah, *no* problem." I had no intention of skipping off on a vampire-ridden underground excursion by myself.

"Let's get on with it, then," Christian said, leading the way. He, Paul, and Demetre had to bend down a little to enter the mine. The opening was overgrown with moss and fern, and part of the upper rim seemed to have sunken in.

"Ugh!" I groaned, running into a spider's web. The smell of earth and mud was rich and cloying as I peered back into the daylight at Clara. She would keep watch on the exterior.

Anna flicked a spider off her shoulder. "This is simply lovely," she said. "We should come here on holiday."

Katrina muffled a giggle. I wondered how far into the darkness their courage would extend. They *must* have seen it all in order to be so at ease in the face of this place. As if thinking in unison, everyone's light surged into brightness and the walls of the mine were illuminated at once.

Perhaps it would have been better if they hadn't.

All manner of creatures, large black beetles, and spiders of varying sizes scurried across the walls and overhead to get away from us. I stifled a shudder and wondered if my reaction would have been stronger if the group wasn't emitting so much calmness.

"Oh, *ugh*." Anna made a face. "Vampires I can handle. This? Not so much."

I grimaced. "I hear you."

"Women." Paul snorted.

Katrina smirked at him. "Is that a millipede in your hair?"

"*What?*" he cried, flipping his head over and batting at it like mad. "Where? Did I get it? Is it gone?!"

She laughed. "Hmm. Never mind. I was seeing things. Didn't mean to scare you. My bad." She walked on, and Paul followed quickly behind her.

"I was *not* scared," he grumbled. "But millipedes, they can kill you!"

"No, they can*not*," she whispered back.

"They have venom!"

"They don't have venom, Paul. You're thinking of centipedes. And it's poison."

"Oh…." But he didn't look much in the way of being relieved.

"If you're going to freak out about bugs," I groused, "I'm not feeling too confident about the vampires."

"I'm not freaking out," he said, his eyes darting in every direction.

"Where's the mine shaft?" I asked. "Where's the slope?"

"Almost there," Demetre answered. "It shouldn't be much farther. To the right, folks…."

We veered right, and sure enough we could see the pathway sloping downward. William waited at the top.

"Was wondering if you got lost," he said.

"Nope. Just distracted by some wildlife," Katrina answered and Paul scowled.

William seemed amused. "Sight-seeing? At a time like this?"

"Unintentional," I whispered. "But regardless, do they know we're here?"

He smiled. "No, not yet. Don't worry."

Demetre nodded. "Let's get down to business, then, before the status changes. Where are they centered?"

"At least a mile down the rightward channel once you reach the end of the shaft." William nodded down the slope. "Their nest extends west. They don't come up here."

Abram nodded. "As soon as you're ready, then, William."

"I'll get moving," William said.

Abram had established that we couldn't safely fight off the entire coven, so the object was to lure out and kill their leaders. William, unfortunately, had been assigned the hazardous task of bringing them to us.

My stomach lurched. "Wait," I whispered, trailing behind William. "Wait a minute."

"What are you *doing*? Go back," he ordered.

"I just wanted to … to …." My voice broke and I started to cry. The group looked away.

William sighed, touching my face. "Wanted to what, sweetheart?"

I reached up and hugged him to me. "Please be *so* careful," I said, only loud enough for him to hear.

He tightened his arms around me, kissing my cheek. "I have to do this," he said. "You know that."

"But what will they do when they find out you've been lying to them?" I clung to him.

"They'll be insurmountably ticked off." He chuckled. "It should be fun."

"Fun?" I pulled away from him. "God, have you lost your fucking mind?"

He smiled. "I love you, Lillian Hunt," he proclaimed without regard to who was listening. "And I'll do anything and everything to deserve you."

The bastard. I hugged him once more, even tighter this time. "Don't be too heroic," I said.

He nodded, putting his hand over his heart. "I swear. I'll be as spineless as the situation allows."

I cracked a smile, and then stood on my toes to kiss him softly. "Go, before I pin you to the ground," I threatened.

He smirked.

"William, you know what I mean," I replied. He chuckled again and headed down the tunnel and away from us until the darkness cloaked him completely.

"All right, Abram." I rushed up to our Seer. "I've trusted you thus far, and I'll continue to do so just so long as you enlighten me a bit."

Abram looked amused. "What particular aspect requires explaining, Lily?"

"Hasn't he done enough? Why have you sent him off to slit his throat in front of a hoard of bloodthirsty maniacs?"

"Very much like your mother, indeed," he said, still smiling. "And I assure you, he will not be revealing his station until he has lured them here."

"So, we just wait?" I crossed my arms. "Is there some kind of signal? How will we know when they're coming?" I persisted.

"Thomas will tell us," Abram answered. "And yes, for now—we wait."

"And after the waiting? Then what?"

"Just follow our lead," Anna said.

Christian peered down at me. "After all this time with Maddox, I expect to see some extraordinary repelling," he warned.

"That's right, Lily," Anna agreed.

"Just stay by my side," Christian added. "And try not to panic. It will only paralyze you."

Granted, part of me was afraid, but, inexplicably, not as much as I should have been. In fact, I feared much more for William than myself and almost prayed for them to arrive so we could get the whole ordeal over with. I was altered. To hell with infatuation … it wasn't being *in* love that held us firmly together, it was simply being loved. Without ever knowing it, William had woven timeless threads into the very deepest parts of my being. His essence had settled into my own. I'd take every member of the coven down myself to protect him … to protect us.

"Rest yourselves," Abram told us, and everyone allowed their lights to fade. I gasped as the cavern fell into darkness. Now I was frightened.

"I'm right here," I heard Christian whisper next to me, and I instinctively reached out for his hand. He grasped mine firmly.

So much time seemed to pass that I was sure William was dead. I was certain he'd said too much, or said the wrong thing, or simply been found out somehow, and they were tearing him apart as we stood here.

"It's been too long," I said finally, switching back and forth between feet. "Where is he? Where are they?"

Abram laid a hand on my shoulder, and I immediately relaxed. "He will be here soon enough, Lillian."

I nodded, knowing full well that my sudden composure was falsely induced. But it helped me clear my head, nonetheless. I had to prepare myself for whatever was about to happen.

"Abram, we'd better hope you're right about Maddox," Christian whispered with an edge. "Or we've just stupidly walked into an ambush."

My hand stiffened in his, but I didn't have a chance to respond further.

"They're moving." Thomas lit up and stood straight, staring down the dark tunnel. "They're definitely getting closer."

"And William?" I whispered pleadingly.

"Mr. Maddox as well," he nodded.

So he was alive.

A few more moments passed—drawn out, excruciating moments in the darkness. Christian still held my hand. Only now did I notice the lack of air. Everything was damp, a chilling suffocation.

"Remain still until I give the signal," Thomas instructed us quietly.

Even at the lake, even face to face with death, I hadn't felt this way. There was something in the imminence of this place, a malevolent inevitability that shook me violently. Suddenly, I knew how brave William was. In fact, I wondered at the sheer magnificence of such character. Would I ever be so triumphant over fear?

Now their approach was audible. There were five, six, maybe more, beings advancing with some speed, their footfalls more like scampering animals than men. Oh, God, the images in my head brought me close to falling apart. Did I really want the lights back? Did I really want to see what was coming?

"*Now*," Thomas ordered. Sudden gold luminance swelled around me … and there was William, standing at the head of what looked like a small cluster of emaciated corpses, white as snow, caked with dirt and completely naked. Every sinewy muscle, every icy blue vein stood out against their flesh. They looked so similar, male or female, who could tell? How could William have been even remotely related to these creatures?

In slow unison, they arched their necks forward at inhuman angles, taking us in. Once again I was struck by the lifeless depth of their eyes, blackened pits where the reflection of a soul should have been.

"What is this, William?" the one in the middle spoke. His voice was grating and shrill, painful to the ears. "A decidedly difficult dinner, don't you think?"

"It's a meal, nonetheless," William shrugged, still watching us.

The vampire snapped his head around to face him. "And would you have us *die* for our food?"

"That's the idea," William said, looking Abram in the eye. Golden light flashed brilliantly and crashed into the vampires, throwing them down the slope. William hurried forward to join us.

Far too quickly the creatures had reassembled, scurrying down the tunnel and away from us on hands and knees.

"Don't let them get too far!" Demetre shouted, and Christian and Paul threw their arms out, catching two of the monsters in a steely grip. The others stopped, deciding whether or not to fight, then ran toward us, screaming obscenely. If they kept this up, we'd have the whole coven on us in no time. Paul wrestled with his victim, still strangling it from a distance. It didn't want to be destroyed, that was certain. Paul had to use two hands and back himself against the mine wall.

I gasped as a taller vampire slunk from behind Anna, locking its eyes with hers. To my horror, she remained completely still, seemingly stunned by his presence. So this is how I'd looked. This was the daze I'd been in when Christian found me. Anna wasn't even blinking. I had to do something, but all I could manage were words.

"Anna needs help!" I cried.

Katrina came to her rescue. "Hey, asshole! Get away from my girlfriend!" she screamed and blasted the vampire with a barrage of heat that sent the thing straight back against the dirt wall with its arms splayed open. Anna came to, shaking for a moment, then her lightline blazed red. Taking a few steps forward, she repelled two vampires at once.

"Nice," I heard myself say.

"Thank you," she breathed.

I'd been lucky up till now. The vampires had been far too distracted to pay me any mind, but that was not to last long. One of them spotted me amid the chaos, and with stilted movements he heaved himself toward me, grinning. William stepped in front of me.

"Out of the way," it hissed at him. "Filthy traitor."

"Traitor?" William scoffed. "No, Edgar. That would suggest I was loyal to begin with." I watched in awe as he repelled the creature to the ceiling, holding him there.

I stared, awe-struck and petrified. Five of the beasts were in various states of writhing agony. Paul had killed one and it lay limply in the shadows with only its withered legs extending into the light. Christian's hostage struggled with wild eyes as he fought to snap its neck.

Finally, I looked away, pained to remember that the humanity of these creatures was long gone. Man or woman once, their lives had since taken leave. All that was left was conscienceless hunger.

With repeated blasts to the ground, Anna continued to torture the smallest while Demetre and Abram glared fervently at their own captures, holding them to the earth with invisible but no less securely bound shackles of light. But where was the last? Paul and I searched the darkness desperately.

"Where is he?" Paul read my mind.

"I don't know!" I said uneasily.

"Son of a bitch. Did he make it back to the coven?"

If he had, a hoard of them could overtake us at any moment…and then what?

A vile crack revealed that Christian had succeeded in killing his vampire. William released Edgar, who fell to the ground, only to have Christian throttle him immediately. I froze, listening. There should have been swarms of the animals all over the place. Another sickening snap later and Edgar was dead.

"He was the leader?" Abram asked William, still holding his vampire down.

"More or less," William answered.

"Let me take care of yours," Paul said to Thomas, aware that the old man's light was lagging. In fact, everyone's light was weakening. Thomas nodded and let Paul take hold of it.

I sighed, feeling ashamed. I'd been utterly useless to them as they'd spent themselves, and we weren't out of danger yet. Surely I could do *something*.

"Can I try to hold him, Abram?" I asked, glancing at his captive.

"Yes … of course," he answered. "Are you ready?"

"I … I don't know."

"I'll help you if you need it," William said.

Abram released the vampire, who in fairness was considerably feeble by now. He attempted to push himself up as I gathered the adrenaline from my fear and stared at him. Again, he collapsed to the dirt while I held him down with unbroken focus, determined that my energy continue its flow. Somehow it was working. He was trapped. And though I was proud of my accomplishment, I felt an undeniable sense of pity. He was beyond redemption, clearly, and would kill me with no regard, but I was tormenting him and the action revolted me.

"Splendid, Lillian," Thomas commented.

"Yes. Nicely done," Christian agreed.

I cringed. Such a macabre victory. "Can I give him to you now, Christian?" I responded.

"Yes, all right," he said, taking over as I broke my concentration. I couldn't watch. Abram was right. This life was not for the weak.

"We need to get out of here," Thomas announced. "They're coming."

Paul stretched his arms out to hold Christian's vampire in place. Together, they wasted no time in killing him and the creature crumbled into a spindly heap.

"Let's go." Christian glanced back down the shaft before hurrying us toward the eastern tunnel.

"Wait!" Thomas held up a hand, and we all stopped. "I think … oh, no, Abram." His face was contorted with worry as he turned to our Seer. "They've blocked our exit."

"Fuck," Paul seethed. "*Fuck*, what do we do?"

"But," I began, wide-eyed. "I thought they didn't go near that part of the mine!"

"They do now," Thomas said grimly. "They must have exited elsewhere and come around."

"But Mum!" Anna said, suddenly horrified. "Thomas, can you feel my mother?"

"One moment…." He furrowed his brows. "Yes. In fact I can. They haven't hurt her."

"Well, I don't trust it," Christian said. "And *shit*. We can't go *that* way." He nodded down the slope. "That's exactly what they'd want. We'd be crippled with them coming at us from both sides."

"Then we head back where we came from and fight our way through," Demetre said.

Abram nodded once. "We have little choice now," he agreed.

I looked at William, and whatever he saw on my face drew him quickly to my side. He laid a hand on my back. "Stay with me," he ordered. "Don't move from my side, okay?"

I nodded, and he took hold of my hand.

"Let's go, folks. Don't get separated," Demetre said. We followed after him, though how I made my legs move I couldn't tell.

"And Lily," William said as we walked, "repel at will. Show no mercy. I promise you they won't."

I was doing everything in my power to gather some tenacity, grasping for the rush of anger, of disgust, that would heave me past fear and into action. It was dawning on me now—really striking me—that I could die here. The last human breath I took as Lillian Hunt could be right here, in this abyss, without ever seeing Frank or Connie again, without ever marrying William, without ever really living my life as a Sentient. I could die just exactly as my mother had in a mortal case of history repeating. The idea saddened and then provoked me. Here was my adrenaline burst, and I was going to need it.

Where light had once filtered into the eastern mouth of the mine, there was none. Instead, an enormous gathering of filthy skin and bone stood, grinning maniacally at our tiny band of heroes. To cap off the effect, the vampire that had escaped us before was now holding an entranced Clara in front of him. She faced us, but she might as well have been asleep. Something flashed across her eyes—a moment of lucidity, perhaps—and she gasped, struggling, before several more of the monsters lay their hands on her shoulders. She relaxed, her eyes rolling back in her head.

"A nice change in circumstances, don't you think?" The vampire sneered at William.

"Luther…let her go," William spoke calmly.

"If you hurt her, I'll rip you to shreds." Christian spit the words like nails.

"And what then? Will you do the same to every one of us here?" The vampire laughed. "I am one, but we are many. Try and fight, and we'll see you decimated."

"Do you think we'll go down that easily?" Christian glared. "Some of us may fall, but only at the expense of half your number."

The vampire ignored him. "Just think! A good meal *and* desirable additions to our little family." The rest of the hoard smirked appreciatively.

Then Abram spoke with the same unquestionable authority that his presence had always commanded. "Do not deceive yourselves. We *will* kill our own kind in order to prevent the spread of yours."

"Kill your own? How valiant," Luther remarked snidely. But the confidence was gone from him. If he was counting on inheriting a troop of Sentient vampires, he was wrong. Murder was plausible; turning…unthinkable.

"You are well aware of the damage we inflicted upon your kind when last we met," Abram continued.

"Oh, most certainly! Though, if I recall, there were twice as many of you," the vampire said. He turned to William, grinding his teeth. "Lolial trusted you so implicitly. He'd have placed you at his right hand…had you been loyal."

"But he wasn't!" another vampire screeched. "Think of what he did to Lolial! Stringing him along when he knew the girl's whereabouts the whole time…filthy deserter!"

"Yes, Ferdinand," Luther agreed. "And as it turns out, an assassin. Tell me, William, did you look him in the eye when you murdered him…or did you sneak up from behind like a snake?"

"That credit goes to me." Christian stood tall. "*I* did away with the bastard."

The group shifted their eyes back to Christian, their expressions simultaneously enraged.

"*You?*" Luther snarled a laugh. "You're a liar. Lolial was far too strong to have been defeated by a human."

"Believe it," Christian said. "I can personally attest that my *very* hands were the last thing he felt before I broke his fucking neck. And you can rest assured you'll meet the same end."

A low growl rumbled through the coven. Either he'd pushed them too far or they realized the degree to which they'd underestimated us as a threat. I prayed for the latter.

Luther smiled. "All right. As I'd hate to see our months of restoration come undone so quickly, shall I make a proposal?"

Paul and Christian scoffed, but Abram raised a hand to silence them.

"What have you to offer?" he asked.

I trembled. Something in me knew to expect the worst.

"William," Luther said. "You'll stay with us, and the rest may leave. And here …." He released Clara from his grasp, pushing her towards us. "To demonstrate the legitimacy of my word."

Clara awoke, blinking quickly and staring at us. "Thomas … what's happening?" she asked. He directed his gaze behind her, and she turned around. Seeing the mass of vampires, she gasped loudly, her memory returning.

"There, you see?" Luther crooned. "She is returned to you. Now, William?"

Impossible, I thought. He'd never agree to their terms in a million years.

But William didn't respond.

I peered at him in disbelief. "*William*," I pleaded, but he was absorbed in deliberation. "Goddamn it, no!" I took his arm.

He looked at me, then Abram.

"No! You're not actually considering this?!" I cried, horrified.

"If he lets the rest of you go, Lily … ," he said.

"Well, well," Luther spoke up, chuckling. "Could this be the girl? Brothers and sisters … I believe we've happened upon the fount of Lolial's fascination."

"Take her!" a particularly shrill vampire demanded. "Lolial won't have died in vain if we take her!"

Christian clenched his fists as William stepped in front of me. "I'll stay with you," he told Luther. "But you have to let her go with the rest."

"Ah," Luther laughed. "So she's your mate! I should have known. Well, in that case, there's a very simple solution to our problem. Both of you come with us, and the rest of your group goes free. Now, can you deny this is a generous and beneficial solution for all?"

"Never," William swore. "I won't let you turn her."

"Why ever not?" Luther smiled. "You two would be together, after all."

"It's not an option," William said. "Take me or fight us all."

Luther considered his words, while I cried, my stomach heaving. This was worse than William dying. I couldn't live with this.

I held onto him fiercely. "*Please, please* don't go. Please, if we die, we die. Don't do this," I begged.

"That's right, son," Demetre agreed. "Don't even think about it."

Paul nodded. "You've already proven you're one of us."

I sniffled against his chest, kissing his shirt. "I won't let you go. You'll have to drag me with you."

William's face was so torn, so full of complexity that I couldn't have imagined what he was thinking.

"Don't be a fool, William," Luther chided in a singing tone.

William looked him in the eye. He seemed to have come to a conclusion, but just as he opened his mouth to speak, Christian interrupted him.

"We don't make deals with monsters," Christian said, glaring at Luther. "Get out of our way or prepare for the consequences."

"Idiots." Luther shook his head. "Stupid, self-righteous idiots."

"We're idiots with souls." Thomas smiled. "Even if we all die, we still win." And I understood how right he was. How far could death remove us? Only as distantly as a breath. We'd all reconnect in the end.

Before I could ready myself, brilliant light was bouncing off the mine walls, surging and ebbing, collecting itself into balls and springing forward. We stood in an unbroken line as Paul and Christian took on two vampires at a time. Never before had I used such a store of energy, and never before had I been so aware of my own lightline. Warmth emitted not only from my fellow Sentients, but from within, and coursed outward, leaving me swimming in perfect calm. I watched as beast after beast approached our line, and I promptly directed the energy forth to knock them back.

I had feared they would all converge on us at once, but this was not the case. They were an undisciplined army, and their rows seemed reluctant to approach too hastily, waiting their turn to advance. As we diminished their numbers, those remaining would scatter, darting out of the cavern and into the daylight. More and more sun was finding its way into the mine, and I felt hope. It seemed we had a chance to escape this nightmare after all ... and not a moment too soon. I was being drained. My light, once white and radiant, was a faded glow. Though nearly one hundred vampires had been reduced to a few dozen through death or flight, my own efforts at repelling them were falling short.

Thomas, even more than I, was in peril now. He held out his arms in a focused attempt at forcing the energy into concentration, but it would not come. Clara, Demetre, and William seemed strong still, but our two combatants stood, drenched in beads of sweat, breathless with exertion.

Only Abram maintained his blinding light, and its endlessness fed our wills, kept us fighting for escape with relentless desperation. Still, so greatly had Thomas been spent that his defenses were failing. Each time he fell behind, Demetre or Abram would slow till he regained his ground. A stronger Thomas would have sensed it coming, and while we saw little but the promise of daylight, something took him from behind and dragged him into deeper darkness.

"Thomas!" Anna cried out, shooting her light into the shadows, but it was too late. He lay on the ground, blood pooling around his head.

"Oh, *God*," I wailed.

"Don't look back, Lily." William pulled me to his side, still repelling what lingering vampires attempted a return. Out of the corner of my eye, I saw Demetre rushing Thomas's body back toward us. Just as quickly, we'd formed a protective circle around them.

Abram set his sights on Luther, who stubbornly blocked our escape.

"Will you stay only to die?" Abram asked the vampire as Christian swept his arm out to capture him.

"No," Luther seethed, choking in the unseen hands of his attacker. "First, I'll avenge my leader." And as we watched, eager to bear witness to his rightful end, a sharp cry tore our eyes away. Christian lay on the ground with a knife protruding from his back as Ferdinand grinned wildly over him. Clara screamed and ran toward the vampire, but Paul held her back.

"Kill him now, Sentient!" Ferdinand squealed. "Strangle him now, dead man!"

Paul released Clara and—shaking with rage—he thrust one hand toward Ferdinand and the other at a weakened Luther and crushed their heads to a pulp. Witnessing this, the remaining vampires sprinted out the main entrance in a panic, dispersing into the nearby woods.

Demetre lay Thomas down and pulled our combatant from the ground, turning him over in his arms. Christian wheezed and gulped with the labor of breathing, and a thin stream of blood trickled from his mouth.

"Get him out of here! I'll carry Thomas," Paul shouted as Demetre swept Christian up and over his shoulder. We rushed the exit, finally free of vampires.

In the sun, Demetre laid Christian on his side, his mother falling over him.

"Not you, too," she cried, kissing his forehead. "Oh, Christian. Not you, too."

Anna held her brother's hand. Her eyes were wide with shock and silent tears flooded her face. I looked on in horror. This couldn't really be happening. Any moment I would wake up and see my dark astral slinking across the bedroom floor.

But no. Christian was really dying, and all we could do was watch it happen. I lost the feeling in my legs and collapsed to the ground.

William knelt before me, taking my face in his hands. "I love you, Lillian. In this life, in every life," he said, his words vehement as he looked me in the eye. I stared dazedly at him for a moment, uncomprehending. Then, just as I had grasped his meaning, he kissed me.

As he stood up, I went numb. So, I would lose him anyway.

Hearing Clara's gasp, I knew what she was reacting to. Though I feared it, I turned my head to see that William had pulled the knife from Christian's back and tossed it to the side. He placed his hands over the wound and closed his eyes. Before long, William was shaking violently.

I ran to where he was, wrapping my arms around his shoulders, and laid my head over his. "I love you," I wept.

His breaths grew shallow as Christian took the first of his own. The color was returning to Christian's face, but William turned ashen gray. Christian took a massive gasp of air and opened his eyes as William slumped back into my lap, his head slung over my arm. He wasn't breathing. He was cold. I stared at him and tried to inhale. The sound was suffocated each time and replaced with something pained and grating. Reality roared over me in excruciating waves.

"*No!*" I screamed, shaking my head. "It's not real. It's not real. Wake up!" I commanded of us both, but his body was dead weight in my arms. I lowered my face to his and kissed his cheek. "Please," I cried. "*Please.* Don't leave me. Please wake up now ... wake up ... William ... *wake* up." I felt Anna's hand on my shoulder, then Clara's. Christian was sitting up, watching, while Demetre and Paul whispered low in his ear.

Abram knelt beside me. "Lily … let me have him."

I refused, pressing William's head to my chest. "*No.* Don't take him away," I sobbed harder. "He's not dead."

"Lillian," Abram spoke firmly. "I will try to help him. But you must let him go. This instant." His words registered immediately, and I unclenched my fingers from his body.

Abram leaned over us. Taking William's head in his hands, he began to breathe on him, slowly, rhythmically.

"Demetre, check for a pulse," he paused, then he continued the action. With every exhalation his light carried forth as golden strands into William's nose and mouth.

Demetre pressed his fingers to William's neck, then shook his head. Abram continued his efforts, breathing and breathing until his body slumped and his light faded. Finally, he fell backward, his hand on his heart. Somehow, though it should have been impossible, Abram looked to have aged ten years.

"That is all…I have," he gasped, the strength gone from him.

"There's a pulse … it's weak, though," Demetre said. Abram nodded faintly.

"We have to get him back to the hotel," Clara said of William.

Anna looked terrified. "What's going to happen to him? What will we do? We can't very well call a doctor!"

Abram lifted a shaky hand. "We'll wait. And pray."

Twenty-Six

*W*e all gathered in William's suite, bone-tired and heartbroken. Clara sat on the sofa, and I rested on the floor in front of her with my back against her legs. She stroked my hair soothingly and kept me warm with her energy.

I tried not to, but I couldn't help staring into William's bedroom…at the place where he lay. He was alive but unresponsive. After I'd spent two hours crying over him, Clara and Ophelia had forced me out of the room, saying that it wouldn't do William any good if he woke to find me this way. Their appeal didn't quell my longing to be with him, though. After all, what if he woke and I wasn't there at all? How would he feel then?

But while William still had a chance, Thomas was lost to us. And arrangements needed to be made, regardless of our mourning.

"Yes. Madelyn, be sure to tell Felix how grateful we are for his intervention. This is such a difficult thing," Abram spoke into the phone.

Before we'd left the park mines, Clara wasted no time in contacting a friend of Abram's—an undertaker from Harrisburg—to arrange Thomas's funeral. Christian and Paul had stayed with the body, shielding our fallen Sentient from retrieval by vampires.

"Felix has sent his man to recover Thomas," Abram said soberly. "The service will be this evening…no authorities have been involved."

Even in dealings of death, Abram had connections. I'd never considered the importance of such a thing until now. How had they explained the deaths of their members in the past? Only Abram knew how to smooth these bumps in the road, regardless of his current condition.

I studied him, trying to unravel the mystery. Our Seer's features were strangely withered. Something unthinkable had occurred in his efforts to save William, something that appeared to have sucked the life right out of him. Our poor Seer, already an elder, had aged even further, right before our eyes.

There were two quick knocks on the door before Christian and Paul entered the suite looking bedraggled beyond words and utterly miserable. Anna and Katrina got up from the couch to let them sit down.

"We'll be back," Anna said, leaving quietly with her girlfriend. Paul sat down, and Christian paused, glancing at me before taking a seat.

"How is he?" he asked, staring at the wall.

"We don't know," Clara replied. "He's still unconscious."

"No physician's desk reference on vampires, huh?" Paul attempted to lighten the mood.

"Unfortunately not," Abram sighed. "In theory, their biology should be similar with regard to the nervous and circulatory systems, but as the digestion of anything short of blood is defunct, one would assume that medications are useless."

"So what are you saying?" Christian went on. "Is there nothing we can do for him?"

"I suppose nothing physiologically," Abram began. "But..." he looked at me, "...there may be other ways to help him along."

"How?" I asked, suddenly alert.

Abram shook his head. "I don't pretend to know, precisely, Lily. But perhaps you do."

I lost my temper. "No lessons, Abram! If you know something, you have to tell me!" I insisted. Everyone gawked. I'd never spoken to Abram like this.

"Lillian," Abram spoke softly. "If I had the answer I would not withhold it. You have my word." And no one could debate that Abram's word was gold. "But nothing is stronger; nothing heals more readily than the love of an empath. And you have enough of this for an army. I have faith that the answer will reveal itself."

"I'm sorry," I whimpered, laying my head on my knees. "I'm sorry. I just ... need to be alone." The tears were starting again. "Please."

"Of course, dear," Clara said kindly, her hand stroking my hair for one last time. "Come on, then. Let's go," she ordered, and all but Christian followed her out of the suite.

He sighed and rose up from the couch to sit beside me on the floor. Then he touched my shoulder. "Lily," he whispered. "I'm so sorry."

I didn't answer him.

"I would never want to see you hurt. And I ... I don't want him to die. You have to believe me." He took my hand, but I remained still. "I know you wish he'd just let me die. *I* wish he had."

His sorrow was real, and it deepened my own. "You need to *stop* that," I said, turning around to hug him. "Never say that again. I don't want you to die! I'm *glad* he saved you."

He clung to the back of my shirt and wept against my cheek. "I don't deserve it, but please forgive me, Lily. Please forgive me."

"There's nothing to forgive," I said, still holding him tightly. "I swear."

He broke away and looked me in the eyes. "There is. There's so much. You know that."

"Then I forgive you," I said without hesitation.

"Will he?"

I sighed. "Yes. He will."

"How do you know?"

"Because I just do. I love him for a reason, you know. He's so good, and ...." I couldn't go on, and Christian held me as a new bolt of pain took my breath away.

"He'll come through this," he said, rubbing my back. "There has to be a way."

Upon learning of Thomas's death, the Northwest Sentients wasted no time. They piled into their rental cars and made a beeline for Wilkes-Barre, ignoring, it seemed, those pesky speed limits. What should have been a seven hour trip, they managed in five.

I sat—Elaine on my left and Anna on my right—and strained to see Abram's face through my tears.

"Of Thomas," Abram began, standing at a podium in the small funeral chapel, "I can rightfully say this: he possessed a quality which even the most gifted of Sentients cannot boast. He was wise … and humbly so.

"Some five years ago, when William joined our group, Thomas was our great ally. When our Society's assembly threatened to turn their back on us, Thomas—risking his own impeccable name—spoke passionately in defense of the decision to allow Mr. Maddox to stay. He was keenly aware of justice and won his battles with a gentle hand. We all knew Thomas's proclivity for sensing evil, but greater than that was his penchant for finding the good. In losing him, we have discovered his legacy and inherited an obligation to carry it on."

Clara nodded, sniffling into a handkerchief, and Christian wrapped his arm around her.

"Furthermore, I realize that his unique influence will reside with each of us singularly. I myself can say, with much feeling, that Thomas was as close to a brother as I have ever known. And none but evil could make of him an enemy."

"That's right," Demetre whimpered. Ophelia rested her hand on his and passed him another Kleenex. Touchingly, it was the lion of our group who had been most deeply broken by his friend's passing.

The next day we laid Thomas to rest. It felt strange to bury him in Wilkes-Barre, since he'd been born overseas, but Abram insisted that this would have been acceptable to Thomas. After all, a Sentient's home was everywhere.

Abram saw to it that the wording on Thomas's gravestone was exactly as he had once requested:

"Seek me not in this place, for we all live on."

❧

"So they've all fled?" Abram frowned across the tiny kitchenette table at Paul.

"Yeah. They're gone. And I figured as much. No way they're sticking around that hole after what happened."

"Into the woods?"

Paul nodded and crossed his hands. "That's right."

"I'll bet they're night-traveling," Elaine suggested.

Abram considered this. "Hmm. It's better this way. The enclosed spaces never bode well for us."

Paul shook his head. "No, they don't. And I'm glad you guys are here," he spoke to Wendell.

"Yes," Abram said. "Yes. I am grateful. We are weaker now, with Thomas gone. And William …."

There was a heavy silence as every eye, inescapably, fell upon me. All the muscles in my body tensed with a strange defensiveness. It was bad enough with Thomas dead. Did they have to speak of William as if he were, too?

"You don't have to look at me like that," I muttered. "He'll wake up."

"Of course!" Clara added, quickly. "Lily, we all know that."

But their light told me otherwise. Their words were comforting, but their confidence was broken. Only Abram's energy differed from the norm. Not once since William had fallen did our Seer's lightline reflect despair, and so long as Abram had hope, I did as well.

I'd thought long and hard about all this. Abram knew so much, he had seen the course of our lives. At first, I could not begin to comprehend why he'd left the Northwest Sentients behind. Wouldn't all of this misery have been avoided if only they had joined us from the start? It seemed, upon surface reflection, to make no sense at all. But Abram was Abram, and in my heart I knew that he knew, understood that he understood, and I clung to my belief in his vision—that every stray breeze had its rightful destination.

"Have you two had a fight, kiddo?" Frank peered at me worriedly, placing his hand on my shoulder.

"No, Grandpa. It's not that …."

Could I tell him??

Frank waited for me to admit what was wrong, and part of me really wanted to tell him. I *wanted* to tell him everything. But, tempted as I was, I knew better. Even if Frank should believe the whole cockamamie tale, it would be too much for him. He looked so small and tired as it was, and I'd already worried him enough to last another eighty years.

"William's fine." I forced the words out. "But … a good friend of mine died."

"Oh, no … Oh, Lily, I'm so sorry, sweetheart," Frank offered.

"And this job is *so* hard, Grandpa. So much harder than I thought it would be."

"I can see that, kiddo. But let me tell you something. Whatever you're doing, you're doing it right. You're conscious, baby doll. And I'm sure I can't explain it right, no matter how I try, but that blank look you used to have—that's gone. There's life in you now. And you know what else?"

"What?"

He stared at me, perplexed. "I hated that look. I've seen it all my life. Nearly everyone that passes through the doors of my store looks that way … like they're sleeping."

I took his hand. Frank was more awake than he realized.

"And your father looked that way, too … until he met Elizabeth, anyway." He paused, thinking. "There was just something about that girl. I always liked her, even if your grandma didn't trust her."

"She didn't?"

"Nope. Connie thought your mother was keeping secrets."

I snorted, laughing loudly. Maybe grandma wasn't so clueless after all. "Well, if Mom had any secrets, I'm sure they were good ones," I said.

Frank nodded, grinning. "I'm sure they were."

Her secret was my secret. It was *everyone's* secret, really, and you didn't need to be a Sentient to figure it out. There seemed to be a purpose in everything—a winding, swaying, knotted, jumbled road that led back to the same door as many times as you needed it to. Until you remembered….

❧

A week had passed since we'd buried Thomas, and still William remained the same. The whole time, I'd wanted nothing more than to shut myself up in his room and talk to him.

I'd seen it before, on TV, in magazines. If your loved one was in a coma, you talked to them. Supposedly it could bring them back. But I'd talked and cried and pleaded myself blue in the face to no avail. There had to be a better way.

Closing his door behind me, I slung my purse on the couch. Everything was so quiet. I hated it. The silence only weighed on my heart, mocking William's condition.

Standing in the doorway, I watched—as usual—for the rise and fall of his chest. He was still alive. That was all I needed. I climbed into his bed and curled up against him, laying my head next to his.

"It's me," I said.

He breathed.

"I went to visit Frank today, and I wanted to tell him what was happening, but I couldn't," I admitted sadly.

Proceeding with what was now a daily routine for me, I touched my lips to his and waited for his breath to tickle my nose. Such a small thing, but it helped.

"You *have* to come back to us, William. I mean it. Stop being difficult."

More breathing.

"God, if I could hear your voice…." I stopped, fighting back tears. "It's *just* like you to leave me groping around in the dark!" I sniffled, and then I pressed my face into his shoulder. "I miss you, and even now—*especially* now—when I think about how I treated you, I can't stand myself. If I could go back and love you from day one, I would. I wouldn't have wasted any time."

I raised myself up on one arm and took hold of his face with my free hand, gazing at him. "Open your eyes, William Maddox," I ordered. Of course this didn't work. I'd tried the tactic countless times to no avail. But that didn't mean I wouldn't *keep* trying. *He* would have.

"I mean it," I said tearfully. "*Please*…open your eyes. For me. Can't you hear me? Don't you feel me here? Where are you?"

His face was so peaceful, so calm, but how fared his consciousness?

Son of a bitch.

There was really only one way to find out, wasn't there? Why hadn't the idea of a soul merge dawned on me earlier?

I took a deep breath, contemplating the possibilities. Could I reach him where the physical had no hold? And what sort of luck would I have without his participation? Would it even work? And even more, could I make things worse? What if William's energy was too weak to be drawn out? Could I somehow harm him in the process?

God, but I had to try *something*, anything, before I lost my mind. So I determined to go for it. Now the only question was how.

Against normal protocol, I closed my eyes and waited for his warmth to come, half-fearing that I'd be met with nothing. My concern was abated, though, when I felt a weak flow of his energy begin to trickle around me. If this worked, it would take forever and exhaust the hell out of me, but I didn't care.

As I drew him in, my head started spinning, and the air became sparse as if I was trying to breathe through a straw. Why was this so difficult? Shouldn't this have been easier than ever without him fighting me? But—wait—*was* he fighting me? I gave up on inhaling and held my breath instead, struggling with an unseen barrier. Finally, something seemed to snap, and a stream of his energy sifted into me. The progress was painstaking, but it was working. In my mind, my body was lifting from the bed and the world was tearing away from me. Then, when hope was at its peak, something cold ripped across my body and sent me slamming to the bed again. William's energy was siphoned away violently.

In my current state, the loss of his energy should have driven me mad… and it *would* have, if I weren't so distracted by the black haze gathering over my body. It held me to the bed, crushing my lungs.

"You can't bring him back," it said.

"Let … me up," I gasped.

"Leave him as he is or I'll kill him."

"You're … doing this?" I shook, wheezing. "Why? To make me suffer?"

"You?" It laughed. "You're nothing. His suffering is far better."

"What are you doing to him?!" I rasped.

"I warn you, I'll kill him. Leave him as he is."

"*You're* keeping him from waking up!" I shouted in realization as the world came crashing in. "You're holding him hostage."

"He suffers magnificently," it hissed.

"I'll kill you!" I roared.

"You won't, Lillian. You're pathetic, just like your mother. She abandoned you, and you'll abandon him. It's your way."

"You're wrong!"

"You're a brazen little wench, aren't you? All of this is your fault, stringing two men along," it snarled. "You selfish little whore. All that fighting did wonders to keep me around."

"Get *off*!" I threw the astral's weight from me, and it crashed against the ceiling, scattering like shards of glass. "Don't try to play head games with me, you disgusting piece of shit!"

As it gathered itself together, I jumped from the bed. "You think I'm weak? You think I'll just sit back and let you hurt him anymore? You *sadistic* motherfucker. Don't you know what I am?"

It lowered itself to the floor and swirled into a tizzy, obviously trying to intimidate me. I laughed at it, and that pissed it off. It growled angrily at my defiance.

"If you're so damned tough, what's with the special effects?" I said, blasting my contempt in its direction. Again, it blew to pieces.

"And you know what else? You're just an astral. You're not a soul; you're not even a vampire. In theory, I could send you straight back to oblivion," I stated.

It screamed so loudly that I was certain everyone for blocks would hear it while it charged toward me. I held out my hand, and, as if hitting a wall, it crumbled. I regrouped, expecting it to repair itself quickly as it had always done, but instead, the astral sloshed together like molasses, converging into a gelatinous blob. Stubbornly, it inched forward, but not before I noticed my lightline was gleaming amber. William had said my abilities would make themselves known when the time was right.

I beamed. "So you're scared of me," I said. "Clever monster."

And as I had in battle, I surged my light through the astral in a rigorous stream, continuing the outpouring until its mass ignited in white flames. I was forced to listen to its howls only briefly, before the door to the suite shot open and Christian and Abram rushed in. They'd made it in time to witness the fire extinguish itself… leaving nothing, not a trace of the astral behind.

"Lily…." Christian gaped on. "What in the bloody hell has happened?"

I laughed. "I killed it. I burned it up."

"*What?*" Christian pressed. "What did you kill? What's going on?"

I sighed and sat on the edge of William's bed. "It was the spirit from Mount Lorna Chapel. It's been stalking me like a bitch, actually."

"Jesus, Lily, and you didn't say anything before now?" Christian complained.

"No. There's been too much happening. I wanted to deal with it myself."

"And it would seem that you *have*." Abram grinned. "Quite expertly, I might add."

"It was easier now. I had to save him," I said.

"Save him?" Abram asked.

I stared in shock at my knees. "William. The astral...it moved on to William. It's been keeping him sick." I looked up, suddenly terrified. "Abram. What do you think it's been doing to him?"

Abram shook his head. "I dare not guess."

"I have to bring him back," I said. "I think I know how...and so did the astral."

"How?" Christian asked, amazement again lacing his words.

"I'm a pathcrosser, Christian. If he can't come out, I'll go in," I said, simply.

Understanding lit in his eyes. "I see."

Abram smiled, but his usual gleam was not there. I frowned. "William's soul," I began. "You've restored it twice in this lifetime, haven't you?"

The old man nodded slowly. "You've caught on, I see."

"Oh...Abram," I breathed and stood in front of him. "You extraordinary man."

"No, Lily. I did only what was intended."

"And that's so easy?" I asked. "Abram. What's happened to you?"

"Nothing to be alarmed about. A Seer's life is very long, and it *must* be for a reason. How old do you think I am? Go on, guess," he teased.

"Seventy? Eighty?"

"I thank you." He laughed. "But no. Next month, I shall be one hundred twenty-four years old."

My jaw dropped. Even Christian seemed surprised. "How is that possible?" I asked.

"Because a Seer is a conduit, Lily. If a soul has not moved on, if it lingers here for its own reasons, there is the chance I can restore it. But there must be some life still in the body, either that or the body must be preserved alive...as with a vampire, for instance. Each time I allow for the transference of a spirit, it takes a bit out of me...if you hadn't noticed. Unfortunately, I can survive only a few such instances before I am finished here."

I kissed his forehead. "Bless you, Abram," I said.

He touched my face. "Thank you, Lillian," he replied. "To be blessed is a gift."

I looked at William. "May I be alone with him?" I asked.

"Of course," Abram said. "We shall wait in the living room, if it's all the same to you."

"That's fine," I commented, as Christian and Abram left me to my last ounce of hope.

This time, there was no barricade. I needed only to breathe and William's energy filled me completely. As my body fell backward and the force settled in, I searched around in the darkness. Where was he?

"William," I thought, but no one responded. "William? William, where are you?"

The world was pitch, impenetrable black.

"I know you're here. It's Lily. It's me. Where are you?"

"Go to hell," thought someone from somewhere.

"What?" I laughed to myself.

"Do you expect me to fall for this again? You're not her. You're *never* her. It's always a lie. So go to hell."

I knew that voice! "William?" I thought joyfully. "Where are you? Come out!"

"I said leave me alone!" This time a figure emerged from the darkness. William's light was feeble, flickering like a dying flame.

"Oh, William," I thought, heartbroken. "What has he done to you?"

He stared at me; then stared at me harder. Something changed in the glow of his face.

"You ... feel like her," he thought.

"I *am* her," I answered and sent forth what essence of myself I could muster.

"But it pretends to be you," he thought, his sadness quite literally becoming mine.

"Not anymore. I killed it."

"Impossible."

"Not so impossible, thank you very much!" I shared a wave of indignation.

"It even *sounds* like you."

"William Maddox!" I thought.

Then I was overcome with elation, with relief, with love.

"William." My spirit rippled with laughter. "It can't keep you here anymore. I'm letting you go now."

"Letting me go? Please don't," he begged.

"But you're free to come out, William. Do you believe me?"

"Yes."

"Then I'm letting go. Just follow me, okay?"

"Okay."

When I opened my eyes, William was still unconscious. I smiled and brushed his cheek with the back of my hand. "Open your eyes now," I whispered.

He groaned sleepily.

"William?" My laughter and tears battled it out and both won.

He sighed, his eyelids opening, and I plastered his face with kiss after kiss. It took him a stunned moment to recognize what was happening, but once he did, he reached up and pulled me on top of him.

"Lily. You found me," he spoke against my lips before he broke away, beaming.

"Don't I always?"

❧

"So, you came here a lot?" William pondered, staring down the trail.

"All the time. Of course, then it started to freak me out, so I stopped coming alone … and eventually, altogether. Apparently, I had the right idea. Last time I was here was a real picnic."

William frowned, and it took a second for me to realize why. Would he ever stop feeling guilty about Lolial?

"Hey …." I touched his arm. After what he'd done for me, for everyone, could I even find the words to express my gratitude?

"Are you still scared of this place?" William asked.

"No."

"Let's walk then," he said.

"Are you okay to do that? It's cold out here." I studied him, pale and gaunt. He was still so weak. It would take him months to fully recover, and a four-mile hike seemed highly unfeasible in his condition.

"For a little while," he assured me.

I nodded. "Okay …."

We walked side by side for a time while I watched for it, the scant patch of trees that concealed a tiny pebble beach … the silent lake.

"This way." I smiled and pulled him from the trail.

He chuckled, ducking beneath the overgrowth. "Where are you taking me?"

"Don't spoil it! Just follow me … here …."

It was as beautiful as I'd remembered. The only difference was that Abram was missing.

"This is where I first met our Seer," I said.

He looked out over the water and smirked. "He likes to make things as dramatic as possible, doesn't he?"

I laughed. "He does. He really does."

Abram would have appreciated this sight. The water reflected fire and blue, the bright-leaved trees and crisp autumn sky on its surface.

"William?"

"Hmm?"

I turned to face him. "I don't think I can begin to forgive myself. I owe you so much more than an apology."

"Lily, don't. You're marrying me, for God's sake," he laughed. "And you saved my life! I know how you feel; everything else is water under the—"

"*No*," I broke in. "No. Under *your* bridge maybe, but not mine."

He watched me.

"I almost lost you," I said. The thought sucked the air right out of me.

"But you didn't." He smiled, as if that would make it all okay, and folded his arms across his chest in an attempt to conceal his shivering.

"Oh, William." I sighed and pulled him to me tightly. He freed his arms from between us, holding me closer still. His trembling ceased.

"I love you," I spoke against his neck, hoping my breath would help warm him. "I love you. And it's awful to think that there was *ever* a time when I *didn't* love you. It'll take years before I'm worthy of you, you know that? I'm so sorry. You're incredible. You don't have to prove yourself to me or anyone else *ever* again, do you hear me?"

He didn't answer, didn't breathe.

"Just say you forgive me," I said. "And you won't sacrifice yourself again … you won't leave me."

I heard him sigh before he unclasped my vice-like grip from his body.

"Lillian …." He took my face in his hands. "There's nothing to forgive. And I'll never leave you," he pledged. "Never again."

"You swear on your soul? You won't go throwing yourself in front of a bus or anything?"

"Wouldn't even consider it. Absolutely *no* buses," he began. "Maybe a Jeep…."

I glowered at him.

"What?" he asked, shrugging a shoulder. "You know my weakness for sports utility vehicles."

There was no keeping a straight face with him. "You're such a pain in the ass," I complained.

Dropping a hand to my shoulder, he brushed my hair between his fingers, and I felt his warmth wash through me. "I love you, angel," he whispered.

Epilogue

I woke to bright morning sunlight that poured in through William's bedroom window, cascading over everything, soaking the bed in heat. Even before opening my eyes, I reached for him. But he was not beside me. Irrational fear shook away the last of my slumber as I sat up quickly.

Only a few times had I really known William to cry. And now, as he sat with his back to me at the foot of the bed—though I couldn't see his face—I sensed his quiet weeping.

"William?" I said hazily. He didn't answer. I moved down the bed to sit beside him, and he lifted his arm to pull me close.

"What is this?" I asked him, noting the paper folded in his hand.

"He left it under the door," he answered in a quiet voice.

"Who did? What is it?"

He handed me the paper and I sat up straight, unfolding it.

Maddox, William,

    I thought about writing this to Lily, but anything I haven't said is rightfully meant for you.
    I ask for your forgiveness. This is a serious request, I know, since I've done nothing but mistreat you for years. Regarding this offense, you should know that it was never personal. I hated you because your soul, your life, had been restored while my father's had not. You were a walking reminder that my father might have been saved had I not done as he asked...had I not killed him.
    I realize you had nothing to do with any of this. I realize that there is no justification for my actions. But harboring a prejudice against you made it easier for me not to despise myself.
    I am certain that, were my father still with us, he'd have wanted me to apologize. And so I am. I owe you my life and perhaps someday I can repay you. But for now, I'll leave you and Lily in peace and find my own way. I've decided to travel with Wendell's group in hopes of doing just that. Take care of my mother and sister while I'm gone, would you?

Your servant,
Christian

❧

The End

Acknowledgements

*T*o Ally, the most patient person I've ever met – thanks for being the toughest critic to please. If it floats your boat, I know I have a chance.

Bev and Kim, oh editors, my editors, what peaches you've been! Thank you for your precious time, thoughts, and effort, and for falling into Lily's world so enthusiastically.

To the inspirational and invaluable friends I've gained from the writing world. What would I do without my girls? Shrivel up and die, that's what.

To Chellie, for believing in me. To Joe, for naming my Seer and to the entirety of my family...especially the crazy members...because you may be far away, but you know where I live, and I'm not taking any chances.

And finally, to Omnific Publishing and its hard-working team for readying this book for the world. I'm forever grateful.

About the Author

*J*ennifer DeLucy grew up in the valley city of Scranton, Pennsylvania, where she developed an obsession with all things literary and musical thanks to the influence of an extroverted and creative family. While in Pennsylvania, Jennifer studied voice and had her first taste of professional writing as editor for a small organization.

Jennifer moved to the Midwest in 2002, and she continues to pursue opportunities as an author and musician. She is determined to put her love of the arts, nature and spirit to good use, broadening minds and opening hearts in every way she can.